W9-BNR-850

WORLD OF WARCRAFT®

THE SHATTERING

PRELUDE TO CATACLYSM

Christie Golden

POCKET STAR BOOKS
New York London Toronto Sydney

The sale of this book without its cover is unauthorized. If you purchased this book without a cover, you should be aware that it was reported to the publisher as "unsold and destroyed." Neither the author nor the publisher has received payment for the sale of this "stripped book."

Pocket Star Books
A Division of Simon & Schuster, Inc.
1230 Avenue of the Americas
New York, NY 10020

This book is a work of fiction. Names, characters, places, and incidents either are products of the author's imagination or are used fictitiously. Any resemblance to actual events or locales or persons, living or dead, is entirely coincidental.

Copyright © 2010 by Blizzard Entertainment, Inc. All rights reserved. Warcraft, World of Warcraft, and Blizzard Entertainment are trademarks and/or registered trademarks of Blizzard Entertainment, Inc., in the U.S. and/or other countries. All other trademarks references herein are the properties of their respective owners.

All rights reserved, including the right to reproduce this book or portions thereof in any form whatsoever. For information address Gallery Books Subsidiary Rights Department, 1230 Avenue of the Americas, New York, NY 10020

First Pocket Star Books paperback edition June 2011

POCKET STAR BOOKS and colophon are registered trademarks of Simon & Schuster, Inc.

For information about special discounts for bulk purchases, please contact Simon & Schuster Special Sales at 1-866-506-1949 or business@simonandschuster.com.

The Simon & Schuster Speakers Bureau can bring authors to your live event. For more information or to book an event contact the Simon & Schuster Speakers Bureau at 1-866-248-3049 or visit our website at www.simonspeakers.com.

Cover design by Alan Dingman, art by John Polidora

Interior art by Glenn Rane (1), John Polidora (2), Glenn Rane (3), and Phroilan Gardner (4)

Manufactured in the United States of America

10 9 8 7 6 5 4 3

ISBN 978-1-4391-7274-2
ISBN 978-1-4391-7143-1 (ebook)

His eyes were open now, watching the path of the tiny flame. *If you continue your path, little spark, you will cause great harm.*

I must burn! I must live!

There are places where your glow and heat are welcome. Find them, do not destroy the dwellings or take the lives of my people!

For a second, he seemed to wink out of existence but then blazed back with renewed vigor.

Thrall knew what he had to do. He lifted his hand. *Forgive me, Brother Flame. But I must protect my people from the harm you would cause them. I have requested, I have begged, now I warn.*

The spark seemed to spasm, and yet he continued on his lethal course.

Thrall, grim-faced, clenched his hand hard.

The spark flared defiantly, then dwindled, finally settling down to nothing more than the faintest of glowing embers. For now, he would no longer do anyone harm.

The threat had ended, but Thrall was reeling. This was not the way of the shaman with the elements. It was a relationship of mutual respect, not of threats and control and, in the end, destruction. Oh, the Spirit of Fire could never be extinguished. It was far greater than anything any shaman, or even group of shaman, could ever attempt to do to him. He was eternal, as all the spirits of the elements were. But this part of him, this elemental manifestation, had been defiant, uncooperative. And he had not been alone. He was part of a disturbing trend of elements that were sullen and rebellious rather than cooperative. And in the end, Thrall had had to completely dominate him. Other shaman were now calling rain to soak the city in case there was another aberrant spark that persisted in its course of devastation.

Thrall stood in the rain, letting it soak him, pour off his massive green shoulders, and drip down his arms.

What in the name of the ancestors was happening?

This book is dedicated to my wonderful and loyal readers. It is you who made Arthas: Rise of the Lich King *Blizzard's (and my own) first* New York Times *bestseller, and you who make it possible for me to do this work I love so much. I will continue to strive to write the very best books I can for you.*

ACKNOWLEDGMENTS

Thanks and appreciation must go to my wonderful and enthusiastic editor, Jaime Costas, who always makes me feel so great about what I do. I must also express my gratitude for the constant support of the Blizzard development team: the deeply appreciated Trio of Awesome—Chris Metzen, Evelyn Fredericksen, and Micky Neilson—with whom I have worked before and with whom I hope to continue working for many moons to come; Justin Parker, Cate Gary, James Waugh and Tommy Newcomer, for editing and various other emergency aid; Alex Afrasiabi for game perspective on the story development; Gina Pippin, who keeps the wheels turning and who has unbridled enthusiasm for seemingly everything I do, and her assistant George Hsieh, who sends me Neat Stuff. You are all without exception creative, fun, and a delight to work with, and I couldn't have done it without you.

WARMAUL HILL
TWILIGHT RIDGE
FORGE CAMP HATE
SUNSPRING POST
FORGE CAMP FEAR
OSHU'GUN

LAUGHING SKULL RUINS
THRONE OF THE ELEMENTS
GARADAR
RING OF TRIALS
BURNING BLADE RUINS
TELAAR
KIL'SORROW FORTRESS

THE
FORLORN
THE
MYSTIC WARD
THE
GREAT
THE
COMMONS
THE
GATES OF IRONFORGE

HE
N CAVERN
HALL OF EXPLORERS
HE
FORGE
TINKER TOWN
THE
DEEPRUN TRAM
THE
MILITARY WARD

PROLOGUE

The sound of rain beating on the tightly drawn hides covering the small hut was like that of a drum played by a swift hand. The hut was well made, as all orcish huts were; no water seeped inside. But nothing could close out the humid chill of the air. If the weather turned, the rain would become snow; either way, the cold damp penetrated to Drek'Thar's old bones and kept his body taut even during sleep.

But it was not the cold, not this time, that caused the elderly shaman to toss and turn.

It was the dreams.

Drek'Thar had always had prophetic dreams and visions. It was a gift—a spiritual sight, as he no longer had physical sight. But since the War Against the Nightmare, the gift had grown teeth. His dreams had worsened during that dreadful time, and sleep promised not rest and refreshment, but terror. They had aged him and turned him from one who had been old but strong into a frail, sometimes querulous elder. He had hoped that with the defeat of the Nightmare, his dreams would return to normal. But while the intensity had lessened, his dreams still were very, very dark.

In his dreams, he could see. And in his dreams, he longed for blindness. He stood alone on a mountain. The sun seemed closer than normal and was ugly and red and swollen, casting a bloody tinge on the ocean that lapped at the foot of the mountain. He could hear something . . . a distant, deep rumbling that set his teeth on edge and made his skin prickle. He had never heard this sound before, but due to his strong connection with the elements, he knew that it indicated something terribly, terribly wrong.

A few moments later the waters began to churn, surging angrily now at the foot of the mountain. The waves grew high, hungry, as if something dark and dreadful stirred beneath their crashing surface. Even on the mountain, Drek'Thar knew he was not safe, knew nothing was safe, not anymore, and he could feel the once-solid stone shuddering beneath his bare feet. His fingers curled tightly, painfully, about his staff, as if somehow its gnarled length would stay stable and secure despite a roiling ocean and a crumbling mountain.

And then, with no warning, it happened.

A fissure zigzagged along the earth beneath him. Roaring, he half-leaped, half-fell out of the way as it opened like a mouth attempting to devour him. He lost his hold on his staff, and it fell into the widening maw. As the wind whipped up, Drek'Thar clung to an upthrust shard of rock and, trembling as the earth trembled, peered with eyes that had not seen in far too long at the blood-red, boiling ocean beneath.

Huge waves crashed against the sheer wall of the mountain cliff, and Drek'Thar could feel the blistering spray as they surged impossibly high. From all around him came the screams of the elements, frightened, tormented, calling out for aid. The rumbling increased, and before his terrified gaze a massive chunk of earth broke the surface of the red ocean, rising, rising seemingly without cease, becoming a mountain itself, a continent, even as the land upon which Drek'Thar stood cracked open yet again, and he fell into the fissure, crying aloud and clutching at air, falling into fire—

Drek'Thar bolted upright in the sleeping skins, his body convulsing and drenched in sweat despite the cold, his hands clawing the air, his again-unseeing eyes wide open and gazing into blackness.

"The land will weep, and the world will break!" he shrieked. Something solid touched his flailing hands, enclosed them, stilled them. He knew that touch. It was Palkar, the orc who had attended him for several years.

"Come now, Greatfather Drek'Thar, it is only a dream," the young orc chided.

But Drek'Thar would not be brushed aside, not with the vision he had had. He had fought in Alterac Valley not so long ago, until he had been deemed too old and weak to serve in that capacity. If he could not serve there any longer, he would serve with his shamanic skills. His visions.

"Palkar, I must speak with Thrall," he demanded. "And the Earthen Ring. Perhaps others have seen what I have . . . and if they have not, I must tell them! Palkar, I must!" He attempted to rise. One of his legs gave way beneath him. Frustrated, he pounded at his betraying, aging body.

"What you must do is get some sleep, Greatfather." Drek'Thar was weak, and struggle as he might, he could not offer sufficient resistance to escape Palkar's steady hands pushing him back on the sleeping skins.

"Thrall . . . he must know," muttered Drek'Thar, slapping ineffectually at Palkar's arms.

"If you feel it necessary, tomorrow we will go and tell him. But now . . . rest."

Exhausted from the dream, and feeling the cold in his aged bones afresh, Drek'Thar nodded and permitted Palkar to prepare him a hot drink with herbs that would send him into a peaceful sleep. Palkar was a good caretaker, he thought, his mind already wandering again. If Palkar thought tomorrow would be soon enough, then it would be. After he finished the drink, he laid his head down, and before sleep claimed him, wondered driftingly, *Soon enough for what?*

Palkar sat back and sighed. Once, Drek'Thar had been mentally as sharp as a dagger, even though his body was growing increasingly fragile under the weight of his years. Once, Palkar would have sent a runner off to Thrall immediately upon learning of Drek'Thar's vision.

But no longer.

Over the last year, the sharp mind that had known so much, had held wisdom almost beyond comprehension, had begun to wander. Drek'Thar's memory, once better than any written record, was becoming faulty. There were gaps in his recollection. Palkar could not help but wonder if, between the twin enemies of the War Against the Nightmare and the inevitable ravages of age, Drek'Thar's "visions" had deteriorated into nothing more than bad dreams.

Two moons ago, Palkar recalled painfully as he rose and returned to his own sleeping skins, Drek'Thar had insisted that runners be sent to Ashenvale, because a group of orcs was about to slaughter a peaceable gathering of tauren and kaldorei druids. Runners had been sent, indeed, warnings issued—and nothing had happened. The only thing that had been accomplished by listening to the old orc was that the night elves had grown more suspicious. There had been no orcs within miles. And yet Drek'Thar had insisted that the peril was real.

There had been other, lesser visions, all equally imaginary. And now this. Surely if the threat was real, others than Drek'Thar would be aware of it. Palkar was not an inexperienced shaman himself, and he had had no such forebodings.

Still, he would keep his word. If Drek'Thar wished to see Thrall, the orc who had once been his student and now was warchief of the very Horde Drek'Thar himself had helped to create, in the morning Palkar would prepare his mentor for the journey. Or he might send a runner so that Thrall would come to Drek'Thar. It would be a long and difficult trek; Thrall was in Orgrimmar, a continent away from Alterac, where Drek'Thar insisted on making his home. But Palkar suspected such a thing would not happen. Come tomorrow Drek'Thar would likely not even remember he had dreamed at all, let alone the content.

Such was usually the case these days. And Palkar took no joy in the fact. Drek'Thar's increasing senility caused Palkar only pain and a fierce desire to wish the world were otherwise, the world that Drek'Thar was so convinced was about to be broken. Little did the old orc know that for those who loved him, the world was broken already.

Palkar knew it was useless to grieve for what had been, for what Drek'Thar himself once had been. Indeed, Drek'Thar's life had been longer than most and certainly full of honor. Orcs faced adversity and understood that there was a time to fight and rage and a time to accept the reality of what was. Since Palkar had been a small child, he had cared for Drek'Thar, and he had vowed to continue until that old orc's last breath, no matter how painful it was to bear witness to his mentor's slow decline.

He leaned over and snuffed out the candle between thumb and forefinger, pulling the furs tight about his large frame. Outside, the rain continued to fall, beating its steady tattoo on the tightly drawn skins.

PART I

The Land Will Weep . . .

ONE

"Land ho!" cried the lookout. The slender blood elf had established a perch for himself in the crow's nest, a place so precarious, Cairne thought, that an actual crow would think twice about alighting upon it. The young elf leaped easily onto the rigging, hands and bare feet entwined with the rope, seemingly as comfortable as a squirrel. The aged tauren watching from the deck shook his head slightly at the sight. He was pleased and unabashedly a bit relieved that the first part of their journey to Northrend was over. Cairne Bloodhoof, leader of the tauren, proud father and warrior, did not like ships.

He was a creature of the good, solid earth, as were all his people. They had boats, yes, but small ones that stayed well within sight of the land. Somehow even the zeppelins, airborne goblin contraptions though they were, felt more secure beneath his hooves than a seafaring vessel. Perhaps it was the rocking motion and the fact that the sea could become hostile in an instant. Or perhaps it was the long, unbroken tedium of a voyage such as the one they had just made, from Ratchet to the

Borean Tundra. Regardless, now that their destination was in sight, the aged bull felt cheered.

He was, as befit his rank, traveling in the Horde flagship, *Mannoroth's Bones*. Sailing alongside the proud vessel were several more, empty now save for kegs of fresh water (and a few of Gordok ogre brew, to promote morale) and nonperishable foodstuffs. Cairne would only enjoy his stay on dry land for a day or so, while the ships were loaded with supplies no longer needed here in Northrend and the last of the soldiers of the Horde, who doubtless were looking forward to the journey home.

His aged eyes could not see the land yet through the thick fog, but he trusted in the sharper ones of the acrobatic sin'dorei lookout. He walked to the railing and closed his hands over it, peering into the mists as the ship drew closer.

He knew that the Alliance to the southeast had chosen to erect Valiance Keep on one of the many islands that dotted that area, which made for easy navigation. Warsong Hold, their destination, was well situated and commanded a good view of the surrounding area—much more important to the Horde than deep harbors or easy access. Or at least, it *had* been more important.

Cairne blew softly through his nostrils as the ship slowly, carefully moved forward. He was starting to make out ships through the peculiarly thick fog—the skeleton of another vessel, her captain clearly not so wise as the troll who captained *Mannoroth's Bones,* that had either come under attack or run herself aground—perhaps both. "Garrosh's Landing," the site was immodestly called, and this was what was left of that impulsive young orc's sailing vessel. It had been stripped down to the bones, the once-vivid scarlet hues of sails sporting the black symbol of the Horde now faded and tattered. Equally weathered was the single watch tower that now came into view, and Cairne could just glimpse the hulking form of what had once no doubt been a great hall.

Garrosh, son of the famed orc hero Grom Hellscream, had been among the first to answer the call to come to Northrend. Cairne admired the youth for that, but what he had seen and heard of his behavior was equal parts encouraging and distressing. Cairne was not so old that he did not remember the fire of youth burning in his veins. He had raised a son, Baine, and had watched the young tauren struggle with the same problems he himself had, and understood well that some of Garrosh's behavior stemmed largely from nothing more unusual—and temporary—than young male bravado. Garrosh's enthusiasm and passion were, Cairne had to admit, catching. In the midst of a disheartening war, Garrosh had stirred the hearts and imaginations of the Horde and awakened a sense of national pride that had spread like wildfire.

Garrosh was, for good and ill both, his father's son. Grom Hellscream had never been known for patient wisdom. Always he had acted first, violent and urgent, his war cry the piercing, unsettling scream that had given him his surname. It had been Grom who had first drunk the blood of the demon Mannoroth—blood that had tainted him and all other orcs who had drunk it. But in the end, Grom had had his revenge. Though he had been the first to drink, and thus the first to fall to demonic bloodlust and madness, he had been the one to end that madness and bloodlust. He had slain

Mannoroth. And with that gesture, the orcs had begun to reclaim their own great hearts, wills, and spirits.

Garrosh had once been ashamed of his father, deeming him weak to have drunk the blood, and a traitor. Thrall had enlightened the youth, and now Garrosh Hellscream embraced his heritage. Perhaps embraced it a little *too* enthusiastically, Cairne mused, although the result of Garrosh's enthusiasm had had positive results among the warriors. Cairne had to wonder if perhaps Thrall, in praising the good Grom had indeed done, had overly downplayed the harm Grom had also caused.

Thrall, the warchief of the Horde and a wise as well as courageous leader, had clashed on more than one occasion with the brash young Garrosh. Before the disaster that was the Wrath Gate had occurred, Garrosh had actually challenged Thrall to fight in the arena at Orgrimmar. And, more recently, Garrosh had allowed himself to be baited by Varian Wrynn's angry taunts and had charged at the king of Stormwind, clashing violently with him in the heart of Dalaran itself.

And yet, Cairne could not argue with Garrosh's success and popularity, nor the joyful zeal and passion with which the Horde responded to him. Granted, unlike some rumors would have it, Garrosh had not single-handedly beaten back the Scourge, slaughtered the Lich King, and made Northrend safe for Horde children to frolic in. But there was no denying the fact that he had led incursions that had been unqualified successes. He had brought back to the Horde a sense of fierce pride and fire for battle. He had managed, every time, to turn what looked like lunacy into a rousing success.

Cairne was too intelligent to dismiss this as coincidence or accident. So bold he could be called reckless Garrosh might be, but recklessness did not yield the results that Grom's son had gotten. Garrosh had been exactly what the Horde needed at what was arguably its darkest, most vulnerable hour, and Cairne was willing to give the boy that.

"Dis be as far as we be goin'," said Captain Tula to Cairne, shouting out orders to have the smaller boats lowered. "Warsong Hold be not far, straight to da east up da hills."

Tula knew exactly what she was talking about, having sailed between here and Ratchet countless times over the last several seasons. This knowledge had been why Thrall had requested she captain *Mannoroth's Bones*. Cairne nodded.

"Open one of the kegs of ogre brew to reward your hardworking crew for their diligence," he said to her in his deep, slow-paced voice. "But save some for the brave warriors who will be making their journey home after so long."

Tula brightened considerably. "Yes, High Chieftain," she said. "Thank ya. We be keepin' it to da one keg."

Cairne squeezed her shoulder, nodding his approval, and then, with not a little trepidation, lowered his great bulk into the seemingly tiny, cramped boat that would bear him the rest of the way to shore. The fog clung to his fur like spider's webbing, cloying and cold. It was with pleasure that, a few moments later, he stepped out into the frigid waters that lapped on the shore of Garrosh's Landing and helped tug the boat firmly aground.

The mist was still present but seemed to thin the

further inland they went. They trudged past broken, abandoned siege engines and discarded weaponry and armor, past the remains of a long-abandoned farm with pig skeletons that had been bleached white by the sun. They continued up the slight incline, the tundra soil covered with some sort of red plant that stubbornly persisted in existing despite the harshness of this place. Cairne respected that.

Warsong Hold loomed ahead, clearly and proudly visible. It appeared to be located in the center of a quarry, the hollow providing a practical barrier. Nerubians, an ancient race of spidery beings, many of whose corpses had been raised by necromantic magic, had attempted attacks at various times, but no longer. What had once been strong, sticky webbing had now been cut or worn down to nothing more than a few ropy strands that danced harmlessly in the wind. Along with the Scourge, they, too, had retreated before the dedicated efforts of the Horde.

Up ahead, Cairne caught a blur of movement as a scout caught sight of the Horde standard at the front of Cairne's entourage and dashed away. Cairne and his group followed along the line of the quarry until they encountered a path that descended into it. It was not an impressive entrance, but a workmanlike one, and Cairne found himself in what had been the forge area.

Now, though, no rivers of yellow molten metal flooded the channels; there was no "tink tink" sound of hammer on anvil. His nose, keener than his eyesight these days, caught the faint, stale scent of wolf. The beasts had been gone for some time, sent home even before their masters. What weapons and ammunition there were seemed to have been gathering dust for a while. Once Cairne could make a proper assessment of what was going on, the several kodos who had also made the sea voyage, excellent beasts of burden, would help transport the cargo back to the ships.

Cairne felt the chill of the place. With the forges running, there would be more than enough heat generated to warm the cavernous, open area, but with them still and silent, the cold of Northrend had permeated. Cairne, seasoned veteran though he was, was almost overwhelmed by the size of the place. Larger certainly than Grommash Hold, probably even larger than some Horde cities, it was massive, open, and empty feeling. Their hooffalls echoed as he and his people moved toward the center of the first level.

Two orcs engaged in deep discussion turned as he approached. Cairne knew them both and nodded respectfully at them. The older one with green skin was Varok Saurfang, younger brother to the great hero Broxigar and father to the late, deeply grieved Dranosh Saurfang. Many had lost a great deal in this conflict; Varok more than anyone's fair share.

His son had fallen, along with thousands of others, at Angrathar the Wrath Gate. On that dark day, Horde and Alliance had fought side by side against the best the Lich King could throw at them—even prompting that monster himself to appear. Young Saurfang fell, his soul consumed by Frostmourne. Moments later, a Forsaken known as Putress unleashed a plague that would destroy both the living and the undead.

More torment lay in store for the Saurfang line. The

corpse of the young warrior was raised by the Lich King, then turned loose to destroy those he had loved in life. A blow more of mercy than of battle had ended his unnatural existence. Only with the fall of the Lich King had High Overlord Varok Saurfang been able to finally bring home the body of his boy—a corpse, now, and nothing more.

Grizzled, strong, Saurfang was everything that Cairne felt was best about the orcs. He had wisdom and honor, a powerful arm in battle, and a cool head for strategy. Cairne had not seen Saurfang since his son had fallen at the Wrath Gate, and he silently took in the aging such a deep pain had wrought. Cairne did not know if he, faced with such a horrific violation of all the tauren held dear in the shape of his child, could have borne the double loss half as well as Saurfang did.

"High Overlord," Cairne rumbled, bowing. "As a father myself, I grieve for what you have had to endure. But know that your son died a hero, and what you have wrought here honors his memory. Anything else is borne away on the winds."

Saurfang grunted acknowledgment. "It is good to see you again, High Chieftain Cairne Bloodhoof. And . . . I know what you say is true. I am not ashamed to say, though, that I am glad this campaign has finally come to an end. We have lost too much."

The younger orc standing beside Saurfang grimaced, as if the words were distasteful to him, and it was clearly an effort for him to hold his tongue. His skin was not green, as was that of most orcs Cairne had met, but rather a shade of rich loam brown, marking him as a

Mag'har from Outland. His pate was bald save for a long ponytail of brown hair. This, of course, was Garrosh Hellscream. No doubt to him it was dishonorable to admit that one was glad that battle had come to a close. The tauren chieftain knew that the passing years would teach him that while it was good to fight for a worthy cause and to earn victory, peace was also a good thing. But for now, despite the long, hard-fought war, Garrosh clearly had not had enough of combat, and this bothered Cairne.

"Garrosh," Cairne said. "Word of your deeds has penetrated to all corners of Azeroth. I am sure you are very proud of your accomplishments here, as Saurfang is of his."

The compliment was genuine, and Garrosh's tense posture eased slightly. "How many of your troops will be returning with us?" continued Cairne.

"Nearly all of them," Garrosh replied. "I leave a skeleton crew with Saurfang, and a few others at outposts here and there. I do not anticipate he will have need even of that. The Warsong offensive has crushed the Scourge and taken the fighting spirit out of the rest of our enemies, as we came here to do. It is my belief that my former advisor will sit and watch spiders spin cobwebs and fully enjoy the peace he so obviously craves."

The words might have stung another. Cairne bridled on Saurfang's behalf—after what the older orc had endured, Garrosh's words were particularly harsh. Saurfang, however, clearly had grown used to Garrosh's attitude and merely grunted.

"We have both done our duties. We serve the Horde.

If I serve by watching little spiders instead of fighting large ones, then I am well content."

"And I must serve the Horde by bringing its victorious soldiers safely home," Cairne said. "Garrosh, which of your soldiers is assigned the task of directing the withdrawal?"

"I," Garrosh said, surprising Cairne. "Such as it is. We all have shoulders to carry items." Once downtrodden and ashamed of his heritage, Garrosh had struck the old tauren as a youth who would require a specially shaped doorway to accommodate his swollen head. And yet he did not hesitate to do the basest task right alongside his soldiers. Cairne smiled, pleased. He suddenly understood a bit better why the orcs Garrosh led admired him so deeply.

"My shoulders are more stooped than they once were, but I daresay they can bear what they need to," Cairne said. "Let us get to work."

It was the work of less than two days to finish packing the supplies that would accompany the troops, load them onto kodos, and transport them to the ship. As they worked, many of the orcs and trolls sang songs in their harsh, guttural tongues. Cairne understood Orcish and Zandali, and smiled at the discrepancies between the actions of the songs and what was actually transpiring. Trolls and orcs blithely sang of chopping off arms and legs and heads while tying boxes onto the backs of the mellow pack kodos. Still, their spirits were high, and Garrosh sang as loudly as any of them.

At one point, as they were walking side by side carrying crates to the ship, Cairne asked, "Why did you leave your landing site, Garrosh?"

Garrosh shifted the weight on his shoulder. "It was never intended to be a permanent site. Not when Warsong Hold was so close."

Cairne eyed the great hall and the tower. "Then why build these?"

Garrosh did not answer. Cairne let him remain silent for a time. Garrosh might be many things, but the taciturn type he was not. He would speak . . . eventually.

And sure enough, Garrosh said after a moment, "We built these when we landed. At first there was no trouble. Then a foe unlike any I have encountered came out of the mists. It does not sound as if you have been troubled by them but, I confess, I have wondered if they would return."

A foe so powerful as to give Garrosh pause? "What is this enemy that gave you such trouble?" Cairne asked.

"They are called the Kvaldir," Garrosh said. "The tuskarr think they are the angered spirits of slain vrykul." Cairne exchanged glances with Maaklu Cloudcaller, the tauren who happened to be walking alongside them. Cloudcaller was a shaman, and as he regarded Cairne he nodded slightly. None of Cairne's landing party had personally seen the vrykul, but Cairne knew of them. They looked like humans—if humans were larger than tauren and sometimes had skin that was covered in ice, or made of metal or stone. They were definitely full of violence and power. Cairne was comfortable with the idea of being surrounded by spirits, but those were tauren ancestors. Their presence was positive. The thought of vrykul ghosts haunting this place was not a pleasant one. Cloudcaller, too, looked a bit uneasy at the notion.

"They come when the mists are thickest. The tuskarr say that is what enables them to manifest," Garrosh continued. He sounded skeptical. Too, there was a strange tone in his voice. Embarrassment?

"They terrified many of my warriors and were so powerful they forced us to withdraw to Warsong Hold. I was finally able to take back this site when the Lich King fell."

And there was the shame. Not in seeing "ghosts," if indeed they were such, but in being forced to run from them. No wonder Garrosh had not mentioned why he had abandoned Garrosh's Landing, a place he might logically feel some pride in and fondness for.

Cairne kept his gaze carefully averted from the scowling Garrosh, who was clearly ready to defend his honor if he heard anything he could perceive as an insult to his courage.

"The Scourge do not come to these shores," Garrosh added, somewhat defensively. "It seems even they do not like the Kvaldir."

Well, if the Kvaldir had not attacked them so far, Cairne would not complain. "Warsong Hold is a better strategic site," was all Cairne said.

It was midday on the second day when Cairne bade farewell to Saurfang. He gripped the other's hand hard. Garrosh might have joked about the peace and quiet of remaining up here with but a skeleton crew, but the reality would be something else. And there would likely be ghosts aplenty to haunt Saurfang, if only in his memories. Cairne knew that, and as he looked into Saurfang's eyes, he knew that the orc knew it, too.

Cairne wanted to thank him again, to offer encouragement, praise for a task so successfully completed. For being able to bear such burdens. But Saurfang was an orc, not a blood elf, and lavish compliments and effusion would not be welcomed or wanted.

"For the Horde," Cairne said.

"For the Horde," Saurfang replied, and it was enough.

The fighters who comprised the last wave of the Warsong offensive to depart Northrend shouldered their weapons and began to trudge westward, through the quarry and up onto the Plains of Nasam.

As had happened every time they went this way, the fog closed slowly about them. Cairne felt nothing supernatural about it; but, as he would freely admit, he was a warrior, not a shaman. Still, he had not endured what Garrosh and his fighters had, nor seen what they had seen, and he knew there were such things as angry spirits.

The fog slowed them down, but nothing unusual rose up to attack them. As they made their way to the beach and the small boats waiting for them, however, Cairne slowed. He sensed . . . something. His ears twitched, and he sniffed the cool, moist air.

As Cairne strained his old eyes to try to see in the obscuring mist, he could make out the faint, ghostly shape of a ship. No, more than one . . . two . . . three . . .

"Kvaldir!" roared Garrosh.

TWO

For a few precious moments, everyone struggled against a sense of fear, forcing themselves to focus on the approaching battle. The ships emerged from the mist's veil, manned by the dead. Pale, they were; pale with a tinge of green, of rot, and wrapped with seaweed, their clothing sodden and torn. The oars went up, and the Kvaldir, crying and moaning, leaped into the water and surged upon the shore.

They were everywhere, enormous and ghastly, moving faster than such supposedly undead things should by all rights be able to move, to interpose themselves between the Horde warriors and Warsong Hold. The second ship pulled up alongside *Mannoroth's Bones,* and the things that some called spirits of the dead began to attack the living. On the shore, others closed the ring about Cairne and Garrosh, moving so swiftly for the attack that some of Garrosh's fighters died before they had even had a chance to swing their weapons.

Cairne, too, moved more swiftly than one would think. Unlike some of the orcs, who were cowering or even running in terror, he had no fear of the dead. Let them come. With a deep bellow he charged one of the giant, undead warriors, attempting to use the rune-covered haft of his ancestral spear to knock some of the others aside. They were swift to evade the spear, and even over the moaning and shrieking, Cairne heard the wind as the spear struck nothing. The runespear was blessed by a shaman, as all Cairne's weapons were; if it encountered even a ghost, it would do harm.

"Stand and fight!" Cairne bellowed. "There is nowhere to flee!"

He was right. They were trapped between the hold and their ship on the ocean, which itself was coming under attack. They were caught out in the open and—

No. Not in the open.

"Retreat!" Cairne roared, reversing his previous command. He pitched his voice as loud as possible over the unearthly cries of the Kvaldir and the battle shouts of the pathetically few who were left of the once-vast Warsong offensive. "Retreat to the great hall at Garrosh's Landing!" They could catch their breaths, plan, regroup. Anything was better than standing and being slaughtered with no real strategy for fighting back.

Considering the orc's penchant for reckless action, Cairne half-expected Garrosh to protest. But instead Garrosh took up the cry, blowing a horn he had strapped to his hip and pointing to the west. At once the Horde members moved in that direction, hacking at the undead creatures as they went. Some of them didn't make it, decapitated or gutted by the double-bladed and very corporeal axes of the Kvaldir. Even Cairne was hard pressed to keep moving forward, and at one point a pale hand closed upon and twined about the runespear, threatening to tug it from his grasp. Cairne did not resist the pull, instead letting the hideous thing haul him to itself.

No enemy would be permitted to abscond with the runespear.

He shouted a battle cry and stabbed.

It sank deep. The Kvaldir's eyes widened. He opened his mouth, spat blood, and sank to the earth. Cairne stared. Flesh and blood and bone! Garrosh was right to be skeptical of the tuskarr stories. The ghostly spirits were nothing more than living beings. And anything that lived . . . could die.

The revelation fueled Cairne as he moved steadily toward the great hall, partially obscured now by the strange mist that was nothing more sinister than a cover for the vrykul—for so they had to be. Some of the others had gotten there before him. Cairne saw with dismay that two of the three doors had been damaged. One was gone completely; the other hung by a single hinge.

His eyes fell upon a table where once, in pleasanter times, the soldiers would gather for a repast. Indeed, a weather-beaten lantern, mug, and bowl still sat on the table. With a single sweep of his huge arm, Cairne sent them flying, then grasped the table in both hands. Grunting slightly, he lifted the table, attached benches and all, and hurried to the doorway as fast as he could.

Garrosh grinned. "You are smart and strong, old bull," he said with admiration that, while grudging, was nonetheless genuine. "You! Grab those crates! Everyone else, hurry, inside, inside!"

They obeyed. Cairne waited, singlehandedly holding aloft the table, until the last one, a troll bleeding badly from a sliced-up leg, hobbled into the great hall. The second he was inside, Cairne ducked in after him and slammed the table into the doorway at a slight angle so that it wedged in firmly. Not a heartbeat later, the makeshift door shuddered under the thump of an attack. There was more pounding and the moans of the "undead."

Cairne gulped in air as he continued to barricade the door. "They are foes, but they are living foes!" he told them. "Garrosh, you were right. The Kvaldir are no more or less than vrykul. They use the mist and costumes as weapons to strike fear into the hearts of their enemies before they attack. It fooled me at first, too—until the runespear impaled one of them and I realized what they were doing."

"Whatever they be, we cannot hold much longer," gasped Cloudcaller, leaning his broad back against the "door" as it shook. Others braced against it. The shaman and druids among the group were desperately trying to attend to the wounded, of which there were many—too many. Fully a third of the already diminished group was injured, some of them seriously. "The crates—any weapons in them? Anything we could use?"

It was a good idea, but one without hope. Most of them had dropped the supplies as they turned to battle their attackers. Carrying the heavy crates with them as they headed for the safety of the great hall would have been foolish.

"We have nothing," Cairne said. "Nothing save our courage."

He had just taken a deep breath, hoping to say a few words to inspire his and Garrosh's people as they fought what would doubtless be their last battle, when Garrosh interrupted him.

"We have our courage, yes," said Garrosh, "but we also have something more. And we will show these false ghosts the price they must pay for attempting to trick us. They think we are vulnerable outside of the hold. And they want to take back this landing. They will know the wrath of the Horde!"

He strode to the center of the hall and flipped back a woven rug that had been lying on the floor. Beneath it was a trap door. With a grunt of effort, Garrosh slowly tugged it open. The trap door fell back with a clang, revealing a small, hollowed-out area.

And in that area, piled high like watermelons, were grenades.

Some of the warriors cheered. The others looked at Garrosh, confused.

"You left them here, just in case, did you not?" Cairne asked, surprised. "In case Warsong Hold fell?"

The orcs were not overfond of contingency plans, Cairne had learned. They did not like to even conceive of possible defeat. And yet it was obvious that Garrosh had done exactly that—left a crate of valuable weapons buried in the sand, in case at some later time, when the orcs were in full retreat, they would have need of them.

Garrosh nodded shortly. "It is not a pleasant thought."

"But it is the mark of a leader, to hold all possibilities, even the unpleasant—even the unthinkable." Cairne said. "It was well done, Garrosh." He inclined his head in a gesture of respect even as a particularly vigorous assault nearly caved his door in.

What was left of the Warsong offensive all scrambled for the small but lethal weapons. The pounding had not ceased all this time. The crates that had been piled up were being pushed ever forward, and the table that served as a door was starting to splinter before the onslaught. Cairne shifted his hooves and repositioned his back to keep up the support as the others loaded themselves down with grenades. Garrosh rose and nodded to Cairne.

"One, two, three!" cried Cairne. On "three" Cairne and the orcs guarding the other two doors stepped back, Cairne dropping the table and the orcs swinging wide the doors. Garrosh was there, a massive battleaxe in each hand, screaming his father's war cry and slashing at the false ghosts, all violence and death. Cairne stepped back, allowing the others to precede him in their race for the ship. They threw the grenades into the cluster of Kvaldir. There were several explosions, and then the path was clear—save of bodies. They had a few precious moments before the next wave of Kvaldir came.

"Go, go!" he urged, turning back to where his spear lay. He quickly strapped it to his back. If he needed to fight in the next few minutes, all would be lost anyway. The real fight would have to take place on the ship. His hands free, he scooped up a badly injured orc as if the warrior weighed nothing at all, and began running as fast as he could toward the ship.

Mannoroth's Bones had been damaged and was under attack, but it looked still seaworthy, at least to Cairne's eyes.

He felt a tug of pain in his heart as a troll fell not four paces in front of him, an axe in his back. There would be time to honor the fallen later, but now there was nothing Cairne could do but leap over the body and keep running.

His hooves sank in the sand. He felt slow, and not for the first time cursed what age had done to his body. There was a hideous cry, and one of the Kvaldir lunged at him, swinging his axe with both brawny arms. Cairne dodged as best he could, but he was not swift enough and grunted in pain as it sliced his side.

And then at last he was there, delivering his charge into one of the small skiffs. It pushed off immediately, crammed to overflowing with wounded. Immediately it became a target, and Cairne had to stand in the small, rocking boat and fight off the Kvaldir while two orcs rowed furiously. At one point, he looked back at the shoreline, dotted with the corpses of "ghosts."

And the corpses of brave members of the Horde.

But some of those "corpses" were still moving. Cairne narrowed his eyes and leaped out of the boat as it pulled up alongside *Mannoroth's Bones.* He turned back, half-swimming, half-wading, slogging onto the shore toward the injured. Cairne intended to do everything he could to keep that number from increasing.

Six times back and forth he went, bearing those who could not get themselves to safety. Garrosh's group had exhausted their supply of grenades, and the shore was equal parts blood and sand now. The horrific, muddy concoction sucked at his hooves as he ran. He heard Garrosh's war cry through it all, the sound heartening his warriors and even Cairne until at last all who could be rescued had been.

"Garrosh!" shouted Cairne.

Bleeding from half a dozen wounds, his breath ragged, Cairne looked about for Garrosh. He was over there, whirling his two axes, shouting incoherently as he severed limbs and was spattered with blood. So lost in the battle haze was he that he paid no attention to Cairne's cries. The tauren hastened over to him and grabbed Garrosh's arm. Startled, the orc whirled, axes raised, but halted the blow in time.

"Retreat! We have the wounded! The battle is on the ship now!" Cairne shouted at him, shaking his arm.

Garrosh nodded. "Retreat!" he cried, his voice carrying over the fray. "Retreat to the ship! We will continue to fight and slaughter our enemies on the water!"

The few combatants left fighting turned at once and hastened to the shore, leaping into the boats even as they pushed off for *Mannoroth's Bones*. A Kvaldir wrenched one hapless orc from inside the skiff and dragged her onto the shore, where he proceeded to hack her limb from limb. Cairne forced himself to shut out her cries, shoving the last boat off with all his strength and clambering into it.

There were several of the giant humanoids on the ship already. Captain Tula was shouting to shove off, and her crew was scrambling to obey. The anchor was hauled up and the ship pushed off toward open water. The Kvaldir vessels, wreathed in the cold, clinging fog, pursued. The sight was less frightening now that everyone understood they faced a living foe, but the danger was still very real. The crew had held its own while the remnants of the Warsong offensive struggled to get to the ship, but now they were able to attend to their duties while the soldiers fought. The Kvaldir ships pulled up alongside, close enough for Cairne to see the leering, furious faces of the murderous enemy.

"Do not let them board!" shouted Garrosh. He dispatched a foe and, leaping over the still-twitching corpse, chopped the hands off of a Kvaldir attempting to climb aboard. The Kvaldir screamed and fell into the freezing waters. "Tula! Push us out to sea! We must outrun them!"

The frantic crew obeyed. Cairne, Garrosh, and the others fought like demons. Archers and gunmen fired at the enemy vessel. Several bowmen lit their arrows on fire, aiming for the sails. A great cheer went up as one of them caught. Bright orange flames pierced the cold gray of the fog, and the sail began to crackle as the fire spread. *Mannoroth's Bones* lurched toward open water. Cairne fully expected the Kvaldir to follow, but they did not. He heard cries in their ugly language as some hastened to put out the fire that was consuming their ship while others rushed to the bow and hurled curses at the rapidly disappearing Horde vessel.

Cairne suddenly felt the pain of his wounds and grimaced. He permitted himself to lie down in the boat and close his eyes for a moment. *Let the pretend ghosts rail. Today, fewer than they expected have fallen to them.*

And for now, Cairne thought wearily, that was enough.

THREE

I am saddened to depart this place," Garrosh said as they stood on the deck of *Mannoroth's Bones* a few hours into their journey.

Cairne stared at him. "Saddened? I would think Northrend symbolized a place of carnage and loss. Many of our best and brightest were slain here. I have never been one to mourn leaving a battlefield."

Garrosh snorted. "It has been a long time since you were on a battlefield . . . *elder.*"

Cairne's brows drew together and he straightened, towering over even Garrosh. "For an *elder,* it seems my memory is sharper than yours, young one. What do you think the last few hours were? Do you disregard the sacrifices that your soldiers made? Do you sneer at the wounds I and others now bear because of it?"

Garrosh muttered something and did not answer, but it was clear to the tauren that Garrosh did not regard a siege in the same light as a no doubt glorious battle on some open plain. Perhaps he thought there was some shame in being trapped in the first place. Cairne had seen too much to be so foolish, but the blood ran hot in the young orc. Garrosh would learn that it was in how one fought, not where or when, that honor was born. And by that standard, the Horde had given a proud accounting of itself.

And so, he had to admit, had Garrosh. His reckless leaping into the fray had paid off—this time. But apparently, according to others he had talked with, even Saurfang, who clearly disliked the young orc, it had paid off a number of times before. Where did boldness become recklessness? Instinct become bloodlust? As he shivered a little in the sharp, biting wind blowing off the arctic seas despite his thick fur, his body stiffening up from its wounds and the exertion, Cairne was forced to admit that it had indeed been a while since he had fought with any regularity, though he had still been able to hold his own when he needed to.

"The Horde won victory against all odds, against a terrible foe in Northrend," said Garrosh, returning to the original subject of the conversation. "Each life counted toward that goal. Toward the honor and glory of the Horde. Saurfang's own son was lost. He and the others shall have *lok'vadnods* composed and sung for them. One day, ancestors willing, I shall have one written for me as well. And that is why I am saddened to depart, Cairne Bloodhoof."

Cairne nodded his grizzled head. "Though I do not think you want a *lok'vadnod* terribly soon, hmm?"

It was an attempt to interject levity, but Grom Hellscream's boy was too earnest to chuckle along. "Whenever death comes, I will meet it proudly. Fighting for my people, a weapon in my hand, my battle cry on my lips."

"Hrmmm," rumbled Cairne. "It is a glorious way to go. With honor and pride. May we each be granted such a dignity. But I have much more stargazing to do, more listening to drumming circles. More teaching the young ones and watching them come of age before I am willing to go with death on that final journey."

Garrosh opened his mouth to speak, but it was as if the wind snatched the words out of his tusked mouth. Cairne, massive and solid as he was, stumbled under the force of the gale that erupted out of nowhere. The ship lurched beneath them, tipping wildly to one side, and suddenly the deck was awash in water.

"What is happening?" Garrosh bellowed, even that loud sound almost drowned out by the abrupt howling of the wind. Cairne did not know the proper seaman's term for this type of storm and thought that identifying it was the least of their worries. Captain Tula rushed on deck, her blue skin pale and her eyes wide. Her functional clothing—black foot wraps, pants, and a plain white shirt—was drenched and plastered to her skin. Her black hair had come undone from its topknot and looked like a mop atop her head.

"What can I do?" Cairne asked at once, unsettled more by her obvious concern than the storm that had quite literally seemed to come out of nowhere.

"Get below so I won't be havin' t' worry about you landlubbers!" she shouted, too focused to worry about rank and courtesies. If the situation hadn't been so dire, Cairne would have chuckled. As it was, he reached out, seized Garrosh unceremoniously by the back of his gorget, and had begun to steer the protesting orc toward the center of the ship when the wave crashed over them all.

Cairne was slammed to the deck as if by a giant hand. The breath was knocked out of him, and even as he struggled, water surged into his lungs to take its place. As quickly as it had come, the wave receded, nearly taking both him and Garrosh with it as easily as if they were but twigs in a stream wending through Quel'Thalas. As one, they reached out to one another, hands gripping painfully hard. They slammed into the curving bulwark, their progress halted for the moment. Cairne rose, his hooves carving a deep gouge in the slippery wooden deck as he stubbornly sought purchase. Snorting and bellowing with the effort, he fought his way forward, hauling Garrosh until the orc could scramble upright. There came a sudden crack of lightning far, far too close and the shattering rumble of thunder almost immediately afterward.

Still Cairne moved forward, one arm around Garrosh, the other reaching out until it grasped the slippery but solid doorframe, and the two half-stumbled, half-slid down into the hold.

Garrosh vomited up water, then stubbornly reached out a brown hand and tried to rise. "Cowards and children stay in the hold while others risk their lives," he gasped.

Cairne placed a hand none too gently on Garrosh's armor-clad shoulder. "And self-centered fools get in the way of those trying to *save* lives," he growled. "Do not be a fool, Garrosh Hellscream. Captain Tula needs to tend the ship so that it won't snap in two, not waste precious energy and time trying to stop us from being washed overboard!"

Garrosh stared at him, then threw back his head and howled his frustration. But to his credit, he did not attempt to rush back up the stairs.

Cairne braced himself for a long, bruising wait at best, a cold, wet death at worst. Instead, the storm abated as suddenly as it had come. They had not even caught their breath when the ship's violent, rocking movements stilled. They stared at one another for a moment, then both turned and hastened up the stairs.

Unbelievably the sun was already coming out from behind rapidly dissipating clouds. It was an incongruously cheerful sight compared to what greeted Cairne's eyes as he emerged.

Sunlight glinted on the calm, silver surface of an ocean littered with debris. Cairne glanced wildly around, counting ships as he saw them. He counted only three, and prayed to the ancestors that the remaining two ships were merely scattered, although the debris bobbing in the water was mute testimony to the fact that some of them, at least, had not made it.

Survivors, clutching the floating crates, were crying out for aid, and both Cairne and Garrosh rushed to assist. This, at least, they could help with, and so spent the next hour bringing gasping, soaked orcs, trolls, and tauren—with the occasional sodden Forsaken or blood elf—aboard the ships that remained.

Captain Tula was grim-faced and taciturn as she barked out orders. *Mannoroth's Bones* had survived the—hurricane? Typhoon? Tsunami? Cairne wasn't sure.

Their ship was largely intact, and was now crowded to the gills with shivering survivors huddled in blankets. Cairne patted a young troll on the shoulder as he handed her a mug of hot soup, then moved to the captain.

"What happened?" he asked quietly.

"Cursed if I know," was the reply. "I be on de ocean since I be a youngster. I be makin' dis voyage dozens of times, resupplying Warsong Hold until dem Kvaldir stopped me. And I never be seein' anyting like dat."

Cairne nodded solemnly. "I hope I do not offend if I say, I guessed as much. Do you think perhaps—"

A howl of outrage that could only issue from the throat of a Hellscream interrupted him. Cairne whirled to see Garrosh pointing at the horizon. He was visibly shaking, but it was clear that it was with anger, not fear or cold.

"Look there!" he cried. Cairne gazed where he pointed, but again, his aged eyes failed him. Not so Captain Tula's. They widened.

"They be flyin' de flag of Stormwind," she said.

"Alliance? In our waters?" said Garrosh. "They are in clear violation of the treaty."

Garrosh referred to a treaty between the Horde and the Alliance, signed shortly after the fall of the Lich King. Both factions had been sorely damaged by the long battle, and both sides had agreed to a cessation of hostilities, including the struggles at Alterac Valley, Arathi Basin, and Warsong Gulch, for a brief time.

"*Are* we still in Horde waters?" asked Cairne quietly. Tula nodded.

Garrosh grinned. "Then by all laws, theirs and ours,

they are ours for the taking! We are allowed by the treaty to defend our territory—including our waters!"

Cairne couldn't believe what he was hearing. "Garrosh, we are not in any condition to be mounting an attack. Nor do they seem to be interested in us. Have you considered the possibility that the same storm that so damaged us blew them off course? That they are not here to attack, but are here only by accident?"

"The winds of fate, then," Garrosh said. "They should face their destiny with honor."

Cairne understood at once what was going on. Garrosh had a perfectly valid excuse for action, and he obviously intended to take it. He could not take revenge on the storm that had damaged Horde ships and taken the lives of many of his people, but he could vent his anger and frustration on the hapless Alliance vessel.

To Cairne's dismay even Captain Tula was nodding. "We be needin' more supplies to replace what was lost," she said, tapping her chin, her eyes narrowed in thought.

"Then let us claim what is rightfully ours. Can *Mannoroth's Bones* engage in battle?"

"Aye, mon, dat she can, wit' a little bit of preparation."

"I am sure you will find many hands eager to aid you," Garrosh replied. Tula nodded and strode off, barking orders left and right. Garrosh's statement had been correct. Everyone leaped to attention, desperately eager to do something, anything, rather than sit and bemoan their fate. Cairne understood and approved of the desire and need, but if his suspicion was correct and the crew of the Alliance vessel were simply innocent victims . . .

The ship turned slowly, its sails swelling, and headed

swiftly for the "enemy" ship. As they drew closer, Cairne could now see it more clearly and his heart sank.

It made no effort to elude their obvious pursuit. It could not have, even if the captain had wished to. The vessel was listing badly to port. Its sails had been shredded by the vicious wind that had played slightly less cruelly with the Horde fleet, and it was taking on water. Cairne could only just make out what was on the ship's standards—the lion's head of Stormwind.

Garrosh laughed. "Excellent," he said. "Truly a gift. Another chance to show Varian how *highly* I regard him."

The last time Garrosh and King Varian Wrynn of Stormwind had been in the same room, they had come to blows. Cairne had no particular fondness for humans, but no true dislike of them, either. Had this ship attacked his own, he would have been the first to issue orders to return fire. But this ship was broken, sinking, and even without their "help" would likely soon vanish beneath the icy waters forever.

"Vengeance is petty and beneath you, Garrosh," Cairne snapped. "And what honor is there in slaying those about to drown? You may not violate the letter of the treaty, but you do its spirit." He turned to Tula, hoping she would see reason. "I am the commander of this mission, Captain. As such, I outrank Garrosh. I order you to give aid to these victims of the storm. Their being here was not provocative, but accidental, and there is greater honor in aiding than in butchering."

She regarded him steadily. "With all due respect, mon, our warchief be appointin' you leader only with regard to overseeing the return of the Warsong offensive veterans. Overlord Garrosh be in charge of all martial decisions."

Cairne's jaw dropped as he stared at her. She was correct. The thought had not occurred to him when they had been fighting tooth and nail against the surprise onslaught of the Kvaldir. Then, he and Garrosh had been thinking completely as one. There was no question but that aggression and battle were utterly necessary, so they had not been in conflict over that, only over how best to defeat the enemy. But now, though he was in charge of the voyage to bring the troops home, they were still obliged to obey Garrosh until such time as Thrall formally relieved Garrosh of his command. There was nothing Cairne could do.

Quietly, for Garrosh's ears alone, he said, "I ask you, please. Do not do this thing. Our enemy is already broken. If we do not choose to assist them, they will likely die here anyway."

"Then a swift kill is a mercy," was Garrosh's reply. And as if to punctuate the statement, the roar of cannons echoed. Cairne was staring straight at the ill-fated Alliance ship as the cannonballs punched holes in its side. From other vessels, a rain of arrows descended, and the sound that no Alliance soldier would ever forget, the sound of the Horde in full battle cry, rose up over the sound of waves and wind.

"Again!" Garrosh yelled, racing forward to the bow, quivering like an eager wolf on the hunt as they drew yet closer to the ship.

The mast was now broken on the Alliance vessel, but Cairne could make out a figure on the deck frantically waving the white flag of surrender. If Garrosh noticed it, he gave no sign. As soon as *Mannoroth's Bones* was close enough, he let out a howl and leaped to the enemy vessel, a weapon in each hand, and began to attack the humans.

Cairne turned away, sickened. Legally Garrosh was right, but by any other reckoning, morally or spiritually, what he was doing was wrong. Horribly wrong, and Cairne darkly wondered how the spirits would exact their revenge upon the Horde, or Garrosh, or perhaps even him, Cairne Bloodhoof, for standing by and permitting it to happen.

It was over quickly, too quickly, as far as the orcs were concerned. Garrosh, somewhat to Cairne's surprise, actually shouted to his troops to "Hold!" after only a few moments. The tauren pricked his long ears up and moved close, straining to see and hear what Garrosh would do next.

"Bring me the captain!" Garrosh demanded. A short while later, a troll, holding a human male tightly by both arms, hurried over and tossed the hapless captain to the deck.

Garrosh prodded the figure with a foot. "You are in Horde waters, Alliance dog."

The man, sinewy, tall for his race, and tanned, with short-cropped black hair and a neatly trimmed beard, simply stared up at the orc. "There is a treaty—"

"Which does not apply to incursions into our territory. That is obviously an act of aggression!"

"You saw what shape we were in," the captain replied, disbelief in his voice. "A rabbit wouldn't have found us aggressive!"

It was the wrong thing to say, and Garrosh kicked him in the ribs. Cairne could hear one or two of them break. The man grunted and his face went pale, then flushed.

"You are in Horde waters," Garrosh repeated. "Whatever state your ship was in, I am well within my rights for everything I do here. Do you know who I am?"

The man shook his head.

"I am Garrosh Hellscream, son of the great Horde hero Grom Hellscream!" The captain's eyes widened, and he paled again. Clearly he did indeed recognize the name—if not the first, then surely the surname. Grom Hellscream was legend in the Alliance as well as the Horde.

"I have defeated my enemies and claimed your vessel for the Horde, and you as prisoners of war. The question is, what should I do with you now? I could set fire to your ship and let you burn," he mused, rubbing his chin. "Or simply leave. It has not escaped my notice that you have no skiffs. There are sharks and orcas in these waters, and I am certain they love the taste of Alliance flesh almost as much as my troll warriors do."

The captain swallowed hard, no doubt keenly aware that it was a troll who had brought him before Garrosh and was now standing beside him. The troll cackled and licked his lips exaggeratedly. Cairne and Garrosh both knew the Darkspear trolls were not cannibals, but clearly the captain didn't.

"My friend Cairne Bloodhoof there," Garrosh continued, jerking his thumb over his shoulder without turning to actually look at Cairne, "urged me to be merciful. And do you know, I think he might be right."

The captain's eyes darted to Cairne. The old bull was certain that he himself looked almost as surprised as the human. What was Garrosh doing? He had swarmed the ship, along with his men, slaying all but a handful of the crew. And he was talking about *mercy*?

"Today, Captain, I have shown you the mighty arm of the Horde, and I also show you its mercy. There are eleven of you who seem to have survived the . . . storm." He smiled a little. "We will give you two skiffs, along with some of our own precious rations. That, and luck, should be enough to see you to safety. And when you reach home, tell them what has happened here. Tell them that Garrosh Hellscream was both death and life to you and your people today."

Without another word, he turned and gracefully leaped back onto the deck of *Mannoroth's Bones*. He spoke quickly and quietly to Tula, who nodded and issued orders of her own. Cairne watched as a few supplies and a single water keg were brought forth from below and two small skiffs were cut loose. At least Garrosh was keeping to his bizarre bargain. The tauren watched with mournful eyes as the humans scrambled into the boats and began to row back in the direction of Northrend.

He shifted his gaze to Garrosh, who stood straight and tall, his arms folded, still in his armor this entire time despite the storm and near-drowning.

Garrosh was a brilliant tactician, a fierce warrior, and loved by those he led.

He also held grudges, was a hothead, and needed to learn the lessons of both respect and compassion.

Cairne would speak with Thrall immediately upon

their return. What Garrosh was had served the Horde well in Northrend, at a time of struggle unlike any they had ever known. Cairne knew it would serve the son of Grom poorly upon their return to Orgrimmar. Those who lived entirely by the sword sometimes did not know what to do in the aftermath of war. Out of their element, unable to channel their passions and energies the way they knew best—sometimes they ended up as belated casualties of the same war that had claimed the lives of their fellows, dying in taverns or in street fights instead of in battle, or simply becoming lost souls who continued to exist without truly living.

Garrosh had too much potential, too much to offer, to end up that way. Cairne would do all he could to prevent such a fate from befalling the son of Grom Hellscream.

But Garrosh would have to be a willing partner in such an endeavor for it to succeed. As he regarded the orc now, standing so certain in his rightness, Cairne was not at all certain that Garrosh would be such a participant in shaping his own destiny.

He looked back at the slowly retreating skiffs. At least Garrosh had spared some lives, although Cairne had a sneaking suspicion it was rooted in arrogance. Garrosh very much wanted words of his deeds to reach Varian, to no doubt further irritate that leader.

Cairne sighed deeply, and turned his face up to the sun, weak in these northern climes but still present, closed his pale green eyes, and prayed for guidance.

And patience. A very great deal of patience.

FOUR

It was a festival the likes of which Cairne had never seen in Orgrimmar, and he wasn't altogether sure he liked it.

It was not that he did not wish to honor the soldiers who had fought so valiantly against the Lich King and his subjects. But he knew as well as others, and better than some, the cost of war on all fronts, and frowned a little to himself at the lavishness with which the veterans were received.

The parade, he had recently discovered, had been Garrosh's idea. "Let the people see their heroes," he had stated. "Let them march into Orgrimmar to the welcome they deserve!"

An unkinder soul than Cairne might have mentally amended, *And make sure everyone knows that Garrosh Hellscream was responsible for the victory.*

Still, Garrosh had insisted that everyone who had been involved with the campaign in Northrend be encouraged to participate. No one expected to see Forsaken or sin'dorei veterans in this parade, although they would not have been denied the right to march had they attended. They had their own concerns and had waged their own campaign in the northernmost continent of the world. No, this parade was mainly comprised of those who dwelt in the hot, dusty lands of Kalimdor—orcs, trolls, and tauren. And it looked to Cairne as if every one of those races who had raised a weapon or a curse against the Scourge had come. The line stretched all the way from the gates of Orgrimmar well past the zeppelin tower.

Scorning the softer traditional rose petals that the Alliance often used on such occasions, Horde workers had paved the road with pine branches that, when crushed underfoot, produced a pleasing scent. Durotar did not offer much in the way of pine branches, so Cairne knew that these had been shipped in from a great distance. He sighed deeply and shook his head at the extravagance.

Grom's boy was at the head of the parade, the first at the gate when it opened, along with his Warsong Hold veterans. Cairne did not begrudge him the position—after all, Cairne had stayed behind in Kalimdor and Garrosh had gone to Northrend, as had all these brave warriors. And most of them were orcs, and this was orc territory. Still, it rankled him that most of the crowd kept pace with Garrosh, cheering him on, seeming to care little for the ranks of other military units who had fought just as hard, and in some cases had sacrificed even more bright young lives to the cause but who lacked a charismatic figurehead.

Thrall himself was standing outside Grommash

Hold. He was clad in the instantly recognizable black plate armor that had once belonged to Orgrim Doomhammer, for whom Orgrimmar was named. In one giant green fist, the warchief of the Horde bore the massive Doomhammer itself. Thrall was an imposing figure whose legend preceded him at every turn, and on more than one occasion a battle had been won simply by his appearance on the field so clad.

Beside him, slightly stooped but still powerful for an orc in his late fifties, stood Eitrigg. Eitrigg had left the Horde after the Second War, in which his sons had been betrayed by fellow orcs and were killed in battle. Sickened by the corruption and waste he saw in the orcs, Eitrigg had felt his duty to his people was over. He had rejoined the Horde when Thrall had risen to command it and return the orcs to their shamanic roots. He was one of Thrall's most valued and trusted advisors and had only just returned from aiding the Argent Crusade in Zul'Drak. In his arms, he bore an object wrapped in cloth.

Thrall's bright blue eyes, rare among orcs, were fastened on the approaching line of warriors. Garrosh drew to a halt in front of him. Thrall looked at him for a moment, then inclined his head deeply in a gesture of respect.

"Garrosh Hellscream," he said in his deep, rumbling voice that carried easily over the crowd, "you are the son of Grom Hellscream, my dear friend and a hero to the Horde. You once did not understand how great an orc he was. Now you do, and it is clear that you, too, are a hero of the Horde for what you have achieved in your campaign in Northrend.

"We stand in the shadow of the armor and the very skull of our great enemy, Mannoroth, whose blood tainted us and clouded our minds for so long. The enemy that your father slew, and in so doing, he freed his people from a terrible curse."

He nodded to Eitrigg, who stepped forward. Thrall took the bundle he bore and unwrapped it. It was an axe—not just any axe, but a named weapon, a famous weapon. Its wickedly curved blade had two notches in it. When the wielder swung it, it sang its own battle cry—just as its owner had once done—which gave it its name.

Many of the spectators recognized it, and murmurs rose throughout the crowd.

"This," said Thrall solemnly, "is Gorehowl. It is the weapon of your father, Garrosh. It is this blade that killed Mannoroth, an almost inconceivably brave deed that cost Grom Hellscream his life."

Garrosh's eyes widened. Joy and pride shone on his brown face. He reached out to accept the gift, but Thrall did not surrender it at once.

"It killed Mannoroth," he repeated, "but it also took the life of the noble demigod Cenarius, who taught the first mortal druids. Like any weapon, it can be used for good or ill. I charge you with being the best of your father, Garrosh. With using this weapon wisely and well, for the good of your people. It is my honor to welcome you home. Receive the love and thanks of those whom you have served with your blood and sweat and spirit."

Garrosh took the weapon and hefted it experimentally. He swung the blade as if he had been born to do so—and, mused Cairne, perhaps he had. It shrieked and howled, cutting the air as it had once and would again cut down the enemies of the Horde. He lifted the axe high above his head, and again cheers swept through the Valley of Wisdom. Garrosh closed his eyes for a moment, as if literally basking in the adoration. Cairne did not think for a moment that it was undeserved, but thought a bit of grateful humility for both the weapon and the accolades might have served Garrosh well.

"Veterans, the taverns are open to you this night. Eat and drink and sing of your glorious deeds, but be mindful that the citizens of Orgrimmar are those whom you have served and not your foes." Thrall allowed himself a smile. "The haze of alcohol can sometimes blur such lines."

Good-natured laughter rippled through the crowd. Cairne had known to expect this. Thrall had agreed to reimburse every inn and tavern for food, drink, and lodging the entire day. However, it was up to the tavern and innkeepers to police their customers—the Horde would not pay for damaged chairs or tables, and there were *always* damaged tables and chairs. Not to mention a few broken noses, but such were borne as a necessary part of the celebrating. Cairne, who did not indulge in such wild behavior—had not even done so as a younger tauren—did not approve, but he had not protested when Thrall had suggested it.

Thrall waved, and several carts pulled by kodos and raptors were brought forth, covered by heavy blankets. At Thrall's nod, several orcs stepped forward and, on the count of three, pulled off the blankets to reveal dozens of kegs of strong beer.

"Let the revelry begin!" shouted Thrall, and wild cheering and applause filled the air.

The parade now officially over, the veterans moved eagerly to the kegs, beginning what was certain to be a long night and likely a hangover-heavy morning. Cairne strode toward the entrance of Grommash Hold, pausing for a moment to eye the skull and armor of which Thrall had spoken.

The armor had been securely chained to an enormous dead tree for all to see. The skull of the great demon lord, which was set atop the tree, had been bleached white by the sun. Long tusks curved out from the pale bone, and the plate armor was gargantuan, unwearable by even the most powerful orc, troll, or tauren. Cairne regarded it for a long moment, thinking about Grom, thanking his spirit for the sacrifice that had set the orcs free.

With a long sigh, he turned and trundled inside. He had, as was his right, brought a retinue with him. He had selected who among his people would have the honor of attending the feast tonight. Ordinarily his son Baine would be among them, but Baine had opted to remain behind in Mulgore.

It is a high honor that you ask me to attend such a ceremony, Baine had written, *but the higher honor is making sure our people are safe until you, their leader, have returned home for good.*

The response pleased but did not surprise Cairne. Baine did exactly as his father would have done in the same situation. While it would have made him happy to have his son by his side, Cairne felt better knowing that the tauren people were watched over and cared for in his absence.

In Baine's stead was the venerable archdruid Hamuul Runetotem, who was a good friend and trusted advisor. Also present were members of several of the individual tauren tribes such as the Dawnstrider, Ragetotem—a tribe with a warrior focus who had sent several of its sons and daughters to fight proudly in Northrend alongside Garrosh—Skychaser, Winterhoof, and Thunderhorn, among others. Included for politics' sake rather than personal preference was the matriarch of the Grimtotem, Magatha.

Alone among the tauren tribes, the Grimtotem had never formally joined the Horde, though Magatha lived on Thunder Bluff and her tribe enjoyed all the rights of being a tauren. A powerful shaman who had come to lead the Grimtotem thanks to the tragic, accidental death of her mate—a death that, it was whispered, was not quite so accidental as it had appeared—she and Cairne had clashed before. Cairne was more than happy to make her welcome on Thunder Bluff and to invite her to important ceremonies such as this one, as he firmly believed in the old adage, "Keep your friends close and your enemies closer." She had not opposed him openly, and he doubted she ever would. Magatha might plot and scheme safely in the shadows, but in the end Cairne believed she was a coward. Let Magatha think herself powerful for merely running her own tribe. He, Cairne Bloodhoof, was the one who truly led the tauren people.

★ ★ ★

Thrall took his seat in the massive throne that afforded him a view of the entire enormous room and watched as the throng filed in. The braziers that normally burned on either side of the throne had been extinguished. In front of the cold braziers were now two lesser, but still ornate, seats that had been moved there for the occasion. Per Thrall's request, Cairne and Garrosh each took one—Garrosh on Thrall's right, as the hero of the hour. In various places about the room, the Kor'kron, Thrall's bodyguards, stood quietly and unobtrusively.

Thrall eyed Cairne and Garrosh, watching their reactions. Cairne shifted slightly in the somewhat too-small chair. Thrall grimaced; the orcish carpenters had tried hard to take a tauren physique into consideration when they had designed the chair but had obviously failed. The old bull was clearly filled with pride as his people settled in. He, like Thrall, knew they had all given, and in some cases forever lost, so much to this war.

The years were starting to take their toll on the tauren high chieftain. Thrall had heard how well Cairne had fought when his group had come under siege, how he had returned again and again to bear more wounded to safety. That did not surprise him. He well knew Cairne's courage, great heart, and compassion. What did surprise him was how many wounds the tauren had suffered in the conflict and how slowly he appeared to be healing from them.

Thrall's heart suddenly hurt. He had lost so many dear to him—Taretha Foxton, the human girl who had shown him that loving friendship could exist between the races; Grom Hellscream, who had taught him so much about what it meant to be an orc; and perhaps soon now Drek'Thar, who, according to the orc who attended him, was growing frail and whose mind was drifting away. The thought of having to say the final farewell to Cairne, who had been so close for so many years, was painful.

He turned his attention to Garrosh. The young Hellscream, Gorehowl across his lap, ate and drank and laughed raucously, fully enjoying himself and utterly present in the moment. But now and then he, too, paused and looked out on those assembled with shining eyes and a chest swelled with pride. Thrall had not missed the enthusiasm with which the population of Orgrimmar had received Garrosh. Not even he, Thrall, had been so completely adored during any kind of ceremony. That was as it should be, Thrall thought. Not all of his decisions were welcome ones among his people, but he knew he led them well and they respected him. Garrosh, however, seemed to have tasted nothing but approbation and the love of his people.

Garrosh caught Thrall looking at him and smiled. "It is good to be here," he said.

"Good to enjoy the accolades you have earned?" Thrall asked.

"Of course. But it is also good to see the orcs. To see them remembering, as I did, what it means to be an orc. To fight the just battle, to defeat your foes, to celebrate your victory with the same passion that let you earn it."

"The Horde is more than just orcs, Garrosh," Thrall reminded him.

"Yes. But we are its core. Its center. And if we hold

firmly to that, to what it means—then you will see more victories from your Horde, Warchief. You will see more than that. You will see chests swell with pride at being who they are. And their war cry of 'For the Horde!' will come not just from their lips, but from their hearts."

Everyone but Thrall, Garrosh, and Cairne sat on the floor, the stone cushioned by thick, soft hides. All three races were used to being close to nature, and the hall was heated by braziers, fires, and body heat. Thrall noticed that only Magatha and her Grimtotem looked put out. Everyone else settled in, happy to be here at this feast, happy to simply be alive after so much pain and hardship and battle.

There was ceremony, but Thrall well knew that humans or elves would not recognize it as such. Servants brought in huge trays heaped high with delicacies. The food was eaten with the hands, and it was simple but nourishing: boar ribs basted in beer, roasted bear and venison, grilled haunch of zhevra turning on a spit, hearty bread to sop up the savory juices, and beer and wine and rum with which to wash it all down. Grommash Hold was filled with much laughter and cheer as the guests ate and drank. The servants cleared out the trays and, sated, those assembled turned their full attention to their warchief.

Now, thought Thrall, *the less than celebratory part begins.*

"We are glad and grateful that so many of our brave warriors have returned safely home, to bring what they have learned to serve the Horde here," Thrall began. "It is right to celebrate and honor their achievements. But war is not without its costs, both in the lives of the fallen, and in the financial costs to provide for the soldiers as they do battle. Due to the peculiar storm at sea that destroyed several of our vessels, we have lost both soldiers and sorely needed supplies.

"The storm not only cost us these precious things, but the strange nature of the event has not been the only one recorded. From all over Kalimdor and indeed in the Eastern Kingdoms, I have heard reports of similar phenomena. Those of you who, like me, call Orgrimmar home need no reminding of the drought that has had so devastating an impact. And we have felt the earth itself tremble beneath our feet from time to time.

"I have spoken with many of my most trusted shaman, and members of the Earthen Ring." Another pang went through him as he thought of the one shaman he had most trusted, whose judgment was now as unreliable as that of a small child. *Drek'Thar, I have never had greater need of your insight than now, and it is too late for you to share it with me.*

"We are doing everything to discover what, if anything, is troubling the elements. Or, conversely, to determine if this is all simply nature going through a completely normal cycle."

"Normal?" came a gruff voice from the back of the crowd. Thrall could not see the speaker, but it sounded like an orc. "Droughts in some areas, floods in others, earthquakes—how is this normal?"

"Nature has its own rhythms and reasons," Thrall said, completely unperturbed by the interruption. He welcomed challenges; they kept him sharp, showed that he was approachable, and oftentimes made him explore avenues previously unthought-of. "It does not adapt to suit us—we must change to accommodate it. A fire may destroy a city, but it also clears space for new and different kinds of plants to thrive. It burns off disease and harmful insects. It returns nutrients to the soil. Floods deposit new types of minerals in places that have never had them. And as for earthquakes, well . . ." He smiled. "Surely the Earth Mother is allowed to grumble from time to time."

There was a ripple of laughter, and Thrall felt the mood change. He himself was not entirely certain that what was being reported was normal; in fact, he was beginning to feel from what connections he could make that it was quite the opposite. The elements seemed . . . chaotic, distressed. They were not speaking clearly to him as they usually did, and he was worried. But there was no need to spread his worry among his people until such time as it was necessary for them to know. He could simply be too distracted by other things to listen as well as he needed to. And, ancestors knew, there were certainly plenty of other things for the warchief of the Horde to be distracted by.

"It is true that this land of Durotar, the new homeland of the orcs, is a harsh place. But that is nothing new. It has always been a difficult environment in which to dwell. But we are orcs, and this land suits us. It suits us *because* it is so harsh, *because* it is brutal, *because* few beings other than orcs could wrest a living from it. We came to this world from Draenor, after warlock magics had rendered most of it lifeless. And we could have done the same to this one. When I rebuilt the Horde, I might indeed have taken a more fertile land. But I did not."

Murmurs rippled throughout the hall. Cairne looked at him with narrowed eyes, no doubt wondering why Thrall was choosing to remind his people that Durotar was a difficult land at best. He nodded almost imperceptibly to his old friend, reassuring him that he knew what he was doing.

"I did not, because we had wronged this world. And yet, we were here in it, we had a right to live. To find a homeland. I chose a place that we could make our own—a land that asked of us all we could give. Living here has done much to cleanse us of the curse that so damaged us as a people. It has made us even stronger, hardier—more orclike than living in a soft land ever would."

Cairne's posture eased as the murmurs turned approving. "I stand by that choice. I well know what the sons and daughters of Durotar were able to give in Northrend. But our land gave, too. No one could have expected the high cost of supplies for the campaign in Northrend. And yet, could we have turned away from the call?"

No one spoke. No one present would have turned away, whatever the cost might be. "And thus it is that our land has given, as we have; given until it has almost given out. The war to the north is over. We must now turn our attention to our own lands, and our own needs. It is an unfortunate consequence of the events of the Wrath Gate that the Alliance has a fresh reason to oppose us. While I realize that to some of you this means nothing, and others are glad of it, I assure you that no one is glad of the fact that the night elves have, for the moment, shut down all trade avenues with us."

Everyone present knew what that meant—no fresh lumber for building, no hunting rights in Ashenvale, no safe passage anywhere the Sentinels patrolled. There was silence for a moment, then unhappy murmuring.

"Warchief, if I may?"

It was Cairne, in his slow, calm voice. Thrall smiled at his old friend. "Please. Your advice is always welcome."

"Our people have a connection with the night elves that the other races of the Horde do not," Cairne continued. "We are both followers of the teachings of Cenarius. We even have a joint sanctuary, the Moonglade, where we meet in peace and converse, sharing what knowledge and wisdom we have obtained. While I understand that they are angry with the Horde, I do not think that all bonds will be severed. I think the druids might be good ambassadors for reopening discussions. Archdruid Hamuul Runetotem knows many kaldorei."

He nodded at the archdruid, who rose to speak. "Indeed, Warchief. I have friendships with them that are years in the making. They may, as a race, resent us, but would take no pleasure in the thought of children starving to death, even the children of their so-called enemy. I have a high position in the Cenarion Circle. Negotiations could potentially be reopened, especially in light of the cooperation we have received with the treaty. If the warchief would permit me to approach them, perhaps we could prevail upon them to—"

"*Prevail* upon them? *Negotiate*? Pagh!" Garrosh actually spat on the floor as he spoke. "I am ashamed to hear such mewling words come from the mouth of any member of the Horde! What happened at the Wrath Gate harmed us all, or has everyone here already forgotten Saurfang the Younger and the many who died with him—and who were later obscenely raised as the walking dead to fight against us? The elves have no greater claim to being attacked than we!"

"Impertinent youth," growled Cairne, turning on Garrosh. "You use the name of Saurfang the Younger to your advantage when you openly disrespect the wisdom of his bereaved father!"

"Just because I disagree with Saurfang's tactics does not mean I belittle his son's sacrifice!" Garrosh retorted. "You, who have seen so many battles in your many, *many* years, should understand that! Yes, I disagreed with him. I said to him as I say to you, Warchief Thrall, let us not fret and whimper like kicked dogs about the night elves' oh-so-delicate feelings. Let us move into Ashenvale now, before my troops are scattered, and simply take what we need!"

The two had been leaning to their sides, shouting over Thrall as if he were not there. Thrall had permitted it because he wanted to judge the relationship between the two, but now he lifted a commanding hand and his voice was biting.

"It is not that simple, Garrosh!"

Garrosh turned to protest, but Thrall narrowed his blue eyes in warning, and the younger orc closed his mouth and sat sullenly silent.

"High Overlord Saurfang knows that," Thrall continued. "Cairne and I and Hamuul know that. You have had your first taste of battle and proved more than worthy at such a noble endeavor, but you will soon learn that nothing is black and white in this world."

Cairne leaned back in his chair, apparently mollified, but Thrall could see that Garrosh was still seething. At least, Thrall thought, he was listening and not talking.

"Varian Wrynn's stance against our people is becoming increasingly militaristic." He did not add, *thanks to you,* because he knew Garrosh would hear the unspoken words. "Jaina Proudmoore is his friend and is sympathetic to our cause."

"She is still Alliance scum!"

"She is still *Alliance,* yes," Thrall said, his voice deepening and growing louder, "but anyone who has served with me or who has bothered to read a single historical scroll over the last few years knows that she is a human with integrity and wisdom. Do you think Cairne Bloodhoof disloyal?"

Garrosh seemed taken aback by the abrupt change of subject. His eyes darted to Cairne, who sat up straighter and snorted.

"I—of course not. No one here questions his devotion and service to the Horde." He spoke carefully, looking for the trap. Thrall nodded. Although his tone was defensive, Garrosh's words did seem sincere to him.

"They would be a fool to do so. Jaina's loyalty to the Alliance does not preclude her working toward peace and prosperity for all who dwell in Azeroth. Nor does Cairne's loyalty to the Horde. His proposition is a sound one. It costs us little and could gain us much. If the night elves agree to open negotiations, well and good. If not, then we pursue other avenues."

Cairne looked over at Hamuul Runetotem, who nodded and said, "Thank you, Warchief. It is my deeply held belief that this is the right path, both to honor the Earth Mother, who seems so distressed, and to obtain what is needed for the Horde to recover from this terrible war."

"As always, my friend, I thank you for your service." Thrall turned to Garrosh. "Garrosh, you are the son of one who was very dear to me. I have heard you called the Hero of Northrend, and I think that an apt title. But I personally have found that sometimes after war, it is difficult for the warrior to find where he belongs. I, Thrall, son of Durotan and Draka, promise you that I will work with you to find a suitable position where your skills and abilities can best be used to serve the Horde."

He had meant this exactly as he said it. He did admire Garrosh's work in Northrend. But those talents were limited, and he needed time to think about where best to position Garrosh to work for the Horde.

Apparently, though, Garrosh did not understand Thrall's intention. His eyes narrowed and he growled softly beneath his breath.

"As the warchief wills, of course. With your permission, great Thrall, I find the air in here a bit stuffy."

Without waiting for the sarcastically requested permission, Garrosh rose, gave Thrall a nod that was only barely courteous enough, and strode outside.

"That boy is a kodo disliking the bridle," Cairne murmured.

Thrall sighed. "But too valuable to give up on."

He lifted his arm and, pitching his voice to carry, announced, "The air is close. More liquid to wet dry throats!"

A cheer went up, and the crowd was momentarily distracted. Thrall thought about Cairne's words and his own, and wondered how in the world he would tame the wild kodo without breaking him.

But Garrosh's role in the Horde, while an important concern to Thrall, was not uppermost in his mind. What troubled him most were the good of his people, of the Horde as a whole, and the unhappiness of the elements. His people were clamoring for more wood to build homes, but the very world itself seemed troubled.

He had chosen Durotar for the exact reasons he had spoken—because it enabled his people to atone for the harm they had done, and because this land had toughened and strengthened them. But he had never anticipated that so many rivers would dry up; that so much of what little forest there was would be denuded by a war that, while utterly necessary, was also utterly damaging.

No, Thrall thought as he sipped at a mug of beer. The taming of a single rebellious kodo was the least of his worries now.

FIVE

Garrosh gulped the night air gratefully. It was dry and warm even after nightfall, so unlike the cold, damp air of Northrend. But this was his home now, not the Borean Tundra, not Nagrand back in Draenor. This arid, inhospitable land, the city named for Orgrim Doomhammer, the land for Durotan, Thrall's father. He reflected on that a moment, nostrils flaring with irritation. The only thing named after him was a tiny strip of shoreline constantly hammered at by false ghosts.

He came to a stop beneath the skull and armor of Mannoroth and felt his agitated spirit calm somewhat. He did feel a swell of pride at looking at what his father had done. It was good to have learned he could be proud of his heritage, but he wanted to make his own path, not ride along in the wake of his father's deeds. Gorehowl, so newly his, was strapped to his back. He reached for it and held the weapon that had killed the great foe of his people, brown hands closing over the shaft.

"Your father was just what the Horde needed, when it

needed it," came a gravelly, deep, feminine voice behind him. Garrosh turned to see an elderly tauren. It took him a moment—her fur was dark, and in the night only the glitter of starlight on her intent eyes and the four stripes of white paint on her muzzle were immediately visible. As his eyes adjusted, he could see that she wore formal robes that marked her as a shaman.

"Thank you, um . . . ?" He waited for her to identify herself. She smiled.

"I am Elder Crone Magatha of the Grimtotem tribe," she said.

Grimtotem. He had heard the name. "Interesting that you speak of what the Horde needs when yours is the only tauren tribe that has refused to officially join it."

She chuckled softly, her rough voice oddly musical. "The Grimtotem does what it will, as it will. Perhaps we have not yet joined the Horde because we do not have sufficient reason to."

Garrosh took umbrage. "What? This is not sufficient?" He stabbed a thick brown finger at the skull and armor of a pit lord. "Our war against the Burning Legion was not? The Warsong offensive was not enough to impress the mighty Grimtotem?"

She regarded him steadily, not in the least put out by his ranting. "No," she said mildly. "It did not impress me. But the tales of what you did in Northrend . . . well, those are the deeds of a hero indeed. We Grimtotem watch. And wait. We know strength and cunning and honor when we see it. It could be that you, Garrosh Hellscream, like your father, are just what the Horde needs, when it needs it. And when the Horde figures this out as well, I think you may count on Grimtotem support."

Garrosh wasn't sure what she was getting at, but one thing was clear. She'd liked what she'd heard inside the keep. Which could mean that she approved of how he wanted to see things happen. That could be good. Maybe somebody could finally start getting something *done* around here.

"Thank you, Elder Crone. I appreciate your words now, and I hope that shortly I'll be worthy of more than words of support."

His mind was already awhirl with ways to bypass the pacifistic Thrall and the crotchety old Cairne and get the Horde what it needed. The trick was to do so without overstepping his bounds.

It was not a time to be cautious. It was a time to be bold. They would understand once he gave them results.

Cairne and his entourage were up and packed before dawn, despite the fact that the celebration had run well into the early hours and he, as a guest of honor, had been required to stay the entire time. He was anxious to return home. The troops he had sent to Northrend when Thrall had issued the call to arms were fierce fighters indeed, and had conducted themselves well. But they, too, were weary of bloodshed and endless nights and days of endurance. Once a nomadic people, the tauren now had a home, Mulgore, and it was dear to them. Today, finally, they began the last leg of the journey to its gentle, rolling hills, proud buttes, and the loved ones there they had left behind.

They had chosen to walk so they could keep the fellowship together for a little longer, but that was no hardship. As dawn was just breaking and other Horde fighters were either sleeping off the revelry or perhaps clutching their heads in payment for said revelry, the tauren were already out of Durotar and heading into the Barrens. Cairne sent ahead Perith Stormhoof to notify Baine that they would be arriving. Perith was one of a select few scouts and messengers called the Longwalkers. They were Cairne's only to command, and were trusted with the most important of messages and information. Not even Thrall knew everything Cairne shared with the Longwalkers. This was hardly a mission of great import. Lives did not depend on it. But Perith's eyes gleamed happily at this particular task, and he departed with his usual steady swiftness.

Late afternoon stretched its thick, golden light on the plains of Mulgore. Perith met them as they neared the turnoff for Camp Narache and Bloodhoof Village, falling into step beside Cairne as they moved slowly toward home.

"I have informed Baine, as you requested," Perith said. "He assures you that all will be ready."

"Good," approved Cairne. "The shops in all the villages should be aware that several travelers will be descending upon them. I would see none of my people go hungry tonight."

"I think you will find what Baine has in mind . . . acceptable."

Curious, Cairne turned to regard Perith. At that moment there was a blast of horns. Several kodos were lumbering toward them. Cairne's aging eyes could not discern who was atop the great beasts, but even his ears could hear the cheering of the little ones. They tumbled pell-mell off the kodos, shouting and laughing, throwing flowers and bundles of herbs at the approaching heroes.

"Welcome home, Father," said Baine Bloodhoof. Cairne turned at the sound of the familiar voice, squinted, and smiled as he made out the shape of his son, riding easily atop one of the great kodos.

Tears stung the old bull's eyes for a moment. This was how one should be welcomed home. With the happy cries of children and family, with the blessings of the natural world. Simpler, better . . . more tauren.

"Well done, my son," Cairne said, keeping the emotion out of his voice with an effort. "Well done."

Baine, calm and steady as his father, nonetheless radiated joy at Cairne's arrival. He dropped easily to the ground and approached his father. They clasped arms warmly, then fell into step, separating out a bit from the cluster of others joyfully welcoming family.

"There are more," Baine said, watching with a smile as several of the warriors took the road to the southwest. These lucky few had already reached their home. "The road home will be lined with those ready to welcome you."

"A sight for sore eyes," Cairne said. "Is all well with them?"

"It will be better once the veterans of the war are home," Baine said. "How was the celebration in Orgrimmar?"

"It did what it was supposed to," Cairne said. "It was very orcish. Much weaponry and feasting and shouting. Our people were not overlooked, though."

Baine nodded. "Thrall would never do so."

Cairne craned his neck over his shoulder, looking about for a moment, then continued in a lower voice. "He would not. He is too wise and too greathearted. I return home with a task that only we can perform to aid the Horde."

He spoke quietly to Baine of Hamuul's suggestion. Baine listened attentively, nodding at times, his ears twitching as he listened. "This is well," he said. "I am a warrior myself, but I tell you, our people have had enough of it. If Hamuul thinks these talks can help, then I am with you, Father. I fully support it."

Not for the first time, Cairne counted his blessings that the Earth Mother and his lifemate, Tamaala, had given him such a gift in his son. Although Tamaala had left to walk with the spirits many years ago, she lived on in their son. Baine was such a comfort to his father. He had his mother's spirituality, perception, and great heart, and his father's calmness and—Cairne was forced to admit—stubbornness. Cairne had not had to think twice about leaving Mulgore in his son's capable hands. He wondered how Thrall bore it, with no mate and no progeny. Even Grom had had a son, for the Earth Mother's sake. Perhaps now that the war had ended, Thrall might turn his thoughts to such things as a mate and an heir.

"How did our favorite shaman conduct herself in my absence?"

"Well enough," Baine replied. They were speaking of Magatha. "I watched her closely. It would have been an opportune time to stir up trouble, but there was none."

Cairne grunted. "There may be. Young Garrosh Hellscream is a hothead, and I saw her slip out to speak with him."

"I have heard he is a magnificent warrior," Baine said slowly, "but . . ." and here he grinned, "*also* a hothead."

The two Bloodhoof grinned at each other. Cairne clapped his hand on Baine's shoulder and squeezed hard. Baine swiftly covered his father's hand with his own.

Just ahead, Thunder Bluff rose majestically into the late afternoon sky.

"Welcome home, Father. Welcome home."

SIX

The day was cool and slightly overcast, and as Jaina Proudmoore walked up the blue and gold carpeted steps of Stormwind's magnificent cathedral, it began to rain. Part of the steps was blocked off, in need of repair after the War Against the Nightmare, and the rain made them slick. She did not bother to put up her hood to cover her bright golden hair, letting the droplets fall gently on her head and face. It was as if the sky itself was weeping at the thought of the ceremony about to be enacted within.

Two young priestesses flanking the door smiled and dropped curtseys. "Lady Jaina," the human girl on the right said, stammering a little, a blush visible even on her dark skin. "We were not told to expect you—do you wish to sit with His Majesty? I am sure that he will be pleased to have your company."

Jaina gave the girl her most disarming smile. "Thank you, no. I'm happy to sit with everyone else."

"Then here," said the dwarf priestess, extending an unlit candle. "Please take this, me lady, and sit wherever ye'd like. We're right glad tae have ye."

Her smile was genuine, if restrained, due to the solemnity of the moment. Jaina took the candle, stepped inside, and dropped a handful of gold coins into the offering plate next to the priestesses.

She breathed deeply; thanks to the dampness in the air, the smell of incense was even stronger here than usual, and it was darker inside than she remembered it being in the Cathedral of Light. The candles smoked as they burned, and Jaina glanced down the rows of pews searching for a space to sit, wondering if she should have rejected the young priestess's offer so quickly. Ah, there was a spot. She moved down the aisle and nodded at the elderly gnome couple who scooted aside to make room for her. From here she had an excellent view, and smiled as she watched the familiar figures of King Varian Wrynn and his son, Anduin, file in as unobtrusively as possible from a separate room.

Although Varian could never be considered "unobtrusive." It was not for nothing that, upon spotting him half-drowned and unconscious over a year ago, the orc Rehgar Earthfury had decided he would make a fine gladiator. With no memory of his past, Varian had adapted well to the brutal lifestyle. Unbeknownst to him at that time, he had actually been split into two separate entities—Varian, under the thumb of the dragon Onyxia, and Lo'Gosh, a fearsome and powerful gladiator. Varian held all of the original man's manners, knowledge, and etiquette; Lo'Gosh, a Taur-ahe word that meant "ghost wolf" and honored a ferocious creature of legend, all of the original Varian's battle skill. Varian was elegant; Lo'Gosh was violent. Varian was sophisticated; Lo'Gosh was brutal.

The two halves were eventually reunited, but imperfectly. Sometimes it seemed that Lo'Gosh had the upper hand in the tall, powerfully built body. More than ever, King Varian Wrynn, dark brown hair pulled back in a topknot and a wicked scar slicing across his once-handsome face, dominated a room.

Anduin was a sharp contrast to his father. He was pale, fair-haired, and slender, and slightly taller than the last time Jaina had seen him. While nowhere near his father's imposing size—and Jaina guessed he would take after his willowy mother and never be quite the large man that Varian was—he was a youth now and not a child. He exchanged smiles and nods with Brother Sarno and young Thomas as he and his father moved to take their seats. Perhaps feeling her gaze, he frowned slightly, looked around—and met her eyes. He was schooled enough in the formalities that princes should abide by that he didn't crack a grin, but his eyes brightened and he gave her a slight nod.

All eyes turned from the king and his son to Archbishop Benedictus, who had entered and was moving slowly to the altar. Of average height and solid, stocky build, the man looked more like a farmer than a holy man. He never seemed to quite fit his splendid robes of gold and white, looking slightly ill at ease. But once he began to speak, his voice, calm and clear, carrying throughout the cathedral, it was obvious that the Light had chosen him.

"Dear friends of the Light, you are all welcome here, in this beautiful cathedral that turns none away who come with open hearts and humble spirits. This place has seen many occasions of joy, and many of sorrow. Today we assemble to honor the fallen, to remember them, and mourn them, and respect their sacrifices for our Alliance and for Azeroth."

Jaina looked down at her hands clasped in her lap. This was one reason she had not wanted to be in a highly visible part of the cathedral. Her romance with Arthas Menethil had not been forgotten—not when he was prince, certainly not when he was the Lich King, and not now that he had been defeated. It was because of him that this sad ceremony was even necessary. A few heads turned her way, recognizing her, and giving her sympathetic glances.

Not a day went by that Jaina did not think of him, wondering if there was anything she could have done, anything she could have said, to have turned the once-bright paladin from his dark path. Her feelings had been turned against her during the War Against the Nightmare, trapping her in a dream in which she had indeed prevented him from becoming the Lich King . . . by becoming the Lich Queen herself in his stead. . . .

She shivered, forcing thoughts of that horrible dream away, and turned her attention back to the archbishop.

". . . the frozen lands far to the north," Benedictus was saying. "They faced a terrible foe with an army that no one ever truly thought we would be able to defeat. And yet, thanks to the blessing of the Light and the simple courage of these men and women—humans, dwarves, night elves, gnomes, draenei; yes, and even the members of the Horde as well—we are safe in our homeland again. The numbers are staggering, and more reports come in every day. To give you an idea of the estimated losses, each worshipper here today has been given a candle. Each candle represents not one, not ten . . . but *one hundred* Alliance lives lost in the Northrend campaign."

Jaina felt the breath go out of her and she stared at the unlit candle, clasped in a hand that suddenly started shaking. She looked around . . . there had to be at least two hundred people in the cathedral, and she knew that others were gathering outside, wanting to participate in the remembrance ceremony even though the cathedral was filled to capacity. Twenty, thirty—perhaps forty or fifty thousand people . . . dead. She closed her eyes for a moment and turned back to the archbishop, painfully aware that the gnome couple next to her was staring at her and whispering something.

When she heard raised voices and startled gasps from the back of the cathedral, it was almost a relief. She turned and saw two weather-beaten Sentinels talking animatedly with the two priestesses. Even as she rose and tried to exit quietly, she saw Varian already on the move.

The human priestess, apparently against the wishes of the dwarf, who looked put out, was steering the two Sentinels into a room on the left-hand side. Jaina hastened to join them. Even as she walked through the entrance to the room, Varian joined her. There was no time for greetings, but the two exchanged acknowledging glances.

Varian turned to the paladins who had also moved to join them. "Lord Grayson," he said to the tall man with black hair and an eye patch, "get these soldiers some food and drink."

"Aye, sir," the paladin said, hastening off to do so himself. Such was the attitude of paladins; any service, however humble, that helped another was of the Light.

"Please, sit," Varian said.

The taller of the two night elves, a purple-skinned woman with white hair, shook her head. "Thank you, Your Majesty, but this is no pleasure errand. We come with dire news and stand ready to report back as soon as possible."

Varian nodded, tensing slightly. "Then deliver your news."

She nodded. "I am Sentinel Valarya Riverrun. This is Sentinel Ayli Leafwhisper. We come with reports of attacks by the Horde in Ashenvale. The treaty has been violated."

Jaina and Varian exchanged glances. "We knew when we signed the agreement that there would be a few holdouts, on both sides," Jaina said hesitantly. "The borders have long been a source of—"

"I would not be here if this were a *skirmish,* Lady Jaina Proudmoore," Valarya said icily. "We were not born yesterday. We know to expect the occasional row. This was not such a thing. This was a *slaughter.* A slaughter, when the Horde claims to be peaceable!"

Jaina and Varian listened, Jaina with ever-widening eyes and Varian slowly clenching his fists, as the gory tale unfolded. A dozen Sentinels had been ambushed as they guarded a convoy of harvested herbs and mineral carts making their way through the green forests of Ashenvale. None had survived. Their deaths were only discovered when the convoy was two days late in arriving at its destination. The carts and all they had contained were gone.

Valarya paused and took a deep breath, as if calming herself. Her sister Sentinel stepped beside her and squeezed her shoulder. Varian was frowning, but Jaina pressed on.

"It is indeed a violation of the agreement," Jaina said, "and as such needs to be brought to Thrall's attention. But even so—I'm afraid I still don't see what makes you call this a slaughter rather than an unfortunately not uncommon incident."

Ayli winced and turned away. Jaina looked from one to the other. These were warriors, who had likely been fighting for longer than Jaina had been alive. What had rattled them so?

"Let me put it this way, Lady Proudmoore," Valarya said through clenched teeth. "We weren't able to recover the bodies."

Jaina swallowed. "Why not?"

"Because they had been methodically chopped into several pieces," Valarya said, "and those pieces were taken away by carrion eaters. This was, of course, *after* they had been skinned. We're not sure if they were alive for that or not."

Jaina's hand flew to her mouth. Bile rose in her throat. This was beyond obscene, beyond an atrocity. . . .

"The skins were hung like linens from a nearby tree. And on that tree, written in elven blood, were Horde symbols."

"Thrall!" bellowed Varian. He whirled on Jaina, glar-

ing at her. "He authorized this! And you prevented me from killing him when I had the chance!"

"Varian," Jaina said, fighting not to be sick, "I've fought beside him. I've helped negotiate treaties with him—treaties he has always honored. There is *nothing* about this that sounds like *anything* he would do. We have no proof whatsoever that he authorized this incursion, and—"

"No proof? Jaina, they were orcs! He's an orc, and he's supposed to lead the damned Horde!"

Her stomach was calm now, and she knew that she was in the right. "The Defias are humans," Jaina said, very quietly. "Should you be held responsible for their actions?"

Varian jerked as if she had struck him. For a moment she thought she had reached him. The Defias were a deeply personal enemy and had taken a great deal from Varian. Then his brows drew together in a scowl that was made terrifying by the brutal scar across his face. He did not look like himself now.

He looked like Lo'Gosh.

"You dare recall that to me," he growled softly.

"I do. Someone has to recall you to yourself." She did not meet the anger of Lo'Gosh, the part of Varian that was cold and swift and violent, with anger of her own. She met it with the practicality that had saved her—and others—time and time again.

"You lead the kingdom of Stormwind—the most powerful in the Alliance. Thrall leads the Horde. You can make laws, and rules, and treaties, and so can he. And he is no more capable of controlling the actions of every single one of his citizens than you are. No one is."

Lo'Gosh scowled. "What if you are wrong, Jaina? And what if I'm right? You've been known to be a poor judge of character in the past."

Now it was Jaina's turn to freeze, stunned, at the words. He was hurling Arthas back at her. That was how Lo'Gosh played, how he had won in gladiatorial combat—dirty, using every tool at his disposal in order to win at all costs. Her nightmare rushed back at her, and she pushed it away. She took a deep breath and composed herself.

"Many of us knew Arthas well, Varian. Including you. You lived with him for years. You didn't see the monster he would become. Neither did his father, nor Uther."

"No, I didn't. But I'm not making the same mistake again, and you are. Tell me, Jaina, if you had seen what Arthas would become . . . would you have tried to stop him? Would you have had the guts to kill your lover, or would you have stood by, peace at all costs, a mewling little pacifist who—"

"Father!"

The word, uttered in a boyish tenor voice, cracked like a whip. Varian whirled.

Anduin stood in the doorway. His blue eyes were wide and his face was drained of color. But there was more than an expression of shock on his face. There was bitter disappointment. Before Jaina's eyes, Varian changed. Gone was the coldly raging anger of Lo'Gosh. His posture shifted. He was Varian again.

"Anduin—" Varian's voice, steady, but tinged with worry and a hint of regret.

"Save it," Anduin said, disgusted. "You stay in here and—do whatever it was you were doing. I'll go back out to provide the sort of royal face that lets our people know *someone* cares about what they've lost. Even if he is a mewling little pacifist."

He turned on his heel and stalked toward the door. He gripped the doorframe for a moment. Jaina watched as his back straightened and he brushed at his hair, composing himself, putting on the face of calmness as he might put on his crown. He had had to grow up so quickly. The two Sentinels glanced at one another briefly. Varian stood for a moment, staring where his son had been. He sighed deeply.

"Jaina, why don't you return as well?" At her look of uncertainty, he smiled a little. "Don't worry. The Sentinels and I will talk reasonably about what's to be done."

Jaina nodded. "Afterward, though—a moment of your time?"

"Of course." He turned back to the two elven females. "Now, you were saying. When did the attacks occur?"

The conversation continued in low voices. Varian was listening to all that was said, but he would not rush to anger again. Jaina turned and slipped quietly from the room. She did not, however, seek out the same pew at which she had been sitting. Instead, she hung toward the back of the cathedral, standing quietly in the shadows, watching and listening and doing what she did best . . . thinking.

SEVEN

An hour later, the service was over. She'd not really wanted to continue to attend. But as the ceremony continued, she realized that she needed to be here for at least two people. One of them was herself. Halfway through the sermon, she found herself with her head bowed, tears slipping down her cheeks as she mourned those who had given all to stand against evil; mourned the young, earnest man Arthas Menethil had once been. And through the tears, she found a sense of peace she had not known until that moment.

As for the other . . .

She returned to the small room where Varian had received the Sentinels. The elves were gone, but the king of Stormwind was still there. He sat at a small table, his head in his hands. He looked up at her approach, even though she had been quiet, and gave her a weary smile.

"I am sorry I so lost control earlier."

"You should be."

He nodded, acknowledging the truth of her comment. "I am. What I said was inappropriate and untrue."

She softened a little. "Apology accepted. And I'm not the only person who deserves one."

He grimaced at that, but nodded. "I would rather he not have seen that, but what's done is done."

She slipped into the chair opposite him, ready to listen. "Tell me what happened."

He did. He had agreed to send several alchemists to Ashenvale to assist the night elves in looking over the site of the slaughter and examining the blood and clothing. An emissary, unarmed and no doubt sweating bullets, would be sent to Thrall to conduct an inquiry.

"That's very . . . restrained of you," Jaina commented.

"My actions should depend on what I know, not what I suspect. If it turns out that Thrall is behind this atrocity, rest assured I will march on Orgrimmar and have his head. I don't care if I'm authorized to do that or not, I will."

"If he is, I'll be marching beside you," Jaina said. She was certain Thrall would be as shocked and horrified by the attack as Varian and Jaina had been. Even if he was not Varian's friend, he would always be an honorable foe. He would never have authorized a violation of the treaty, let alone so gruesome an attack.

"I wanted to talk about Anduin," she said, changing the subject.

Varian nodded. "Anduin is a born diplomat. He understood the necessity to go to war in Northrend, but he yearned—still yearns—for peace. And I seem to be unable to cease yearning for war. Things were good when I came back, but . . ."

"Well, he *is* a teenager," Jaina said lightly.

"He took Bolvar's death hard. Very hard."

At the name, Jaina shifted uncomfortably.

"I realized how close they had become while I was gone. Bolvar was like a father to Anduin."

"Does . . . he know?" Jaina asked quietly.

Varian shook his head. "And I hope he never does." When the Lich King was finally slain, dreadful news came with the victory—the revelation that there must always be a Lich King, or else the Scourge would run rampant across the world. Someone needed to don the helm, become the next Lich King, or else everything they had all fought for would be for nothing.

It was Bolvar—his life saved by the red dragons' flames but his body hideously deformed, seeming a living ember shaped vaguely like a man—who had insisted on undertaking the dreadful task. And it was Bolvar who now wore the Lich King's crown, sitting atop the roof of the world, forever destined to be the jailor of the undead. Even now, Jaina's blue eyes filled with quick tears at the thought.

"Anduin has had a difficult time of it," Jaina said, her voice thick. She cleared it and resumed. "But Bolvar was not his father. You are, and I know he's glad to have you back. But—"

"But he wants his *father* back, not Lo'Gosh. Completely understandable. But Jaina . . . sometimes I'm not sure where one ends and the other begins. I . . . do not like having the boy around, living with me, while I try to determine this."

"I've been thinking the same thing. And I have an idea. . . ."

* * *

Jaina slipped her hood over her head as she exited the cathedral. It was still raining, and in fact had picked up. It did not distress her unduly; living in Theramore, she was well accustomed to such damp weather.

Having teleported to Stormwind, she had no palfrey, so she strode quickly through the wet streets toward Stormwind Keep. It was not a long walk, but her feet found a few puddles, and when she did arrive, she was quite thoroughly soaked and shivering.

The guards knew her and nodded politely as she entered. Servants stepped up to her quickly, offering to take her cloak and get her something hot to drink. She waved aside the offers, smiling kindly, and thanked them for their attentiveness. As she was a well-known visitor, they did not question where she wished to go in the keep when she asked directions.

Jaina made her way past the formal rooms and the throne room into the private areas of the castle. She reached her destination, smoothed her soggy hair, and knocked on the door to Anduin's quarters.

There was no immediate response. She tried again, this time saying quietly, "Anduin? It's me, Jaina."

She heard the quiet tread of feet approaching the door, and then it opened a crack. Solemn blue eyes peered up at her and then flickered past her.

"It's just me," she assured him. He nodded his fair head and then stepped back to admit her.

Stormwind Keep was lavish enough, she supposed, though it did not hold a candle to Lordaeron's once-magnificent palace. She remembered what Prince

Arthas's chambers had been like as she took in Anduin's rather sparse room. He had been prince all his life, and king for a time, during Varian's absence, and yet this room was simple and spare. The bed was small, better suited to the child he had been rather than the youth he was. He'd need a larger one soon, she thought; he was growing like a weed. The bed frame lacked ornate hangings, the walls paintings, save for one—a portrait of Anduin and his mother, Queen Tiffin, when the boy was still an infant. Jaina guessed she had died not long after that portrait had been painted, slain by a rock thrown during a Defias riot. It was this incident that she had referred to earlier with Varian, in an attempt to get him to understand the position Thrall was in. Tiffin's son had never known her.

There was a simple nightstand with a pitcher of water and a basin next to the bed on one side. An unlit brazier stood a few feet away, to take the chill off the room in winter. A door opened presumably to another room where Anduin's clothing and other regalia were stored, as Jaina saw nothing here, not even a wardrobe. In the center of the room there was a single chair next to a small table upon which sat books, parchment, ink, and a quill. Politely Anduin eased the chair out for her, reaching to take off her cloak and hang it up, then stood next to the chair, his arms folded. He was obviously still upset from his earlier conversation with his father.

"You're drenched," he said flatly. "Let me order you some hot tea."

"Thank you. That would be most welcome." She gave him a smile.

He returned it, but it was forced and did not reach his eyes. He tugged on a braided rope beside the door.

"I swear, you'll be as big as your father the next time I see you," Jaina teased, hoping to ease him out of his mood. She settled into the chair.

He grimaced slightly. "Which version of my father?" His voice was evenly pitched, carefully modulated as befit a prince, but the words had a bite to them that Jaina, who knew him so well, winced at.

"Your father is chagrined that you witnessed that," she said gently.

"I'm certain he is," Anduin said in that same voice. "But there are many things I have witnessed at my age."

He stood straight and tall, his hands clasped behind his back. Was he betrothed yet? She realized she didn't know. She hoped not. Anduin was right. He had seen a great deal in his short life, and she had rather hoped that he would yet have some time to be a boy, at least.

"Oh, for pity's sake," she said, waving a slightly annoyed hand at him. "You're unsettling me, standing there like you have a polearm for a spine. Go hop on the bed and talk with me. You know I'm not much for ceremony."

Like ice cracking under the first warm rays of a spring sun, a slight smile curved Anduin's lips. She winked at him. The smile became a full-fledged grin, a slightly sheepish one, but a grin nonetheless.

There was a soft knock on the door. A gray-haired servant stood in the doorway.

"What can I do for you, Your Highness?"

"Some peacebloom tea. Two cups. Oh . . ." He turned

to Jaina. "Are you cold? I can have Wyll light the brazier for us."

Jaina quirked an eyebrow, lifted a hand, and fluttered it in the direction of the brazier. At once the kindling in it caught.

"Not necessary, but thank you."

He laughed at the display. "I forgot. Just the tea, then. Oh, and some bread and honey. And some cheese, Dalaran sharp. And a couple of apples." Jaina was touched. Anduin had remembered apples and cheese were Jaina's favorite snack. "Thank you."

Jaina hid her smile. Definitely a growing boy. Once Wyll had left, Anduin obeyed her earlier request, settling himself comfortably on the bed, regarding her with those bright blue eyes that saw more than adults suspected.

"There, that's better. I've not come to lecture you or to apologize for your father," Jaina continued. "I've come to give you an opportunity for a little fun, if you like."

He raised a golden eyebrow at that. "Oh? Fun?" He pronounced the word with exaggerated awkwardness. "What, pray tell, is that?"

"Something you need more of. Your father *is* upset that you had to see that. He and I talked for a bit, and we both decided that you might like to have the chance to get away from things from time to time."

He eyed her curiously. "What exactly did you have in mind?"

"How would you like to come visit me at Theramore?" Anduin had been to Theramore once, during a terrible storm, to attend peace talks that had been violently disrupted. She hoped to change his association of the place to a more positive one.

But Anduin apparently had the resiliency of youth, for instead of looking unhappy, he brightened. "Visit the frontier again? I'd like that very much! I didn't get to see very much of it at all. Is there any dragon fighting going on?"

"Hardly any at all," Jaina said with a mock sigh. "But I'm sure there is some trouble a thirteen-year-old boy can get into."

"Thirteen and a half, almost," Anduin admonished her in all seriousness.

"I stand corrected."

"But . . . it's a very long journey."

"Not for magi."

"Well, no, of course not, I didn't mean for *you,* Aunt Jaina, I meant for me."

She smiled at him. "I've got a little something that might make traveling a bit easier." She fished in the pouch clipped to her belt and came out with a small oval crystal covered with soft blue runes. "Here. Catch!"

Jaina tossed it to Anduin, who caught it easily. "It's pretty," he said, examining it and tracing the runes with his fingers.

"Pretty, and rather rare. Hold it lightly for now. Don't close your fingers over it. Recognize the runes?"

He peered at it. "It has your name and the word . . . 'Home,'" he said.

"That's right. I see you've been keeping up with your studies. I had this created just for you. Even before . . .

today . . . I had thought that you might enjoy coming to visit your old Auntie Jaina."

He scowled at her, brushing a lock of blond hair off his face. "You're not old," he said.

"And you've been keeping up with your diplomacy, too," she said, grinning. "But yes. It's called a hearth-stone."

"But the *rune* means 'home.'"

"Yes, it does, but 'homestone' sounds so ugly. 'Hearthstone' is more musical."

He chuckled, turning the hearthstone over in his hand, and said in a slightly supercilious tone, "Trust a *girl* to worry about such things."

"Kingdoms have risen and fallen over less," Jaina said.

"True enough," he allowed. "So, how does this hearthstone work?"

"Close your hand tightly over it, and concentrate."

Anduin obeyed. Jaina rose and went to him, placing her hand over his. A faint blue light limned her hand, then his.

"This will bind the stone to you," Jaina said quietly. He nodded his understanding. "Focus. Take the stone into yourself. Make it yours."

She felt the shift, from her to him, and smiled softly to herself as she let go. "There. It's yours now."

Anduin looked at it again, grinning. He was clearly fascinated. "It's purely magical, right? It's not a gnomish construct?"

Jaina nodded. "And I'm afraid it will only take you to Theramore. From there, we can port you back home."

"Wouldn't want to put the dwarves and their gryphons out of business I suppose," Anduin said with that odd streak of pragmatism that surfaced now and then.

"Be mindful of when you use it," she said, rising. "It will literally take you right to my hearth. Midafternoon is a very good time."

He continued to regard the stone, smiling, and Jaina's heart lifted. This was definitely the right thing to do. She held out her arms to him. Anduin slipped off the bed and hugged her. He was growing up, she thought to herself, her arms around shoulders that were broader than she remembered, his head resting on her shoulder. This boy had known nothing but challenge, hardship, and loss, and yet he could laugh, could embrace his "auntie," could be excited at the prospect of visiting the frontier.

Light, let him stay a boy a little longer. Let him know at least something of peace before he has to take on adult responsibilities . . . again.

"You might regret this, Aunt Jaina," he said, pulling away and regarding her seriously.

Her heart lurched at his tone of voice. "Why do you say that, Anduin?"

"Because I'm probably going to be visiting you *all the time.*"

Relief swept through her. "That hardship I think I can handle." Jaina Proudmoore, ruler of Theramore and a powerful sorceress, laughed like a girl and mussed the prince of Stormwind's bright golden hair.

EIGHT

For a change, the weather was dry and the skies were partially clear as the pair of orcs rode their wolves through Dustwallow Marsh. The orcs were male, one older, one younger. Both looked as though they had been wandering for weeks in the swamp with their old, stained clothes. They wore oversized cloaks wrapped around their frames, a wise precaution in a place usually so rainy. Their wolves, though, were surprisingly sleek coated and healthy looking to belong to such obviously down-on-their-luck masters, although they, too, were now muddy from many sessions of plodding through the muck and mire.

The trek ended in a swim out to one of the little islands off the coast, in a place called Tidefury Cove. The riders dismounted and swam side by side with their wolves. When the orcs emerged on dry land, they moved a safe distance away from the vigorous shaking that ensued as the wolves clambered ashore.

The younger orc took out a spyglass and lifted it to his face. "Right on time," he said.

A dinghy was approaching. In it was a single, slender figure, wearing a cloak that concealed its form as the orcs' cloaks had. But pale hands that were small and uncallused revealed that the lone occupant was female—and human.

The younger orc waded into the water as the human woman's vessel approached. Easily he grabbed the bow and pulled the boat firmly onto the shore, extending a hand to help her out. Without hesitation, she grasped the huge, rough hand, her own barely curling around two fingers, and permitted herself to be assisted.

Once out of the boat, she slipped off her hood, revealing bright golden hair and a smile equally as bright.

"Thrall," Jaina Proudmoore said warmly. "Someday we shall meet under better circumstances."

"Ancestors willing, that day will not be long in coming," Thrall rumbled, his voice deep and affectionate. He slipped off his own hood, revealing a strong, bearded, orcish face and eyes as blue as her own.

Jaina squeezed his hand and then released it, turning to his companion, an older orc with white hair pulled back in a topknot and a sparse beard. "Eitrigg," she said, and dropped a small curtsey.

"Lady Jaina." His voice was cooler than Thrall's, but still kind. With a nod, he moved slightly away to higher ground, to keep watch while his warchief and the human sorceress spoke.

Jaina turned back to Thrall, her brow furrowing. "Thank you for agreeing to meet me here. In light of . . . recent events, I thought a meeting site other than our usual one at Razor Hill would be a good idea.

Word has reached Stormwind of the . . . incident in Ashenvale."

Thrall grimaced and ground his teeth. "Word has reached *me* of the incident in Ashenvale." His voice simmered with barely contained anger.

Jaina let herself smile. "I knew that you couldn't possibly be behind it. That the rumors you were involved weren't true."

"Of course they're not true!" Thrall spat the words. "I would never condone such barbarity. And if I make a treaty with the Alliance, I intend to see that it is kept." He sighed and rubbed his face. "Still—I cannot lie. Orgrimmar, the Barrens—they are in desperate need of supplies. And there are plenty of both to be had in Ashenvale."

"But that's not the way to get them," Jaina said.

"I know this," Thrall snapped, then added more gently, "but others apparently do not understand such—subtleties. Jaina, I did not authorize that incursion, and I am furious at the level of brutality displayed toward the Sentinels. I deeply regret the violation of the treaty. But the results have proven . . . very popular."

"Popular?" Jaina's eyes widened. "I know some of the Horde have bloodthirsty natures, but—I confess I had thought better of them as a whole. I had thought you—"

"I have done what I thought best," Thrall said, then added under his breath, "though now sometimes I question." More loudly, he said, "We have a violent history, Jaina. And the more fate forces us toward simply surviving, the closer to the bone we must pare."

"Have you received Varian's courier?"

The grimace deepened. "I have." They both knew what the courier's letter had said. Varian had been very controlled in the missive—for him. He had demanded that Thrall issue a formal apology, reaffirm his dedication to the treaty, denounce the actions, and turn over those responsible to Alliance justice. Varian would then agree to overlook the "blatant violation to a treaty designed to promote peace and cooperation between our two peoples."

"What are you going to do? Do you know who did it?"

"I do not have proof, but I have my suspicions. I cannot approve of the action."

"Well, of course you can't," Jaina said, looking at him uncertainly. "Thrall, what's wrong?"

He sighed. "I cannot approve of it," he repeated, "but I will not do as Varian demands."

She stared at him for a moment, mouth slightly open in shock. "What do you mean? Varian believes you deliberately broke the treaty. His request wasn't unreasonable, and he will have the perfect excuse to escalate the situation. We could be looking at outright war!"

He held up a large green hand. "Please. Listen to me. I will send a letter to Varian, stating that I did not condone the incursion. I will seek out those responsible. I've no desire for war. But I cannot apologize for the violence, nor will I turn over any suspects to the Alliance. They are Horde. They will be judged by Horde. To give them to Varian—no. It is a betrayal of my people's trust on far too many levels. And frankly . . . it is wrong. Varian would never stand for such a request from me, nor should he."

"Thrall, if you didn't give the order, then you're not responsible, and—"

"But I *am* responsible. I lead my people. It is one thing to rebuke my people for violating a law. It is another to appear to attack their sense of self. Their very identity. You do not understand how the Horde thinks, Jaina," Thrall said quietly. "That is one thing my unique upbringing granted me. To understand how things are perceived from both sides. My people hunger, they thirst for clean water, they must have wood for housing. They believe they were wronged when the night elves closed the trade routes. They see this unwillingness to fill basic needs as a brutal act—and someone, somewhere, decided to retaliate in kind."

"Slaughtering night elves and removing their skins is in-kind retaliation for closed trade?" Her voice rose.

"Closed trade permits children to starve, to be exposed to the elements, to become sick. The logic . . . I can follow it. And so can others. If I were to condemn this attack openly, when it successfully provided something so desperately needed—it would seem as though I am condemning that need. I would look weak, and believe me, there are plenty who would like to take advantage of such a moment of perceived vulnerability. It is a treacherous path I walk, my friend. I must rebuke them—but only to a point. I will apologize for the violation of a treaty, but not for the theft, or even the murders or how they were performed."

"I am—disappointed that you choose this path, Thrall," Jaina said, being completely honest.

"Your opinion matters to me. It always does.

Nonetheless, I will not grovel before Varian, nor play down the desperate survival needs of my people."

Jaina was silent for a long moment, her arms folded tight across her chest, looking down at the ground. "I think I understand," she replied finally, the words coming slowly, bitterly. "Light, how I hate to say that. But one thing *you* need to understand is how very badly the Wrath Gate incident harmed your relationship with the Alliance. We lost almost five thousand at the Wrath Gate alone, Thrall. And in particular, the loss of Highlord Bolvar Fordragon was personally felt by so very many."

"As was the loss of Saurfang the Younger," Thrall said. "The best and brightest sliced down in his prime, then raised to . . . well. Do not think the Horde escaped lightly from this conflict."

"Oh, I don't. But—it is hard to bear. Especially when so many of the fallen died at Horde hands and not Scourge."

"Putress was not of the Horde!" Thrall growled.

"It's a distinction that not a lot of people make. And even now, there are doubts. You know that."

Thrall nodded, growling a little in the back of his throat. Jaina knew it was not directed at her but at Putress and the rest of those who had been behind the attack. Those who had claimed allegiance to the Horde while plotting behind its back.

"First that, and now this. It's going to be hard for the Alliance leadership to trust you," Jaina continued. "A lot of people, Varian included, felt that you didn't do enough to address the situation after it happened. Publicly decrying all aspects of this incursion would go a long way to mending the Alliance's image of you and the Horde both. And let's face it—it wasn't a little scuffle. This was horrific."

"It was. And turning over suspected criminals to Alliance justice would be a horror that my people would never recover from. It would shame them, and I will never do that. They would seek to overthrow me, and they would be right in doing so."

She regarded him evenly. "Thrall, I don't think you fully appreciate the direness of the situation. It's not going to do much good for you to tacitly approve something you deplore if it brings war upon the Horde. And Varian—"

"Varian is a hothead," Thrall snapped.

"So is Garrosh."

Thrall suddenly chuckled. "Those two are more alike than they know."

"Well, their hotheaded similarities may end up getting more people killed, far too soon after Northrend."

"You know I do not wish war," Thrall said. "I led my people here to avoid senseless conflict. But truth be told, from what you have said, it does not sound like Varian is inclined to listen to me anyway. He would not believe me even if I *did* publicly denounce the attack. Would he?"

She did not answer, her brow furrowing deeper in her unhappiness. "I . . . I would encourage him to."

Thrall smiled sadly and gently dropped a huge hand on her narrow shoulder. "I will condemn the breaking of the Horde's word . . . but nothing more." He looked around at the dismal swamp environment in which they stood.

"Durotar was the place I chose to give my people a fresh start. Medivh told me to bring them here, and I chose to listen to him, though I knew nothing of this place. When we arrived, I saw it to be a harsh land, not verdant like the Eastern Kingdoms. Even places with water, such as this, are difficult in which to dwell. I chose to remain here despite that, to give my people a chance to pit their spirits against the land. Their spirits are still mighty, but the land . . ." He shook his head. "I think Durotar has given all it can. I must tend to it, to my people."

Jaina's eyes searched his. She brought her hand up to brush a lock of golden hair out of her eyes, a girlish gesture, but her expression and words were those of a leader. "I understand that the Horde works differently than the Alliance, Thrall, but—if you can find a way to do what I urge you to, you will find a path open to you that would otherwise not be."

"There are many paths open to us at all times, Jaina," Thrall said. "As leaders of those who trust us, we owe it to them to examine every one."

She extended her hands to him, and he clasped them gently. "Then I shall just have to hope that the Light guides you, Thrall."

"And I hope your ancestors watch over and protect you and yours, Jaina Proudmoore."

She smiled up at him warmly, as another fair-haired human girl had in the not-so-distant past, then Jaina returned to her small boat. Still, Thrall thought as he gave the dinghy a good shove, he saw a little furrow in her forehead that told him she was still troubled.

So was he.

He folded his arms and watched the water take her back toward her home. Eitrigg came quietly down to join his warchief.

"It is a pity," Eitrigg said, apropos of apparently nothing.

"What is?" asked Thrall.

"That she is not an orc," Eitrigg said. "Strong and smart and greathearted. A leader all on her own. She would bear strong sons and brave daughters. A fine mate she could make someone someday, if she so chose. A pity she is not an orc, and so cannot be yours."

Thrall couldn't help it. He threw back his head and laughed loudly, startling some crows resting in a nearby tree into cawing angrily and flapping away in a flurry of black wings to a quieter perch.

"We are coming off wars with the Lich King and nightmares themselves," Thrall said. "Our people are starving, thirsting, and reverting to barbarism. The king of Stormwind thinks me a brute, and the elements turn deaf ears to my pleas for understanding. And you speak of mates and children?"

The old orc was completely unruffled. "What better time? Thrall, everything is unsettled now. Including your place as warchief of the Horde. You have no mate, no child, no one to carry on your blood if you were suddenly to join the ancestors. You have not even seemed interested in such a thing."

Thrall growled, "I have had more on my mind than dalliances and getting a mate with child," he said.

"As I say . . . those reasons are precisely why that is so

important. Too—there is a comfort and a clarity to be found in the arms of one's true mate that can be found nowhere else. The heart never soars as high as when listening to the laughter of one's children. These are things you have put aside for perhaps too long—things that I have known, though they were taken from me. I would not trade that knowing for anything else in this or any other life."

"I need no lecture," Thrall grumbled.

Eitrigg shrugged. "Perhaps that is true. Perhaps it is you who needs to speak, not I. Thrall, you are troubled. I am old, and I have learned much. And one of those things I have learned is how to listen."

He slogged into the water, his wolf following. Thrall stood for a moment, then followed. When they reached the shore, both orcs swung onto the backs of their wolf mounts and said nothing more. They rode in silence for a while, and Thrall collected his thoughts.

There was something he had not shared with anyone, not even Eitrigg. He might have shared it with Drek'Thar, had that shaman still been in possession of his faculties. As it was, though, Thrall had kept it to himself, a cold knot of a fearful secret. Inwardly, he was at war with himself.

At last, after they had ridden for some time, he spoke. "You may understand after all, Eitrigg. You, too, have had interaction with humans that has been more than slaughter. I straddle two worlds. I was raised by humans, but born an orc, and I have gleaned strength from both. I *know* both. That knowledge was power, once. I can say without boasting that it made me a unique leader, with unique skills, able to work with two sides at a time when unity had been utterly vital to the survival of all of Azeroth.

"My heritage served me, and through my leadership, the Horde, very well then. But . . . I cannot help but wonder . . . does it still serve them now?"

Eitrigg kept his eyes on the road before him and merely grunted, indicating that Thrall should continue.

"I want to care for my people, provide for them, keep them safe so that they can turn their attention to their families and rituals." Thrall smiled a little. "To finding mates and getting children. To the things all thinking beings have a right to. To not have to constantly see their parents or children going off to war and never returning. And those who still spoil for battle do not see what I do—the Horde population now consists largely of children and elders. A whole generation almost entirely lost."

He sensed the weariness in his voice, and Eitrigg obviously did, too, for he said, "You sound . . . soul sick, my friend. It is not like you to so doubt yourself, or to fall so far into despair."

Thrall sighed. "It seems most of my thoughts are dark these days. The betrayal in Northrend—Jaina cannot imagine how stunned, how shocked I was. It took all my skill to keep the Horde from splintering afterward. These new fighters—they have cut their warrior's tusks on slaughtering undead, and that is a very different thing from attacking a living, breathing foe, who has family and friends, who laughs and cries. It is easy for them to become inured to violence, and harder for me to temper them with arguments that call for understanding and perhaps even compassion."

Eitrigg nodded. "I once walked away from the Horde because I grew sickened by their love of violence. I see what you see, Thrall, and I, too, worry that history will repeat itself."

They had emerged from the shadows of the swamplands and onto the road heading north. Heat from the baking sun seared them. Thrall glanced around at the place so aptly named the Barrens. It was drier than ever, browner than ever, and he saw few signs of life. The oases, the salvation of the Barrens, had begun drying up as mysteriously as they had appeared.

"I cannot recall the last time I felt rain on my face in Durotar," Thrall said. "The silence of the elements at this time when something is clearly so very wrong . . ." He shook his head. "I remember the awe and joy with which Drek'Thar pronounced me a shaman. And yet, I hear nothing."

"Perhaps their voices are being drowned out by these others you are listening to," Eitrigg offered. "Sometimes, in order to solve many problems, you must focus on only one for a time."

Thrall considered the words. They struck him as wisdom. So much could be eased if he understood what was wrong with this land and was able to help heal it. His people would eat, would have shelter again. They would not feel the need to take from those who already had bitterness and hate in their hearts. Tensions would be eased between the Horde and the Alliance. And maybe then Thrall could focus on, as Eitrigg had said, his own legacy, his own peace and contentment.

And he knew exactly where to go to listen.

"I have been to the land of my father only once," he told the elder orc. "I wonder if now another journey is in order. Draenor was a world that saw more than its fair share of elemental pain and violence. What it is now—Outland—could still remember that. My grandmother, Geyah, is a powerful shaman. She could guide me as I attempt to listen to the wounded elements there. And perhaps they have some knowledge bought from the pain of their own world that could help ease Azeroth."

Eitrigg grunted, but Thrall knew him well enough to know the gleam in the other's eyes was that of approval.

"Sooner you do that, sooner you'll have a little one to dandle on your knee," he said. "When do you leave?"

Thrall, his heart lightened by the decision, laughed.

NINE

Jaina rowed steadily, deep in thought. Something was troubling Thrall. Something more than the current situation. He was an intelligent, capable leader, with a great heart as well as a great mind. But Jaina was convinced that this tacit acceptance of the graphically violent attack in Ashenvale would lead to nothing positive. He might keep the goodwill of his people, but he would lose that of the Alliance—well, what little was left, anyway. She had to hope that he would find out who was behind it and deal with them swiftly. A second occurrence would be disastrous.

She docked, secured the little dinghy, and walked toward the keep, lost in thought. She was worried about Thrall and his relationship to the Horde. In all the time she had known him, he had never seemed so . . . uncertain about his control over it. She had been stunned at the conclusions he had reached about how to proceed. Thrall would never in his heart condone such unnecessary violence. And, therefore, how could he publicly?

She smiled perfunctorily at the guards and ascended the tower that housed her private quarters. And Varian—he was still dealing, poorly, it was clear, with the integration of his separated selves. It would have been better if he had been granted some period of calm, but such was not fate's decree. The Alliance had been plunged into war with a man—if you could still call him that—who had once been her childhood friend, and who had slaughtered tens of thousands. And what of young Anduin? He was a capable youth, perceptive and smart. But he wanted a father who could—well, *father* him.

She entered the sitting room, where a cheerful fire burned in the hearth. It was late afternoon, so she was not surprised to see that the servants had laid out the tea things.

She was, however, surprised to see a fair-haired young man, a cup and saucer in his lap, who turned to her with an impish grin.

"Hello, Aunt Jaina," he said. "Your hearthstone worked perfectly."

"Goodness, Anduin!" Jaina said, startled but pleased. "I only just saw you a few days ago!"

"I did warn you that you'd be seeing me all the time," he said jokingly.

"Well, lucky me." She stepped forward, mussed his hair, and went to the sideboard to pour herself her own cup of tea.

"Why are you wearing that ugly cloak?" Anduin asked.

"Oh, well," Jaina said, caught off guard, "I didn't want to attract attention. I'm sure you don't always want people knowing it's you when you're out riding or such."

"I don't mind," Anduin said. "But then again, I don't have secret meetings with orcs in the middle of nowhere."

Jaina whirled, splashing tea. "How did—"

"Yes!" Anduin looked delighted. "I was right! You were out meeting Thrall!"

Jaina sighed and wiped at her robes, grateful that they were, actually, the rough and dirty ones rather than her nice, everyday clothes. "You're too perceptive for your own good, Anduin," she said.

He grew sober. "It's how I've stayed alive," he said matter-of-factly. Jaina felt her heart lurch in empathy for the boy, but he was not seeking pity. "I've got to admit, I'm surprised that you're seeing him. I mean, what I overheard from the Sentinels about the attack seems pretty brutal. Not the sort of thing Thrall would endorse."

She moved toward the fire with her cup of tea, pulling up her own chair. "That's because he *didn't* endorse it."

"So he's going to apologize and turn over the killers?"

Jaina shook her head. "No. An apology—but only for breaking the treaty. Not for how it was broken."

Anduin's face fell. "But . . . if he wasn't responsible, and he doesn't think it's a good thing—why not? How does that help earn trust?"

How indeed, Jaina thought, but did not say. "One of the things you'll learn, Anduin, is that sometimes you can't always do what you'd like to do. Or even do what you think is the right thing—at least not right away. Thrall certainly doesn't want war with the Alliance. He wants to cooperate for all our benefits. But—the Horde thinks differently from the Alliance about a lot of things, and displays of power and strength are absolutely key to a leader's ability to govern them."

Anduin frowned into his tea. "Sounds like Lo'Gosh," he murmured.

"Ironically, yes—that aspect of your father would have fit quite well into the Horde mentality," Jaina said. "One of the reasons he was so popular as a gladiator during his brief . . . er . . . career."

"So Thrall can't risk coming out and denouncing it right now, is that what you're saying?" Anduin popped a small cream-and-jam-laden biscuit into his mouth. For a pleasant instant Jaina was more concerned about whether they'd have enough pastries and small sandwiches to appease a growing boy's appetite than about the possibility of war. She sighed. Would that filling Anduin's teenage belly was the most pressing of her cares.

"Essentially that's correct." She did not wish to reveal specifics and so simply added, "But I know he didn't do it, and I know that personally he is appalled."

"Do . . . you think he will let it happen again?"

It was a serious question, worthy of a serious, thoughtful reply. So she took the time to give him one.

"No," she said at last. "This is just my opinion, but . . . I think this took him by surprise. He's aware of it now."

Anduin drained his cup and went to the sideboard to pour himself a second serving. While he was there, he piled small cakes and sandwiches on his plate. "You're right, Aunt Jaina," he said quietly. "Sometimes you just can't do what you want. You have to wait until the time is right, until you have enough support."

And Jaina smiled to herself. The youth in front of her had been king at age ten. True, he had a sound advisor in the form of Highlord Bolvar Fordragon, but she'd seen enough to know that he'd wrestled with many things by himself. Perhaps he had never been faced with the sort of choice Thrall had, but he could certainly empathize with it.

She found herself, as she often did, missing the wise, wry presence of Magna Aegwynn. She wished that great lady, the former Guardian of Tirisfal, was still alive to give her sound, if sometimes tart, advice. What would Aegwynn have done now, with this boy sitting at her hearth, this too-serious but good-hearted young man?

A smile touched Jaina's lips. She knew exactly what Aegwynn would have done. Lighten the situation.

"Now, Anduin," Jaina said, almost sensing the presence of the wise old woman in the room. "Fill me in on all the court gossip."

"Gossip?" Anduin looked perplexed. "I don't know any."

Jaina shrugged. "Then make some up."

Anduin returned to Stormwind three minutes late for dinner, materializing in his room to discover that Wyll had laid out his clothing. He splashed his face quickly with water from the basin, then threw on the formal dining clothing and scrambled quickly downstairs to join his father.

There were rooms for enormous banquets, but ordinary dinners for the two of them were held in one of Varian's private rooms. The last few meals they had shared together had been stiff and uncomfortable.

Looming between Varian and Anduin Wrynn was the shadow of Lo'Gosh. But now, as he slipped into his chair and reached for his napkin, Anduin looked down the length of the table and saw his father without the haze of resentment that had clouded his vision earlier. His visit to Jaina had enabled him to clear his mind, to just . . . be away from all of this, even for a little while.

And as he looked at his father, he did not see Lo'Gosh. He saw a man who was starting to get faint lines at the corner of his eyes, the marks of age and weariness and not battle. He saw the strain of the crown, of the countless decisions that had to be made daily. Decisions that cost money, or even more precious a currency, lives. He felt not pity for his father—Varian did not need it—but compassion.

Varian glanced up and gave his son a tired smile. "Good evening, Son. How was your day? Do anything fun?"

"Actually, yes," said Anduin, dipping his spoon into the rich, thick, turtle bisque. "I used Aunt Jaina's hearthstone to pay her a visit."

"Did you now?" Varian's blue eyes flickered with interest. "How did that go? Did you learn anything?"

Anduin shrugged, suddenly filled with doubt. It had seemed so exciting at the time, but now that he had to recount the incident to his father it . . . well, it was just having tea, mostly.

"We talked about some things. And, um . . . had tea."

"Tea?"

"Tea," Anduin said, almost defensively. "It's cold and wet in Theramore. There's nothing wrong with having tea and eating something."

Varian shook his head, reaching for a slice of bread and cheese. "No, there's not. And you certainly were in fine company. Did you talk about the current situation?"

Anduin felt the heat rise in his face. He didn't want to betray Jaina, even inadvertently. But he also didn't want to lie to his father. "Some."

Keen eyes flickered to Anduin's face. Lo'Gosh wasn't completely present, but Anduin sensed he wasn't completely absent, either. "See any orcs?"

"No." That at least he could answer honestly. He toyed with his soup, his appetite suddenly gone.

"Ah, but Jaina did."

"I didn't say—"

"It's all right. I know that she and Thrall are thick as thieves. I also know Jaina wouldn't betray the Alliance."

Anduin brightened. "No, she never would. Never."

"You . . . sympathize with her, don't you? With the orcs and the Horde?"

"I . . . Father, we've just lost so many already," Anduin blurted out, putting his spoon down and regarding Varian intently. "You heard Archbishop Benedictus. Almost fifty thousand. And I know that a lot of our people died at the hands of the Horde, but a lot of them *didn't*, and the Horde also suffered terrible losses. They're not the enemy, they—"

"I do not know what other term you would use to describe someone—some *thing*—that could do to those Sentinels what the orcs did to them."

"I thought—"

"Oh, Thrall replied, condemning the breaking of the treaty and assuring me he had no desire for it to happen again. But as for what was done to those elves? Nothing. If he is as civilized as you and Jaina seem to think, then why would he stay silent on something so atrocious?"

Anduin looked miserably at his father. He couldn't say what he knew, and even if he could, the information was secondhand. He wondered if he'd ever truly grasp politics. Jaina, Aegwynn, and even his father had all praised his insight, but he felt more confused than clear on . . . well, pretty much everything. What he knew was more intuition than logic, and that was something that neither Varian nor Lo'Gosh would really understand. He just knew, somehow, in his bones, that Thrall wasn't as Varian saw him. And he couldn't explain it any better than that.

Varian watched his son keenly and sighed inwardly. He liked Jaina; he respected her; but she was not a warrior. He was not opposed to peaceable relationships with former foes, as Anduin seemed to think. His agreement to the armistice in the first place was proof of that. It was just that his people's safety came first. Only a fool extended the hand of friendship if it was likely to be sliced off at the wrist.

Anduin wasn't weak. He had proved that again and again in situations that would have made someone twice his age give in to panic or despair. But he was . . . Varian groped for the word and found it: soft. He was not the best with heavy weapons, although his archery and dagger throwing skills were superb. Perhaps if he had more ability, more understanding, of what a warrior endured, he would be less inclined to be kind-hearted when such gentler emotions might result in the deaths of said warriors.

"I'm glad you're taking advantage of this chance to visit Jaina," he said. He finished the soup and wiped the bowl clean with a bit of bread, nodding at the servants who came to remove the bowl and used utensils. "I think it's a good idea."

Anduin glanced up at him. Varian realized, with a pang of pain, that the boy's expression was wary, guarded. "But?" Anduin said bluntly.

Varian had to smile. "But," he agreed, emphasizing the word, "I think it would also be a good idea if you spent some time elsewhere. With people other than me and Jaina."

The guarded expression shifted into one of curiosity. "What do you mean?"

"I was thinking of Magni Bronzebeard," Varian said. "You're fond of him, aren't you?"

Anduin looked relieved. "Very much so. I like the dwarves. I admire their courage and tenacity."

"Well, would you like to go stay with him for a while in Ironforge? You've not spent much time there, and I think it's time you did. The dwarves—except for the Dark Irons, of course—have close ties with us. Magni likes you and I'm sure would teach you all kinds of things. You wouldn't be too far away either, in case you wanted to come visit your lonely old father."

Anduin grinned now, and Varian felt better. This was a good idea. "The Deeprun Tram can bring me right back to Stormwind," he agreed.

"Absolutely," Varian said. "So it's settled, then?"

"Yes, that sounds like a lot of fun, actually," Anduin said. "I've wanted to spend some time learning more about the Explorers' League, and the display of their most precious exhibits is right there in Ironforge. Maybe I'll even get to talk to some of the members."

The servers came with the second course, roast venison in a rich sauce. Anduin dug in, his appetite, which had seemed a bit off to Varian, clearly having returned.

If the boy wanted to spend time with the Explorers' League studying, Varian would not try to stop him. It was a good pursuit for a future king. But he'd also have a quiet word with Magni and emphasize the need for Anduin's battle training to be stepped up. Magni would understand. Varian himself had studied under the skilled tutelage of a dwarf and knew that the same training would benefit his son. Maybe it would help make this promising but delicate boy become a man.

TEN

Thrall awoke, instantly alert to the sound of horns blowing a warning. He leaped out of his sleeping furs immediately, the acrid smell of smoke telling him what the emergency was before he heard the words that he knew would strike terror into the heart of every citizen of Orgrimmar:

"Fire! Fire!"

Even as he threw on clothing, two Kor'kron burst into the room. It was obvious that they, like Thrall, had only just heard the news.

"Warchief! What would you have us do?"

He pushed past them, barking orders as he did so: "Bring me a wyvern! All hands to the pond near the Spirit Lodge save the shaman—rouse them and direct them to the site of the fire! Form a bucket brigade to sluice down any nearby buildings!"

"Yes, Warchief!" One of them kept pace with Thrall while the other ran ahead to carry out his warchief's orders. Thrall had barely left the shadow of the hold when the reins of a wyvern were pressed into his hand. He leaped atop the great beast and directed him straight up.

Thrall clung as the creature rose nearly vertically, giving him a good view of where the fire raged out of control. It was not far. He had ordered many of the bonfires that burned night and day in Orgrimmar to be extinguished because of the extreme drought that was parching the land. Now he realized he should have allowed none of them.

Several buildings had caught fire. Thrall grimaced at the stench of burning flesh, reassured that it likely came from a place called the Chophouse; it was the stench of burning animal meat that he smelled. Even so, three buildings were already going up, vast sheets of flame illuminating the night.

By the light of the conflagration Thrall could see forms scurrying about. The shaman, as he had ordered, were converging on the site of the active blazes, while others were soaking surrounding buildings to ensure that they did not catch.

He guided the beast in the direction of the fire, patting his neck proudly. The wyvern had to be smelling the smoke, sensing the danger, yet he obeyed Thrall trustingly, never shying as Thrall guided him closer and closer to the source. The smoke was thick and black, and the heat was so fierce, he wondered for a moment if it might burn his clothing right off him or scorch the courageous wyvern. But he was a shaman, and he could tame this blaze if anyone could.

He landed, leaped off, and released the beast to the air. The wyvern flew away immediately, happy to put distance between himself and the danger now that he had served his rider well. Figures turned toward Thrall as he approached, parting to make way for their warchief. The other shaman did not move, though, standing still, eyes closed, arms lifted, communing with the fire as Thrall was about to do.

He emulated them, calming himself and reaching out to this individual elemental flame.

Brother Flame . . . you can do great harm and great good to those whose lives you choose to touch. But you have taken for your fuel the dwellings of others. Your smoke sears our eyes and lungs. I ask you, return to the places where we hold you with gratitude. Harm no more of our people.

The fire answered. This elemental was but one of many who were angry and erratic, fierce and uncontrolled.

No, we do not wish to return to the confinement of the bonfires or braziers or small family hearths. We like being free; we want to race across this place and consume all in our path.

Thrall felt a flutter of worry. Never before had such a direct request of his, one from the heart and filled with concern for the safety of others, been so flatly refused.

He asked again, putting more of his own will into the query, emphasizing the damage that the element was doing to people who had ever welcomed it into their city.

Reluctantly, sullenly, like a sulky child, the blaze began to die down. Thrall sensed his fellow shaman lending their aid, their concentration, their pleas as well, and was grateful if unnerved by the incident.

The fire did consume seven buildings and a great deal of personal property before it finally subsided. Fortunately, no lives were directly lost, although Thrall knew that several were affected by the smoke. He would—

"No," he whispered. A spark, dancing defiantly, was wafting on the wind, heading for another building, to wreak more havoc. Thrall reached out to the spark, sensed in its erratic intent its refusal to respect Thrall's entreaty.

His eyes were open now, watching the path of the tiny flame. *If you continue your path, little spark, you will cause great harm.*

I must burn! I must live!

There are places where your glow and heat are welcome. Find them. Do not destroy the dwellings or take the lives of my people!

For a second the spark seemed to wink out of existence, but then it blazed back with renewed vigor.

Thrall knew what he had to do. He lifted his hand. *Forgive me, Brother Flame. But I must protect my people from the harm you would cause them. I have requested, I have begged, now I warn.*

The spark seemed to spasm, and yet it continued on its lethal course.

Thrall, grim-faced, clenched his hand hard.

The spark flared defiantly, then dwindled, finally settling down to nothing more than the faintest of glowing embers. For now, it would no longer do anyone harm.

The threat had ended, but Thrall was reeling. This was not the way of the shaman with the elements. It was a relationship of mutual respect, not of threats and control and, in the end, near destruction. Oh, the Spirit of Fire could never be extinguished. He was far greater than anything any shaman, or even group of shaman, could ever attempt to do to him. He was eternal, as all the spirits of the elements were. But this part of him, this elemental manifestation, had been defiant, uncooperative. And it had not been alone. It was part of a disturbing trend of elements that were sullen and rebellious rather than cooperative. And in the end, Thrall had had to completely dominate it. Other shaman were now calling rain to soak the city in case there was another aberrant spark that persisted in its course of devastation.

Thrall stood in the rain, letting it soak him, pour off his massive green shoulders, and drip down his arms.

What in the name of the ancestors was happening?

"Well, of course we can do it," said Gazlowe. "I mean, we're goblins, of course we can *do* it, you know what I'm saying? We did it in the first place, after all. So yes, Warchief, we can rebuild those parts of Orgrimmar that were damaged. Don't you worry about that."

Two Kor'kron stood a few paces away, massive axes strapped to their backs, powerful arms folded, watching the scene and silently guarding their warchief. Thrall was talking with the goblin who, along with several others, had helped construct Orgrimmar several years ago. He was clever, intelligent, more scrupulous and less annoying than most of his brethren, but even so, he was a goblin, so Thrall was waiting for the other boot to drop.

"Well, that's good. And how much are we looking at?"

The goblin reached into the small sack he had brought with him and pulled out an abacus. His long, clever, green fingers flew across it as he murmured to himself,

". . . carry the one . . . factor in the cost of supplies at a postwar rate . . . and of course labor's gone up . . ."

He retrieved a piece of charcoal and a sheet of parchment and scribbled down a number that made the orc's robust green skin turn sickly. "That much?" Thrall asked, disbelieving.

Gazlowe looked uncomfortable. "Look . . . tell you what . . . you've been awfully good to us, and you've been more than scrupulous in your business affairs. How about . . ."

He wrote a second figure down. It was less than the first figure, but only marginally. Thrall handed the paper over to Eitrigg, who whistled softly.

"We will need more supplies," was all Thrall said. He rose and left without another word. The Kor'kron fell into silent step behind him. Gazlowe looked after Thrall.

"I am guessing that's a yes. That's a yes, isn't it?" he asked Eitrigg. The elderly orc nodded, his eyes narrowing as, from out of the open door, he watched Thrall's shape grow smaller and smaller as he left Grommash Hold.

Though Thrall was a well-known figure in Orgrimmar, the inhabitants of the city were always courteous enough to give their warchief space. The Kor'kron who shadowed him helped encourage that attitude. If Thrall wanted to wander the streets of his capital city, well, then, good for him. So it was that Thrall found his feet taking him on dusty roads still covered in ash, breathing air that was still thick and smelled of char. He needed to walk, to move, to think. His bodyguards knew him well enough to keep back and let him do so.

The sum Gazlowe quoted was astronomical. Yet it would have to be done. Orgrimmar was the capital of the Horde. It could not be permitted to stay damaged. Unfortunately, the tragedy only emphasized the two great issues that consumed Thrall's thoughts every waking moment and during his dreams as well: Why were the elements so agitated, and how best could he lead this postwar Horde?

The decision he had reached during his conversation with Eitrigg was the right one. Thrall realized he needed to go to the home of his people—to Nagrand, where a legacy of shamanism had been practiced and understood for so long its origins had been swallowed by time. Geyah was wise and her mind still sharp. She, and those she had personally trained, would have answers he could not possibly find here in Azeroth. Answers to questions Thrall didn't even know he should be asking. The more he thought about it, the more it called to his soul as the right thing, the absolutely perfectly right thing, to do. The shaman of Outland had learned how to help a broken world. They could help the distressed elements in Azeroth.

Thrall also knew this was no self-indulgent vision quest for his own peace of mind. His people were enduring great hardships. Even verdant Mulgore was starting to feel the effects of the drought creeping westward from the Barrens. And the fire of the previous night was undoubtedly testimony to the dire need to do something now, before the next fire perhaps razed Orgrimmar, or

Thunder Bluff. Before the next storm swept Theramore, and Jaina Proudmoore with it, off the map. Before any other lives or livelihoods were lost.

And in this way, Thrall realized, he could best serve the Horde. He knew he was unique—a warrior, a shaman, of the worlds of humans and orcs both. No one else could be who he was. No one else could do what he could do. Because no one else had the experience and skills he had.

But the Horde must not be paralyzed while he was not at its head. One day Thrall would pass, as all things must, to walk with the ancestors. For a moment he permitted his thoughts to wander to the things Eitrigg had said. To the thought of a child, and a lifemate. Someone courageous and strong and great of heart, as Draka had been to his father, Durotan. He had not known his parents, but he had heard the stories. Theirs had been a fine match, one of the heart. They had loved each other and stood by each other through the darkest of times, even giving their lives together to protect Thrall. Walking on the streets of the Horde capital, Thrall realized that he did, as Eitrigg had implied, long for such a stalwart companion, to share the hard times and the joyful both. And for a child of that union, a fine son or daughter.

But he had no mate, no child. Perhaps that was just as well, for now—he would leave no brokenhearted family if he passed. Only the Horde, which would have to learn to do without him. Perhaps it could do without him now. For a short time, anyway. Long enough for him to go to Nagrand and find out what was amiss with the elements and somehow put an end to the aberrant behavior that was claiming so many lives.

He closed his eyes for a moment. Handing over control of the Horde that he had founded was like entrusting the care of a loved child to another. What if something went wrong?

But something *was* going wrong, terribly wrong. Another would have to lead the Horde for a time. He nodded his head once, firmly, and felt his soul and heart settle somewhat. Yes, this was the right thing to do. There was no longer a question of if he should go, or even when—as soon as possible. The only question that remained was to whom would he surrender care of this loved "child."

His first thought was Cairne. His oldest friend here in Kalimdor, Cairne and he thought alike on many things. He was wise and ruled his people well. But Thrall, like Cairne himself, knew there were those who thought him old-fashioned and out of touch with what was needed. If there was slight unrest in the form of the Grimtotem in Cairne's own city, then there would surely be unrest and murmuring if Thrall appointed an elderly tauren to lead the Horde now.

No, Cairne would definitely have a part to play, but it could not be the role of leader. An orc would be better. One the people knew and liked already.

Thrall sighed deeply. The perfect choice was one he could not have—Saurfang the Younger. Youthful, charismatic, and yet wise beyond his years, he had been the brightest star in the sky of Horde warriors before the Lich King had slain him. His father, though not quite broken, had been emotionally devastated by the recent events. Too, the orc was too old, as was Cairne, as was the deeply trusted Eitrigg. Thrall realized that there could be only one choice, and he made a sour expression.

There was only one who could do it. Only one who was young and vibrant, who was well known and loved, who was a warrior without equal. Only one who could on such short notice bring the disparate factions of the Horde together and keep their spirits high and proud.

A perfect figurehead.

Thrall's glower deepened. Yes, Garrosh was loved and a fine fighter, but he was also rash and impulsive. Thrall was about to deliver him the ultimate power. A word floated to his mind, *usurper,* but he did not truly believe such a thing would happen. Garrosh needed something to placate an ego as mammoth as his legend—an ego that Thrall now realized he might have unwittingly helped to inflate. He had been concerned when he learned that Garrosh despised his father, and had wanted to show the son of Grom that Hellscream had done great good. But perhaps he might have made Grom look better than he was. If so, then the younger Hellscream's arrogance might be, at least in part, due to Thrall himself. He had not been able to save Grom's life; he had hoped to inspire and guide his son.

Still, Eitrigg would be there to temper Garrosh, as would Cairne, if Thrall asked it of his old friends. Thrall would not be gone long. Let Garrosh sit in his place temporarily in Grommash Hold, with Cairne and Eitrigg on either side. If the rumors were true, Garrosh had already tipped his hand with the Ashenvale incident, and Thrall knew Cairne would sit on the orc before he'd let anything like that get by him, now that he knew to be watchful of it. There wouldn't be a lot that Garrosh could do, really, to harm the Horde, and—Thrall had to admit—there was much Garrosh *could* do to inspire it.

Their leader would be gone. They would be worried and afraid. Garrosh would remind them that they were proud and fierce and unconquerable, and the Horde would cheer and be content until Thrall returned with the real answers to the problems that besieged them. Calm the land, and all would have a chance to become better. Ignore the land, the elements, and no glorious victory in battle could ever make up for the disasters that would inevitably follow.

Garrosh saluted as he stood before Thrall. "I am here as you have asked, Warchief. How may I serve the Horde?"

"It is precisely to request such service that I have summoned you here. Walk with me."

Thrall had been seated on his throne when Garrosh arrived, flanked by four of the large, intimidating Kor'kron. He had sent one of them ahead to deliberately make the younger orc wait for a while, and made no effort to stand when he did enter. Now Thrall rose, slowly and in control of the situation, and spread out his arms in a welcoming, friendly, but slightly patronizing gesture. Garrosh needed to understand his place before Thrall could change it.

He nodded to the Kor'kron, who saluted smartly and

stayed where they were as Thrall guided Garrosh to the private areas of Grommash Hold, where they could speak without being overheard. "You know I am a shaman as well as a warrior," Thrall said as they walked.

"Of course."

"You have seen enough to know that the elements are deeply disturbed. The strange waves you encountered coming home from Northrend. The fire that raced through Orgrimmar."

"Yes, I am aware of these things. But how can I possibly change them?"

"You cannot. But I can."

Garrosh narrowed his eyes. "Then why do you not do so? *Warchief?*"

"It is not as warchief that I can do these things, Garrosh. It is as a shaman. And you ask the very question I have been wrestling with—why do I not do it? The answer is, to do so would mean I would need to leave Orgrimmar. To leave Azeroth altogether."

Garrosh looked alarmed. "Leave Azeroth? I don't understand."

"I intend to travel to Nagrand. The shaman there deal with elements that have suffered terribly, yet there are places where the land is still verdant. Perhaps I can learn why that is . . . and apply that understanding to our troubled elementals here."

Garrosh smiled around his tusks. "My homeland," he said. "I would like to see it again. Speak with the Greatmother before she leaves us to walk with the ancestors. It was she who healed me and so many others when the red pox was upon us."

"She is a great treasure," Thrall agreed, "and one whose wisdom I would seek."

"You will be returning soon?"

"I—do not know," Thrall said honestly. "It may take time to learn what I must. I trust I will not be gone too long, but it could be weeks—even months."

"But—the Horde! We need a warchief!"

"It is for the Horde that I go," Thrall said. "Do not worry, Garrosh. I do not forsake it. I travel where I must, to serve as I must. We all serve the Horde. Even its warchief does so—perhaps especially its warchief. And well do I know that you serve it loyally too."

"I do, Warchief. You were the one who taught me that my father was someone to be proud of, because of what he was willing to do for others. For the Horde." Garrosh's voice was earnest, the naked emotions plain on his face. "I have not been part of it for long. But even so, I have seen enough to know that, like my father, I would die for it."

"You have already faced and cheated death," Thrall admitted. "You have slain many of its minions. You have done more for this new Horde than many who have been part of it since the beginning. And know this: I would never leave without appointing someone able to take care of it, even during so brief a sojourn."

The younger orc's eyes widened, this time in excitement. "You—you are making me warchief?"

"No. But I *am* instructing you to lead the Horde on my behalf until I return."

Thrall had never expected to see Garrosh lost for words, but now the brown-skinned orc seemed struck dumb for a moment. "I understand battle, yes," he said. "Tactics, how to rally troops—these things I know. Let me serve that way. Find me a foe to face and defeat, and you will see how proudly I will continue to serve the Horde. But I know nothing of politics, of . . . of *ruling.* I would rather have a sword in my fist than a scroll!"

"I understand that," Thrall said, slightly amused that he found himself reassuring the normally proud Garrosh. "But you will not be without sound advisors. I will ask Eitrigg and Cairne, both of whom have shared their wisdom with me through the years, to guide and advise you. Politics can be learned. Your obvious love for the Horde?" He shook his head. "That is more important to me than political acumen right now. And that, Garrosh Hellscream, you have in abundance."

Still Garrosh seemed uncharacteristically hesitant. Finally he said, "If you deem me worthy, then know this. I shall do all that I can to bring glory to the Horde!"

"No need for glory at the moment," Thrall said. "There will be enough of a challenge for you without any extra effort. The Horde's honor is already assured. You just need to take care of it. Put its needs before your own, as your father did. The Kor'kron will be instructed to protect you as they would me. I go to Nagrand as a shaman, not as warchief of the Horde. Make good use of them—and of Cairne and Eitrigg." He paused, and amusement quirked his lips. "Would you go into battle without a weapon?"

Garrosh looked at him, confused at what, to him, seemed a sudden change of subject. "That is a foolish question, Warchief, and you know it."

"Oh, I do. I am making sure you understand what powerful weapons you have," Thrall said. "My advisors are my weapons as I struggle to always do what is best for the Horde. They see things I do not, present options I did not know I had. Only a fool would scorn such things. And I do not think you a fool."

Garrosh smiled, relaxing slightly as Thrall's intention became clear. With a touch of his former arrogance, he said, "I am not a fool, Warchief. You would not ask me to serve so if you thought me one."

"True. So, Garrosh, do you agree to lead the Horde until such time as I return? Taking advice from Eitrigg and Cairne when they offer it?"

The young Hellscream took a deep breath. "It is my true longing to lead the Horde to the best of my ability. And so, yes, a thousand times yes, my warchief. I will lead as well as I can, and I will consult with the advisors you suggest. I know what a tremendous honor you do me, and I will strive to be worthy of it."

"Then it is done," Thrall said. "For the Horde!"

"For the Horde!"

Ancestors, Thrall thought as he watched Garrosh stride away, chest swelled with pride and pleasure, *I pray I am doing the right thing.*

ELEVEN

Two weeks later, his things already having been sent ahead on an earlier train, Anduin Wrynn stepped off the Deeprun Tram and was immediately almost crushed by a pair of powerful, short arms.

"Welcome, lad!" exclaimed King Magni Bronzebeard. Anduin tried to reply but was unable to actually take breath into his lungs and so stayed silent for a moment more while Magni continued. "We've been excited about hosting ye. Ye've sprouted up right tall, ye have. I barely knew ye!"

Magni released Anduin, who gasped in air with a whooshing sound. Even so, he was smiling at both the king and the young dwarf lady who stood next to him. He suspected that his reasons for coming here were not the same as his father's for sending him, but it didn't matter. He was away from home, a boy being exposed to an entirely different culture after having been confined to the city of Stormwind for far too long.

"It's good to be here, Your Majesty," he said. "Thank you for agreeing to host me."

"No thanks needed, me lad. I think we needed a wee kick in th' pants. Place has gotten too stodgy." Magni clapped him on the back. "Come now, I've got yer chambers all ready. Now, I know ye've sent ahead a few servants, and they've been made most welcome. But I'd like to assign Aerin here," and he indicated the young dwarf woman, "tae be yer bodyguard, though I doubt the folk o' Ironforge will be bothering ye much."

Aerin gave him a cheerful grin. "Great tae meet ya," she said, bowing politely.

She was a fine specimen of dwarven womanhood, curvaceous and pink-cheeked with a long brown braid running the length of her back. She wore her armor as if it were no more of a hindrance than a frock, and as she stuck out her hand to shake his heartily, Anduin saw that most of her curves were muscle. "Aerin is one of my personal retinue. She'll take good care o' ye."

"Aye, and I'm also an Ironforge native, born an' bred," Aerin said with pride. "I'll be happy to be yer guide while ye're here as well, Yer Highness."

"Thank you," Anduin said. "And please—call me Anduin." While the dwarves were fiercely devoted to their royal family, there was a pleasant ease in their attitude toward them that Anduin liked.

"All right then," Aerin agreed, "Anduin it is."

"Let's go to yer quarters an' get ye settled in," Magni said, turning and striding off at so brisk a pace that Anduin was hard put to keep up with him. "I think ye'll like what I've picked out for ye," he said, a twinkle in his eye.

"Would you mind if we visit the Great Forge first?" asked Anduin. "I'd like to see it again."

"O' course not!" said Magni. "Always proud tae show it off."

Ironforge was, quite literally, centered around a giant forge. The air was thick and almost stiflingly hot, a contrast to the cold freshness of the snowy environment right outside the dwarven capital's towering gateway. But the harsh scent was different and not evocative of human cities in any way, and Anduin loved it. As they approached the forge, Anduin winced a little at the oppressive heat rolling off it in waves and removed his jacket. He glanced down at Aerin furtively. He was wearing only a light linen shirt and breeches, carrying the jacket slung over his shoulder, and he was drenched with sweat. Aerin and Magni were in full armor and seemed completely unaffected. Such was the constitution of the dwarves.

The discomfort was quickly forgotten at the powerful sight of the forge, with its streams of molten metal splashing like water and glowing in shades of red and yellow and orange. It was so overwhelmingly vast, the mind almost couldn't grasp it. At least his had a hard time with it.

"Aye, that's a grand sight," Magni said. Anduin agreed. After a while the heat was too much, and he was grateful to continue on through the relative cool of a corridor. Several dwarves and gnomes moved about purposefully, and the guards posted here and there nodded polite greetings to their liege.

Anduin slowed, confused at the direction they were taking. He had assumed that he would be staying in the royal quarters located near the High Seat. He was, after all, a prince, and such would be expected of him. He had wondered if he'd be able to get any sleep, as the High Seat was located right next to the forge. Which, in addition to being incredibly hot, was also active day and night. But it looked as though they were going away from that part of Ironforge.

He opened his mouth to ask about this when he came to a dead stop, mouth still hanging open. Not at the structure that was before him—from the outside it looked like merely another part of Ironforge architecture. There was nothing remarkable about the arched doorways. It was what he glimpsed inside that made Anduin's heart skip a beat.

It was the skeleton of a giant winged reptile, held together by wiring and suspended from the ceiling. Enraptured, Anduin walked toward it. "What is it?"

"It's a pteradon," Aerin said. "Unearthed in Un'Goro Crater. Nasty place. Spent too much time there meself."

"Now, now, lad, we've got to go tae yer quarters afore ye can do much sightseeing," Magni chided. His eyes were bright, as if he were in on some joke that Anduin wasn't quite getting.

Anduin sighed and cast a final wistful glance at the pteradon and nodded. "Of course, sir. I'll be here for several weeks at least. Plenty of time for amusement later. Let's go to my quarters."

"All right," Magni said. He didn't move.

"Your Majesty? My quarters?" Now Aerin was smothering a grin. What was going on?

Slowly Magni lifted a finger and pointed to his left. "We're already there!" He threw back his head and laughed. Aerin joined in, and Anduin felt a foolish grin spread across his face. "I've arranged for ye and yer folk to have apartments right here. Directly across from the library. I thought ye might be a wee bit tired o' living in royal dwellings. And I know summat o' what ye're interested in."

"Thank you, Your Majesty!"

"Psssh," Magni said, waving a hand dismissively. "I've known ye since ye were a wee bairn. This is me home. And here, ye can call me Uncle, if ye'd like."

A fleeting expression of sorrow, old and well-worn, danced across his face. For a moment, Anduin thought it related to the term *uncle,* but realized at once it was another term of affection that Magni Bronzebeard was missing: *Father.*

Magni had only one child, a daughter, Moira. A few years ago, servants of the Dark Iron emperor, Dagran Thaurissan, had spirited Moira away. Magni believed that Dagran had seduced his daughter through magical means, enchanting her so that she thought she was in love with him. When Magni sent in a team to kill Thaurissan and retrieve the ensorcelled Moira, she had refused to come home. She had announced that she was pregnant, and that the murder of her husband had created a terrible, fiery rage within her heart. Magni had been devastated. Nothing had been heard of Moira or her child—heir to two kingdoms—since.

Becoming a grandfather should have been an occasion for rejoicing. Magni should have had his daughter with him here in Ironforge, his grandchild—Anduin didn't even know if it was a boy or a girl, and he was not about to ask if Magni knew—playing on his knee. Instead, child and grandchild were estranged from him, still caught in the throes of what Magni firmly believed was the emperor's dark spell even from beyond the grave.

The somber moment passed quickly, and Magni smiled again, although the mischievous glint had gone from his eyes. "Dinner's at eight sharp, mind. Dun be late. Ye're training with Aerin first thing on the morrow."

Anduin was surprised. Fighting? His shoulders sagged slightly. He supposed that he should have expected his father to set up something like this. Well, at least Aerin seemed like good company, and there should still be time to investigate the library and learn more about the Explorers' League.

"Yes, Uncle." Anduin smiled at the dwarf, pleased to see that the term eased Magni's taut features, at least a little. Magni nodded, patted Anduin's arm, and turned and strode back toward the High Seat. Anduin watched him go, then turned to Aerin.

"So, my attendants are all settled in?"

"Och, aye, some time ago."

He grinned. "Then I'm going to the library!"

The following morning Anduin was lying on his back, staring at the ceilings of an out-of-the-way area of the High Seat, bruised and filled with both great pain and a fresh admiration for the fighting abilities of the dwarves.

"Down again, li'l lion?" A tsk-tsk of disapproval. "That's three times in a row."

Every muscle aching with the effort, Anduin lifted his arm and grasped Aerin's smaller but stronger one. She hauled him to his feet as if he weighed nothing at all. His left arm dangled at his side, the shield still strapped to it. His sword was at least two yards away on the floor. Sighing, Anduin lumbered over to pick it up. He closed his hand painfully around the hilt and with great effort lifted the sword.

Aerin's blue eyes darted to the shield, and she raised her eyebrows meaningfully. It still hung down.

"I, uh . . . can't lift it," Anduin said, feeling the hot color rushing into his cheeks.

Aerin looked exasperated for just an instant, then smiled cheerily. "No matter, li'l lion. Today was just about checkin' yer strength an' judging yer skills. Ye'll be with us for a while. We'll send ye back tae yer father all properly dwarf-tempered, ye'll see!"

She had started calling him "li'l lion" yesterday afternoon when they had been ambling around Ironforge together, and he hadn't minded. And he knew her comment just now was intended to be encouraging. Instead, he winced inwardly.

He knew his father did not think he was "warrior material," knew that one of the reasons Varian had sent him here at all was to "toughen him up" and have the dwarves "make a man out of him." Anduin was painfully aware—now literally—that he really *wasn't* warrior material. He was good at archery and knife throwing, because he had a keen eye and a steady hand, but when it came to the heavier weapons, his slight build just couldn't seem to manage it. But that was not all there was to it. The swords and polearms never seemed to feel comfortable in his hands. And no matter how hard he trained, no matter how many hours he sparred with this stout, cheerful female dwarf, despite her words, he was *not* going to become "all properly dwarf-tempered."

"I'm sorry," he said. "You're a fine trainer, Aerin. I'm sure I'll improve."

"Och, I ken ye will," she said, winking at him, and for the first time he realized that she was really quite pretty. He smiled back, sorry to have lied to her. He wasn't at all sure he would improve, and he felt his mood darken as he anticipated disappointing Aerin. But she had already begun putting things away, whistling and bustling about industriously. He assisted her, hanging up the training weapons and shrugging out of the padded armor, trying not to gasp as overly strained muscles protested.

"I think I'll go back to my quarters and take a bath," he said, dragging a hand across his sweaty forehead.

"Aye, I was going to say something," she said bluntly. He stared at her for a full half a minute, mortified, before a telltale smile curved her lips and he realized she was just teasing him—again. He laughed sheepishly. "Let me know if ye need anything," Aerin said. "I'll be happy tae take ye out for a ride later."

The thought of bouncing around on one of the giant rams that the dwarves favored as mounts made Anduin turn pale. "No, I may just stay inside for a bit, keep up with my studies."

"Well, if ye want some fresh air, simply send fer me."

"I will. Thank you again."

"O' course, any time!" She bustled off cheerily.

Anduin could not help but notice that she hadn't even really broken a good sweat. He sighed and went back to his quarters.

A good hot bath and a change of clothes later, his mood much improved, he decided to take a walk to the Mystic Ward. He was feeling in need of a little Light.

He knew he'd made a good decision when he felt the constriction around his chest ease as he approached. Somehow, whether it was a trick of the light or the actual materials used in construction, the Mystic Ward seemed brighter to him. Too, the softly lapping pool in the ward was soothing. He wasn't sure exactly what its purpose was, if indeed it had any other than decorative. He fished out a coin, made a wish, and tossed it in, watching the gold glint in the light for an instant before slowly sinking downward. He was reassured when he peered into the depths and saw that it had many monetary companions. There were stairs—was the pool for swimming, or ritual bathing? He'd have to ask Aerin. For now he was not going to commit any kind of social error.

He walked through the open doorway into the Hall of Mysteries, smiling gently as blue-purple-white light fell upon him. Five pillars, each adorned with a repeating geometric pattern wrought in gold and blue, supported an upper story and a ceiling. Now that he was inside, he found the place not quite as sacred-feeling as the cathedral—but the Light was still there. It had seemed to him yesterday and earlier today that everyone in Ironforge wore plate armor even going about day-to-day tasks. It was a relief to see rooms filled with gnomes and dwarves in soft, flowing robes.

Something small and hard and moving fast slammed into his thigh, and he stumbled backward. "What—"

"Dear me!" came a small squeak. "Dink, look out for—"

"Ouch!" A second something small and hard and moving fast slammed into Anduin's thigh, causing his legs—already weak from the training he'd received earlier—to buckle. Before he could recover, he'd fallen on his knees on the cold stone floor. He winced, but did not utter a cry as he slowly rose.

"Terribly sorry about that!" Anduin peered down at two gnomes. They looked like brother and sister. Both had white hair and blue eyes that were now wide with embarrassment. They both wore robes in shades of yellow and blue. The female was holding a book and starting to blush. "I'm afraid I got caught up in this. Wasn't looking where I was going. Don't know what Dink's excuse is!"

"I was following you, Bink!" said the male, who was apparently named Dink. "Sorry, young fellow. Sometimes we get a little too focused around here for our own good!"

"Our good and others," Bink said, smiling winningly. She attempted to brush the dust off Anduin's knees solicitously. Anduin winced and stepped back, forcing a smile. "So terribly sorry!"

"That's all right," he said. "I should be more careful, too."

They both beamed up at him at the same instant, then bowed and scurried off. Amused but hurting, Anduin watched them go.

"Here now, lad," came a deep, kindly voice. "Let me take care o' that for ye."

A sudden pleasant warmth seeped gently through Anduin, and he turned to see an elderly dwarf chanting softly while moving his hands. His long, white beard had two braids and a third ponytail. The top of his head was quite bald, with a ponytail in back and long fringes on the side. His green eyes crinkled in a smile. A heartbeat later, Anduin realized all the pain was gone—the stinging of his bumped knees, the aches and stiffness of his training. He felt rested, refreshed, as if he'd just awoken from a good night's sleep.

"Thank you."

"Ye're welcome, lad. Might ye be th' young prince o' Stormwind we've been told tae expect?"

Anduin nodded and stuck out his hand. "Pleased to meet you . . . ?"

"High Priest Rohan. Light's blessing be on ye. How do ye find our glorious city?"

"By taking the Deeprun Tram," Anduin quipped, the old joke escaping before he realized it. His eyes widened, and his cheeks reddened. "I—I'm sorry, I didn't mean—"

To his surprise and relief, the high priest threw back his balding head and laughed heartily. "Och, I've not heard that one in far too long. I walked ri' into it, did I not?" The guffaw subsided to a chuckle.

Anduin relaxed, grinning a little himself. "It's a *really* bad joke. I apologize."

"Well, I'll fergive ye if ye can come up with some better ones," Rohan said.

"I'll try. . . ."

"Far too little laughter these days, says I. Och, the Light's serious business, but then again, ye cannot be *Lighthearted* without a little humor, can ye?"

Anduin eyed him dubiously, wondering if it would be disrespectful if he groaned at the pun. His expression did not go unnoticed, but Rohan only smiled the more. "Aye, I ken, 'tis a poor joke, which is why I hope ye'll teach me some new ones. In the meantime, what brings ye to the Hall of Mysteries?"

Suddenly serious, Anduin said, "I just . . . I just missed the Light."

The old dwarf smiled gently, and this time his voice was soft and serious, though no less full of joy. "It is never far, lad. We carry it in ourselves, although 'tis true, seeking the company of others in a special place feeds th' soul. Ye are welcome here any time, Anduin Wrynn."

No title. Anduin knew he did not have one before the Light, and neither did Rohan. He remembered his father saying once, after he had been home for a time, that if it were not for Anduin, and for the people of Stormwind who relied upon him, Varian would have been content to remain Lo'Gosh, fighting in the ring. It was an uncomplicated and straightforward, if short and brutish, existence, lacking all the complexities of royal life.

As he walked up the curving stairway to the quieter rooms above, the soft blue light augmented by the glowing orange of the braziers here and there, he realized that he understood his father's longing. Not for the violence of the ring and the threat of sudden death each day: his father might crave the fight, but not he. No, what Anduin longed for was the seemingly elusive luxury of peace. Peace to sit in quiet contemplation, to study, to help people. A priestess brushed past him, smiling gently, her face calm.

Anduin sighed. It was not his fate. He was born a prince, not a priest, and no doubt his destiny included more war, more violence, and would demand of him politicking and maneuvering.

But for now, here in the Hall of Mysteries, Anduin Wrynn—no title at the moment—sat quietly and thought not of his father, or Thrall, or even Jaina, but of a world where anyone could walk into any city and be welcomed there with open arms.

TWELVE

Drek'Thar tossed and turned in his sleep. Visions plucked at him, pinched and teased and tormented him. Half-glimpsed, uncertain, unclear; visions both of peace and prosperity and disaster and ruination playing out simultaneously in the theater of his mind.

He could see in this vision. He stood, and yet there was nothing beneath his feet. All around him were stars and inky black sky, above and below. Images of the Spirits of Earth, Air, Fire, Water—all angry, all unhappy, all raging at him. They reached out to him, pleading, and yet when he turned to them, heart open and trying to understand, rebuffed him with fury so profound he staggered. If they had been children, they would have wept.

Water crashed around him, whipped by Air manifesting as wind. Storms, strong and powerful, catching up ships and snapping them like child's toys. Cairne and Grom's boys were on such a ship . . . no, no, it was Thrall . . . then it did not matter *who* was on the ship, for it had been smashed to sodden kindling.

Fire was next, its sparks diving at Drek'Thar like birds protecting a nest. He was powerless under the onslaught, crying out as his clothing caught and burned. He beat at it frantically, but the flame refused to be extinguished.

Just as it seemed that Drek'Thar would succumb to Fire's attack, it ceased. He was whole and sound. Drek'Thar breathed heavily, trembling. The moments stretched out. Nothing happened, yet the vision continued.

And that was when he felt the rumbling beneath his feet. And he knew, somehow, that Air and Water and Fire had already voiced their pain. And while they might yet again, this trembling of a sobbing Earth beneath his feet was, Drek'Thar knew, yet to come. And he sensed it would be terrible. Images flashed through his mind—a place of snow, a place of forests—

He shouted and bolted upright, blinking eyes that once again, mercifully, saw only darkness. His reaching hands met those of Palkar, as they always did.

"What is it, Greatfather?" asked the younger orc. His voice was clear, strong, untroubled by all that haunted Drek'Thar.

Drek'Thar opened his mouth to answer, but suddenly his thoughts were as dark as his eyes. He had dreamed—something. Something important. Something he needed to share—

"I . . . I don't know," he whispered. "Something terrible is about to happen, Palkar. But . . . I don't know what. *I don't know!*"

He shook with frustrated, fearful sobs.

The tears that streamed down his face were warm.

* * *

Anduin developed a routine as the days unfolded. Mornings were spent training with the seemingly inexhaustible and eternally chipper Aerin. When they were not sparring, she and Anduin went for rides out in the countryside. While rams would never be his favorite mounts, Anduin loved the chance to get outside; the clear air made him feel almost giddy, and the snowy land was so very different from the temperate clime of Stormwind. He grew to become very fond of Aerin. He could trust her to not pull a punch, physically or verbally, and found that very refreshing. Once, he asked about Moira.

"Och, that's a convoluted business, that," she said.

"Sounds straightforward to me. She got kidnapped, was enchanted, and broke Magni's heart."

"I'll certainly agree that he misses her," Aerin said, "but he was no the best daddy tae her either."

Anduin was stunned. He'd always imagined the bluff dwarf as the perfect father. Surely he would appreciate someone for who they were, not who he wanted them to be.

"Not cruel, or anything, mind. But . . . well, Her Highness was the wrong gender. Magni always wanted a son tae rule after him. Felt that a female just wouldna do th' job right."

"Jaina Proudmoore is a wonderful leader of her people," Anduin said.

"Aye, and it wasn't long after Moira disappeared that His Majesty put me an' a few others in his elite guard," Aerin said. "I think he finally understood that he'd been a bit unfair. 'Tis my hope that one day, father an' daughter will have a chance tae make things right."

Anduin hoped so, too. It would seem that father–child difficulties were not limited to humans.

As they rode together, he got to know the people of the neighboring areas of Kharanos and Steelgrill's Depot. Once they even rode as far as Thelsamar in Loch Modan, where they broke for lunch and Anduin, exhausted, fell asleep by the loch and awoke two hours later to an exquisitely painful sunburn.

"Och, ye humans, not smart enough tae come in out o' the sun," quipped Aerin.

"How come *you* aren't burned?" asked Anduin crossly. Ninety percent of the time he saw her, Aerin was in full armor, and the rest of the time she lived underground. What skin was now revealed was even paler than his own.

"I went and napped in the shade o' yon rock outcropping," she said.

He gaped at her. "Why didn't you suggest that to me?"

"Thought ye'd figure it out for yerself. Ye will in the future, won't ye?" She smiled placidly at him, and although he was in terrible pain and the color of a crab when it was boiled, he found he could not be angry at her. He hissed as he put his shirt back on; the fine runecloth fabric, soft as a feather, was agony. Aerin was right. He would never let himself drift off on a sunny day without making damned sure he was well protected by the shade.

He returned to his quarters to find a letter waiting

for him. It was in Magni Bronzebeard's own bold handwriting:

Anduin—

Come to the High Seat as soon as you return. Bring Aerin, too.

He'd hoped to ask High Priest Rohan for some help with his sunburn, but Magni's summons clearly brooked no delay. He showed the letter to Aerin, whose eyes widened. She nodded, and as one they turned and hastened to the High Seat. Despite the pain of his sunburn, Anduin broke into a trot. Worry flooded him. Had something happened to his father? Had war finally broken out between the Horde and the Alliance?

Magni was there, leaning over a table. Two other dwarves, their garb travel stained, were on either side of him. A third dwarf looked on eagerly. Anduin recognized him as High Explorer Muninn Magellas, the head of the Explorers' League, a dashing dwarf with red hair and beard who liked to sport goggles most of the time. On the table were three stone tablets. Anduin skidded to a halt, exchanging a quick, confused glance with Aerin, who shrugged, clearly just as confused as he.

"Ah, Anduin, lad, come here, come here! Ye'll want tae see this!" Magni waved him forward, his eyes alight with excitement. Relief filled Anduin, leaving him feeling momentarily drained, and then he felt a twinge of annoyance.

"Your message sounded urgent, Your M—Uncle

Magni," he said, moving forward, feeling the sunburn with renewed awareness.

"Och, not urgent, but most intriguing! Come take a look for yerself!"

One of the dwarves nodded and stepped out of the way so Anduin could stand beside Magni and Magellas. He looked at the tablets, realizing now that there were not three, but only one, which had been broken into pieces. There was writing on each part of the shattered tablet. Anduin knew several languages, but this was unfamiliar to him.

"Me brother Brann sent this tae me," Magni said. He pulled off one of his gloves and ran bare, powerful fingers over the texts with a startlingly light touch. "He was intrigued and thought I might be as well." He glanced at Anduin. "And as soon as I saw these, I sent for ye. I imagine ye've no idea what ye're looking at."

Anduin laughed a little and shook his head. "I've never seen this before."

"I'm not sure anyone has, at least not in a long, long time. This writing . . . it is of the earthen."

Anduin's skin erupted in gooseflesh and he stared at the broken pieces with new respect. The earthen were creations of the titans, long, long ago. And it was from the earthen that the current dwarves were descended. The stone in front of him was unspeakably old, perhaps as old as ten thousand years—maybe even older. He, too, reached a trembling hand to touch it, lightly, as Magni had, with profound respect.

"Do you know what it says?"

"Nay, I'm not schooled in such things. Even Brann

had a wee bit o' trouble with this. That's why he sent it here, to the experts at the hall. He got something . . . let me see . . ." Magni picked up a piece of paper that lay on the table. "Something about . . . becoming one with the earth."

"Hmph," said Aerin. She was, as Anduin was learning, all about practical matters. She did not have much in the way of imagination and had gotten so bored with the repeated visits to the Hall of Explorers that Anduin had officially relieved her of duty when he spent time there. "Becoming one with the earth? Sounds like bein' buried in it tae me."

Anduin shot her a glare that had no malice in it and returned his attention to the tablet. "What do you think it means? That's kind of vague."

"Indeed, and one must have clarity in such things," Magni said, nodding. He eyed Anduin speculatively. "Ye're a right sharp lad, Anduin. Have ye been paying attention to what's been going on in th' world?"

Anduin was confused. "I know there's a lot of tension between the Alliance and the Horde," he said, wondering if that was what Magni was getting at. "That the Horde has been stirring up trouble because its supplies are depleted on account of the war."

"Good, good." Magni nodded approvingly. "But not just because of the war. Follow the chain, lad."

Anduin furrowed his brow. "Well . . . because Durotar is a pretty harsh land," he said. "There were never many supplies to begin with."

"And there are fewer now because . . . ?"

"Because of the war and . . ." Anduin's eyes widened

as comprehension dawned. "Because of the unusual droughts."

"Exactly."

"Now that we're talking about it . . . Aunt Jaina said there had been a violent storm right before I visited her. Even she said it was one of the worst she'd seen. And there were reports of a strange hurricane that damaged many ships trying to come home from Northrend."

"Yes!" Magni almost cheered in his excitement. "Ferocious storms, floods in some places, droughts in the other . . . Something's wrong, lad. I'm no shaman, but th' elements are definitely not happy these days. This tablet could possibly hold th' key tae what's wrong wi' them."

"Do—really? You really think something that old can help us today?"

"Anything's possible, lad. And at the very least . . ." Magni said in an exaggeratedly conspiratorial whisper, "we've gotten our hands on something that's not seen the light o' day in a while, eh?"

He clapped Anduin on the back. Right on the sunburn.

The translation process was slow and painful, with many false starts. It didn't help matters that the translators struck Anduin as a touch self-important and unwilling to admit they might be wrong—and each one had a slightly different interpretation.

High Explorer Magellas kept insisting it was a metaphysical union. "'Become one with th' earth,'" he repeated. "Tae join wi' it. Tae sense its pain."

Advisor Belgrum, a wizened elder with hands that trembled but a voice that, when raised, could be heard almost throughout all of Ironforge, scoffed. "Bah," he said. "Muninn, ye're too taken wi' the lasses. Ye see 'becoming one' in everything."

Magellas, who had been casting sidelong glances at the comely Aerin the whole time, laughed boisterously. "Just because ye've nae been wi' a lass in decades, Belgrum, doesna mean—"

"Now, now, all this salty talk's not fit fer young royal ears!" chided Aerin, who was completely unruffled by the conversation.

Anduin, however, colored slightly. "It's okay," he said. "I mean . . . I know about these things."

Unable to resist, Aerin winked at him. "Do ye now?"

Anduin quickly turned to Belgrum. "What do *you* think it means?" he asked, hoping to change the subject.

"Well, I think we canna really know until we get all of it translated. Th' interpretation of a phrase is often dependent upon what else is around it. Fer instance, take . . . 'I am hungry.' If ye put it in a paragraph like, 'Me wife is cooking dinner in th' other room. I can smell th' beer-basted boar ribs. I am hungry,' well, that's a literal hunger, isn't it?"

"Belgrum, ye're toying with me. It's past lunchtime," Aerin said.

"But if the paragraph is more like, 'I have been imprisoned fer four years. All I see are the gray walls. I dream o' open spaces and sunlight. I am hungry.' That's quite a different thing."

"Goodness, ye're a poet," said Aerin, impressed. Anduin was, too.

"I see what you mean," he said. "I've never thought of it that way. What—"

A deep rumbling interrupted him. Anduin gasped as the floor beneath him vibrated ever so subtly, as if he were standing on a giant purring animal, except it signaled nothing so benevolent. Another sound came from above—Anduin glanced up to see the hundreds of books trembling as they slowly moved out from their shelves.

Three thoughts struck him simultaneously. One, that he suspected all those books, and all the priceless knowledge they contained, were about to topple unceremoniously from tremendous heights to almost certain damage, if not destruction. Two, that the books that were about to topple unceremoniously were about to fall from tremendous heights on top of their heads. And finally, if the tablet pieces were to slide off the shaking table, they would shatter. He lunged forward and grabbed them, pressing the irreplaceable pieces of knowledge close to his heart.

"Look out!" Aerin cried, grabbing the arms of both Anduin and Belgrum and dragging them along to the large archway that separated the library from the main display hall. Anduin misunderstood and thought she meant for them to flee the hall completely, and he kept going until, with a grunt, Aerin flung herself bodily on him. Frantically he twisted and landed hard on his hip, Aerin at his back, the tablet protected still.

"Nay, Anduin! Not out there! Stay in th' archway!"

The warning came not a second too soon. He had

fallen directly under the pteradon skeleton. It was rattling violently, the chain suspending it swinging and making the bony wings flap as if it had suddenly come to unlife. The bindings that positioned it in such a pose had never been meant to hold against anything more demanding than gravity, and even as Anduin watched, the wiring snapped and the skeletal wings crashed down. For a long, slow, horrified moment he simply watched as death toppled toward him.

Then stout, strong arms wrapped around his shoulders and his face was pressed into cold plate as Aerin draped herself atop him. She uttered a pained "oof!" as one of the fossilized bones clanged against her armor and forced the wind out of her lungs.

A heartbeat later, it was all over. Aerin leaned back, her face drawn in pain but otherwise seemingly all right. Anduin sat up and looked around cautiously. The books, as he had expected, were on the floor, as were most of what had adorned the tables.

"The tablet!" cried Belgrum, hurrying to his feet.

"I have it," Anduin said.

"Good lad!" exclaimed Magellas.

Aerin got to her feet, wincing slightly. Anduin followed, his legs shaking, clutching the tablet pieces to his chest still. He stared at her.

"You saved my life," he said quietly.

"Och," she said, waving it aside. "Ye'd have done the same. Besides, I'd be a poor bodyguard if I wasna prepared to save yer life when I needed to, now wouldn't I?"

He nodded, grateful, and gave her a smile. She winked back playfully.

"Everyone else all right?" Anduin asked, handing the tablet over to Belgrum.

"Looks like . . . och, the poor books," Magellas said, real pain in his voice. Anduin nodded solemnly.

"I should see if anyone else needs help," Aerin said.

"Good idea. Let's go."

"I'm nae takin' ye into danger," Aerin said.

"Well, you have to stick with me, so you can't really go off alone, can you?" He had her there, and she gave him a scowl. "Let's go to the Hall of Mysteries," Anduin continued. "If anyone's hurt, they're going to need healers."

He left the Hall of Explorers and went quickly to the Hall of Mysteries, Aerin, seemingly completely recovered, trotting along beside him. They slowed as they approached.

Dozens of people were clustered about the hall. Some were walking on their own. Others were being carried, or were borne on the backs of rams. Some were lying on the cold stone floor while their loved ones wept frantically, calling for the priests, who seemed very scarce and were murmuring healing prayers at a rapid rate.

"Oh, dear," Aerin said. "Looks like we were lucky."

Anduin nodded. "Rohan's not here," he said. "That means there's a worse situation somewhere else." He gently grabbed ahold of one priestess as she scurried past. "Excuse me, but where is High Priest Rohan?"

"He's been called away," she said.

"Where?"

"Kharanos. It hit harder there. Now please, let me tend tae these people!"

"Come on," Anduin said to Aerin.

"What?"

"We're going to Kharanos. I've been taught how to help in emergency situations," Anduin said. "I can tend wounds, set bones, bandage—help until the real healers can get to people."

"And how many bones have ye actually set?"

"Um . . . none. But I know how to!" At her uncertain look, he grabbed her arms and shook her. "Aerin, listen! I can help! I can't just stand around here and watch!"

"Help these fine folk, then," Aerin said practically.

Anduin glanced around. Now that he looked at them, he realized that what he was seeing was the blood left by a healed injury, not an injury itself. Most of those still actually injured were mobile, upright, and talking. This was not an emergency site, although it was clear that the priests were being kept busy and would be for some time.

"They don't need it," he said quietly. "I want to help those that really *do*. Please—let's go to Kharanos."

Her eyes searched his and she sighed. "All right. But I'm nae letting ye wander into danger, got that?"

He smiled. "Fine, but let's hurry, all right?"

THIRTEEN

Anduin hung on tightly to the great ram as it took the slick, icy path from Ironforge to the small villages in its shadow at a full gallop. He had no choice but to trust in the ram's sure hooves, and he realized somewhat to his surprise his trust seemed to be well placed. There wasn't a single stumble. The large beasts were actually more comfortable to ride than horses, he had found, but that still didn't mean he enjoyed the breakneck pace of the trip.

As they approached Kharanos, they were greeted by several of the mountaineers stationed there.

"Hurry! Several are trapped in town!" one of them cried. "Give me yer ram, lass! I've got tae ride tae Ironforge and get more help!"

Immediately Aerin slipped off and handed the reins over to the mountaineer, who vaulted into the saddle and took off. Without a word Aerin quickly climbed up behind Anduin and they hurried on grimly.

The injuries were much more severe here. Anduin saw nearly a dozen people being treated right out in the open, as almost all of the buildings were damaged in some way. He looked around for Rohan, and found him kneeling over an elderly dwarf female. Anduin slipped off the ram and hurried to the high priest just in time to see him pull a sheet over the still form.

Rohan looked up, his eyes looking older than Anduin had ever seen them. "Prince Anduin," he said, "I thought ye might come. Know some first aid training, do ye?"

Anduin nodded. "And I'm no dwarf, but I've got a pretty strong back," he said. "I hear people are trapped inside."

"Aye," he said, "but it's healers we're short of, nae strong backs. Aerin, lass, go help the others; I'll put our boy tae work here."

"Aye," Aerin said, "let's get these people out o' danger and into th' fresh air!"

And for the next several hours Anduin was indeed put to work. As more and more victims of the quake were pulled from the rubble, Rohan healed those with the most grievous injuries, leaving those with minor wounds to Anduin. He bathed and bandaged and smiled and reassured, and at one point saw Rohan looking at him approvingly.

He thought about his father as he worked. Varian was a warrior. Anduin knew that he was not. Sparring and the thought of dealing injury had never made the human prince feel the way he did now, when he was doing something concrete to ease pain instead of cause it, to help people instead of harm them. Oh, war was a dark and dire necessity sometimes, as was the case in Northrend, but Anduin knew in his heart that he would always long for, and strive for, peace. The injuries here, caused by nature and unavoidable, were bad enough. Anduin did not want to think how he would feel if he were treating those wounded in battle and not by the accidental fall of rocks.

Someone had set up a cauldron and filled it with snow. The resulting water was hot and clean. Anduin poured a small bit of a healing potion into a mug of water and added a few leaves of peacebloom to steep, then handed the mug to a young gnomish mother. She let her two children, a baby and a toddler, sip it first before taking a drink herself.

"You're very kind, sir," she said. "Thank you."

"You're very welcome," he said, patting the baby's tiny head and moving on to a cantankerous middle-aged dwarf male who was arguing with another healer. The priestess, a visiting night elf, was dabbing at a cut on the dwarf's forehead that was bleeding profusely.

"I'm fine, curse ye, go an' tend tae someone who's really wounded, or I'll make ye next in line wi' a broken nose!"

"Sir, please, if you'll just hold still—"

"I'll no waste yer precious healing abilities on a wee cut!" the dwarf bellowed. "Why don't ye—"

The earth rumbled again. This time Anduin did not feel that he was standing on a large purring creature, but attempting to balance atop a bucking horse. His feet went out from under him and he hit the frozen ground hard. It rumbled beneath him, angry and aggressive this time, and he covered his head and held his breath and waited for it to be over. All around him he heard screaming, high-pitched and terrified, and a low, rumbling, cracking sound. Anduin fought against a primal terror as he squeezed his eyes shut and prayed to the Light. He hadn't anticipated this. He'd handled the first quake just fine, but now reason seemed to have deserted him. He realized that the screaming he heard around him now included his own voice.

Something warm and calming touched him, and he felt the familiar sensation of the Light. His chest suddenly loosened and he was able to breathe. The earth still heaved beneath him, but he could think now, could ride it out in control of his emotions, not they in control of him. Others, too, seemed to calm, and the awful sound of screams no longer mixed with the sounds of a shaking earth.

It seemed to go on forever, but finally the aftershock ended. Anduin lifted his head cautiously. His breath misted in the cold air as he looked around. The gnome woman and her children—they were all right. So were the cranky dwarf and the night elf female, although both were pale. Where was—there was Rohan. It must have been he who had calmed him and the others, using the Light to protect them from the crippling attack of fear. Anduin put hands to the earth to push himself up and splashed in something wet. For a horrible second he thought it might be blood, but it was brown and cool. What . . . Slowly Anduin got to his feet, staring at the liquid on his hands. He sniffed it cautiously.

It was . . . *beer.*

For a second, it made no sense, and then he realized what had to have happened. He whirled to look behind him, seeing several shattered casks that had rolled away and a blanket of ominous white where a building had once been.

The Thunderbrew Distillery had caved in, and snow and collapsing earth from the hill behind it had smothered it all.

"Oh, Light," Anduin breathed, the words a panicked prayer as he broke into a run and went toward the mound of snow that had once been a pleasant little inn. Others joined him, calling out reassurances, grabbing shovels and starting to dig with a will. A gnome mage rushed forward, robes fluttering in agitation. "Don't worry! I can melt the snow!" she cried, preparing to suit action to words.

"No!" Anduin cried. "You'll flood it!"

The gnome, bright red hair tied back in two pigtails, glared at him, but nodded, seeing the logic in the words.

"Wind," came a soft voice. An elegant, long-legged draenei woman stepped forward, looking at Anduin. He wondered how it was that a thirteen-year-old boy had suddenly been put in charge and thought frantically. Yes—properly directed and controlled, the wind could blow away the enveloping snow without causing harm to anyone trapped inside. They could then see how much earth was piled atop the rubble.

"Uh—yeah," he said inelegantly. "But be careful!"

She closed her eyes and fluttered long, blue fingers, tossing her blue-black hair. Despite the direness of the situation, for a moment Anduin simply stared at her, enraptured by her beauty and grace, then blushed and concentrated his attention on the magic she was summoning.

He heard a slight thump and a small shape appeared. It was jar shaped, filled with a glowing light, and he knew it to be a totem—a method for shaman to contact, summon, and control the elements. Radiant jewels seemed to swirl about it, and runes he did not recognize moved in a slow circle.

A heartbeat later, a little dust devil formed, blue-white and whirling. It grew larger as the shaman began to chant, and with a flick of her wrist she released it. It did not move. The draenei opened her eyes, puzzled, and said something in a language Anduin did not understand. Still the little elemental she had summoned did not obey her.

Her face showed her confusion and a trace of fear. She spoke again, imploringly, and finally it moved forward, whirling, sending the snow flying so that the onlookers had to take a step back. A few moments later it was done. The snow was gone, revealing the gray stone that had once been the distillery's roof. The elemental whirled in place, faster and faster, until it suddenly vanished. Out of the corner of his eye, Anduin saw the young draenei shaman lift a trembling hand to her face.

The crowd rushed forward again, eager to begin assisting those trapped inside. Anduin was among them.

"Wait, wait!" It was Rohan this time. "Silence!" Everyone obeyed, staring at the high priest, who closed his eyes and listened. Anduin heard it after a moment of straining—a faint tapping and clanking. Someone was still alive down there. There was also the sound of muffled voices, their words too faint to be heard.

"Dinna waste yer breath shouting!" Rohan said in a deep voice. "We can hear ye an' we're coming fer ye!"

People began again to dig by hand. Others brought in some equipment to help with the process. Unsurprising to Anduin, Aerin was in the forefront of the recovery, her arms quivering with strain after a time but her determination overriding her exhaustion. Bit by bit, the rock was lifted away, revealing dusty, wounded bodies beneath it. Rohan moved about as needed, attempting as best he could to see and heal those he could not physically touch. His concentration was utter, his eyes sharp and focused, his hands moving in a swift motion that belied his age. Anduin felt tears sting his eyes, tears of joy and gratitude for this dwarf and the blessing of the Light, as victim after victim of the earthquake was removed alive and well.

"How many levels?" Anduin asked, pausing at one point to wipe his forehead. It was cold, but he was sweating profusely from the hard physical labor.

"Three," someone said.

"Nay, f-four," someone else corrected. It was the innkeeper, Belm, sitting off to the side with a blanket wrapped around him and a mug of hot tea. His hands were wrapped around the mug for warmth, and he trembled as he spoke. "There are rooms deep b-below for those stayin' overnight. We had no guests and I d-dinna think anyone was in them."

"Thank the Light fer wee favors," muttered Rohan. "Three levels tae worry about, then."

"Och, nae so great a task," Aerin scoffed, although the strain on her face belied it. "The sooner we rebuild, the sooner we can raise our mugs wi' good Thunderbrew ale!"

Laughter rippled through the crowd, and for the first time since the whole ordeal began, Anduin saw smiles on some of the faces. It did not detract from the dire need to recover the wounded, but it eased the tension and the workers moved the swifter for it.

The first level was cleared out now, of rubble, injured, and, more somberly, bodies. Again someone tapped a rhythmic tattoo, and again the reassuring sound of a response made people sigh in relief. Several gnome volunteers were the first to wriggle through a small cleared area into the next level, ropes tied around their tiny waists. A few tugs told those above how many survivors: three. A cheer went up, the hole was widened, and even as others worked to clear it, Aerin and a second dwarf dropped down.

Hopes were high. The recovery was going well. More and more people were coming to offer aid. Food and hot drinks and blankets were being passed around. At one point Anduin glanced over at Rohan, who caught his eye and nodded.

"Dinna worry, lad, we'll rebuild. We dwarves are tough, an' so are our friends the gnomes. And believe me, the distillery will be th' *first* thing that gets rebuilt!"

Anduin laughed along with all the others and returned, smiling, to the task at hand. It began to snow again, which helped nothing at all. He was soaked and cold, but the activity helped keep him warm. His fingers were scraped and bleeding. He could have had Rohan heal them with a quick prayer, but he knew that others were in far more dire straits than he. His fingers would recover. The injuries suffered by others would be harder to—

It came again, another aftershock, and Anduin barely had time to leap out of the way as the floor beneath him buckled. He landed hard, the wind knocked out of him, gasping like a fish for air even as he winced when small chunks of stone pelted his body. The earth finally ceased its angry shaking, and for what felt like the thousandth time Anduin got to his feet and wiped a trickle of blood from his eyes to peer at the distillery. He blinked sticky lashes, and for a moment refused to believe what he saw.

There was no distillery. Not anymore. There was only a dreadful hole in the ground, a hole covered with pieces of walls, and ceiling, and tables. Dust was still rising, mingling incongruously with the peaceful image of falling snow.

Aerin. . . .

Rohan clambered up and tapped on the stone, cocking his ear to listen. After a few seconds he tapped again. Then he sighed heavily and stepped back, shaking his head slowly.

Something snapped in Anduin.

"No!" he cried, surging forward. Fear gave him new strength, and he forced his cold fingers to obey as they grasped a large chunk of stone and hurled it away only to reach for another one. "Aerin!" he cried, his voice hoarse. "Aerin, hang on, we'll get you out!"

"Lad," came a gentle voice.

There was something in that tone that Anduin refused to acknowledge. He ignored Rohan's voice and kept going, his breath coming in hitching sobs. "Aerin, just hang on, okay? We're c-coming!"

"Lad," came Rohan's voice again, more insistent.

Anduin felt a hand on his shoulder and angrily shook it off, glaring with blurred vision at the priest, seeing the compassion and sorrow on the aged visage and denying it utterly. He looked around at those who were supposed to be helping him. They stood still. Some of them had tears running down their faces. All of them looked stunned, shocked.

"There's no tapping," Rohan persisted inexorably. "It's . . . over. No one could have survived that. Come away, lad. Ye've done all ye could an' then some."

"No!" shrieked Anduin, lashing out with his arm and barely missing Rohan. "You don't know that! We can't just give up! They're not answering because they're wounded, maybe unconscious. We have to hurry—have to get them out—have to get *her* out. . . ."

Rohan stood quietly by, making no further attempt to stop the young human prince. Anduin, tears flooding down his face, kept going, for how long, he did not know. Stone after stone he moved, until his slender shoulders screamed in white-hot agony, until his hands bled furiously and numbed and cramped until finally he crumpled on the snowy stone and sobbed violently. He reached one hand out, palm flat, trying to contact his friend, who was trapped beneath the implacable stone hurled upon her by the violently agitated earth.

"Aerin," he whispered, for her ears alone, wherever she might be. "Aerin . . . I'm sorry . . . I'm so so sorry. . . ."

Now he did not resist the gentle hands slipping about his exhausted body and lifting him up. He accepted, unable to fight anymore, his heart hurting and his body too drained to protest. The last thing he knew before merciful unconsciousness finally claimed him was the gentle touch of gnarled hands upon his heart and forehead, and the soft voice of Rohan telling him to rest now, rest and heal.

And the last thing he saw in his mind's eye was a cheerful dwarven face framed by brown hair, smiling, as Aerin always was, and in his heart always would be.

FOURTEEN

Magni looked older than Anduin had ever seen him.

In the two days since the disaster at the distillery, Anduin had learned that those who had fallen at Kharanos had had a great deal of company. The quake had not been localized. It had shaken towns throughout Khaz Modan. Part of Menethil Harbor now lay at the bottom of the ocean, and excavation sites from Uldaman to Loch Modan had been buried, at least partially. It had gone from being a localized incident to a national crisis.

The tragedy had aged the dwarven king, but there was a determination in his eyes that told anyone who looked into them that Magni Bronzebeard would not be kept down. He glanced up as Anduin entered the High Seat and waved him forward, not with the enthusiasm he had displayed on the first occasion, but with blunt command. Anduin hastened to the king's side.

"I dinna wish to act precipitously," Magni began, "but by th' Light, now I wish I had. We might have been able to save all those lives. Including Aerin's."

Anduin swallowed hard. A service for the Khaz Modan dead had been conducted yesterday. It was harder to sit through than the one in Stormwind had been; that was a commemoration of many thousands of lives lost over a long period of time. Anduin had mourned the death of his friend Bolvar Fordragon, but the loss had been many months old by the time of the service. The loss of Aerin was new and raw and, dammit, *hurt* so badly. . . . He focused his attention on Magni's words.

"I—don't understand," he said. "This is about the tablet?"

"Och, aye," Magni said. "I've been pushing th' translators and they're pretty sure as to what the tablet says. Let me read tae ye." He cleared his throat and bent closer, his eyes flickering over the strange letters. His heavily accented voice deepened as he read the formal, archaic-sounding words aloud.

"'An' here are the why an' the how, tae again become one wi' the mountain. For behold, we are earthen, o' the land, and its soul is ours, its pain is ours, its heartbeat is ours. We sing its song an' weep fer its beauty. For who wouldna wish tae return home? That is the why, O children o' the earth.

"'Here is the how. Go ye tae the heart o' the earth. Find ye these herbs three: mountain silversage, black lotus, and ghost mushroom. Wi' a finger's pinch o' the soil that nourished them, consume the draft. Speak these words wi' true intent, an' the mountain shall reply. And so it shall be that ye shall become as ye once were. Ye shall return home, and ye shall become one with the mountain.'"

He turned his intense gaze to Anduin. "Do ye see?"

Anduin thought so. "I . . . think so . . . this—this rite will let you speak to Azeroth itself?"

"It seems so, aye. An' if we can talk tae Azeroth itself, then we can ask what th' bloody Nether is going on wi' it. Help find a way tae—tae fix it, tae heal it somehow. An' maybe then there'll be nae more o' these unnatural floods an' droughts an' . . . and earthquakes. Anduin—there's more goin' on here than a simple cave-in. Summat big is happening. Did ye know that reports o' tremors are coming in from as far awa' as Teldrassil?"

"That . . . shouldn't be possible . . . should it?"

Magni shook his head. "Not normally, no. 'Tis not how such things work . . . not naturally, at any rate."

Anduin was silent for a moment, thinking. Something occurred to him. "But . . . aren't some of those herbs toxic if ingested?"

"That's why they want ye tae take it wi' soil," said Magni. "Certain soils neutralize certain poisons. Dinna worry, I've checked wi' the top herbalists in Ironforge. I've no desire tae keel over clutching me throat."

Anduin stared. "You? You're going to try this? This sounds like something a shaman should do."

"Nay, lad. 'Tis me realm that is hardest hit. 'Tis the dwarves who are suffering the most. I lead them. We are the children of the titans, lad. We are already of the earth, more than any other race. It's right that I be the one to do this. Besides, what kind o' a king would I be, tae let others face the danger o' th' unknown while I cowered in safety? That's nae the way o' the dwarves, lad."

"Nor would it be my father's way," Anduin said, realizing the words were true as he spoke them.

"No, it wouldna be Varian's way either," Magni agreed. "Now, the scholars have agreed that it should work right here in Ironforge. I'll just need tae go as deep as I can, right tae the heart o' the earth." He smiled a little at Anduin. "Not everyone knows about th' secret places, but I think ye can be trusted. Ye've th' stout heart o' one of our own, lad, even though ye're reed thin an' far too delicate, bein' a human stripling."

Anduin found himself smiling a little, something that two days ago he wondered if he'd ever be able to do. Aerin would be the first to chide him for being such a sad fellow, he knew. "Aerin promised to dwarf-temper me," he said, his voice catching a little, but still surprisingly light.

"Ah," Magni said, giving him a smile tinged with sorrow. "I'd say she did, from what I see before me."

Anduin swallowed again.

"Now," Magni said, "I've sent for some herbalists tae gather th' necessary ingredients. All should be ready tae do this tomorrow morning."

"So soon?"

"Aye, the sooner the better, I think. Azeroth had better start talking tae me, so that I can do what I can to take care of it. Do ye not agree?"

Anduin nodded. Light alone knew if there would be any more aftershocks.

Anduin started to head back to his rooms, but instead found his feet taking him to the Hall of Mysteries. He had avoided it for the past two days. For some reason he didn't want to see Rohan again. He wasn't sure why. Maybe it was because he felt he had failed the high priest in the effort to save lives. Maybe because of how angry he had been at Rohan when he had tried to urge Anduin to come away from the wreckage. But now he stood before the hall, took a deep breath, and went inside. At once, as always, the Light offered comfort. Even so, he still did not wish to speak with anyone, and ascended to the upper level where there were fewer people. At one point he heard a soft voice and winced slightly as he recognized it as Rohan's. He kept his eyes closed and his head bowed, hoping that the dwarf wouldn't notice him. He heard the tread of feet approach and then fall silent, and a hand was gently placed on his shoulder.

Anduin did not reply, but felt a gentle warmth stealing through him. Softly, Rohan said, "Ye're a good lad, Anduin Llane Wrynn. Ye've a good heart. Know that even if it breaks, it will mend again."

And as the dwarf withdrew, Anduin realized that there had been no magic performed on him at all. And yet he felt better.

Healing, it would seem, took many forms.

When he returned to his rooms, he found Wyll waiting with a note from Magni asking Anduin to come to his quarters. Anduin was confused but immediately went.

Magni was waiting for him. The room in which he greeted Anduin was surprisingly small and cozy, very dwarven in its snug feeling, unlike the large, airy, human rooms. A brazier burned cheerily, and the table was piled with simple but hearty fare. Anduin's stomach growled quite audibly, and he realized he hadn't eaten for several hours. Ever since Aerin's . . . death, he had not had much of an appetite, but now, looking at the assortment of roast meats, fruits, breads, and cheeses displayed on the table, it seemed to return with a vengeance. Life, it would appear, did go on. The body had needs that had to be satisfied, even if, as Rohan said, one's heart was broken.

"There ye are, lad," Magni greeted him. "Pull up a chair and dive right in." His own plate was already piled high, and Anduin did as he was bid, enjoying the roast lamb, Dalaran sharp, and grapes.

"I wanted tae have a few words wi' ye afore the ritual on the morrow," Magni said, reaching for his tankard and downing a big swig of ale. "Afore the earthquake, I had a wee chat with Aerin."

The food stuck in Anduin's throat, and he reached for his own glass of juice to wash the suddenly tasteless food down.

"She said she'd never seen anyone try harder at sparring, and she's trained quite a few warriors. But . . . she also said the weapons weren't yer friends. That ye dinna have a real feel fer them."

The human prince felt his face grow hot. Had he so greatly disappointed Aerin?

"An, being the sharp lassie that she is . . . was . . . Aerin knew a born warrior when she saw one. And one that wasna born tae it."

The king took a bite of a crisp apple and chewed, watching Anduin's reaction. The boy put down his knife and fork and simply waited to hear what Magni had to say. Something kind but dismissive, no doubt. Something to make it sound like Anduin hadn't disappointed him.

"I've also been talking wi' Rohan," Magni continued. "If ye can get past his terrible jokes, th' fellow has a lot of wisdom. He couldna say enough about ye—how ye seemed tae thrive whenever ye visited. How ye felt compelled tae go to the aid of those who'd been harmed. How ye worked long past the time when ye should have dropped from exhaustion." He took another long pull on the tankard, then set it down and turned to face Anduin with his whole body. "Lad . . . have ye ever considered that ye just might not be cut out fer the life of a warrior? And that there's summat else that might be just exactly what ye're supposed to be doing?"

Anduin stared down at his plate. Given what Aerin had told him about how Magni wished that he had had a son, not a daughter, he wasn't sure how criticism of his father would be received. Finally he just spoke simply and truthfully. "Father wishes me to be a warrior," he said. "I've always known that in his heart, that's what he wants for me."

Magni placed his hand on Anduin's shoulder. "Och, he might want that, right enough, because it's what he is. But yer father is a good man. In the end, he'll want ye to do what's right for ye, and fer the kingdom. There's no shame in healing, lad, in loving th' Light, in inspiring people and giving them hope. None at all. That's looking out fer the good o' yer kingdom just as much as fighting for it is."

Anduin felt a shiver run through him, but it was not

unpleasant. Far from it; it was a shudder almost of . . . knowing. And it left in its wake a strange calmness and contentment. A priest. Someone who worked with the Light to do its work to heal, not harm, someone who inspired others by clearing their heads and asking them to give their best, rather than inflaming their darker emotions. He thought about the peace that always bathed him any time he entered the cathedral or the Mystic Ward here in Ironforge. A longing seized his soul for more of that. It felt almost like coming home to hear the dwarven king speak so. He looked at Magni, his eyes searching those of this powerful warrior and great king.

"Do . . . do you really believe that?"

"Aye, I do. And while we'll find another arms trainer fer ye, I'd be right pleased tae see ye start talking seriously wi' High Priest Rohan."

Anduin didn't want another arms trainer. He wanted Aerin, cheerful and pragmatic and blunt. But he nodded. "I will, sir."

"Good!" They finished their meal, chatting quietly, and when the last grape had been popped into Anduin's mouth and the last drop of ale had been consumed by Magni, the dwarf patted his belly and smiled at the human prince. "Now, then, we should both get some sleep. But afore then, I've got summat fer ye."

He slid out of the chair and trundled over to an old chest. Anduin followed, curious. The chest groaned in protest as Magni lifted the lid. Inside were several cloth-covered items whose shapes led Anduin to believe they were weapons. Magni selected one and lifted it out, carefully unwrapping it.

It was indeed a weapon, a mace, gleaming as bright as the day it was made although it had to be quite old. The head was silver, wrapped in intersecting bands of gold that had runes etched into it. Small gems dotted it here and there. It was altogether a lovely and graceful thing of beauty and power.

"This," said Magni reverently, "is Fearbreaker. It is an old weapon, Anduin. Several hundred years. This was handed down through the Bronzebeard line. It's seen battles in Outland and here in Azeroth. It's known th' taste o' blood, and in certain hands, has been known tae also stanch blood. Here, take it. Hold it in yer hand. Let's see if it likes ye." Magni winked.

More than a little intimidated—the weapon was large for one so slight as he to wield—Anduin extended a hand and grasped the shaft of the mace. At once he felt a cool calmness spread from the weapon to his hand, and from there throughout his whole body. He found himself inhaling and letting the breath out as a sigh, found his body—tense for so long from effort and pain both emotional and physical—relaxing. Uncertainty and worry were not banished, not quite, but they receded through Fearbreaker's touch of metal against skin.

Just as he opened his mouth to comment on the sensation, he could have sworn the weapon . . . glowed, slightly.

"As I suspected," Magni said. "It does like ye."

"It's . . . alive?"

"Nay, nay, but, lad, ye know as well as I, as well as anyone who wields a weapon—they have their likes an' their dislikes, same as people. They can be persnickety at times. I thought ye and Fearbreaker might be a good match. 'Tis yers."

Anduin gaped. "I—I couldn't possibly—"

"Oh, aye, ye can, an' ye will. Fearbreaker has sat here fer some time now, waiting fer the right hand tae wield it. Ye may not be an armsman like yer father, but ye can fight the good fight. Fearbreaker proves it. Go on, lad. If ever a thing was meant fer someone, that weapon was meant fer ye."

Anduin blinked. He teared up quickly these days, but somehow, holding the beautifully wrought mace, he was not ashamed of the quick emotion as he had been. Fearbreaker. That was what Rohan had done for him when he had panicked—broken his fear. Called forth his best. "Thank you. I will treasure this."

"O' course ye will. Now, off tae bed wi' ye, lad. I've got a few last-minute things tae prepare, and then I'm tae bed meself. Got tae have a good night's sleep if one is tae have long conversations with one's world, eh?"

Anduin laughed a little. He left Magni's quarters not cheered or happy, but more reconciled to what had happened. He placed the precious weapon on the nightstand by his bed. In the darkness of the room after he had blown out the candles, it emitted a barely perceptible radiance, and as he drifted off to sleep, Anduin wondered if he was being silly to think that it might be watching over him.

FIFTEEN

Anduin realized that Magni's compliment wasn't an idle one. He was indeed the only human—indeed, the only person who wasn't a dwarf or a gnome—present as those who would witness and participate in the ritual assembled in the High Seat. Magni had donned his most formal armor. Gone was the avuncular dwarf whom Anduin had become so fond of. Today Magni was fully embracing what he needed to be for his people, and he was every inch, short though it might seem to Anduin, a king. Anduin, too, had dressed in the finest clothes he had brought with him, but still felt a bit out of place. Fortunately, he knew many of the dwarves.

One, though, was not present, and he missed her keenly. He wondered what she would have thought about this. Would Aerin have deemed it superstitious nonsense, or a practical method of finding out information? He would never know.

Magni's eyes swept the assembled gathering. There were not many—High Priest Rohan, several herbalists, High Explorer Magellas, and Advisor Belgrum from the Explorers' League. "Would that me brothers were here," Magni said quietly, "tae witness this. But there was no time tae notify them. Come, let us go. Each moment we linger distresses poor Azeroth th' more."

Without another word he strode toward a large door toward the entrance of the High Seat. Anduin had noticed the door there before but had never asked about it, and no one had ever mentioned it. Magni nodded, and two attendants stepped forward bearing a huge iron skeleton key between the two of them. Another brought out a large ladder; the door was so gargantuan even the slightly taller Anduin would not have been able to reach the lock. The dwarves cautiously ascended and hefted the mammoth key into position. Working together, they twisted it. With a deep, protesting groan, the key turned and the lock yielded. The dwarves descended and moved the ladder out of the way.

For a moment nothing happened, and then slowly the door magically swung open of its own accord toward the onlookers, revealing a yawning darkness.

The two attendants who had opened the door had set aside the giant's key and now moved ahead of the small procession, lighting sconces along the way as they went to reveal a simple descending corridor. The air was cool and moist, but not stale. Anduin realized that there must be huge open areas beneath Ironforge.

They followed the corridor in silence as it led them ever downward. It was precise and linear; no twining path this, not for the dwarves. One of the attendants moved up ahead of them, and when they reached the end of the hallway, there was a brazier burning brightly ready to greet them. The hallway opened into a large cavern, and Anduin gasped.

He'd been expecting the neat hallway, but what he saw startled him. Beneath his feet was a platform that branched out to two paths. One was a set of stairs, carpeted and surprisingly new looking, which led upward. Another path led downward, this one plain, unadorned stone. What took his breath away was what was on the walls and above.

Clear, gleaming crystals jutted from the walls and ceiling. They caught the light of the brazier and the torches the attendants held, sparkling and seeming to radiate clean white illumination of their own, though Anduin knew that was but a trick of the imagination. Nonetheless, it was beautiful, this blending of the glories of the natural formations of this place and the simple lines of dwarven architecture.

"The crystal—it's so beautiful," Anduin said softly to Rohan, who was walking next to him.

The priest chuckled. "Crystals? Lad, these are no crystals. Ye're looking at *diamonds*."

Anduin's eyes widened, and his head whipped back up to regard the gleaming ceiling with new respect.

Magni was purposefully striding up the stairs to a broad platform large enough to accommodate a group several times their size. He turned and nodded expectantly.

"I think it no accident that right when we needed it, we have uncovered a tablet that contains information that might be of great help," he said, his voice echoing in the cavern. "Nearly everyone present here today lost someone he or she loved dearly three days past. Reports come from all over Azeroth that summat is mightily wrong. The earth is wounded, an' is shaking—cryin' out fer aid. We are dwarves. We are of th' earth. I have faith in the word of the earthen. I believe that what I do here—this rite that is unspeakably old—will let me heal this poor, hurtin' world. By my blood an' bone, by the earth an' stone, let this be done."

The hair on the back of Anduin's neck prickled. Even though Magni's speech had been spontaneous, there was something about it that made his breath catch. He felt that just as he had descended into the heart of the earth, so he was about to descend into a ritual that was deep and unfathomable.

Belgrum stepped forward, a scroll in his hand. Magellas stood beside him, his hands clasped behind his back. Beside these two stood Reyna Stonebranch, a dwarf herbalist, holding a crystal vial full of a murky-looking liquid. Belgrum cleared his throat and began to speak a strange language that sounded hard and blunt and made Anduin shiver. It seemed colder here now, somehow.

After each phrase, Magellas translated for Anduin's benefit. The young prince remembered Magni reading the same phrases to him just yesterday.

"An' here are the why an' the how, tae again become one wi' the mountain," intoned Belgrum. "For behold, we are earthen, o' the land, and its soul is ours, its pain is ours, its heartbeat is ours. We sing its song an' weep fer its beauty. For who wouldna wish tae return home? That is the why, O children o' the earth."

Home. Azeroth was truly home to all of them, Anduin thought as Belgrum continued with the specific directions on how to prepare the draft. Home wasn't Stormwind, or even with his father, or Aunt Jaina. Home was this land, this world. Here they now stood, in the "heart of the earth," embraced by diamonds and stone that felt sheltering rather than oppressive. Magni was about to speak to the wounded Azeroth and find out best how to heal it. It was truly a noble goal.

"Wi' a finger's pinch o' the soil that nourished them, consume the draft. Speak these words wi' true intent, an' the mountain shall reply. And so it shall be that ye shall become as ye once were. Ye shall return home, and ye shall become one with the mountain."

Reyna now stepped forward, handing the muddy-looking elixir to Magni. Unhesitatingly the dwarven king took the transparent, slender vial, brought it to his lips, and drank it down. He wiped his lips and handed it back to Reyna.

Magellas now handed him a scroll. With a bit more hesitation than Belgrum had displayed, Magni read aloud in the ancient language while Magellas translated.

"Within me is th' earth itself. We are one. I am o' it and it o' me. I listen fer th' mountain's reply."

Magni handed back the scroll, then spread his hands imploringly. He closed his eyes and furrowed his brow in concentration.

No one knew what to expect. Would the mountain suddenly begin to talk? If so, what would its voice be like? Would it speak only to Magni, and what would he hear? Could he speak to it? Would—

Magni's eyes flew open. They were wide with wonder, and his mouth curved in a soft smile. "I . . . I can hear . . ." He lifted his hands to his temples. "Th' voices are in me head. Lots o' 'em." He chuckled softly, his expression one of stunned joy and triumph. "It's not just one voice. It's . . . dozens, maybe hundreds. All the voices o' the earth!"

Anduin shivered, his own lips curving in a smile. Magni had been right! He could hear the earth itself—themselves? It was so confusing!—speaking to him.

"Can ye understand them?" asked Belgrum excitedly. "What are they saying?"

Magni suddenly threw his head back, arching. He seemed to try to stagger backward, but his feet were held as if rooted in place. No, not rooted . . . Anduin realized his black boots were turning almost translucent, as if they were suddenly made of glass—as if his feet themselves were suddenly made of glass—

—or crystal . . . or diamond . . .

One with the mountain . . .

No, oh, no, it couldn't be—

Suddenly Magni's foot quivered and a bulge of clear stone formed atop it. Like a living ooze of rock, it began moving upward, along his legs, his torso. It spiked here and there with a sudden groaning sound, forming long crystal spears, as if Magni Bronzebeard was a crystal forming crystals of his own. Magni opened his mouth in a long, wordless cry and lifted his arms high over his head. Diamond ooze scurried to wrap around his hands, shooting out to encircle his body. Magni screamed, a gut-wrenching cry of pure horror. But the merciless clear liquid stone poured into his mouth, silencing him in midscream, hardening so quickly he didn't even have time to close his eyes.

Everyone had been staring, open-mouthed, but now was galvanized into action by the sound, echoing in the diamond cavern, bone-chilling, like no cry of pain or horror they had ever heard.

Rohan began to cast healing spells. Magellas and Belgrum moved forward, seizing Magni's arms, trying foolishly to somehow pull him away from where he stood. But it had all happened too fast, and now it was too late. The echoes of his single shout died away. Magni looked like he had been both turned to stone and encased in it, his head thrown back, his arms spread, the tendons in his neck standing out in pain. And over him, like some bizarre costume, were ragged, gleaming chunks of jagged crystal.

Anduin broke the shocked silence. "Is he . . . can you . . ."

Rohan stepped close to Magni, placing a hand on his king's arm and closing his eyes. A single tear leaked beneath the closed lids as he stepped away, shaking his head.

Anduin stared. Disbelief rushed through him, the same disbelief he had experienced after the land trembled and buried Aerin beneath the crushing weight of tons of rock. But . . . this wasn't possible!

He dragged his gaze to Magellas, who stared as aghast as he.

"I was certain," he murmured, "that it was not literal . . . we checked every source. . . ."

"You mean—it *worked*? This is what the ritual was *supposed* to do?" Anduin cried, his voice treble with his shock and horror.

"Not literally," Magellas said, looking like a panicked hare. "But we—we d-did perform it precisely correctly. . . ."

Unable to help himself, Anduin sprang forward. With a cry, he took the hilt of his ceremonial dagger, and before anyone could stop him, had struck the figure on the shoulder. The hilt shattered beneath the impact, part of it whirling erratically away. The impact jarred his hand, and he dropped the part of the hilt he still held. Clutching his stinging hand, he stared.

There was not a single mark on the image. Magni had been turned into one of the hardest known materials in the world.

As Anduin stared at the diamond lump that had once been a vibrant, hale dwarf, some of the words of the ritual floated back to him. *For behold, we are earthen, of the land . . . For who would not wish to return home? . . . And so it shall be that you shall become as you once were. You shall return home, and you shall become one with the mountain.*

The dwarves were descendents of the titans. Magni had become what he had once been—and paid for it with his life. "He's gone home," Anduin whispered past a throat tight with grief. Tears welled in his eyes and blurred the image of Magni Bronzebeard. As the torchlight glinted off the statue, Anduin saw only beautiful, fractured lights dancing before his gaze.

He blinked hard, gulping, tears trickling down his face for the kindly dwarf who had only wanted to do what was best for his people, who had wanted to talk to a wounded world in order to help it heal. And for that goal, he had been lost to them.

What were the dwarves going to do now?

SIXTEEN

Anduin didn't realize how much comfort the constant ringing of the forge had provided until it was silenced.

He hadn't thought of Ironforge as a lively, bustling city, not the way Stormwind was. And yet when the sound of the forge ceased, and the halls no longer echoed with the distinctive sound of dwarven laughter, he realized that the city once did have a cheerfulness to it. Now, even though more people than ever were in Ironforge coming to pay their respects to Magni Bronzebeard, it was somber and bleak.

Within the hour of the disaster, the question of succession had become pressing. Gryphons were sent out immediately in search of Brann and Muradin, Magni's brothers. Thus far, they had met with no success.

Anduin had wanted to go home, but instead his father had come to him. All the leaders of the Alliance had either come in person to honor Magni's memory or else had sent representatives. The young prince had always wanted to meet High Priestess Tyrande Whisperwind, who for so long had led the night elves and been forced to be apart from her great love, Archdruid Malfurion Stormrage. And Anduin had been curious about Far Seer Nobundo, the Broken who had been touched by the elements and brought shamanism to his people. Velen, leader of the draenei, had sent Nobundo to honor the reason Magni had fallen—trying to heal the earth, to understand the elements.

So it was that Anduin stood beside Jaina and his father, a few paces away from the night elf high priestess and Malfurion, the archdruid of legend, and the first shaman the Alliance had known. Under any other circumstances he would have been delighted. Now, though, as they stood solemnly gazing at the diamond figure that had once been Magni Bronzebeard, he bitterly wished that he had never met the distinguished personages, if the privilege had been bought at so high a cost.

Even the goblins, too, had sent representatives, and so had the Horde. It was a deep show of respect from Thrall and the Horde in general, and although many eyes looked upon the blood elf and the tauren unfavorably, Anduin found nothing in their behavior to warrant hostility.

Advisor Belgrum had stepped up to fill the void until such time as Muradin or Brann could be found and brought to Ironforge. He was selected for the duty because he had no political agenda other than finding—and serving—a new king, knew Ironforge and its people inside and out, and because his loyalty to the dwarven people themselves was beyond question. He was clearly deeply uncomfortable with the honor, but also knew that someone had to take the reins of power until the rightful leader could be contacted.

Now he stepped forward and looked at the representatives in turn. "Yer presence here is a great honor," he said, his voice rough with emotion. "Would that we were celebrating a happy occasion. Magni was no' just a great dwarf—plenty o' leaders have been great. Magni . . . was *good.* And that's much harder tae find. He would have been so pleased tae see all o' ye . . . aye, even ye, too," he said to the Horde emissaries, "for ye've come wi' good hearts an' plenty o' respect." The blood elf seemed to be debating whether or not to be offended, but the tauren nodded solemnly.

"High Priestess Tyrande . . . yer faith and patience were well known tae Magni, and he spoke with great respect o' yer people. Archdruid Malfurion—ye've done so much tae help our world. Magni would have been right pleased to ken ye had come."

His eyes fell on the humans. "Lady Jaina . . . sometimes he dinna ken what tae make o' ye, but he was always fond o' ye. King Varian, ye were as a brother tae him. And Anduin . . . ah, lad, ye've no idea how dear ye were tae Magni."

Anduin bit his lip hard and thought of the exquisite mace, likely invaluable, that Magni had so readily gifted him with, and thought he maybe had at least an inkling of how the late king regarded him.

The elderly dwarf cleared his throat. "Well, er . . . thank ye fer coming." When those assembled blinked askance at him, Rohan stepped up smoothly.

"Please . . . all are welcome tae come t' the High Seat

and share yer stories about Magni. We'll have some refreshments fer ye."

Gentle murmurings could be heard as the honored guests moved down the stairs, away from the contorted, gem-encrusted figure that was so much more than diamond, and yet nothing more than diamond.

He didn't realize he was staring until a gentle hand closed on his shoulder. "Prince Anduin, come along," Jaina said kindly.

"Yes, come, Son," said Varian. "Our presence is required for some time yet."

Mutely, Anduin nodded, dragging his gaze away and praying quietly to the Light that Muradin or Brann would be found soon, and come to Ironforge, and chase away at least some of this awful solemnity that lay like a shroud upon the city. Although he suspected that the dwarves would never quite get over the shockingly strange, unforeseen, and violent end their beloved leader had met.

"Well, that is the last of it," Thrall said. He set down the quill and regarded the parchment solemnly. This was the last official business he would conduct for some time—signing the approval to begin work on repairing Orgrimmar. Again. It seemed to Thrall that the city had only just begun to recover from the War Against the Nightmare when another blow had been dealt it. Gazlowe had dropped his price a second time, and Thrall was quite moved by the gesture, even though it was still almost ludicrously high. Too, the goblin had agreed to be paid in increments instead of in advance, and had indicated he'd be willing to adjust the fee if he didn't need to also provide certain supplies. Thrall felt a small, somewhat petty twinge of satisfaction leaving such annoying details as budgets, construction, and supplies to Garrosh. Such "boring" things were of necessity part of being a good leader, and Garrosh needed to learn that.

Nodding, he left the scrolls for Garrosh and rose. He would be making this journey alone. By his orders, no Kor'kron would accompany him. Their duty was now to defend Garrosh Hellscream, the acting warchief of the Horde. They would not be needed to guard a lone shaman journeying to another world to seek knowledge. His leave-taking was not being announced with fanfare or spectacle. For one thing, such frivolities were too expensive. For another, he did not wish to make this any kind of an "event." He was simply going away for a time, and he had no desire to make his departure anything of consequence for the average Horde citizen. While he made no secret of it—that would be as counterproductive in his mind as trumpeting it—he wished it to be perceived as a minor event.

He had sent word ahead to Cairne, of course, informing his old friend of his decision and reasoning behind it, and requesting that Cairne advise Garrosh when needed. He had as of yet received no response, which surprised him. Cairne usually was quite prompt in such matters. He supposed that the tauren leader, too, had his hands full with the aftermath of Northrend.

"Farewell for now, my old friend," Thrall said to Eitrigg. "See that the boy does the little things as well as the large."

"I shall, Warchief," Eitrigg said. "Do not tarry in our homeland overlong. Garrosh will do his best, but he is not you."

Thrall embraced his friend, clapping him on the back, then picked up the small sack that was all he planned to carry with him on the journey. With little notice even being taken of him, the warchief of the Horde walked out of Grommash Hold into the still-hot night air, heading for the flight tower.

"You are making a grave mistake," came a deep, rumbling voice in the darkness.

Surprised at the words, though recognizing their speaker, Thrall checked his brisk stride and turned to Cairne Bloodhoof. Cairne stood beneath the towering dead tree that bore the skull of a demon and his once-impregnable armor. The tauren high chieftain was straight and tall, his arms folded across his broad chest, his tail swishing slightly. His face showed disapproval.

"Cairne! It is good to see you. I had hoped to hear from you prior to my departure," Thrall said.

"I do not think you will be glad, for I do not believe you are going to like what I have to say," the tauren said.

"I have ever listened to what you have to say," Thrall replied, adding, "which is why I requested you advise Garrosh in my absence. Speak."

"When the courier arrived with your letter," Cairne said, "I thought I had indeed, at long last, finally become senile and was dreaming fever dreams as poor Drek'Thar does. To see, in your own writing, that you wished to appoint Garrosh Hellscream as leader of the Horde!"

The voice had begun quiet, but stern. Cairne was slow to anger, but it was clear he had had some time to think on this matter and it disturbed him greatly. His voice deepened and grew louder as he spoke. Thrall glanced about quietly; so public a place was not where he would have wished to have this particular conversation.

"Let us discuss this in private," Thrall began. "My quarters and ears are open to you at all—"

"No," replied Cairne, and stamped a powerful hoof for emphasis. Thrall glanced at him, surprised. "I am here, in the shadow of what was once your greatest enemy, for a reason. I remember Grom Hellscream. I remember his passion, and his violence, and his waywardness. I remember the harm he once did. He may have died a hero's death by slaying Mannoroth; I am the first to acknowledge that. But by all accounts, even your own, he took many lives, and gloried in the doing. He had a thirst for blood, for violence, and he quenched that thirst with the blood of innocents. You were right to tell Garrosh of his father's heroism. It is true. But also true were the less savory things Grom Hellscream did, and his son needs to know these things as well. I stand here to ask you to remember these things, too, the dark and the bright, and to acknowledge that Garrosh is his father's son."

"Garrosh never had the taint of demonic blood that Grom had," Thrall said quietly. "He is headstrong, yes, but the people love him. He—"

"They love him because they only see the glory!" Cairne snapped. "They do not see the foolishness." He softened somewhat. "I, too, saw the glory. I saw tactics and wisdom, and perhaps with nurturing and guidance those are the seeds that will take root in Garrosh's soul. But he finds it far too easy to act without thinking, to ignore that inner wisdom. There are things about him I respect and admire, Thrall. Mistake me not. But he is not fit to lead the Horde, any more than Grom was. Not without you to check him when he overreaches, and especially not now, when things are yet so tenuous with the Alliance. Do you know that many secretly whisper that now would be a fine time to strike at Ironforge, with Magni turned to diamond and no leader yet visible?"

Thrall did know it. He'd known that the whispers would begin the moment he had learned the news. It was why he had moved quickly to send formal representatives to what amounted to a funeral service, and why he had chosen a sin'dorei and a tauren whom he knew to be moderate individuals.

"Of course I know this," Thrall sighed. "Cairne—it won't be for very long."

"That does not *matter*! The child does not have the temperament to be the leader you are. Or should I say, you were? For the Thrall I knew, who befriended the tauren and helped them so greatly, would not have blithely handed over the Horde he restored to a young pup still wet behind the ears!"

Thrall's jaw tightened, and he felt anger growing within him. Cairne had set his great hoof squarely on Thrall's own worries. Worries that he could not shake. Yet he knew there was literally no other choice. No one else could take on the responsibility. It had to be Garrosh.

"You are one of my oldest friends in this land, Cairne Bloodhoof," Thrall said, his voice dangerously quiet. "You know I respect you. But the decision is made. If you are concerned about Garrosh's immaturity, then guide him, as I have asked you. Give him the benefit of your vast wisdom and common sense. I—need you with me on this, Cairne. I need your support, not your disapproval. Your cool head to keep Garrosh calm, not your censure to incite him."

"You ask me for wisdom and common sense. I have but one answer for you. Do not give Garrosh this power. Do not turn your back on your people and give them only this arrogant blusterer to guide them. That is my wisdom, Thrall. Wisdom of many years, bought with blood and suffering and battle."

Thrall stiffened. This was the absolute last thing he had wanted. But it had happened, and when he spoke, his voice was cold.

"Then we have nothing more to say to one another. My decision is final. Garrosh will lead the Horde in my absence. But it is up to you as to whether you will advise him in that role, or let the Horde pay the price for your stubbornness."

Without another word, Thrall turned and strode off into the darkness of the sultry Orgrimmar night. He half-expected Cairne to come after him, but the old bull did not follow. His heart was heavy as he retrieved a wyvern, slung the sack across his saddle, and mounted. The wyvern leaped skyward, his leathery wings beating quietly and rhythmically and creating a cool breeze that brushed the orc's face.

* * *

Cairne stared after his old friend. Never had he thought it would come to this—an argument over something that was so obviously a mistake. He knew Thrall saw it, too, but for whatever reasons the orc felt it necessary to persist in this course of action.

The parting words wounded Cairne. He had not expected Thrall to dismiss his concerns so quickly or so thoroughly. There was virtue in the boy. Cairne had seen it. But the recklessness, the deaf ear he turned to sound advice, the burning need for acknowledgment and accolades—Cairne flicked his tail, the thoughts agitating him. These were qualities that needed tempering. And, of course, Cairne would be there. His words would be ignored, doubtless, but he would offer them.

He looked up again at Mannoroth's skull, gazing into the shadowed eye sockets.

"Grom, if your spirit lingers, help us guide your son. You sacrificed yourself for the Horde. I know you would not wish to see your son destroy it."

There was no response; if Grom was indeed here, lingering beside the great evil he had destroyed, he was providing no answers. Cairne was on his own.

PART II

. . . AND THE WORLD WILL BREAK

SEVENTEEN

Aggra ran lightly over the surface of Skysong Lake, her bare, brown feet making only the faintest of splashes. Normally she walked, enjoying the feel of this place of power, but the wind had whispered in her ear a moment ago, with the words of Greatmother Geyah: *Come, child, I have news.*

Gentle as the words were, it was a summons that Aggra hastened to obey. She had come to the Throne of the Elements to sit quietly at the feet of the great Elemental Furies—Aborius, Gordawg, Kalandrios, and Incineratus—in the hope that perhaps today they would speak to her. She had barely settled down near Kalandrios, the Fury of Air, when Geyah's words had come to her. So now she was heading back toward Garadar, the Horde fortress in this land of Nagrand, to hear the news that was so important it could not wait.

Aggra was a shaman, but as fit, healthy, and strong as most warriors. She was therefore only slightly out of breath from her exertion when she entered the building atop the highest rise of Garadar and dropped to her knees in front of the Greatmother, her head respectfully lowered.

"The wind bade me come, Greatmother. What is the news?"

Geyah smiled and patted the threadbare rug. Aggra moved to sit beside her. Geyah touched the younger orc's face gently. "So prompt. Perhaps the wind let you fly, eh?"

Aggra chuckled and leaned into the gnarled hand. "No, but the water spirits let me run over the lake."

Geyah laughed. "That was kind of them. As to my news, I have just heard from my grandson . . . and he wishes to come here to Nagrand, to learn what I have to teach."

Aggra blinked. "He . . . what? Go'el?"

"Yes, Go'el."

Aggra frowned. "Does he still go by that hateful slave name?"

"He does," Geyah said, unperturbed by Aggra's seeming rudeness. Aggra knew Geyah had realized long ago that it was easier to direct the elements to help one than it was to curb Aggra's sharp tongue. "And that is his choice. Perhaps you can ask him why he so chooses when he arrives."

"Perhaps I will," Aggra agreed readily. She had never met the famous Thrall, as she had been away from Nagrand when he had come once before. All she knew of him was what others had told her. Now it seemed she would get the chance to make up her own mind about him. "I did not think he would ever return."

"Nor I, save to bid me farewell when it is my time to join the ancestors," Geyah said. "He has asked for my help."

"Help? What does the oh-so-powerful Thrall need help with?"

"Healing his world."

Aggra fell silent. "He tells me in this letter that the elements are distressed in Azeroth, and he seeks my wisdom," continued Geyah. "He says that if anyone understands how to work with a world in turmoil, it is I."

"Hmph," sniffed Aggra. She was embarrassed by her earlier comments but was trying not to show it. "The green fellow does have wisdom in him, for all his humanlike ways."

Geyah laughed, a cheerful cackle. "I look forward to seeing the two of you meet," she said. "But he is not quite correct."

"What do you mean? Greatmother, you have more wisdom than the rest of us combined. You have seen so much more."

Geyah laid a hand on the girl's smooth, brown arm. "I have seen more, yes. And I know much, yes. But there is someone who might understand such things even better than I."

Aggra cocked her head in a confused look. "Who?"

"You, child."

The brown eyes flew open wide. "Me? Oh, no. I know some, but—"

"Never have I seen a more natural shaman than you," Geyah said. "The elements all but sang lullabies to you, Aggra. They claimed you for their own long ago. I am proud that I have been able to teach you, but if you had not had me, another would have served you just as well. When it is my time to join the ancestors, I will do so contentedly, knowing that you are here to take my place."

Aggra blinked quickly. "May that day be many years in

the future," she said. "I am sure you have much to teach me and the others. Including your slave-named grandson."

"Actually," mused Geyah, a glint of mischief in her eyes, "I was thinking of leaving most of the instruction to you. If for no other reason than this old orc will get a great deal of amusement watching the two of you interact."

Aggra could not see her own expression, but judging by the way Geyah tilted back her head and laughed, it was one of comical dismay.

Thrall had forgotten how beautiful Nagrand was.

It was closing in on sunset, and it was as if the sky had decided, like an exotic bird proud of its plumage, to put on a display to impress him. Blues and purples of all shades hosted pink-tinged clouds that looked like seed-pod fluff. Below this spread, the earth, too, was beautiful. The grass was a carpet of thick, verdant green, and Thrall could catch the movement of large animals in the distance. He could hear the sounds of running water and the calls of birds settling in for the night, and he felt an unexpected tug on his heart.

This was the way he had been told so much of Draenor had once appeared. Elsewhere, Thrall knew, the land was damaged, desolate, scarred. But not here, not in Nagrand. And he could not help but wonder, as he drank his fill of the celestial display of sunset, if there might be some way that Durotar, too, could be made to flourish so. If the Barrens and Desolace might one day cease to deserve their ominous names.

"Lok-tar," came a voice.

Thrall had requested that there be no ceremony to

announce his arrival. He had come here to learn, to work, not to be feted. There was no time to waste on such frivolities. Therefore he was not surprised, and was actually pleased, when he turned around and discovered that only one female orc was awaiting his arrival.

She was young, perhaps a little younger than he, and bore a piece of bundled cloth in strong brown arms. Her shiny, reddish-brown hair fell loosely to her shoulders in an untidy, almost wild fashion, and she was dressed very casually, in a leather kilt and vest. She would have been quite beautiful, in a strong-jawed, straight-backed sort of way, had it not been for the scowl of disapproval that twisted her lips down.

"You are Thrall, son of Durotan," she said without preamble.

"I am," he replied.

"A filthy name. Here you will be called Go'el."

The bluntness of her statement took him aback slightly. He had not been ordered around for many a year, not since he had proved his worth to the Frostwolf clan and to Orgrim Doomhammer one night long ago.

"Go'el might be the name my parents intended for me, but fate chose otherwise. I prefer Thrall."

She turned her head and spat. "A human word that means 'slave.' It is not fit for any orc to bear, least of all one who claims to lead us—even the ones who don't live in his world."

Thrall's nostrils flared at the insulting gesture, and his words had a sharp edge to them. "I am warchief of the Horde, shaman, and I have made the Alliance fear the name that once meant 'slave.' To them, it now means the glory and power of the Horde. I would ask you to use the name I have chosen to keep."

She shrugged. "You can keep it, but we won't use it. Unless I am mistaken, you come not as warchief of the Horde to order us about, but as a shaman seeking wisdom."

"This is true." Thrall forced down the righteous anger that bubbled up inside him. He had chided Garrosh for giving in to such things; he would follow his own advice and remain calm. "I have come to learn from my grandmother, Greatmother Geyah. Will you take me to her, please?"

His voice was courteous, but not subservient, and the orc girl seemed slightly—ever so slightly—mollified.

"I will," she said. "And without a doubt you will learn much from her. But she has instructed that you will have another teacher for most of your lessons, as she tires easily."

"Anyone Geyah thinks is fit to teach me, I will humbly learn from," Thrall said with utter sincerity. "What is his name?"

"*Her* name is Aggra," said the girl, turning away and striding off briskly, clearly expecting him to follow.

"I look forward to meeting this Aggra."

She shot him a quick glance over her shoulder and smiled archly around her tusks. "You already have."

Thrall stumbled slightly as her words registered. *Ancestors give me strength,* he thought.

The meal was a simple one: roast clefthoof, Mag'har grain bread, various fruits and vegetables, and pure, clear water to wash it down with. Thrall had never developed a taste for luxurious food, having spent most of his life eating the plain, albeit nutritious, fare served to the gladiators, and had no objection to the meal. Indeed, its lack of ostentation was reassuring, as was Geyah's simple presence. She had been growing frail when he first met her, and the last year had taken its toll, but she was yet far from fragile in body, and her spirit was still vital and strong. Her mind, too, was clear and sharp, and Thrall could not help but contrast her with Drek'Thar. Sometimes fate seemed kinder to some than to others.

He could have wished that it was just the two of them at the meal. Aggra sat beside Geyah and was clearly, and to Thrall's mind perplexingly, a favorite of the older woman. Aggra did not speak much, but when she did, the words were clipped and often barbed. Geyah seemed to not mind the apparent disrespect at all, and once when Aggra left to get more water for them, he leaned in to his grandmother and spoke quietly.

"This girl is not showing you the respect due to one of your rank, Grandmother," he said.

"Some would say that you do not, calling me Grandmother and not Greatmother," she replied.

"If you wish, I will happily do so."

Geyah waved a hand dismissively. "I *am* your grandmother, Go'el. Why should you not address me as such?"

"But this . . . Aggra cuts off your sentences, she flat out says you are wrong, she—"

"Sneers at you, even though you are the great warchief of the Horde?" Geyah chuckled quietly. "Come, my grandson. Tell me you do not have those you trust to pull your head out of the clouds and hold your feet to the fire when you need it, and I will call you a liar.

Because you are a fine leader, and fine leaders do not surround themselves with those who only fawn upon them. Aggra challenges me because she thinks for herself. Sometimes she is right, and I am the one who must change what I held to be true or correct. Sometimes she is not. But I have never attempted to silence her, and I have never regretted it. The day that I am unable to listen to others' truths is the day I should pass to the ancestors, for all that I value in myself will have died."

Thrall nodded, understanding her words, and thought about Eitrigg and Cairne. Just the other night Cairne had used a tone of voice and words that any bystander might have interpreted as disrespect—indeed, insult. But Thrall had known them for what they were—honest, if blunt, expressions of genuine concern. He shifted uneasily on the threadbare rug, which provided no padding at all from the ground beneath it. He had taken offense from Cairne, even though he knew better, and he did not like himself for that. He decided he would apologize to Cairne upon his return and thank the old bull for his blunt truth.

"Already the lessons begin with you, Grandmother," Thrall said quietly.

"Oh, good," said Aggra, returning with a filled pitcher. "You need lessons."

Thrall took a deep, calming breath. Learning to work with Aggra, he thought, would be chief among the "lessons."

"Aggra, I have told you and Go'el that I wish you to be his primary teacher during his time in Nagrand. I will still instruct you, Thrall, but our lessons will be carried out here. My body no longer has the strength to travel the breadth of this land. Aggra's does. She can take you to places you need to visit."

Thrall nodded with what he hoped was courtesy to the younger orc female. "I understand, and I welcome her training."

Aggra lifted a black eyebrow and made a small, dismissive, grunting sound.

"And, Aggra . . . you may not agree with Go'el on everything. You do not have to. You simply need to instruct him as well as you can, with true willingness to impart information. His land is suffering. He has turned over his duties in Azeroth to Garrosh Hellscream—"

"Garrosh? That child is not fit to—"

"*—in order to learn how to help his world,*" Geyah continued implacably, letting her voice grow louder and more stern. "Who he has appointed to lead the Horde does not matter to me or to you. What matters to us should be *that* he has done so. Do you think yourself above trying to aid the elements when they are in torment?"

Aggra's cheeks darkened. She looked about to retort, but then folded her hands in her lap. "You are right, Greatmother. I have dedicated my life to listening to them and working with them, even the elements of another world. I will serve by teaching Go'el all that I know." Clearly unable to resist, she added, "Whatever I may think about him personally."

Thrall gave her a polite smile. "And I, for my part, am willing to listen and learn all that I may, for the sake of my world. Whatever I may think about Aggra personally."

EIGHTEEN

The weeks crawled past. Varian had insisted that Anduin remain in Ironforge.

"You have a chance to help the people of Ironforge now," Varian had said. "You've made some good friends there. And the fact that the prince of Stormwind is staying there throughout this difficult period sends a strong signal about how highly we regard the dwarves. I know it's not a very pleasant place to be right now, but not everything you do as king will be pleasant either."

Anduin had nodded and returned to Ironforge within the hour of the conversation. He knew his father was right, and he did want to help.

Still, he knew it would be best for all involved if Muradin or Brann took up the role their brother had so tragically laid down.

Soon.

He continued to speak with Rohan and train with several of Magni's personal guards. He was with the

high priest one day when Wyll hastened up to him, limping a little from the run and out of breath.

"Your Highness! Come quickly!"

Anduin was on his feet instantly. "What is it? What's wrong?"

"I—I'm not sure," panted the elderly servant. "You are both . . . wanted at the High Seat. . . ."

Rohan and Anduin exchanged glances, then rose and hurried off. Anduin wondered if Muradin or Brann had finally come to assume leadership. It was a thought that filled him with relief, but at the same time he felt a twinge that such a thing was necessary. Still, it would be what Magni wanted. He forced himself not to run.

He rounded the corner and couldn't help himself; he broke into a trot the last few feet.

And slid to a halt, disbelieving what he saw.

Neither Muradin nor Brann Bronzebeard had answered the summons to return to Ironforge to take up the crown. But another Bronzebeard had come.

Advisor Belgrum stood looking as if he, like Magni, had been turned to diamond, except for his wide, alarmed eyes. The guards who had always stood protectively near Magni Bronzebeard now clustered over on one side, looking confused and distressed. Their positions were now being held by other dwarves with long black beards and skin as gray as their armor. They bristled with weapons. But Anduin only gave them the most cursory of glances. He stared, instead, at a young dwarf female.

She was pretty, with reddish-brown hair neatly pinned up in circular buns on either side of her head. She was dressed in fine but somewhat old-fashioned clothing and held a small toddler in her lap. Anduin knew he had never seen her before, but she looked strangely familiar to him.

And she was seated on Magni Bronzebeard's throne.

"Ah, High Priest Rohan," said the stranger in a mellifluous voice, smiling gently. "So *very* good to see you again. And this young human must be Prince Anduin Wrynn. How very courteous a young man you are, to come so promptly. Your father has done such a fine job of teaching you in the niceties. Oh, but we haven't been properly introduced, have we?"

He smile widened, and her eyes glinted, ever so slightly. "I am Queen Moira Bronzebeard."

Anduin couldn't believe what he was hearing, or seeing. But now that Moira had announced her name, he could see the resemblance to her father. And he understood why there had been no challenge to her, even though she had clearly come with several dwarves whose glowing eyes and gray skin proclaimed them Dark Irons. Her claim was legitimate—she was the only surviving heir, and her child after that. There was nothing anyone could do.

And . . . *did* they want to do anything? Anduin wondered after the shock had worn off. This was Magni's daughter, after all. A Bronzebeard was again sitting upon the throne to Ironforge. Anduin had by now recovered at least somewhat and bowed the proper deepness for a prince toward one of equal rank. Heir she might be, but she had not been crowned queen, despite what she had said. And until that time, she was a princess, and his equal.

She lifted a red-brown eyebrow and inclined her head. She did not bow. And that told Anduin all he needed to know.

"Far too long has it been since I have dwelt within these walls," she said. "It was foolish for my dear, late father to have let things come between us. I married an emperor, surely no dishonor to the Bronzebeard name. This child—Dagran Thaurissan, named for his father, is Magni Bronzebeard's grandson, and heir to two kingdoms." She cradled the child, a smile of genuine love softening her brittle visage. "After so long, this little boy will bring unity between two proud peoples—the Dark Irons and the Bronzebeards." She glanced up, and the peek into a mother's heart was immediately replaced by a sly, false charm. "Isn't it wonderful, Rohan? You are a dwarf of peace, a priest of the Light. Surely you must applaud this new era you are about to witness!"

Rohan replied politely, "Indeed, Your Highness. I—"

"Majesty." Again, the brittle smile. Anduin felt a chill run down his spine.

Rohan hesitated just long enough to let his disapproval register. "Majesty. Peace certainly is a goal worth striving for."

The old priest, it would seem, was also a politician. It was an artful reply.

Moira turned her gaze to Anduin, her smile widening. Anduin thought she looked like a fox ready to pounce on a rabbit.

"And Anduin," she said, almost purring. "What great friends we shall doubtless become! Two children of royalty here in Ironforge. I am so very interested in getting to know you! You simply *must* stay for a while, so that we can become better acquainted."

"My father asked me to stay in Ironforge until such time as the proper heir to the throne was found," Anduin said, keeping his voice calm and polite. This much was true. "I have duties awaiting me at home, now that this solemn task is complete."

Also true. But the implication—that he was being summoned home by his father—was all of his own making.

Her smile didn't move. "Oh, no, I wouldn't *dream* of such a disappointing thing. I am certain that your father will understand."

"I believe that—"

She held up an imperious hand. "I won't hear of it, Prince Anduin. You are my guest, and you'll not be leaving for Stormwind until we've had a good, long visit." She smiled and nodded, as if everything was settled.

And with a clench in his gut, Anduin realized that everything was.

He murmured something polite and flattering, and she gave him a wave of dismissal. He, Belgrum, and Rohan moved out. Anduin was in a daze.

"Did . . . was that just . . . a *coup*?" he asked, pitching his voice very low.

"It's perfectly legal an' aboveboard," Belgrum said. "In th' absence of any male heir, th' legitimate female heir has rights tae claim th' throne. Moira even outranks Muradin an' Brann, because she's the direct heir. So it's nae a coup if it's a legitimate claim."

"But . . . she and Magni were estranged. And they're

Dark Iron dwarves!" Anduin was struggling to make sense of it all.

"Well, Magni never disowned her, lad," Rohan said. "He always wanted her tae come home. Even if he—well, that's water under the bridge now. Though I'm sure he'd be all kinds o' furious at seeing the Dark Irons in his city. But they are our cousins . . . perhaps this will turn out tae be a good th—"

He halted in midword. They had emerged from the High Seat into the Great Forge area. The forge had become operational again shortly after Magni's funeral. And right over there was where the gryphons flew in and out of Ironforge.

Except . . . they were gone.

So were the flight masters. Only the empty roosts padded with straw remained at the site where several gryphons had previously waited to bear riders to various places around the Eastern Kingdoms. Anduin glanced around and saw a tufted tail and yellow, leonine hindquarters disappearing in the direction of the gates. Without thinking, Anduin broke into a run, ignoring the calls for him to stop.

He caught up with a flight master and one of the gryphons as they stepped out into the cold, snowy day. "Gryth!" he cried, laying a hand on the dwarf's broad shoulder. "What's going on? Why are the gryphons gone?"

Gryth Thurden turned to Anduin, scowling. "Better not get too close, lad, or ye might get sick!"

Ordinarily that would be a warning to cause some concern, but the way in which Gryth uttered it, it sounded more like a bad joke, so thick with sarcasm was his voice.

"What?" Anduin wasn't sure if a prank was being played, and looked askance at the gryphon. "Well, this one's wing looks injured, but he doesn't look ill. . . ."

"Och, nay, nay, they're terrible sick!" Gryth literally rolled his eyes. "At least, that's what th' new queen's Dark Iron bruisers told us. They're all very ill, it seems. And it's catching! Tae everyone—imagine that! Dwarves, humans, elves, gnomes, even draenei, who aren't even from this world! What a *powerful* disease! They'll have to be quarantined fer months. No gryphon flights in or out. This one dinna like th' Dark Irons and took a bite out o' one. Got a nice wee injury tae his wing fer his trouble. The others have already flown tae their new pens. Light alone knows when they'll be back."

"But—you know that's not true!" Anduin blurted.

Gryth turned slowly toward him. "Of course it's nae true," he said, his voice deep and angry. "An' yon pretender queen is a fool tae think we'd believe it. But what am I supposed tae do? Moira doesna want th' gryphons flying, and those Dark Iron bastards threatened to kill this beastie right on the spot when I protested. Better they're alive and landbound fer a wee bit, until things can get set right again. Light willing, that's soon."

Anduin watched them continue down the road from Ironforge. He wondered distractedly if the animals would indeed be simply quarantined or if they'd be put down. He drew a trembling hand across his forehead, which was damp with sweat despite the cold air outside.

Belgrum and Rohan had caught up to him. They

looked troubled. Another, a gnome wearing a bleak expression, was with them. "The gryphons are being quarantined," Anduin said dully, turning to them. "Apparently they are quite sick, and the illness is contagious."

"Oh, really?" Rohan said, scowling. "Perhaps it was a sick gryphon who damaged th' Deeprun Tram, too, then?"

"What?" Anduin was shivering, and he folded his arms tight. He was pretty sure he was only shaking from the cold as they went back inside. At least he hoped so.

The gnome spoke up. "The tram. It's been determined to be 'unsafe' and ordered closed until repairs can be made to it. But there's nothing unsafe about it! It's just fine! I work on that tram every day; I'd know if there was anything amiss!"

"Unsafe trams and unwell gryphons," Anduin said, narrowing his eyes. "Ways to get out of the city . . ."

Rohan scowled. "Aye, we figured that out, too. But there are other ways to—"

"What do you think you're doing, you brute?" came a shrill female gnome voice.

"Yes indeed!" echoed another gnome's voice. "We're fine, reputable citizens!"

A male gnome. Both voices sounded familiar to Anduin. He exchanged worried glances with his friends, and as one they picked up their pace to reach the Commons.

Four Dark Iron dwarves had firm grips on the arms of two gnomes, both of whom were wriggling in protest and voicing their distress loudly.

"Bink and Dink," Anduin said, remembering the brother-sister mage pair.

"Let them go!" A handful of Ironforge guards were running up, axes and shields drawn.

"Orders from Her Majesty," one of the Dark Irons snarled. "They'll nae be harmed." His voice was deep and sinister and made Anduin instantly think, *Liar!* "We're just takin' them away fer questioning about a few suspicious things, that's all."

No, they weren't, and Anduin knew it. They were taking them in because they were magi . . . and magi were able to create portals out of Ironforge. And Moira didn't want *anyone* getting out of Ironforge.

"She's not *our* Majesty, not yet," said the guard, his voice dangerous and soft. "Let. Them. Go."

For answer, the Dark Iron who had spoken shoved Dink at another of his fellows, drew his sword, and attacked.

It happened so quickly. Dark Irons and Bronzebeards seemed to come from all directions, the simmering resentment and fear and anger boiling up all at once. The air was filled not with the ringing of hammer on anvil, but with angry shouts and the clash of steel. Anduin surged forward, but a powerful hand on his arm pulled him back.

"Nay, lad! This is dwarf business!" cried Rohan. He stepped forward and lifted his arms, uttering a prayer and emanating calm. "Hold yer weapons! Ironforge should never see dwarf against dwarf again!"

"Stand down, guards of Ironforge! Stand down!"

The voice was thickly accented, used to being obeyed,

and thankfully belonged to Angus Stonehammer, the captain of the Ironforge guards. He was at the head of several of them, all with hard, angry eyes, all hastening toward the conflict.

The guards were well trained, and it only took a few seconds before they obeyed, leaping back and standing in a defensive position but nonetheless not attacking. The Dark Irons pressed the attack for a bit, but finally they, too, paused. In the confusion, the gnomes had been forgotten, and now they scurried up to Anduin and Belgrum, clinging to them in fright. Rohan quickly stepped in to heal the wounded while Stonehammer continued speaking. Anduin saw that there were indeed many, some of them quite seriously injured, Dark Iron and Bronzebeard alike. Despite the heat of the place, a chill swept through him, and he couldn't help but wonder if he was looking at the first bitter stirrings of a second dwarven civil war.

"Guardsmen!" the captain was bellowing. "Moira is th' heir tae th' throne until and unless a better claim can be made, ye will respect her an' those she chooses to protect her as such! Do ye understand?"

There was a mumbled chorus of "ayes," some of them sounding very reluctant.

"And ye!" Stonehammer stabbed a stubby finger at the Dark Irons. "Ye canna take proper citizens and just haul them off. There's law tae be observed. I dinna think ye've even charged these wee ones. We guard the people of Ironforge an' enforce its laws. No matter who is on th' throne!"

The Dark Irons shifted uneasily. Anduin smiled bitterly, but with some hope. It was one thing to force a tram to close, or to kill or threaten animals in order to keep Ironforge isolated. It was another to lock up its citizens without cause and due process of law. Moira might be able to achieve some of her plans—and Anduin suspected that the mail and all other methods of communication with the outside world would be suspended—but she hadn't bargained on the sheer guts and will of the dwarves of Ironforge.

Growling, the Dark Irons glared at the gnomes, and nodded. "If it's the law ye want, then ye will have it," one of them growled. "We'll obey it. Because, ye see, Her Majesty is the *legal* heir. And ye'll find out just what that means soon enough."

He spat at the other dwarf's feet, then he and his companions turned and marched away. Anduin watched them go. He should have felt relieved, but he did not. This conflict was far, far from over, and he feared that before it had all been settled, dwarven blood would flow in Ironforge as the hot metal flowed in the forge—freely, and in large quantities.

NINETEEN

Thrall leaned forward and scratched the long, fawn-colored neck of the talbuk he rode. The animal bobbed its head in pleasure, but remained alert, ready to bear Thrall wherever he wished. He had come desiring to learn new things, and already he was doing so, sitting astride an animal he had only seen in glimpses before now. The Mag'har still rode wolves, as most orcs did, but the talbuk were dear to them, special creatures that only a chosen few were allowed to ride.

Aggra's talbuk was a beautiful blue hue, and seemed feistier. Thrall's was, as she had told him earlier, "A mount suitable for novices like you, Go'el." Another slight from one who seemed to take great pleasure in insulting him just enough but not too much. He looked upon Aggra as one more test he must endure for the good of his people.

He liked his talbuk, Shuk'sar, well enough, and had no complaint to offer. The ride was bumpier than the smooth stride of the wolf, but he was growing used to it.

"Nagrand was lucky. It has not suffered as other parts

of what was once Draenor have," Aggra said as they paused for water by a small, clear pool. "Other places are broken and harmed. We do what we can to learn here, and help others to help the elements elsewhere. It will never be the same as before, but it will heal as much as it can."

"I wonder if my world will be able to say the same," Thrall said. "You mentioned a place called the Throne of the Elements?"

Aggra nodded. "When we ask for aid from the elements to enact our will, we touch the spirits of those elements. Spirits of Earth, Air, Fire, and Water."

It was Thrall's turn to nod, and he did so, a little impatiently. "I know this. It was one of the first things Drek'Thar taught me."

"Oh? Good. Just making certain. I do not know how rudimentary your knowledge is, after all." She smiled with false sweetness and he gritted his teeth.

"Geyah said something about the elements having names here," he continued. "On Azeroth, having a name often denotes that these are particularly strong elementals. What is the role of these beings?"

"That's actually a good question," she said, though she offered the praise grudgingly. "These named beings are called Furies. They are extremely powerful elementals, but they are no more all that it is to be earth, or water, than a handful of soil or a drop of water is all that it is to be earth or water. It is a complex idea to hold in one's head."

Thrall sighed. "Whatever you think of me, Aggra, you cannot possibly think that I lack intelligence. Your continual insults are eventually going to harm your ability to instruct and mine to learn, and neither of us wants that."

Her eyes narrowed and her nostrils flared, and he knew he'd hit the mark. Her strong jaw clenched.

"No. You are not stupid, Go'el. I question your choices, your decisions, but I know there is a brain in your skull."

"Then, please, teach me as if I actually have the capacity to learn. It will go much faster and I will be able to return home that much sooner. And surely that is something we both want."

"True," she said bluntly. "If you grasp what I am telling you—"

"Which I do," Thrall said, barely able to be civil.

"—then let us spend the day traveling away from Nagrand. I will show you some of the other parts of Outland. I will show you polluted water elementals and poisoned earth elementals. You can try to talk to them—or engage in battle with them, for they will not come to your call—and see how they feel to you."

"I have worked with corrupted and twisted elementals before," Thrall replied, nodding.

"Good. Perhaps you will find something familiar in their illness that can help you heal Azeroth."

He blinked. When it wasn't dripping sarcasm or contempt, her voice was husky and melodic. And her face, when not scowling, had a calm beauty that reminded him of Geyah. It was too bad she was so determined to dislike him. He would have liked to have her return with him to Azeroth, use her skill to help the Horde and

Azeroth both. But even as these thoughts occurred to him, she seemed to remember how much she disliked Thrall, and frowned.

Clucking her tongue, she turned her talbuk's head with unnecessary vigor and headed south.

"Come, Go'el," she said. "We ride to the end of the world."

"Things are changing," said Archdruid Hamuul Runetotem. He sat quietly with Cairne outside of Thunder Bluff, in the area known as Red Rocks. This place of jutting, rust-colored stones was considered a sacred site to the ancestors of the tauren. Cairne came here when he needed to think calmly.

He had therefore been coming here often since Thrall left.

"I agree," Cairne said. "When Garrosh proposed rebuilding Orgrimmar as soon as Thrall left rather than launching some kind of invasion somewhere, I was pleased. I commended him. Told him that showed he was a leader who cared about the well-being of his people, not an orc who was a personal glory-seeker." Cairne snorted. "I wonder, now. Considering what he did with the money."

Orgrimmar had indeed been rebuilt, but it was barely recognizable. All of the damaged buildings had been replaced, but not with the wooden, thatched, or hide-covered roofs that had been in place before. Citing a need to keep Orgrimmar "safe from future fires," Garrosh had commissioned metal instead of combustible materials. One could argue that his choice was a reasonable one.

One could also, as Cairne had upon beholding the new buildings in Orgrimmar, feel a shiver of unease at how very, very much the new architecture resembled the old. He had never traveled to Draenor himself, but he had seen images of Hellfire Citadel and some of the other buildings created by the orcs when they were in the grip of the demonic bloodlust. Black iron, wrought into jutting, pointed, brutal-looking buildings that were practical but unwelcoming. Now, here in the Horde capital city, one could imagine tools of torture lurking within, rather than the simple groceries and items the buildings actually housed.

He had left Thunder Bluff for Orgrimmar upon Thrall's departure to be physically accessible to the new young leader Thrall had appointed against Cairne's advice. As ruler over their people in his absence, Cairne had appointed his son, Baine, a fine warrior with a cool head like his father's. Baine had had no difficulties in his father's absence.

As the time stretched on, Cairne had found his advice was not particularly welcome, and indeed was often ignored. As he watched the hostile-looking architecture go up, Cairne had realized that this was no longer a place for him to be. He had asked to see Garrosh, explained that he was returning to Thunder Bluff, and had been surprised at Garrosh's reaction.

He had expected relief or indifference. Instead, Garrosh had risen and gone to him.

"We fought together well once, in Northrend," Garrosh said.

"That we did," Cairne agreed.

"And yet I know you did not agree with many of my decisions."

Cairne peered at him for a moment. "Both things are true, Garrosh. But I think that my disagreement with your decisions interferes with my ability to aid you."

"I . . . Thrall entrusted me with the care of the Horde. He is a symbol of it, as are you. I have no wish to offend you, but I have to make my own decisions. And I will do so. I will do what I think best for the honor and glory of the Horde . . . and its overall well-being."

Cairne liked the words. And he was willing to believe that Garrosh actually meant them. But he knew Garrosh perhaps better than the orc knew himself. Cairne had known of Grom, had known countless other hotheaded youths and watched so many of them come to violent and often senseless ends. He had no wish for Garrosh to join their number, and worse, drag down the Horde along with him.

But it was pointless for him to stay. Garrosh would do exactly as he wanted. If he wished Cairne's advice, he would find a way to justify requesting it so he could do so without losing his pride. And Cairne would let him keep it.

He bowed, courteously, and Garrosh bowed lower, and then Cairne returned home to Thunder Bluff.

The Kor'kron, the elite guards that were always near the warchief though usually unobtrusive, had shown him out. Cairne had always thought them fiercely loyal to Thrall; indeed, Thrall had revived the order. But it would seem that while their loyalty was certainly fierce, that loyalty was not to any one individual, but to whoever led the Horde. Cairne had listened carefully for any quiet protests or grumblings from them about the new direction the Horde was taking, at least in Orgrimmar, and heard nothing. Indeed, if there were any whisperings or mutterings, they would likely echo approval of the "glory days attitude" that Garrosh had brought to his style of leadership.

"I have not seen Orgrimmar since the rebuilding, nor do I have any desire to," Hamuul Runetotem rumbled, jolting Cairne back to the present moment. "But, old friend, I do not think you asked me here to comment upon architecture."

Cairne chuckled. "Would that were the reason, but you are correct. I wished to inquire as to how the negotiations with your kaldorei contacts in the Cenarion Circle are proceeding."

At the feast to honor the returning veterans, Cairne had spoken up with a suggestion to reestablish relations with the night elves through the Circle, an area of mutual connection. Garrosh had exploded, and Thrall had had to try to calm him down. The end result was that, officially, nothing had happened.

But, unofficially, Thrall had given Hamuul permission to do whatever he thought would benefit the Horde. And Hamuul had spent the last several months clandestinely sending letters, couriers, and even representatives.

"Surprisingly well, considering everything," Hamuul replied. "It took a while to even get an initial response from the kaldorei. They were deeply angry."

"So were we."

"I explained that to them, and fortunately there are those among them who still call me friend and believed my words. It has been slow, Cairne. Slower than I would have liked, slower than I think was necessary, but things ripen in their own time. I did not wish to force a meeting, but it seems that the kaldorei now would be amenable to one such."

"This news makes an old bull happy," Cairne exclaimed, his heart swelling. "I am pleased to hear that there are some who hear the whispers of reason over the shouts of aggression."

"It is easier to hear such things in the Moonglade," Hamuul said, and Cairne nodded.

"When and where would such a meeting take place?" Cairne inquired.

"Ashenvale. A few more days of letters, and then I think it will happen."

"Ashenvale? Why not the Moonglade itself?"

"Remulos does not get involved in these sorts of affairs," Hamuul replied. Remulos was one of the sons of the demigod Cenarius, who had taught druidism to Malfurion Stormrage. A powerful, beautiful being, Remulos's form was that of a night elf and a stag; his hair and beard made of moss; his hands not flesh, but leafy, wooden talons. In this tranquil place he oversaw, peace reigned.

"He cannot prevent casual discussions, but we would not bring such potentially explosive issues to the Moonglade without his blessing. If this goes well, however, Remulos has indicated that he would permit a second meeting in the Moonglade."

"That would be good," Cairne said. "Ashenvale is still too volatile a place for my liking. You will be attending, I take it?"

"I will. I will be leading the meeting, along with an archdruid who is essentially my counterpart among the kaldorei."

"Take some of my best warriors with you," Cairne urged.

"No." Hamuul shook his head firmly. "I will not give anyone an excuse to take up arms, saying that I myself come to do so. The only weapons will be the claws, teeth, and talons we all possess in our bestial forms. My counterpart has agreed to do the same. Swords do not befit those who come with peace in their hearts."

"Hrrm," rumbled Cairne, stroking his beard. "What you say is true, though I could wish it otherwise. Still, I would not want to see anyone attack you in your bear shape, old friend. They would not end up the victor."

Hamuul chuckled. "Let us hope we do not find out. I will be careful, Cairne. More than my own life is riding on the outcome of this gathering. We are all aware of the risk we take, and we deem it worth it."

Cairne nodded and spread his arms, indicating the sacred grounds before them. "I hope I do not have to come here to commune with you afterward."

Hamuul threw back his head and laughed.

TWENTY

Five bears, their fur of varied shades but all shaggy and huge, walked the verdant forests of Ashenvale. They paused to snuffle or paw at something that interested them here and there, and did not appear to be together. Bears seldom were. Still, if one had watched them long enough, and followed their apparently aimless wandering, one would have noticed that they all seemed to be heading in the same direction.

One also might have noticed that they had horns.

They reached a certain spot in the mountains slightly west of the Talondeep Path. One, a larger, more grizzled-looking beast than the others, scouted about for a few minutes, sniffing cautiously, then rose up on its hind legs and lifted its forepaws to the sky.

Claws, black and shiny, turned to long, strong fingers. Brown and white fur rippled and shortened. The bear muzzle elongated, horns now jutting from a larger head with calm, deep-set eyes. Skeleton and organs shifted within the short-furred skin. Hind legs turned to long, strong limbs with hooves and not paws, and the short tail elongated and grew whiplike, with a tuft at the end.

"I can smell them; they are coming," Hamuul Runetotem assured his fellows. "And they are alone."

Beside him the other druids emulated him, their bodies twisting, but not disharmoniously, from bear to tauren. They stood, ready, only their tails and ears moving now and then.

A few moments later five nightsabers, their coats varying shades of dark hues, crested the hill, running swiftly and elegantly. Almost at once they, too, shifted their shapes. Long, lithe, feline bodies became long, lithe, night elf bodies. Ears grew longer, hands and feet replaced paws, and their tails disappeared altogether. They stood regarding the tauren solemnly. Hamuul bowed low.

"Archdruid Renferal," he said. "I am so pleased you have come, my old friend."

"It was not without a great deal of soul-searching," Elerethe Renferal said. Hamuul noted that she did not call him "friend" in return. She was tall and graceful, with short green hair and purple skin. It was clear, though, that she had seen battle; lavender scars marred the darker violet, and her body was sinewy and muscular rather than lush.

"Your soul has guided you and your companions to this meeting, as my soul has guided me and mine," Hamuul said.

"The blood of the butchered Sentinels still calls for justice, Hamuul," Renferal replied, but even as she spoke, she stepped forward to close the distance between herself and Hamuul.

"And justice it shall have," Hamuul assured her. "But unless there can be conversation, and peace, and healing, justice cannot come." He took the initiative, sitting on the soft green grass. The other tauren druids emulated him. The kaldorei exchanged glances, but when Renferal sat, they did as well. It was a circle, of sorts, albeit one that could be divided neatly in half by race.

The coldness and precise division of races pained Hamuul. This was not a gathering of strangers, but of erstwhile friends. The ten of them had worked together for years as part of the Circle. There had been a bond that had transcended race and political divisions, a bond of what it meant to take on the form and touch the spirit of the beasts of this world, to unite with nature in a way no others understood. But that bond had been sorely tested. Hamuul sent a silent prayer to the Earth Mother that the work they did here today would make strides toward reforging that bond, perhaps even make it stronger.

"I am sure word has reached you that Thrall has departed—temporarily. And I am equally sure you know his mission."

Renferal frowned. "Yes, we have heard. And we know who he has appointed in his stead."

"Rest assured that Thrall does not intend to be gone long and that he has asked Cairne to counsel young Hellscream," Hamuul said. "You know that Thrall's wish is for peace."

"Is it? Truly?" Another night elf spoke up, anger in his voice. "Then why does he leave at all? And appoint Garrosh to rule in his absence? *Garrosh,* who has openly spoken against the treaty? Who we believe was behind the attack in the first place?"

Hamuul sighed. There had been no conclusive evidence one way or the other that Garrosh had instigated the brutal attacks on the Sentinels. But it was easy to believe those rumors.

"Thrall is in Nagrand to better understand what is wrong with the elements. Come now—we druids are closer to the natural world than most, though we are not shaman. I cannot believe that anyone present does not think this world is in pain."

That seemed to mollify the night elf contingent. "If Thrall can return quickly with anything that can help calm the elements—and if Garrosh can refrain from any more needless slaughter," said Renferal, "then perhaps good can come of this."

"I will remind you that we do not know for certain that it was Garrosh's doing, and thanks to this gathering, good has already come," Hamuul said. "May peace begin here, now."

Various expressions flitted across the faces of those assembled: hope, worry, mistrust, fear, determination. Hamuul looked about and nodded. It was going as well as he had expected, though not as well as he could have wished.

With careful deliberation, he reached into one of his bags and brought out a long, thin object wrapped in decorated leather. He lifted it high for a moment, then stood, placed it in the center of the circle, and unwrapped it.

"This is a ceremonial pipe," he said. "It is shared

among the participants at the beginning of peace talks. For ages has this been the custom of my people. I brought this to my first meeting of the Cenarion Circle. Some here remember that meeting. I bring it again now, to formally show my desire for healing and unity."

Renferal watched closely, nodding her green head quietly. Then she reached in her own bags and brought forth a cup and a waterskin.

"It seems you and I are of the same mind," she said quietly, lifting the cup. It was a simple, ceramic goblet. It had been glazed blue, and runes were etched on it, but otherwise it was unadorned. Hamuul smiled softly. Long ago, she had brought this, as he had the pipe. "This cup is ancient. We do not know its original owner, but it has survived since the Sundering, passed down from hand to hand with love and care. The water is from the Temple of Elune. It is pure and delicious." She poured some water into the goblet reverently, then she, too, rose and set it in the center.

Hamuul nodded, pleased. The night elves were taking this meeting as seriously as the tauren were. He could feel the tension start to die, feel respect and hope start to replace resistance and antagonism.

He rose, bowed to Renferal, and bent to pick up the pipe. As he filled it with herbs, he began to speak.

"Once lit, the pipe will be passed around from person to person," he explained for the benefit of those younger night elf druids who had never seen the tauren ceremony before. "Please, when it reaches you, hold it for a moment. Think of what you wish to achieve here. Then bring it to—"

He froze.

The breeze had shifted, carrying to his sensitive tauren nose a scent. Strong, familiar, not unpleasant at any other time, but he knew that now, at this delicate juncture, it could spell the death of everything.

Orcs.

"No! Hold!" cried Hamuul in the orc's native tongue, but it was too late. Even before the words had left his mouth, the deadly arrows sang out on their lethal flight. Two night elves dropped, throats neatly pierced.

Cries of rage and alarm from tauren and night elf erupted. Renferal whirled for just an instant to affix Hamuul with a stare of fury and loathing that pierced his heart as surely as any spear.

"We came in good faith!" was all she said before she transformed into a cat and launched herself on the nearest orc, a huge, bald, snaggle-toothed warrior with a giant two-handed sword. He fell beneath her, his sword knocked from his hand and lying useless in the grass as her claws laid open his abdomen.

"Get the purple skins!" cackled their leader. Where had they come from? Why? Was this Garrosh's doing? It didn't matter. By accident or design, the peace conference had been destroyed beyond imagining. All that was left to Hamuul was to protect the three—no, he amended as another orc impaled Renferal with a polearm, pinning her to the earth—*two* night elf druids who still survived.

Surrendering to his anger and pain, he shifted quickly into bear form, and lunged for the nearest orc in this barbaric war party. His fellow tauren did likewise, each of them changing into various bestial forms. The orc female, brandishing two shortswords, never stood a chance against Hamuul's bulk. Her cry was cut short as his weight crushed her rib cage. He wanted to clamp his massive jaws down on her throat, crunch her windpipe, taste the coppery flavor of her blood, but he restrained himself. He was better than they.

All around him the druids were shifting into various forms to defend themselves—storm crow, diving and slicing at the orcish faces with razor-sharp talons; cat, with teeth and claws to rend and tear; and bear, the strongest of the bestial forms. Blood spattered everywhere, and the scent of it drove Hamuul almost mad. He hung onto his sanity by the barest of threads, remembering why he had come here, how close they had been to the dream of peace a few short, violent, minutes ago.

"Hold, hold, these are tauren!" came a cry, piercing the red haze of battle. Summoning every bit of restraint he possessed, Hamuul leaped off the orc he was fighting and reverted to his true shape.

Belatedly he realized he had been injured; in bear form, he had not felt the wound. He pressed a hand to the gash in his side and murmured a healing spell, his eyes widening in horror as he assessed what had happened.

It seemed almost impossible to him, but all five night elves were slain and lay where they had fallen. Almost all the tauren had been wounded, and he grieved to see that one of them lay on the grass, an arrow in her eye, flies already buzzing around her limp form.

He whirled on the orc who seemed to be the leader. "In the name of Cenarius, *what have you done*?"

The orc was pale green and seemed completely unperturbed by Hamuul's outburst. He merely shrugged. "We saw five of those filthy night elves running in those cat shapes and thought they might be attacking."

"Attacking? *Five?*"

The orc continued to regard him steadily and remained silent. How had they even known for certain they were druids and not just nightsabers? Hamuul wondered.

Slightly unnerved by the orc's sullen, silent stupidity, Hamuul's voice rose even more with outrage. "Who sent you? Was it Garrosh?"

The orc shrugged again. "Who is Garrosh?"

Impossible. Hamuul could not believe anyone could be so ignorant. Love him or loathe him, everyone knew Garrosh. The orc had to be toying with him for some reason.

"You have interrupted a secret and vital meeting that could have ensured the Horde the rights to harvest wood in Ashenvale without risking lives! I will personally report you to Cairne Bloodhoof and see that this incident is made public. I will not be responsible for another black mark on the Horde's honor. These elves, these *druids,*" and he pointed a shaking finger at the cooling corpses, "came here at my request. They trusted I would keep them safe. And now our best hope for peace lies as dead as they do because *you* thought they were attacking. What is your name?"

"Gorkrak."

"Gorkrak," Hamuul said, relishing the name and emblazing it upon his memory. "Any chance you stood of advancing in the Horde, Gorkrak, ends right here."

Gorkrak's expression shifted slightly. His piggy eyes moved coldly, deliberately, from the night elf druids, to Hamuul, to something behind the tauren. A crafty smile spread across his face, and too late Hamuul realized what was about to happen.

"Not if I end you first," Gorkrak crowed.

And Hamuul heard the twang of an arrow taking flight.

Gorkrak of the Twilight's Hammer looked about with satisfaction.

"I thought druids were supposed to be smart," one of his brethren said, tugging his sword out of the body of a white tauren female.

"All are foolish who do not embrace the coming destruction," Gorkrak said. He dropped the stupid expression he had worn to trick Hamuul. "It is inevitable and beautiful. We will bury the corpses, but not so well that the carrion eaters will not find them. We want the bodies discovered." He smiled darkly. "Eventually."

He was glad that Hamuul had mentioned Garrosh. It meant that already suspicion had begun to spread about the acting warchief. Some were already whispering that it had been Garrosh who butchered the Sentinels. Now they would believe him behind this slaughter as well.

"For the nothingness that awaits," Gorkrak said. "Dig."

Hamuul Runetotem regained consciousness slowly. He blinked awake, then wondered if he really was awake.

Where was he? What had happened? He could see nothing, and something pressed in on him from every angle. Breathing was difficult; what little air there was smelled of old blood and earth. He tried to move and realized that he was pinned. His body was in agony, and thirst clawed at his throat. He was in his bear form; he imagined he had had a split second to change shapes before he had been shot—

—in the back—

—by fellow Horde members.

Memory crashed down on him like an avalanche, and he suddenly realized where he must be, and what was pressing on him.

He was in a mass grave.

Adrenaline shot through him, giving his tormented body fresh strength. Which way was up? Corpses draped lifeless arms across his shoulders, pressed cold torsos against his back, as if trying to force him to join them in death. Hamuul opened his sharp-toothed mouth, gasping in fetid air and dirt, and pressed his paws against the bodies of his friends. He clawed his way upward, causing the corpses to bleed sluggishly, to where the freshest air was coming, using all his strength to shoulder aside bodies and dirt, until his head broke the lightly packed surface and he gulped in fresh air. Grunting, now feeling anew the pain of his wounds, he climbed free and collapsed, white and light brown fur clotted with blood and other gory fluids, gasping and shivering in horror at the atrocity.

He tried to shift back to tauren, but the first attempt made him pass out a second time. When he came to what seemed like a few minutes later, he was able to make the change and heal his wounds, at least somewhat. It would take time for him to recover completely.

Grimacing, he got to his hooves and moved, wincing, to examine the grave, wondering if anyone else had managed to survive. It was night by this point, but he did not need the sun's radiance to behold the tragedy.

Dead. All dead. Night elf and tauren alike. He had been the only one to survive. His great heart broke. His knees gave way, and for a moment he collapsed beside the hole in the earth that held his friends, weeping for the slain, weeping for the future wounds this would cause to any hope for peace.

He lifted his face, his muzzle streaked with tears, and beheld the sacred ritual items he and Renferal had brought with such high hopes. They had been broken, the beautiful pipe, the simple, ancient goblet. Trampled beneath careless feet and falling bodies. Shattered beyond repair, as his dream for peace had been.

Closing his eyes, Hamuul clambered unsteadily to his hooves again, raising his hands to the sky and asking for aid. It came in the form of an owl, hooting quietly as it perched on a branch nearby. Hamuul fumbled for a piece of parchment in his bags. In his own blood, for the ink bottle he had carried had been crushed in the conflict, he wrote a brief message. He bound it around the owl's leg. It fidgeted, bobbing its head and fixing Hamuul with a glare from lambent eyes, but accepted the strange sensation.

Hamuul whispered Cairne's name, and held an image of the old high chieftain in his mind's eye. When he was satisfied that the owl would obey his request, he released it with a blessing. It headed southwest.

In the direction of Thunder Bluff.

He closed his eyes in relief and gratitude, and slumped quietly to the earth, letting its embrace take him, for the moment, or forever, he did not know.

TWENTY-ONE

The pain was so much more than Garrosh had anticipated, and he embraced it joyfully.

He was pleased with how his decisions to rebuild Orgrimmar had been received. While some seemed unhappy, like Cairne and Eitrigg, most seemed to revive at the idea of returning to old orcish ways. Garrosh was glad of it. Often he walked out to gaze at the skull of the enemy his father had slain, and one day he had rubbed his chin thoughtfully and decided to take yet another step to honor his late father.

The decision had been easy, but the reality was painfully red-hot. He lay faceup on the floor of his quarters, forcing his body to stay relaxed and calm and not tense. Hovering above him was an elderly orc whose powerful muscles and steady hands belied his wrinkles and snowy ponytail. In one hand he held a sharp, narrow blade, the tip of which he repeatedly dipped in black ink. In the other he held a small hammer. The only sounds in the room were the crackling of the brazier which provided illumination and the tap-tap-tap of the hammer as the orc tattooist used it to slice into Garrosh's face.

Most designs were simple. A family design, a word, the Horde insignia. Garrosh, however, wanted his entire jaw tattooed solid black—just to begin with. His desire was to eventually have his chest and back decorated with elaborate tattoos so that both friend and foe alike would see and know that he had willingly inflicted pain upon himself. At the rate of a single piercing of the flesh with each tap, this would take hours—hours when every puncture was like being jabbed with a white-hot needle.

At one point Garrosh swallowed. He also realized he was sweating—from the pain or the heat in the confined, firelit room, he did not know. The tattooist paused and glowered down at him. "Do not move," he said. "And do not sweat so. Your father did not sweat."

Garrosh wondered how it was that Grom was able to control sweating. He would strive to do so as well. He said nothing, as speaking would force him to move his mouth, but merely blinked to show he understood.

The tattooist, an apprentice to the orc who had ritually tattooed Grom Hellscream, stepped aside to let his own apprentice dab at the sweat on Garrosh's brown forehead and wipe away the excess blood and ink from his chin. Garrosh breathed deeply during the reprieve. It had already been four hours, and only three fingers' breadth of ink had been applied. The tattooist bent over him again. Garrosh willed himself still once more, and the torment—the sweet, honor-bought torment—resumed.

* * *

"Garrosh!"

Cairne's bellow was loud and deep and echoed as he strode into Grommash Hold. The guards moved to him, allegedly to assist, not quite to intercept. He glared down at them balefully and snorted in derision, and they stepped aside.

"Garrosh!"

There was always somebody awake in Grommash Hold, tending the fires that never went out, making preparations for the following day, so it was not quite deserted, if still. Cairne's shouting roused those who had been sleeping, and the rooms slowly filled with curious, still slightly drowsy onlookers rubbing their eyes and dressed in clothes that were obviously hastily donned.

"Garrosh, I demand to see you!"

"Nobody *demands* to see the leader of the Horde!" one of the Kor'kron spoke up, snarling.

Cairne whirled on him with a speed that belied his age. "I am High Chieftain Cairne Bloodhoof. I helped create this Horde that Garrosh is currently undermining. I will speak with him, and I will speak with him *now*!"

"Old bull, you will wake the dead with your angry snorting and pawing!"

Garrosh's voice was as sharp as Cairne's and dripping sarcasm. Cairne turned, the Kor'kron forgotten, and fixed his gaze upon Garrosh Hellscream. The tauren's eyes widened slightly.

"So," he said quietly, regarding Garrosh's tattoos, "you have adopted more than your father's weapon."

"His weapon," said Garrosh, "and the markings on his face and body that struck fear into his enemies." He moved his mouth slowly, as if it still caused pain. The tattoos looked recent.

"Your father did much ill, but he died doing a great good," Cairne said. "And he would be ashamed of you right now."

"What?" growled Garrosh. "What are you talking about, tauren?"

"I warned Thrall about you," Cairne said, his voice as quiet as it had been loud before, ignoring the question for the moment. "I told him he was being foolish to give you so much power. I thought that one day you might be ready for it, but you needed experience and tempering. I was wrong. You, Garrosh Hellscream, are not fit to lead a pack of hyenas, let alone this glorious Horde! You will ride us to ruin, screaming and beating your chest like one of the gorillas of Stranglethorn the entire way."

Garrosh paled, then flushed with anger. "You will regret those words, old bull," he hissed. "I will make you eat them, along with handfuls of dirt."

"It was you who attacked the Sentinels in Ashenvale, wasn't it?" Cairne cried, moving forward to where the orc stood clenching his brown fists. "And it was you who authorized the mass slaughter of nearly a dozen druids of the Cenarion Circle, gathering together to achieve a peaceful solution to the needs of the Horde."

Disbelief and then fury crossed Garrosh's face. "What in the names of the ancestors are you talking about? How *dare* you accuse me of such despicable acts?"

Cairne snorted. "Garrosh, you have been open in

your contempt of a treaty agreed to with honor and in good faith, and of Thrall's so-called appeasement of the Alliance."

"Yes! I do despise this appeasement. But I would not sneak around the treaty! I would be proud of any attack on the Alliance I authorized! I would shout it from the rooftops to prove to the Horde that all is not lost! The honor of the Horde—"

"How can you even utter that word?" growled Cairne. "Honor? Even now, you lie, Garrosh. You have not the honor of a centaur. At least admit what you have done. Own your foolish, selfish choices!"

Garrosh suddenly grew cold. "You are an idiot to think me a schemer. Age has addled your wits. Because of the esteem in which Thrall inexplicably holds you, I shall ignore your prattlings as that of a madman. Thrall put me in charge of the Horde, and I will always do what I believe is best for it. Go now, and spare yourself the indignity of being bodily tossed out on your tail."

For answer, Cairne backhanded Garrosh right across the face, striking the fresh tattoo. So powerful was the blow that Garrosh staggered and nearly fell, crying out sharply in pain and flailing his arms in an attempt to keep his balance.

"It is I who shall toss *you* out on your tail, impudent pup," Cairne said. "That blow has been long in coming."

Blood was flowing freely down Garrosh's split and swelling lower lip. He reached automatically to touch his cheek, then hissed and pulled his hand away. The orc seemed almost confused for a moment, and then anger descended visibly upon him.

"You challenge me then, old bull?"

"Did I not make myself clear? Perhaps I ought to try again. I challenge you to a duel of honor, Garrosh. I challenge you to a mak'gora."

Garrosh sneered. "The mak'gora has been weakened. Watered down. Since Thrall's decree, it has become nothing more than a show. You want to fight me? Then fight me truly. I am in charge of the Horde now, and I say I will accept your challenge of the mak'gora—the *old* mak'gora. The way it once was, with all the old rules. *All* of them."

Cairne's eyes narrowed. "To the death, then?"

Garrosh grinned. "To the death. Perhaps now you will apologize."

Cairne stared for a moment longer, then threw back his head and laughed. That caught Garrosh by surprise.

"If you ask me to fight under the old rules, son of Hellscream, then know that you have done nothing but unfetter my hands. I sought only to teach you a lesson. I will regret depriving the Horde of such a fine warrior, but you cannot be allowed to destroy everything Thrall has worked for. To undermine the sacrifices the honored dead have made. All in the name of your own personal glory. I will not have it, do you hear me? I repeat my challenge. The mak'gora—the traditional way. To the death!"

"I accept," Garrosh snarled, but there was the briefest moment of hesitation. "With pleasure. I used to feel sorry for you, but not anymore. It is time that the Horde was rid of old parasites like you, hanging on by the grace of those who actually went and fought and died in battle."

"It is time the Horde was rid of a young, arrogant fool like you, Garrosh," Cairne replied, unperturbed. "I regret the necessity of doing so. But I must. In truth, I am glad you have pushed for the traditional way. You have killed innocents, and you are planning nothing less than killing any hope for peace. I cannot permit this to continue."

Garrosh was laughing now, dabbing gingerly at his chin, then bringing his bloodied fingers up to his mouth and licking at them gently. The movement had to have been exquisitely painful, but he had recovered and gave no sign of the torment he had to be enduring.

"You know what you need, of course."

Garrosh hesitated.

"What weapon? What garb to wear? How many witnesses?" asked Cairne.

When Garrosh, his cheeks darkening in embarrassment, shook his head, Cairne snorted. "You call for a traditional fight, yet I, a tauren, understand your orcish traditions better than *you*!"

"You are caught up in details," growled Garrosh. "Whatever you wish I will do. Only let us begin this fight!"

Cairne regarded the orc with contempt, then shook his head and composed himself. "We each may select one weapon. A shaman of our own choosing is permitted to bless it. No armor—no clothing, indeed, save a loincloth. And we must each have at least one witness." He smiled bitterly. "I daresay we will have more than that."

Garrosh nodded curtly, recovering. "I will follow all these rules."

"In the arena. One hour." Cairne turned to go. At the doorway he paused. "Make what arrangements you may, Garrosh Hellscream. Do not fear that I will desecrate your body. In death, I will give you the honor you should have earned yourself in life." He inclined his head.

Garrosh's laughter followed him as he marched out.

One hour later the arena was packed. Torches and braziers were lit, providing light and stifling warmth. Word had spread just as the fires had before Thrall's departure, and it was clear that sides had been chosen. Some came to sit in support of Cairne; others—many others—came to cheer on Garrosh.

Cairne looked up, straining to recognize faces with his aged eyes. Most of those on his side of the stands were tauren, not unexpectedly. There were a few of other races, too, but one thing tended to stand out about them—they were older. He could not see far enough to distinguish individuals on Garrosh's side, but he could see clearly in the orange light that, mixed among the green, purple, gray, and pink skins of orc, troll, Forsaken, and blood elf, were the black and brown and white coats of tauren.

Cairne sighed. He believed he could win this fight, or else he would not have issued the mak'gora. Life was not so pale and devoid of delight for him that he was ready to relinquish his grasp upon it. Far from it. He had made the challenge—and accepted Garrosh's decision to return to the "old way"—because he needed to end Garrosh's arrogant, shortsighted, dangerous rule over the Horde Cairne loved so much. He planned to take Garrosh's place until Thrall returned to mete out whatever justice he saw fit. Cairne was ready to accept it.

He was under no illusion, however, that this would be an easily won battle. Garrosh was one of the best warriors the Horde had. But one-on-one combat was a different thing from battle, and Garrosh was impetuous. Cairne would fight in his own manner, and that manner would give him victory.

Over in his area of the huge arena, Garrosh was preparing. Per the ritual rules of the mak'gora, he was naked save for a loincloth, and his brown body had been oiled till it shone. He cut a striking figure of orcish power, muscular and proud, warming up for the fight with the mighty axe that had slain Mannoroth. It, too, had been oiled, and glinted darkly.

Cairne would be fighting with the weapon of his lineage—the runespear. He, too, had stripped to a loincloth. If his fur was slightly gray with age, it was still sleek and thick, shiny with the anointing oil. Beneath his pelt was solid muscle. His joints might ache in the rain or snow from time to time, and his eyes might strain to see, but he had lost none of his strength and little of his speed. He now hefted the runespear, offering it to each of the four directions and elements, thumping his chest with the hand that clasped the spear to salute the Spirit of Life within himself and all other beings, and then turned to Beram Skychaser for his blessing.

Just as the bodies of the warriors were anointed with oil for their battle, so, too, were the weapons. Beram murmured something softly, dipped a finger in the vial of holy oil, and then gently smeared the glistening liquid onto the spear tip.

"I am saddened it has come to this," he said quietly, for Cairne's ears alone. "But as it has, I know that your cause is the just one, Cairne Bloodhoof. May your spear strike straight and true."

Cairne bowed deeply, humbly, his thick, powerful fingers curled tightly around the shaft of the spear. Twenty generations of Bloodhoof chieftains had wielded this runespear in battle, as he was about to do. It had tasted the blood of many noble enemies, and indeed had always struck straight and true. For a moment he allowed his gaze to linger on the runes. He had carved most of his own story into it some time ago, as was the tradition. But there was still much left to tell. He promised himself that when this battle was over and things had settled down a bit, he would take the time to finish his story.

"Old bull!" came Garrosh's taunting voice. "Are you going to stand there all night lost in thought? I thought you had come to kill me, not stare at an old spear."

Cairne sighed. "Your words are borne upon the winds of fate, Garrosh Hellscream. They will be among your last. I would choose them with more care."

"Pagh!" Garrosh spat. He picked up Gorehowl, bowing to the shaman who had blessed—

Cairne's eyes narrowed as he strained to see at this distance. It was a tauren shaman who had blessed Garrosh's weapon with words of ritual and sacred oil. That surprised and pained Cairne, who had assumed another orc would perform that rite. It was a female, black-coated. . . .

"Magatha," he breathed. She was a powerful shaman, but so was Beram. While her blessing would help Garrosh, Beram Skychaser's blessing would help Cairne. She had to know that; it was a gesture, nothing more. All she had done was, finally, openly state where her loyalties lay.

Cairne nodded to himself, confident now more than ever of the rightness of his path. This challenge really did need to happen, before more fell under Garrosh's spell. At least Magatha now had shown her true colors. He would have to address the disloyalty; he had no choice now. The Grimtotem would need to be banished from Thunder Bluff, unless they finally chose to swear allegiance to the Horde. It had become a necessity, not a desire.

Magatha looked up. Cairne could not see her expression, but he imagined she was smirking. He allowed himself a quiet smile. She had chosen the wrong combatant to support.

He turned to regard his opponent.

Garrosh balanced on the balls of his feet, shifting his weight lightly, hand wrapped around the hilt of the axe, his golden-brown eyes alight with excitement.

Earth Mother, guide my blows. You know that I fight for more than myself.

Cairne threw back his head, opened his mouth, and uttered the deep, wordless bellow of the challenge to the traditional mak'gora. For his part, Garrosh responded by uttering an earsplitting shriek that was almost as loud as the cry of his father, and, as Cairne had expected, charged at once.

Cairne stood his ground, letting the youth run toward him, axe aloft. Garrosh whirled the mighty Gorehowl over his head. Cairne knew that the grooves in the axe head would cause it to make the shrieking sound that had given it its name. It was a sound that had struck fear into the hearts of Grom Hellscream's enemies, but Cairne was unmoved by it. At the last moment, with a grace that belied his bulk, the tauren moved aside and let Garrosh's own speed propel him harmlessly past. The orc tried to halt his forward movement and almost succeeded, but not before Cairne had brought up the spear and plunged it into Garrosh's right bicep.

Garrosh cried out in surprise, affront, and pain. His grip on the weapon loosened. Cairne lowered his horned head and rammed it into the wound, knocking Garrosh off his feet and causing him to nearly lose his grip on Gorehowl. If he had, all would have been lost for the orc. Once a weapon was dropped, the rules clearly stated that it could not be retrieved by either party.

Cairne raised the runespear and plunged it straight down. Garrosh rolled to the side at the last minute. The spear sliced a furrow down the orc's side and embedded itself into the earth of the arena. Cairne lost a precious second wresting it free, and by then Garrosh was on his feet. Garrosh, the most highly acclaimed warrior of the Horde, had nearly lost his weapon, and Cairne had drawn first blood.

"Well played, old bull," Garrosh said, panting just a little. "I admit, I underestimated your speed. It would seem that it's just your wits that are slow."

"Your jeers were not that clever to begin with, and

less so now, son of Hellscream," Cairne replied, never taking his eyes off his opponent. "Save your breath for battle, and I will save mine to speak well of you at your funeral."

It was almost too easy to enrage Garrosh, Cairne thought. The orc's heavy brow furrowed in offense, and with a growl he charged. He swung Gorehowl skillfully, and Cairne felt the rush of air and heard the weapon's angry song as he barely dodged the blow. Garrosh was not a fool; he learned from his mistakes. He would not underestimate Cairne a second time.

Cairne lowered his head, pawing the earth with his right hoof, and charged. Garrosh shrieked a war cry and lifted his axe to slice the bull in the throat. At the very last instant, however, Cairne halted, veered to the left, and thrust outward with his spear toward Garrosh's exposed torso. Garrosh's eyes widened. He had just enough time to turn slightly so that his right shoulder met the spear's bite instead of his chest. The blow was dangerous, but not the killing blow it would have been otherwise. Even so, with a wound to his right bicep and now to that same shoulder, Garrosh's arm was badly weakened.

Garrosh cried out, in pain and in fury, his free hand clapping over the wound while his other hand clutched Gorehowl. Cairne pulled the spear free and felt the faintest twinge of pity. Garrosh's death would be a loss to the Horde—of a fine warrior, if nothing else. If only Thrall had not appointed the younger orc leader! This tragic necessity could have been so easily avoided.

His brief hesitation enabled Garrosh to, almost

impossibly, heft the two-handed axe with his badly wounded arm. Quickly Cairne grasped the runespear with both hands, holding it up to block the blow. Strong and sturdy, the ancient weapon had witnessed countless battles, and Cairne had used it to block in such a manner before.

Gorehowl shrieked its eerie cry as it descended.

The runespear—the weapon of twenty generations, the pride of the Bloodhoof, which had slain so many and defended the tauren people so well—shattered into pieces.

Its force slowed but not stopped, Gorehowl bit into Cairne's chest, slicing a shallow groove in his fur and flesh, continuing onward to cut his arm. The strike was only a flesh wound; the spear had stayed the worst of the blow.

Cairne recovered from the horror of seeing the ancestral weapon destroyed. He was not yet done. His hand tightened around the lower third of the spear. Its single tooth could still bite. Garrosh was still fighting, but he was badly wounded. The blow that had shattered the runespear had drained him, and he would not last much longer. And one good thrust with the remnants of the spear would—

Cairne blinked. His vision was blurring. Had he gotten dust or sweat or blood in his eyes? He took a precious second to wipe the back of his hand across his eyes, but it aided nothing. His hand shook as he lowered it. And his legs . . . they felt weak. . . .

Stunned, he stared at Garrosh. The orc was sweating profusely and breathing hard. As Cairne watched,

Garrosh gripped the axe and met Cairne's gaze evenly. Cairne clutched his own weapon. It weaved in his hands. It felt so strangely heavy—

And then he knew exactly what had happened to him.

And so, I, who have lived my whole life with honor, die betrayed.

He could not even cry out with his last breath to accuse his murderer. It was through an act of sheer will that he was able to even hold on to the shattered spear so that he would not be struck down unarmed.

Garrosh's eyes narrowed as he beheld the furrow he had carved in Cairne's chest and the pieces of the runespear lying on the earth. For a moment surprise flitted across his features, then he set his jaw in determination. He began running toward his opponent, lifting Gorehowl in both hands and bringing it down. Unable to deflect the blow or move out of its path, his life fading with every heartbeat, Cairne Bloodhoof, high chieftain of the tauren, mutely watched it descend.

TWENTY-TWO

Magatha watched from a distance, her calm visage betraying nothing of her increasing excitement. The two warriors were well-matched, though very different in all aspects. Cairne had strength, wisdom, patience, and experience; Garrosh had energy, the fire of youth, and speed. The simmering cauldron of conflict between the old and the new had reached a boiling point tonight. Only one would walk away, and the victor would dictate the future of the Horde. All present knew that they were bearing witness to history, and Magatha observed as emotions ran the gamut from horror and shock to enthusiasm and delight.

It was a fierce battle, closer than anyone had expected.

Anyone, of course, except Magatha.

She had been waiting for the opportunity for years, and like a leaf that had slowly and unexpectedly drifted down from the tree into her lap, it had finally come. Her spies in Orgrimmar had been able to reach her in time for her to travel from Thunder Bluff to the arena, and it had been ease itself to offer her services as shaman for the ritual blessing of the weapon.

Earlier, when Garrosh and several of the Kor'kron were in a private area below the main seating level, she had requested and been given permission to see him. "I told you once before, Garrosh Hellscream, that I suspected you were just what the Horde needed when it needed it. And that if the time was right, I would give you my support and that of the Grimtotem tribe. Let me bless your weapon in preparation for its trials today."

Garrosh had eyed her. "You would turn against Cairne? A fellow tauren?"

Magatha had shrugged. "I want to do what is best for my people. I believe that is following you, Garrosh Hellscream."

He nodded. "That makes sense, and marks you as a wise leader of your tribe. The future lies with me, not with an old bull, hero though he might have been once." His brows had knotted for a moment. "I . . . do respect him. I would rather not be the instrument of his death, but he was the one who called for the challenge, and he has insulted my honor."

"Indeed he has," said Magatha. "That blow that staggered you so . . . *Everyone* is speaking of it. Shameful. It cannot stand unavenged."

Garrosh had growled softly, and his face, where it was not tattooed black, flushed with anger and embarrassment. Magatha kept her expression neutral, but inwardly she smiled. This was almost too easy.

"So, will you accept my blessing of your blade and the support of my Grimtotem?"

He eyed her up and down for a moment, then nodded. "Let all who see know of your decision, then, Elder Crone. You may bless my blade before the fight begins."

Shortly afterward, in full view of the crowd, he had offered up Gorehowl. Magatha could barely suppress her excitement as she intoned the ritual blessing, removed the stopper from the vial that had been prepared for her scant minutes earlier, and dropped three drops of oil on the blade. Tradition demanded that she use her hands to apply the oil. She did not. Garrosh did not know the difference.

Nor did he know how he was being used by her. Which was good—the orc would have slain her on the spot had he known what she had planned. Had he known his oh-so-precious Gorehowl was slicked with poison.

Yes, she mused as she watched Cairne suddenly stumble and blink a few seconds after Gorehowl shattered the ancient runespear into bits and sliced into the tauren's chest and arm. *Almost too easy. But so much else I have striven for has been too hard. It is the balance.*

Garrosh seized the opportunity. Gorehowl shrieked as the orc whirled it over his head before bringing it down for the final blow. The blade bit deep at the juncture between head and shoulder, cutting through muscle and flesh. Blood spurted from the severed artery, and the mighty Cairne Bloodhoof's legs buckled, then collapsed. He was dead by the time his torso struck the floor. Thunderous applause mixed with gasps and sobs filled the arena.

Thus ends one era. With his death, a new one is birthed.

Cairne's loyal followers rushed into the ring, grieving. They lifted the body of their fallen leader. Magatha knew what everyone expected would happen now. They would ritually bathe it, washing away the dirt and blood and sweat and oil, then prepare it for cremation by wrapping it in a ceremonial blanket. There would be a long, mournful walk back to Thunder Bluff from Orgrimmar, so that all could pay their respects before the body was burned, the ashes offered to the winds and rivers, to become one with the Earth Mother and Sky Father.

And those expectations, however false they would prove to be, would give her the opportunity for which she had hungered so long.

She turned to one of her apprentices and whispered in Taur-ahe, "Now. Send the word now. Cairne has finally fallen. Tonight the reign of the Grimtotem begins."

The moon was full over Thunder Bluff, the night clear and cloudless. The tauren were mostly diurnal, and while some activity of some sort was going on at all times, day or night, at this hour of the early morning it was mostly still. The wind wafted the smoke of a few fires upward to the star-filled skies. In their tents, the tauren drowsed.

The Grimtotem moved, shadowlike and stealthy, black blots of ink against the moon-silvered night. Some of them arrived in Thunder Bluff on wyvern back, the beasts' wings almost as silent as the still night air. Some of them walked, avoiding the lifts and instead climbing the sheer bluff with deadly intent and a grace that belied their bulk. They had been in position for years awaiting this call and had leaped into action within seconds of their notification.

They all carried weapons—garrotes, knives, swords, axes, bows. No guns, nothing that would make noise. Sound meant discovery; discovery meant resistance; and that was not what their matriarch wanted. Their mission was to kill in silence and move to the next victim.

They kept to the shadows, taking their time, moving behind the tents of the first, lowest level of the mesa until they were all in position. Soft hooting sounds then gently punctuated the night; sounds that, even if they were heard, would be disregarded. And then, coordinated, they struck.

Swiftly the Grimtotem assassins moved into the tents. Some targets were known to them—those who were experts in weapons, or were particularly powerful druids or shaman. What good was the power of the bear when one never awoke in time to transform? What did it aid one to be lethal with a sword when one's chest was already pierced by it? How easily throats were slit when no resistance was offered.

They moved into the center by the small pool, checking their numbers, giving hand signals. They split into two groups. One darted off to Spirit Rise, the other to Hunter Rise. Elder Rise they ignored. That was where Magatha had made her home until this night of nights, and she had left behind loyal subjects who had doubtless already executed every one of the hapless druids unlucky enough to have been present. The old boards of the bridges creaked slightly under the attackers' weight as they crossed, but these bridges creaked even in the wind, and they had no worries of discovery.

Straight to their victims they ran, leaping atop the shaman who awakened only long enough to gasp and then die. Skychasers they were, a family—dead, down to the last one. There was no need to worry about the Forsaken in the Pools of Vision just below the main level of Spirit Rise. Most of them tacitly supported Magatha, and those who did not had no particular attachment to the tauren or who led them.

On to Hunter Rise.

These were more physically brutal battles. Quick to awaken and extremely strong and fit, the hunters put up a good fight. But they were no match for the Grimtotem, who had the element of surprise on their side, or, eventually, the poison on their blades. Soon enough, the rise was silent, and the assassins moved back to the heart of Thunder Bluff.

Those who posed the greatest threats to Elder Crone Magatha had been slain. It was now time to kill without specific need, to strike fear into the hearts of what tauren still remained. They needed to know that the rule of the Grimtotem would have no margin for error and no place for the gentler notions of forgiveness or compassion.

Thunder Bluff, like a child, would be rebirthed in blood.

"Wait," said a Grimtotem shaman, holding up a hand. Although his given name was Jevan, others had taken to calling him Stormsong due to his affinity with the elements of air and water. While he led the party that had surrounded Bloodhoof Village, he had told those under his command that he would not utilize his formidable powers until the last moment. Now his second-in-command, Tarakor, was awaiting the signal to attack.

"Wait?" replied Tarakor, confused. "We have been given our orders, Stormsong. We attack!"

The shaman sniffed the air, his black ears twitching. "Something is not right. It is possible they have been alerted to our presence."

Tarakor snorted. "Unlikely. We have trained for years for this night."

Stormsong eyed him. "If we have our spies and ways of delivering messages, you may rest assured that Cairne did, too."

The mission to Thunder Bluff had been extensive—to slaughter everyone who posed a threat to the matriarch. It was a long list, and many who embarked on that mission would not complete it. But there was only one goal here in Bloodhoof Village—only one who needed to die. But that one must die, or else the entire blood-soaked night would have been for nothing.

Baine Bloodhoof, Cairne Bloodhoof's son and only heir, lived here, not with his father on Thunder Bluff.

The tauren now sleeping securely in their tents, or even on the earth underneath the moons' light, were in peaceful ignorance of the fact that that their beloved chieftain had joined the ancestors. The Longwalkers who had witnessed the fight in Orgrimmar and planned to report to Baine had all been quickly, quietly dispatched ere they could do so. Magi and others who could get word to Thunder Bluff swiftly had been silently followed, watched carefully—or otherwise taken care of. The roads had been blocked. Magatha had planned well and left absolutely nothing to chance.

The village had been the first tauren settlement to be established on an open plain rather than on a protected mesa. It was evidence of how the tauren had become secure in a land that had once been so new to them.

It was indeed secure, from predators and attacks from other races.

It was not secure from the Grimtotem.

"If anyone was alerted as to Cairne's untimely death in the arena, surely it would be his son," said Stormsong. "A single messenger might have escaped our net. I will go ahead, quietly, and scout out the area to make sure we are not walking into a trap. If it is not safe, we will need to adjust our tactics. Do nothing until you hear from me, do you understand?"

Stormsong was of an age with Cairne, and like that late bull was still strong and sharp despite the gray starting to dot his black pelt. Tarakor shifted uneasily. He was younger, and hot-blooded, and had been dreaming of this night for a long, long time. He did not want to wait another minute, but finally he nodded.

"You are the leader of the mission, Stormsong," he said in a voice that clearly revealed his wish that it were otherwise. "I will obey. But make haste, eh? My blade is thirsty for Baine's blood."

"As is mine, friend, but I'd like to not shed my own if I can help it," Stormsong said. The group of two dozen who had been assembled for tonight's task chuckled quietly. "I will be back as soon as I can."

Tarakor watched him go, moving quietly, his black hide swallowed by the shadows.

He waited.

And waited. And waited, shifting uneasily from one hoof to the next, his ears twitching with ever-increasing anxiety. Beside him his warriors also fidgeted impatiently. They were all hungry for battle, and this sudden imposed pause did not sit well with any of them. Tarakor did not know how long he stood, eyes straining to see in the dark, when finally something inside him snapped.

"He should have been back before now," Tarakor growled. "Something has gone wrong. We can wait no longer. Grimtotem, attack! For the elder crone!"

Something had woken Baine Bloodhoof. He lay restless in his sleeping furs, an odd chill racing along his spine. A dream had come to him, one he could not recall, but that had unsettled him greatly. And so when he heard voices outside, he rose, threw on some clothing, and stepped out to find out what the problem was.

Two of the braves held another tauren between them. Even in the dim moonlight Baine recognized him.

"I know you," he said. "You are one of Magatha's people. What are you doing here this time of night?"

The other tauren was elderly, but there was nothing frail about him. He made no effort to resist the firm grip the braves had on him. Instead, he gave Baine a compassionate yet concerned look.

"I come to warn you, Baine Bloodhoof. Your father is dead, and you are to be next. You must leave, quickly and quietly."

Pain shot through Baine, but he tamped it down. This was a Grimtotem. This had to be a trick.

"You lie," he rumbled. "And I do not take kindly to jests about my father's well-being. Tell me why you are really here, and perhaps I will overlook your poor taste in jokes."

"No lie, Chieftain," the Grimtotem insisted. "He fell in the arena against Garrosh Hellscream, whom he challenged in the mak'gora."

"Now I know you lie. Thrall has forbidden such things. The mak'gora is no longer a duel to the death."

"What was old is new again," said Stormsong. "Cairne made the challenge, and Garrosh agreed—providing they fought under the old rules. It was indeed to the death."

Baine froze. It was all indeed possible, from what he knew, both of his father and of Garrosh. He knew that his father had not approved of Thrall's appointment of Garrosh—nor, truth be told, had Baine. He knew that both Hamuul Runetotem and Cairne thought it likely that Garrosh was behind the attacks on the Sentinels in Ashenvale. It was entirely like Cairne to have challenged Garrosh if he felt that the orc was a true danger to the well-being of the Horde. And entirely like Cairne to not back down if Garrosh decided to change the rules.

"My father would have won such a battle," he said, his voice shaking slightly.

"He might well have," the shaman agreed, "had not

Magatha poisoned Garrosh's weapon. She used her position as shaman to bless Gorehowl and coated its blade with poisoned oil. A single strike was all that was needed." He said the words bitterly, angrily. "My pack—open it. There is sad proof within."

Baine nodded at one of the braves. The tauren opened the pack they had taken from the Grimtotem, and his eyes widened. Baine felt a deep chill within. Slowly, the brave reached inside—and produced a small fragment of what looked to be little more than a broken stick.

Baine extended a hand, and the brave placed the splinter of the legendary runespear in Baine Bloodhoof's palm. Trembling, he closed his fingers about it, feeling the runes, known and familiar, against his skin. He staggered. His powerful yet gentle father—whom he had envisioned either passing gloriously in battle or peacefully in his sleep—murdered by treachery . . .

Anger began to swell inside him as the Grimtotem continued. "Two dozen Grimtotem warriors are waiting just beyond the firelight to attack. I was to lead the mission myself. Instead, I come to warn you. Your father was a great tauren, even if I disagreed with some of his decisions. He did not deserve such a death, nor do you. Long have I served the matriarch, but this time . . ." He shook his head. "This time she has gone too far. She has disgraced what it means to be a shaman. I will not participate in her plans any longer."

Baine closed the distance between him and the Grimtotem in two strides and jerked the other tauren's head up by his beard. The Grimtotem grunted slightly but met Baine's gaze evenly.

The strange dream . . . the sense of unease . . .

A great pain filled Baine's chest, lancing his heart, and he could hardly breathe. "Father," he whispered, and even as he said the word, he realized that the Grimtotem defector had spoken the truth. Tears stung his eyes, but he blinked them back. There would be time to properly mourn his father later. If what the defector said was true—

"What is your name?"

"I am known as Stormsong, Chieftain."

Chieftain. He supposed he was chieftain of the Bloodhoof now. . . . "I will stand and fight," Baine declared. "I will not run from danger. I will not abandon the people of the village that bears my family's name."

"You are outnumbered," said Stormsong, "and yours is more than simply another life to be thrown away in battle. You are the last Bloodhoof, and, too, you would be the obvious choice to lead your people as well as your tribe. You have a responsibility to the tauren to stay safe and reclaim what has been stolen from you. Do you think Bloodhoof Village is the only tauren settlement under attack tonight?"

Baine's eyes widened in growing horror as Stormsong continued. "Even now, slaughter goes on in Thunder Bluff! Magatha will rule the tauren by the time the sun peeks its head over the horizon to regard the bloody aftermath of this shameful night. You must survive. You do not have the luxury of dying to avenge your father! Come, please!"

Baine snorted angrily, gripping Stormsong by the front of his leather vest, then releasing him. The shaman was right.

"This could be a trick, a trap!" one of the braves said. "He could be leading you into an ambush!"

Baine shook his head sadly. "No," he said. "No trick. I can feel it. The shaman speaks the truth." He opened his hand, which he had clenched hard around the rune-spear fragment, and regarded it for a moment before tenderly placing it in a pouch. "My father is slain, and I must survive tonight if I am to take care of our people as he would have wanted me to. Stormsong Grimtotem, you risk much, coming to warn me. And so I risk much in trusting you. Know that if you betray me, you will die within seconds."

"Well do I know that," Stormsong agreed. "I am one and you are many. Now . . . the Grimtotem are on three sides, but I think I know a way to scatter them. Follow me."

The Grimtotem charged the village. They were met not by sleeping, unaware tauren, but by warriors in training, fully armed and ready for them. Tarakor was not altogether surprised; he had assumed that Stormsong had been captured and Baine had been alerted to the attack. Still, they were Grimtotem, and they would fight to their deaths.

Many fell beneath Tarakor's axe, but there was one he did not see—Baine Bloodhoof. Every Grimtotem present knew that killing Baine was the sole objective, and as the moments ticked by and Baine did not appear, Tarakor began to panic.

There was only one explanation.

"Grimtotem!" he cried, brandishing his axe over the

body of a druid he had sliced almost in two as she attempted to transform into cat form. "We are betrayed! Baine has escaped! *Find him! Find him!*"

Now the battling villagers were not a target, but a nuisance, as the Grimtotem tried to move past the boundaries of Bloodhoof Village. And then suddenly the earth began to shake. Tarakor whirled, axe at the ready, and stared for a split second in horror.

Nearly a dozen kodos were charging directly at him and his men. Some of them were being ridden by Bloodhoof villagers, but others only had saddles and harnesses. Some, not even broken for riding yet, did not have that much. They bellowed, eyes rolling, frightened out of their wits, and gave no indication that they were even considering slowing down.

There was only one option. "Run!" cried Tarakor.

They did. The kodos followed, seeming to pick up speed, and the Grimtotem literally ran for their lives. Up ahead was Stonebull Lake, and potential safety. Tarakor did not slow as he plunged into the cold water, sinking beneath the weight of his armor. The kodos followed, but their stampede slowed as they hit the water. Tarakor swam as strongly as he could, struggling to the surface, his armor, donned to protect him, threatening to drag him down. The kodos were straggling back to the land now, still snorting, shaking water off their coats. The Grimtotem treaded water as Tarakor counted heads. Some had not emerged from the depths of the lake, and some had not even made it that far this night. They would be grieved later. For now the ones who had survived struck out to the far side of the lake.

It was slow going. They emerged, drenched and shivering and disheartened.

They had failed. Baine had escaped. Stormsong had betrayed them. Tarakor was not looking forward to telling Magatha the news.

Baine watched the stampede, nodding to himself. It had been a good plan, to agitate the herd, and it had bought them the opportunity to escape. While generally placid even in the wild, agitated, frightened kodos were a force that could not be stopped. The kodos were driving the enemy westward, trapping them against the mountains. They had nowhere to go. Some would be killed, but others would escape and come after them; it was a delay, but even a brief delay would help Baine and his followers.

"Camp Taurajo has not fallen to the Grimtotem, has it, Stormsong?"

The Grimtotem shook his head. "No. Our main targets were Thunder Bluff, Bloodhoof Village, Sun Rock Retreat, and Camp Mojache."

"Then we head for Camp Taurajo and hope it has not become a secondary target. We can arrange transportation from there."

"Transportation where?" Stormsong asked.

Baine's eyes were hard as he urged the kodo he rode to greater speed. His heart was full with the missing of his father and the anger he bore toward the Grimtotem for the bloodshed this night.

"I do not know," he said honestly. "But I know this. My father will be avenged, and I will not rest until the

Grimtotem have been revealed for the traitors they are. My father permitted them to live with us, though they refused to join the Horde. Now I will expel them from every aspect of tauren society. This, I vow."

Baine had not traveled much outside of Mulgore in the last few years, and he had forgotten just how open and exposed the aptly named Barrens were. Jorn Skyseer greeted them and brought them into the camp, making sure the orc guards were not alerted. Baine did not know yet whom he could trust. They gathered together in the back of one of the great lodges: Baine; the four braves who had come with him from Bloodhoof Village; the recovering Hamuul Runetotem, who had a bitter tale to tell of an attack on a peaceful druidic gathering; and the defector, Stormsong. Jorn joined them, carrying a tray of food—apples, watermelon, Mulgore spice bread, and chunks of cooked meat.

Baine nodded his thanks to the hunter. He took a bite of fruit and regarded Hamuul. "I trust your word, Hamuul, and that of Stormsong, Grimtotem though he is. It is cruel that our leader betrays us so, whereas my trust must fall to an old enemy."

Stormsong lowered his muzzle. It was awkward for him to be here, but he was gradually winning the respect and trust of Baine and those around him.

"I do not know what Garrosh knew of the attack, but I do know that it was an oversight that I survived," Hamuul said. "They left me for dead, and I nearly was. As for the challenge," and he eyed Stormsong, "Garrosh may have consented to the use of the poison, he may not. It does not matter. Magatha has what she wanted—control of Thunder Bluff, Bloodhoof Village, probably Camp Mojache, and unless we stop her soon, all the tauren."

"But not Sun Rock," Jorn said quietly. "They have sent a runner. They were able to repel the attack."

Baine nodded. It was good news, but far from sufficient. Baine growled softly and forced himself to eat. He needed to keep his strength up, although his stomach did not wish the food.

"Archdruid, my father ever trusted your advice. I have never been in more need of it than now. What do we do now? How do we fight her?"

Hamuul sighed, thinking. A long silence fell. "From what we can learn, most of the tauren are now controlled by Magatha—willingly or not. Garrosh might be innocent of treachery, but he is most certainly a hothead, and one way or another he wished your father dead." Baine took a deep breath, and Hamuul gave him a compassionate look before continuing. "The Undercity is not safe for you, not patrolled as it is by orcs likely loyal to Garrosh. The Darkspear trolls are likely trustworthy, but they are not many. And as for the blood elves, they are much too far away to offer any aid. Garrosh will likely reach them before we could."

Baine laughed without humor and gestured at Stormsong. "So it seems that our enemies are more trustworthy than our friends," he said drily.

Hamuul was forced to agree, nodding. "Or at least more accessible."

A thought struck Baine, daring and dangerous. As his father had taught him, he sat with the thought for a long moment, turning it over in his head rather than simply blurting it out. Finally he spoke.

"I will take an honorable enemy over a dishonorable friend every time," he said quietly. "So let us go to an honorable enemy. We will seek out the woman Thrall trusted."

He looked at them each in turn, seeing dawning comprehension on the long-muzzled faces.

"We will go to Lady Jaina Proudmoore."

TWENTY-THREE

"Have you ever gone on a vision quest, Go'el?" Geyah asked one night as they shared a simple meal of clefthoof stew and bread. Thrall ate hungrily; the day had been long and intensely wearying, emotionally and physically. He had spent the day not communing with or aiding the elementals of this land, but destroying them.

Thrall understood that very few elemental spirits were balanced and in harmony with themselves and the other elements. Some were in true alignment with their natures, chaotic though those natures might be. Others were sometimes sick and corrupted. Often, a gentle but firm hand could bring them back into line. But sometimes the entities were too damaged. One such had been the little spark in Orgrimmar, who would not listen to reason, or even to begging.

The shaman could not be selfish. They must always show honor and respect for the elementals, to ask humbly for their aid and be grateful when it was offered. But they also had a responsibility to protect the world from harm, and if that harm came from an uncontrollable elemental, their duty was clear.

And Outland was apparently overrun with them.

Aggra had leaped into the fray with the surety of one who had done this dozens, perhaps hundreds of times. She took no joy in the task, but neither did she hesitate to defend herself or him, her charge, even if she would rather he was not so. It was a bitter fight, Thrall thought, a shaman using the power of a healthy elemental to slay its tainted . . . brethren? Peers? He was not sure of the word, only that it made his heart ache to watch it. In the back of his mind was the nagging question: *Is this the future of Azeroth's elementals? And is there nothing I can do to prevent it?*

He turned to Geyah, to answer her question. "When I was young, and under Drek'Thar's tutelage, I met the elements," Thrall said. "I fasted and did not drink for a full day. Drek'Thar took me to a certain area, and I waited until the elements approached me. I asked each of them a question, as part of my test, and pledged myself to their service. It was . . . very powerful."

Aggra and Geyah exchanged glances. "That is well," said Geyah, "though not a traditional rite of passage. Drek'Thar did the best he could under challenging circumstances. He was one of only a handful left, and when you came to him, the Frostwolves were too busy simply trying to survive, and so he could not prepare a traditional vision quest for you. You have done well on your own, Go'el, astonishingly well, but perhaps now that you have come back to your homeland to learn, it is time for you to have a proper ritual quest."

Aggra was nodding. She looked solemn and did not regard him with her usual barely concealed disdain. In fact, quite the opposite—she seemed almost to have acquired a new respect for him, if her body language was any indication.

"I will do what I must," Thrall said. "Do you think it is because I have not had this particular rite that I am not learning what I have come here to learn?"

"The vision quest is about self-knowledge," Aggra said. "Perhaps you need that before you are ready to accept other knowledge."

It was hard not to take umbrage at her slightest word. "More than most I am self-made," he said stiffly. "I think I have learned a great deal about myself already."

"And yet the mighty Slave cannot find what he seeks," said Aggra, tensing slightly.

"Peace, the two of you," Geyah said mildly, though she was frowning. "The worlds are in enough chaos without two shaman sniping at one another. Aggra, you speak your mind, and that is well, but perhaps holding your tongue from time to time might be a good exercise for you. And, Go'el, surely you admit that anyone, even the warchief of the Horde, would benefit from knowing himself better."

Thrall frowned slightly. "My apologies, Grandmother. Aggra. I am frustrated because the situation is dire, and I as of yet can do nothing to help. It serves no one to take my irritation out on you."

Aggra nodded. She looked annoyed, but somehow Thrall sensed that—for once—it was not with him. She seemed annoyed with herself.

The young shaman confounded him, he had to admit. He did not know what to make of her. Thrall was not unaccustomed to dealing with intelligent, strong women. He had known two—Taretha Foxton and Jaina Proudmoore. But they were both human, and he was coming to realize that their strength came from a place that was very different from where orc females drew their strength. He had heard stories of his mother, Draka, who had been born sickly but through her own will and determination had become as strong physically as she was mentally and emotionally. "A warrior made," he had once heard Geyah say of Draka with admiration. "It is easy to be a good warrior when the ancestors gift you with speed and strength and a strong heart. It is not so easy when you must wrest these things from a world that does not want to give them to you, as Draka did."

Now she spoke to Thrall, though it was upon Aggra that her gaze was fixed. "Your mother's spirit is within you, Thrall. Like her, everything you are, you have made of yourself. What you gave your people was not an easy thing—you had to fight for it. You are your mother's son as well as your father's, Go'el, son of Durotan—and Draka."

"I came here to do whatever was necessary to learn how to help my world," Thrall said. "But I would be about this vision quest as quickly as possible."

"You will stay as long as it takes, and you know it," Aggra said.

Growling slightly to himself, Thrall said nothing, because he did know it.

* * *

Anduin knew well that he was not "an honored guest." He was, in fact, a hostage, and the single most valuable one Moira had.

The envelope, written in a flowing hand, was on the table of the main room when Anduin came back after an hour spent with Rohan four days after Moira and her Dark Iron dwarves had swept into the city. He gritted his teeth as he saw that the red wax was sealed with the royal seal of Ironforge. He opened it while Drukan, the "special guard" assigned to Anduin to "make sure he was well taken care of, as he was such an honored guest," looked on sullenly.

The Pleasure of your Company is requested at Twilight this Evening. Formal Attire is required and Promptness is appreciated.

Anduin resisted the urge to crumple the letter and throw it away. Instead, he smiled politely at Drukan.

"Please tell Her Majesty that I shall be happy to attend. I'm sure she'll want to hear from me as soon as possible." At least, he thought, this would send off the watchdog for a few moments. He waited until Drukan determined he couldn't get out of the errand. The dwarf scowled and stomped off.

Anduin realized he actually found Drukan's lack of pretense, interest, and concern refreshing. At least Drukan wasn't lying about his feelings.

Anduin bathed and dressed. Moira may have thought she was pulling the strings on a puppet by demanding his attendance, but by insisting on formal attire, she was giving Anduin permission to wear his crown and other regalia that marked him as her equal. Anduin was well aware of the power such subtleties could convey. Wyll helped him dress, adjusted his crown with about a dozen delicate, infinitesimal tweaks, and then produced a mirror.

Anduin blinked a little. He always hated it when adults said he had "grown so much since the last time I saw you," but he was forced to see the evidence now with his own eyes. He hadn't paid much attention to what he looked like in the mirror recently, but now he could see that there was a new somberness to his eyes, a set to his jaw. He'd not had anything resembling a sheltered childhood, but he just hadn't expected the stress of the last few days to be so . . . visible.

"Everything all right, Your Highness?" Wyll inquired.

"Yes, Wyll. Everything is fine."

The elderly servant leaned forward. "I am certain your father is working diligently to find a way to secure your release," he said, pitching his voice very soft.

Anduin merely nodded. "Well," he sighed, "time for dinner."

Anduin was led past the High Seat and discovered that there were only two place settings at a surprisingly small table. Apparently it was to be an intimate gathering.

In other words, he was going to be interrogated.

He assumed Moira would take the head of the table, so he stood politely beside his chair awaiting her arrival.

He waited. And waited. The minutes crept past,

and he realized that this, too, was all part of the game that was being played. He understood it better than she thought. He was young and he knew it, and he knew that people underestimated him precisely for that reason. He could use that to his benefit.

And, being young, he could stand for a long time without discomfort.

At last a door was flung open. A Dark Iron dwarf clad in the livery of Ironforge stepped forward, puffed out his chest, and announced in a voice that would carry in a crowd of hundreds, "Rise to greet Her Majesty, Queen Moira of Ironforge!"

Anduin gave the dwarf a half smile and spread his hands slightly to indicate that he was already standing. The prince bowed as Moira entered, still maintaining the proper depth of the bow to an equal. When he straightened, smiling politely, he saw a flicker of annoyance cross Moira's usually set-in-stone expression of false cordiality.

"Ah, Anduin. You are right on time," Moira said as she swept into the room. A servant pulled out her chair for her, and she settled in, then nodded to Anduin that he might do likewise.

"I believe punctuality to be a great virtue," he said. He did not need to mention that she had kept him waiting. They both knew it.

"I trust you have been having a pleasant and enlightening time conversing with my other subjects," she said, permitting the servant to place the napkin in her lap.

Other subjects? Was she implying that Anduin was—no, she wasn't, but she wanted him to think she was. Anduin smiled pleasantly, nodding thanks to the servant who poured him a glass of water. Another was pouring blood-red wine for Moira. Beer, apparently, was not high on the list of the queen's favorite beverages.

"By that, of course, you mean the Dark Iron dwarves, not just the dwarves of Ironforge," he said pleasantly. "I've not had much conversation with Drukan. Kind of a quiet fellow."

Moira lifted a delicate hand to her mouth, hiding a smile. "Oh, dear, why yes, that is very true. Most of them aren't talkers, you know. Which is one reason I am so terribly glad that *you* are here, my dear friend."

Anduin smiled politely and dipped his spoon into the soup.

"I am very much looking forward to the long conversations we are certain to have as the weeks and months unfold."

He forced himself not to choke on the soup, swallowing hard. "While I am sure they would be fascinating," and that at least was not a lie, "I think that my father will need me back before then. I fear you must get as much stimulating conversation as you can with me now."

A flicker in the depths of Moira's eyes, then the brittle smile. "Oh, I daresay your father will indulge me. Tell me of him. I understand he's had quite the ordeal."

Anduin was very certain indeed that Moira knew everything there was to know. She did not strike him as someone who would have waited this long to find out what she wanted to learn. Nonetheless, through the soup course and the salad, he told her what was general knowledge of his father's adventures.

"That must have been quite hard on you, Anduin."

He didn't think she really cared, but a thought occurred to him. He decided to run with it.

"It was," he said, utterly honest. "It's been even harder to know that he doesn't approve of the direction in which I wish to take my life. Rumor has it that's something you would understand."

For the first time since he saw her, she looked at him with a completely unguarded expression, the spoon partway to her mouth, her eyes wide in astonishment. She looked—vulnerable, flustered, and hastened to recover.

"Why, whatever do you mean?" She uttered a false laugh.

"I hear that Magni wasn't the best father in the world, even though he might have wanted to be—just like mine," Anduin said. "That he never quite forgave you for not being the son he wanted."

Her eyes went hard, but they were oddly shiny, as if with unshed tears. When she spoke, it was as if Anduin's words had broken a dam. "My father was indeed quite disappointed in my *flaw* of being born female. He could never believe that I might not want to stay here while constantly being reminded that I'd failed him simply by being born. He decided that the only way I could possibly fall in love with a Dark Iron dwarf was if my husband had enchanted me. Well, he did, Anduin. He enchanted me with the concept of respect. Of having people listen to me when I spoke. Of believing that I could rule, even as a female, and rule well. The Dark Irons welcomed me when my own father dismissed me."

She laughed without humor. "*That's* the only magic Dagran Thaurissan and the Dark Irons used on me. My father thought them only to be despised, only good enough to fight and kill. Well, they are dwarves, just like any other clan of dwarves—heirs to the earthen. The other dwarves could stand to be reminded of that, and that's what I intend to do."

"You are the rightful heir," Anduin agreed. "Magni should have recognized and raised you as such from the day you were born. I'm sorry you only found welcome among the Dark Irons, and you're right—they're dwarves, too. But you aren't going to promote harmony by forcing the people of Ironforge to think like you do. Open up the city. Let people see who the Dark Irons really are, as you have. They can have—"

"They can have what I say they can have!" snapped Moira, her voice strident. "And they will do what I say they will do! I have the right of law on my side, and Dagran—the boy that Magni so wished I had been—will rule when I am gone. His father and I . . ."

She paused, and the artificial good cheer suddenly replaced the honest anger. "Do you know," she said, "that is really the first time this thought has occurred to me."

Discouraged at her reversion to her previous demeanor, Anduin asked, "And what thought might that be?"

"Why, that I am an empress, not just a queen."

A chill ran down Anduin's spine.

"Goodness! This changes everything! I have two peoples to rule over. As will my little one, once he comes of age. Such opportunities to be had to build bridges, to bring peace. Do you not agree?"

"Peace is always a noble goal," he said, his heart sinking. He'd had her, just for a moment, had gotten her speaking honestly. But the moment had passed.

"Indeed. My, my. Sometimes I think I am just a silly little girl still."

No, you don't, and neither do I. "I can sympathize. Sometimes I think I'm just a thirteen-year-old boy," he said.

Moira tittered again. "Ah, your humor delights me, Anduin. While I am certain your father misses you, I am quite, quite sure that I cannot *bear* to part with you just yet."

He gave her a smile that he sincerely hoped did not look quite as fake as it actually was.

Several hours later, finally alone in his quarters, Anduin closed the door and leaned against it heavily.

Moira wasn't mad, or under any spell. He wished she were. She'd been wronged, he had to admit, but instead of turning that into a strength, she'd let her resentment eat away at her. She was calculating, in control, and intent upon bequeathing an empire to her son. Some of what she said made sense. Peace *was* a good thing. But so was liberty.

He had to get out of here. Had to let someone know what was going on. He took a deep breath, ran his hand through his hair, and then began to throw things into a small pack he'd brought for day trips with . . . Light, how he missed Aerin, even now. But he was also glad that she wasn't here to see what Ironforge had become.

He wouldn't need much—a change of clothing or two, some money. He had brought a few special things from Stormwind, but now he realized that he could live without them in the face of the urgent need to get away as soon as possible. But there was one thing that meant too much, that was too precious, to part with.

He'd kept it under the bed since Magni's death, wrapped in the same cloth as it had been when the dwarven king had presented it to him. He hoped word had not reached Moira about the gift. Somehow he suspected the idea wouldn't sit well with her.

He took a moment to unwrap it and touch the beautiful mace. Fearbreaker. He could use its comfort now. Anduin permitted his hand to close about the weapon for a moment, then he rewrapped it and placed it carefully in the pack.

It was time. He had decided not to tell Wyll. The less the elderly servant knew, the easier they would be on him. Anduin took a deep breath, reached his hand in his pocket, and closed his hand about the hearthstone Jaina had given him. Squeezing his eyes tightly shut, Anduin filled his mind with images of Theramore, of Jaina's cozy little fireplace—

—and materialized there.

Jaina stared at him. "Anduin, what are you doing here?"

The prince of Stormwind didn't have a thought to spare for her. All he could do was gape at the enormous, angry-looking tauren clad in armor and feathers who stood directly in front of him.

TWENTY-FOUR

"What is this—" the tauren rumbled, in heavy but intelligible Common.

"Baine, Anduin—hold on!" Jaina reached a hand out to each of them.

Baine? "Baine Bloodhoof?" Anduin managed.

"Anduin Wrynn?"

"Everyone hold on!" Jaina cried, more loudly this time. "Baine—I gave Anduin a gift, a stone that enabled him to come visit me whenever he wanted. And given what we've heard from Ironforge—or rather, *not* heard from Ironforge—I'm very, very glad to see you." She gave him a quick but heartfelt smile. "And Baine—I apologize for his unexpected arrival, but I believe you can trust Anduin."

"His father has no love for the Horde," Baine said. "I believe you did not anticipate this, Jaina, but—"

"I am not my father," Anduin said quietly. He was calming down now, starting to figure out what was going on. Baine Bloodhoof was the son of the tauren high chieftain, Cairne. Cairne and Thrall were good friends, and the tauren were not as hostile to the Alliance as some of the other races that comprised the Horde. If Jaina was on good terms with Thrall, it stood to reason that she would not be averse to meetings—even secret ones—with a representative of Cairne's.

His composure seemed to impress the young bull. Baine relaxed slightly, regarding him with more curiosity than hostility now. "No," he said, "we are not our fathers. Even if we wished to be."

There was something in the tone that alerted Anduin that something was very wrong here. He glanced at Jaina, questioningly. Now that he looked at her, she looked strained and unhappy.

"Sit down, both of you," she said, indicating the hearth. Baine was far too big to fit into any of the chairs. "I think you two have long stories to share."

"I intend no offense," Baine said, continuing to stand, "but I risk a great deal even coming to see you, Lady Jaina. To confide in the heir to the crown of Stormwind? I fear you ask too much."

"I understand your trepidation," said Jaina, "and I know right now you're both focused on your own problems. But bear in mind I am harboring *both* of you right now, and so you're just going to have to get along."

"How can you *harbor* a fellow Alliance member?" Baine snorted.

"Because Magni Bronzebeard is dead; his daughter, Moira Bronzebeard, has returned to Ironforge from Shadowforge City with a bunch of Dark Iron dwarves and is declaring herself empress; she's got Ironforge in a lockdown; and she's going to be very, very upset that I got out," Anduin said bluntly. Baine was right. There was no reason he should trust Anduin, prince of Stormwind . . . unless Anduin gave him a reason to. Besides, if he didn't know already, he soon would. Moira couldn't keep her intent secret forever. Baine's massive, horned head swiveled around, and he blinked at Anduin for a moment.

"Some would call you traitor for revealing that information, young prince," he said quietly.

"What Moira is doing is wrong, even if she is the legitimate heir," Anduin said. "Some of her goals and plans make sense. But how she's going about them—I can't approve of that. Just because she's a dwarf and the daughter of a friend doesn't mean I blindly support her. And just because you're a member of the Horde doesn't mean I wouldn't support *you*."

He kept his gaze on Baine, but out of the corner of his eye he saw Jaina relax slightly, hopefully.

"He has met Thrall, and they like and respect each other," Jaina said. "You could ask for no better endorsement, Baine."

Baine nodded, though his ears flapped, presumably in distress. "Had not Thrall left, though, I would have no need of your aid, and . . ." He paused, and took a deep breath, blowing it out through his nostrils. "And my father would still be alive."

Anduin gasped and looked at Jaina. Her eyes were sad, and she nodded. "Baine already told me," she said quietly.

"I'm so sorry," he said, and meant it. Whatever anyone thought of the Horde, everyone agreed that Cairne had been a good, decent leader and a good . . . man?

Person? But it was not unexpected. Cairne was old. It seemed strange that Baine seemed so upset. No, not upset—anyone who loved his father would be upset at his passing—but . . . agitated. Distressed. "What happened?"

"Sit down," Jaina said, not unkindly. This time Anduin and Baine complied, taking seats on the floor. Jaina poured tea for all of them, put the cups on a tray, and sat down on the floor, cross-legged, herself. Anduin took a cup, and, after a moment, so did Baine. He regarded the tiny cup in his massive hand and gave a little chuckle—possibly the first, Anduin suspected, he had uttered since learning of his father's death.

Jaina glanced from one to the other. "Neither of you knows how much I wish we three were meeting under different circumstances," she said quietly, "particularly yours, Baine. But at least we are meeting. Maybe this conversation tonight will lay the groundwork for future, more formal conversations between our people."

Anduin lifted his cup. "To better times," he said. Jaina lifted hers and clinked it gently. After a moment Baine did so, too.

"I think . . . my father would be glad of this," he said. "Prince Anduin. Let me tell you what suffering this past day has brought."

"I'm listening," the prince of Stormwind said.

"Are you listening to me?" Moira screamed.

"Aye, Your Excellency, I—"

"How could you let him escape?"

"I dinna ken! We've arrested th' magi. . . . Perhaps a warlock summoning frae outside?" Drukan was reaching here, and he knew it.

"We have wards up against such a thing!" Moira was pacing now. It was early morning, and this was not the sort of news she had wished to awaken to. Not at all. She had simply thrown on a wrap when Drukan had sent her an agitated message that her prize pet had escaped. "No, it must have been something else. Perhaps you simply drank too much and slept while he tiptoed past you!"

Drukan frowned but bit back a retort. "I dinna drink on duty, Yer Excellency. And even if he had slipped past me, he would not have gotten past the guards stationed at every entrance."

Moira placed a hand to her throbbing temples and massaged them. "*How* is not important. We . . ." A crafty smile curved her lips. "Perhaps we are mistaken. Perhaps my pretty little caged bird of a prince has not escaped after all."

Drukan looked at her, perplexed. She sighed. "He has clearly left his quarters, yes. But perhaps he is still in Ironforge, simply hiding. There are many places for one to hide in this city."

"Indeed there—oh."

She smiled sweetly. "I will send you as many additional guards as you need to search for him. But you must not attract undue attention! No one must know that he is missing. You have taken the doddering old servant in for questioning?"

Drukan brightened somewhat. "Oh, yes indeed."

"Take care he is not mistreated. We want Anduin . . . cooperative."

"Of course."

"This must stay as quiet as possible. We shall put out word that Anduin is ill. . . . No, no, then that pesky Rohan will insist upon seeing him. What to do, what to do . . ." Moira paced the room, pausing beside her son's cradle and rocking it absently.

"Ah . . . we shall say he has gone to visit Dun Morogh. Yes! That's just the thing." This would accomplish two purposes. It would provide a plausible cover for why Anduin was not available and would give the impression that, at least in some cases, there was contact with the outside world that Moira approved of. Continuing to rock the cradle, she waved a hand at Drukan. "Go, shoo. Be about your task. Oh, and Drukan?" She lifted her eyes from her child and regarded him coldly. "You must make certain that no one knows about Anduin's disappearance and no one knows what has happened here. I will reveal my agenda in my own time, and in my own way. Is that clear?"

Drukan swallowed audibly. "Y-yes, Yer Excellency."

Palkar returned with fresh meat to prepare for his and Drek'Thar's evening meal and found a bedraggled tauren courier waiting for him. He was one of Cairne's Longwalkers, which meant that the news he bore was important indeed. He was weather stained, and Palkar could see dried blood on his clothing. It was uncertain at first glance if the blood was the tauren's or that of another.

"Greetings, Longwalker," he said. "I am Palkar. Come inside and eat with us, then share your news."

"I am Perith Stormhoof," the Longwalker replied. "And my news cannot wait. I will share it with your master now."

Palkar hesitated. He did not like to talk about Drek'Thar's declining health with anyone. "You can share it with me. I will make sure that he receives it. He has not been well as of late and—"

"No," said Perith flatly. "I have instructions to deliver the news to Drek'Thar, and deliver it I shall."

There was no other option. "Drek'Thar's mind is not what it once was. I tend to him. If you speak only to him, your words will be lost."

The tauren twitched an ear, his harsh expression softening slightly. "I regret to hear this news. You may hear it with him, then. But I must speak with him."

"I understand. Come in."

Palkar held open the tent flap, and Perith entered, having to duck as the flap was not designed to accommodate one of his size. Drek'Thar was awake, and his body posture seemed attentive and alert. He was, however, seated a good six feet away from his sleeping furs.

"Drek'Thar, we have an honored guest. It is one of Cairne's Longwalkers, Perith Stormhoof."

"My sleeping furs . . . why did you move them? You are always disturbing my things, Palkar," he said, his voice displaying his confusion.

Palkar gently helped the elderly orc to his feet, guided him to the furs, and helped him into a comfortable seating position.

"Now," Palkar said to Perith, "you may share your news with us."

Perith nodded. "The news is grave. The heart of the matter is that our beloved leader, Cairne Bloodhoof, is murdered, and the Grimtotem have taken over many of our cities in a bloody coup."

Drek'Thar and Palkar both stared at him, horrified. The news seemed to jolt Drek'Thar into one of his lucid phases.

"Who slew the mighty Cairne? What caused this?" the elderly orc demanded in a voice that was surprisingly clear and strong.

Perith recounted the tragedy of the attack on the druids in Ashenvale, and of Hamuul Runetotem's narrow escape. "When Cairne heard of this atrocity, he challenged Garrosh Hellscream to the mak'gora in the arena. Garrosh accepted—but only if Cairne adhered to the old rules. He demanded a battle to the death, and Cairne agreed."

"Then he fell, in fair battle. And the Grimtotem saw the opportunity," Drek'Thar said.

"No. There are rumors circulating that Magatha poisoned Garrosh's blade so that the noble Cairne was felled by nothing more than a nick. I saw her anoint the blade; I saw Cairne fall. I cannot say if Garrosh knew of the deception or was himself deceived. I do know that the Grimtotem did all they could to prevent word from reaching Thunder Bluff. It was only with the greatest care, and the blessing of the Earth Mother, that I eluded their net."

Palkar stared at him, his mind reeling. Cairne assassinated by the matriarch of the Grimtotem? And Garrosh was either duped or a willing participant—either was terrible to contemplate. And now the Grimtotem ruled the tauren.

He tried to gather his thoughts, but Drek'Thar, alert and fully present now, spoke more quickly than he. "Baine? Any word of him?"

"There was an attack on Bloodhoof Village, but Baine escaped. No one has heard from him yet, but we believe he lives. If he were dead, rest assured that Magatha would announce it—and back it up with his head."

Something was bothering Palkar, more than the obvious horror at the news. Something else that Perith had said—

"Then there is still hope. Is Garrosh choosing to aid the usurpers?"

"We have not seen evidence of that."

"If he truly was a participant in the dishonorable murder of Cairne," Drek'Thar continued, "it is unlikely that he would not do all he could to silence Baine and see that those Garrosh supported continued to hold power. The warchief must be advised of these developments at once."

The warchief must be advised. . . .

I must speak with Thrall. . . . He must know. . . .

Ancestors . . . he had been right!

Sweat broke out on Palkar's brow. Two moons ago, Drek'Thar had had a wild, feverish vision in which he proclaimed that soon a peaceful gathering of druids, both night elf and tauren, would be attacked. Palkar had believed him and sent guards to "protect" the gathering, but nothing had happened. He had thought that the "vision" was nothing more than an expression of Drek'Thar's increasing senility.

But Drek'Thar had been right. Now, speaking lucidly with Perith Stormhoof, the old shaman did not appear to even recall the vision. But it had happened, exactly as he had predicted. A peaceable gathering of night elves and tauren had indeed been attacked—and the results had been disastrous. The incident had simply occurred much later than anyone could have expected.

Frantically Palkar recalled Drek'Thar's most recent dream in which he had cried, "The land will weep, and the world will break!" Could it be that this "dream," too, had been a true vision? That it would come true, just as the dream of the druid gathering had?

Palkar had been a fool. Better to have told Thrall of the dream and let the warchief decide for himself whether or not to pay attention to it. Palkar clenched his hands in anger directed not at Drek'Thar, but at himself.

"Palkar?" Drek'Thar was saying.

"I'm sorry—I was thinking—what did you say?"

"I asked if you would write a missive," Drek'Thar said as if he had uttered this request several times. Which, for all Palkar knew, he might have. "We must tell Thrall right away. Even so, it will take time for a Longwalker to find him. We can only hope we are not too late to help Baine."

"Of course," Palkar replied, leaping up to obey. He

would write whatever Drek'Thar and the Longwalker wished. And then, at the end, he would confess to the warchief all that he had kept from him and why, and let things fall as they might.

He would not risk Drek'Thar's being right a second time.

TWENTY-FIVE

Thrall was surprised at the level of involvement and effort it took to prepare for the vision quest. He understood now Geyah's comment about Drek'Thar's doing his best as one of the last shaman the orcs then had. It would seem that a "proper" vision quest involved nearly the entire community.

Someone came to measure him for a ritual robe. Someone else offered the herbs for the rite. A third orc came to volunteer to lead the drumming and chanting circles, and six more offered their drums and voices. Thrall was surprised and moved. At one point he said to Aggra, "I do not wish for any favors to be done to me because of my position."

She gave him a slight smirk. "Go'el, it is because you are in need of a vision quest, not because you are the leader of the Horde. You do not need to worry about any favors."

It both relieved him and embarrassed him, and he wondered, not for the first time, how it was that Aggra was so adept at getting under his skin. Maybe it was a gift from the elements, he mused drily as he watched her stride off, head high.

He chafed at the delay, but there was little he could do about it. And there was a part of him, a not insignificant part, that anticipated the ritual eagerly. So much had been lost to the orcs in the years before he became a shaman himself. His own experience of such communal rites was lacking, he knew.

At last, three days later, all was prepared. Torches were lit at dusk. Thrall waited at Garadar to be escorted to the prepared ceremonial site. Aggra came to get him, and he did a double take at her.

Her long, thick, reddish-brown hair was braided with feathers. She wore a leather vest and kilt embroidered with feathers and beads, and symbols in white and green paint decorated her face and elsewhere where her brown skin was revealed. She stood tall and straight and proud, the tan of the leather setting off the dark brown of her skin to perfection. In her arms, she bore a bundle of cloth as brown as her skin.

"These are for you, Go'el," she said. "They are plain and simple. Initiate's robes for an initiation."

"I understand," Thrall said, reaching out to take the bundle from her.

She did not surrender it to him. "I am not certain that you do. I admit, you are a gifted and powerful shaman. But there is much you still do not know about it. We do not wear armor in our initiations. An initiation is a rebirth, not a battle. Like the snake, we shed the skins of who we were before. We need to approach it without those burdens, without the narrow thoughts and notions that we have held. We need to be simple, clean, ready to understand and connect with the elements and let them write their wisdom on our souls."

Thrall listened intently and nodded respectfully. Still, she did not give him the robes, not yet. "You will also find a necklace of prayer beads. This will help you reconnect with your inner self, so you may touch them as you feel called."

Now, finally, she extended the bundle to him. He accepted it. "I will return shortly," she said, and left.

Thrall regarded the plain brown garment, then slowly and respectfully put it on. He felt . . . naked. He was used to wearing the distinctive black plate armor that had once belonged to Orgrim Doomhammer. He wore it nearly every waking moment and had grown accustomed to its weight. This garment was light. He slipped the prayer beads around his neck, rolling them between his fingers, thinking hard on what Aggra had said. He was to be reborn, she had told him.

As what? And as who?

"Well," said Aggra, startling him out of his reverie, "it would seem initiate's robes suit you after all."

"I am ready," Thrall said quietly.

"Not quite yet. You are not painted."

She stepped forward, with her usual brusque manner, to a small chest nestled against the hide wall, rummaged about, and emerged with three small pots of colored clay. "You are too tall. Sit."

Somewhat amused, Thrall did so. She stepped toward him, opened one of the jars, dabbed some clay on her finger, and began applying it to his face. Her touch was deft, strangely gentle for someone Thrall had known to be so forceful, the clay cool; and this close to her, Thrall could smell the sweet, light scent of the oil with which she had anointed herself. She frowned slightly at him.

"What is wrong?"

"These colors do not look the same on green skin."

"I fear I cannot change that, Aggra, no matter how much studying with you I do," he said, his voice and expression utterly sincere and concerned.

She looked him right in the eye for a long moment, irritation furrowing her brow. And then she smiled. A hearty chuckle rumbled from her.

"Ancestors know, that is true," she said. "It seems as though it is I who must change the colors of the paint, then."

They both smiled, looking at one another, then Aggra dropped her gaze. "Perhaps blue and yellow instead," she said and retrieved the appropriate jars. She continued painting his face in silence. Finally she nodded her approval, then frowned again. "Your hair . . . one moment."

She wiped her hands. Long, clever brown fingers undid the two long braids that Thrall usually wore, and she quickly braided feathers into the hair. "Now. Now you are ready, Go'el."

Aggra fetched a polished sheet of metal that would serve as a mirror.

Thrall almost did not recognize himself.

His green skin was now adorned with dots and swirls of yellow and blue, as if he wore a mask. His hair, braided with bright feathers from the windroc, fell about his shoulders in a thick mass. Normally he was contained, controlled. Now, he realized he looked . . .

". . . wild," he said quietly.

"Like the elements," she said. "There is little that is calm and orderly about them, Go'el. You now begin your vision quest kin to them. Come. They are waiting."

Thrall had been through a great deal in his life. He had been taught to fight while still a child, had learned about friendship and hardship in the same formative years. He had liberated his people and fought demons. And yet now, as he followed Aggra outside to the prepared site next to the lake, he found that he was nervous.

The drumming started as soon as he appeared. Aggra straightened. She lost both her lightness and her aggressiveness, and for a moment she seemed to him to be a younger version of Geyah. She moved with a graceful, solemn step, and he slowed his own pace to match hers. It seemed the entire population of Garadar had turned out, standing to form a line on either side of the path. The torches kept the darkness at bay for a few feet, but after that the shadows waited. Up ahead, standing waiting for him, propped up on a staff, was Geyah. She looked beautiful, if fragile, and her wrinkled face was luminous and smiling. He drew up to her, then bowed deeply.

"Welcome, Go'el, son of Durotan, who was son of Garad." Thrall's eyes widened slightly. Of course—he should have realized it earlier. Garad was his grandfather, and he now stood in Garadar, a place named after him. "Child of and chosen of the elements. Not so far from this site, the Furies watch over us. They will behold the ceremony held this night."

Thrall glanced out over the black water. He could see only one of the Furies—Incineratus, the Fury of Fire, moving slowly about. But he knew the others were there.

"It is well," he said, as he had been instructed. "I offer my body, mind, and spirit to this vision quest."

Aggra took his hand, led him forward to the center of the pile of skins that had been placed on the ground, and brought him down with her.

"When you embark upon this quest," she said, "your soul leaves your body. Know that while you journey in the world of spirit, your people will keep careful watch over your physical form. Here. Take this draft. Drink it down swiftly."

She handed him a cup of a vile-smelling liquid. Thrall accepted it, his fingers brushing hers as he did so. He gulped the liquid down as quickly as possible, then swallowed again, hard, to keep the unpleasant concoction in his stomach. Even as he handed the cup back to Aggra, he began to feel light-headed. He did not protest as she reached for him and settled his head on her lap. It was an oddly tender gesture, coming from one who had previously been so curt, but he accepted it.

His head spun, and the drumming seemed to throb through his veins, as if it were not heard so much as felt. As if the sound were merging with his own heartbeat.

Cool fingers caressed his hair. Again, unusual for Aggra. Her voice—deep, soft, kind—came to him as if from far, far away.

"Go within yourself and outside yourself, Go'el. Nothing shall harm you here, though you may be afraid of what you see."

Thrall opened his eyes.

A shimmering, misty figure stood before him. It had luminous eyes, four legs, sharp teeth, and a tail. It was a spirit wolf, and he knew, without understanding how he knew, that it was Aggra.

"You will lead me?" he asked the wolf, confused. "I thought Grandmother—"

"I was chosen to guide you. Come," said Aggra, her voice husky and somehow suited to issuing from a wolf's muzzle. "It is time. Follow me!"

And suddenly Thrall, too, was a wolf. The world changed in front of him, some things becoming insubstantial, other things taking on a new, strange solidity. He shook himself, feeling lighter than air, part of the nothingness that was everything, and followed her into the swirling mist.

They emerged into the bright light of a noonday sun, in an arena. Thrall, in spirit wolf form, blinked in confusion.

He was looking at himself.

"What . . ." the now-Thrall said, his voice sounding strange in his own ears. "I thought I was to meet the elements and—"

"Silence!" Aggra's reprimand was a harsh, short bark, and Thrall obeyed. "Observe only. Do not try to interact. No one here can see or hear you. This is your vision quest, Go'el. It will show you exactly what you need to know."

Now-Thrall nodded and watched.

Younger Thrall was clad in a few pieces of armor. His body was fit and toned, sweat gleaming on green skin, and he was armed with a sword in one hand and a mace in the other. Now-Thrall knew where he was—he was in the arena at Durnholde Keep. The sounds of both cheers and boos were thunderous, and he knew that somewhere up there, eating fruit and drinking wine, was the hated Aedelas Blackmoore. The man who had taken him as an infant and turned him into a gladiator. Anger burned in him, even as he watched his younger self fighting a huge bear.

"Fire," Aggra said. "It was the first of the elements to choose you, Go'el. It gave you the anger, the outrage, to fight fiercely. It gave you the passion to fight well, for the right causes, as soon as you could do so. It burns deep within you, sustaining you even in your dark moments."

Thrall listened, watching himself, surprised at just how strong and graceful and, yes, impassioned he was when he was in the ring. Knowing that he had taken those skills and used them to free his people, to protect them.

This was not what he had expected to see, but he nodded to Aggra's words. Fire had indeed come to him as a youth, and he thought back to the concern that burned high in him even now to aid his world. He smiled, with perhaps just a touch of understandable pride, as his younger self defeated his opponents and raised his arms in victory.

The mist crept back into the scene, swirling about the shouting, victorious younger Thrall until it obscured him completely. Thrall waited, curious as to what other unexpected visions he would see in this strange journey.

The mist cleared. The arena, with its brightness and noise, was gone. In its stead was a forested nightscape, the only sounds the soft ones of wind and insects. Thrall again saw himself, but this time he looked wary. Hunted. He stood before a stone formation that, viewed from the right angle, resembled a dragon standing guard over the woodlands. The younger Thrall turned his head, regarding the dark oval mouth of a nearby cave, and Now-Thrall suddenly knew, with a jolt of deep, old pain and a new spike of torment, what was about to happen.

Nightmares. He had been at war with them. The whole world had.

"Must I watch this?" he asked quietly, knowing the answer even as he voiced the question.

"If you wish to understand, to become a true shaman, then yes," Aggra said implacably.

Younger Thrall entered the cave, and both incarnations of himself beheld a young human woman named Taretha Foxton. Tari . . . Blackmoore's mistress, Thrall's "sister" of the spirit. Who had risked everything to free him, and who would eventually lose her life for that act. But she was alive, now, alive and vibrant and so beautiful. His nightmare had been about her—about trying, repeatedly, to save her. Again and again he had tried, in the dream coming up with a new idea in which she would live, laugh, love, as she should have. And each time he had failed and been forced to experience her death over and over and *over*. . . .

But she was not dying, not now, not here. She leaned

against the wall, waiting for him, and when he spoke her name, she gasped, then laughed. Her face was lovely, all the more appealing for the genuine warmth of affection lighting it.

"You startled me! I did not know you moved so quietly!" She moved toward him, stretching out her hands. Slowly, Younger Thrall folded them in his own.

"It still hurts," Now-Thrall said to Aggra. She did not chide him, not this time, but merely nodded her ghostly wolf's head.

"That hurting, and the healing of the hurting, is the gift of Water," she said. "Deep emotion. Love. The heart wide open, to joy and pain both. It is why we weep . . . water is moving with and through us."

He listened quietly, remembering the words he and Taretha had shared at this, their first true meeting, as he heard them again. She gave him a map and some supplies, urging him to go find his people—the orcs. They spoke of Blackmoore. Now-Thrall, knowing what was to come, wanted to turn away but found he could not.

"What is happening to your eyes?" Younger Thrall asked.

"Oh, Thrall . . . these are called tears," Taretha said quietly, her voice thick as she wiped at her eyes. "They come when we are so sad, so soul sick, that it's as if our hearts are so full of pain there's no place else for it to go."

And even though he was traveling in the spirit world and had no physical body, Now-Thrall felt tears welling in his own eyes.

"Taretha understood," Aggra said, her own voice soft

with understanding. "She knew pain and love both. The heart swells to overflowing, and Water flows forth."

"She should not have died," Now-Thrall growled. Unspoken were the words: *I should have found a way to stop it.*

Aggra's response staggered him as surely as if she had struck a powerful blow.

"Truly? Shouldn't she?"

He whirled on her, stunned and furious at her callousness. "Of course not! She had everything to live for. Her death accomplished nothing!"

Aggra's wolf form regarded him implacably. "How do you know this was not her destiny? That perhaps she had done all she had been born to do? Only she knows. Maybe you would not have been moved to the same action, had she lived. It is arrogance to believe you can know all things. Perhaps you are right. But perhaps you are not."

Her words left him staring in mute silence. He had been racked with guilt ever since the moment he saw Taretha's severed head lifted in a ghastly display by Aedelas Blackmoore. The nightmares had only served to hammer him with the message: *I should have done something more.*

But there truly had been nothing he could have done. And now, for the first time, he was forced to consider the idea that maybe what had happened . . . had been right. Painful, horrible, racking. But maybe . . . right.

He would never forget her. Never stop missing her. But that sense of guilt was lifting.

"For you," Aggra continued as he stood silently trying to understand the shift in his soul, "she was the blessing of Water in your life. This time, this female—this, Go'el, was when the element moved into your being."

He struggled for words. All that came out was, "Thank you."

The mist began to swirl at the feet of the figures of the past. Although he initially had not wished to relive this incident, now that it was about to slip away, Now-Thrall wanted to cry out, to beg for a few moments more with Taretha, but he knew better. This had been a bittersweet gift from the elements, along with the insight Aggra had given him.

Farewell, dear Taretha. Your life was a blessing, your death not a waste, and there are not many in this world who can say that. And you will always be remembered. I can let you go with peace in my heart, now.

The elements had more to show him.

The mist swirled, obscuring his vision, and then once again he was beholding a younger version of himself. It was winter, and he was with the Frostwolves. He and Drek'Thar were seated by the fire, reaching their hands out to it. Drek'Thar was certainly not young at this time, but his mind was still sharp, and Now-Thrall knew sadness as he watched his friend and tutor. His younger self listened raptly to Drek'Thar as he spoke with deep eloquence about the bond between the shaman and the elements. Snow fell softly. Now-Thrall, even merely watching, felt still and centered, felt the heartache of the recent vision of Taretha ease ever so slightly.

"Grounded," he said, understanding for the first time where the word came from. "Like the earth. This is Earth's gift, isn't it?"

The wolf that was Aggra nodded, and with a hint of her old acerbicness added, "You only now are discovering this? No wonder you are having difficulties."

This time Thrall found that he was not irritated, only amused. Perhaps, he thought, it was the calmness and steadiness of Earth moving through him. All too soon, it seemed to Now-Thrall, the mists inexorably rose up again, hiding the scene. Thrall understood, though, that Earth was within him now. He could go to this place of peace inside anytime he needed to . . . and he smiled . . . ground himself.

There was one element left. He understood by this point that the vision quest was supposed to show him how the elements were already integrated in him, living with and through him. He understood the fiery passion of battle, the loving nature of Water, and the calmness and steadfastness of Earth. But he was curious as to how Air would manifest.

The mist formed, and cleared, and he saw himself in Grommash Hold. It was again late at night, but braziers, torches, and oil lamps provided more than enough illumination and warmth. He stood in front of a table spread with maps and rolled-up scrolls, and beside him stood his old, dear friend Cairne Bloodhoof.

He could not pinpoint this moment, as he had all the others, because this scene had happened in various ways over the last several years. He smiled, watching as his other self and Cairne spoke animatedly about negotiations, land rights, treaties. How they worked through problems, and found solutions. The scene shifted quickly, and he was standing with Jaina, as he had also done many times, and together they spoke of peace and how to achieve it.

There was no deep emotion, other than concern for the safety of the people he led. No great sense of rootedness, or burning passion for an outcome. With Jaina and with Cairne at these moments, Thrall used his head rather than his powerful body or emotions. This was rational, intellectual conversation—talk of new beginnings. Of hope.

Now-Thrall nodded, understanding it all. Of course. Air—the element of clarity of thought, of inspiration, insight, and fresh starts. He had begun again with Cairne when the orcs had arrived on Kalimdor, and had forged a tentative peace with Jaina Proudmoore. All with words, and careful thought. Attributes that some did not expect to find in orcs, but which Thrall had cultivated all his life—from his youngest days devouring books to this moment, where he had made a difficult decision to leave his world and come here, to Outland, to Nagrand.

He smiled a little, and as the scene began to fade, he let it go easily. Because he knew that with Air, there would always be something new to come, to challenge and inspire him.

He stayed, in the strange being-not-being place, with Aggra in spirit wolf form, waiting either for the fifth element, the elusive spark that enabled the shaman to connect with the other elements, to manifest, or for some sign to be given that would aid him. The time passed, but nothing happened. Thrall began to feel agitated. Finally he turned to Aggra, confused. His voice echoed in the not-place. "Will I be able to save Azeroth? The Horde?"

The mist cleared suddenly. Thrall saw himself wearing the black armor that Orgrim Doomhammer had bequeathed him as leader of the Horde. He carried that late orc's great weapon, looking every inch the warrior. But there was fear on his green face—fear, and a terrible sense of loss. The Doomhammer split into several chunks, each piece hurtling away as if it had been fired from a gun. The armor cracked and fell off, and Thrall fell to his knees, clad only in what he wore now—the simple brown robe of an initiate.

"No," Thrall breathed. And that quickly, he was awake. He found himself staring up into a dark-skinned orcish face bending over his, with gorgeous paint, kind eyes, and wide, smiling lips curving over two small, sharp tusks. He reached and gripped her arm.

"Aggra, I failed! Or, rather, I'm going to! They showed—"

"Shh," she soothed, shaking her head, calm in the face of his panic. "They showed you an image. It is up to you to decide what it means."

He started to get to his feet, then caught himself, dizzy. Gently she eased him into a sitting position. "It seemed clear enough to me."

"I saw it, too," she said. "And trust me when I say that the clearest visions are often the most confusing. But—there is a way to find clarity. I think you are ready to see the Furies. You have completed the vision quest. You realize that you have integrated the elements within you now. You are ready."

"They will help me understand the vision at the end?"

She shrugged. "Maybe not. It certainly couldn't hurt, now, could it?"

He found himself smiling. Her tongue-in-cheek brusqueness was exactly what he needed.

"When?"

"Tomorrow," Aggra said. "Tomorrow."

TWENTY-SIX

Thrall was surprised that the Throne of the Elements was so easily accessible, and so close to Garadar. It was but a short run across Skysong Lake to a small island nestled against the mountains. As they drew closer, he saw moss-covered standing stones arranged in a pattern.

"Why are the Furies so close?" he asked Aggra as they ran.

She gave him a wry smile, but her eyes had more mischief than anger in them as she replied, "If *you* were a giant embodiment of an elemental force, would you be worried by anyone disturbing you?"

Caught off guard, Thrall laughed, a short, amused bark. Aggra's smile widened. "There are members of the Earthen Ring there who make certain that the Furies are not bothered by trivialities. Only those who have need of their wisdom or who are sincere in offering their aid may speak with them. Even so, it is just a courtesy. The Furies can certainly handle themselves."

They left the lake, and their feet now trod upon marshy soil.

And suddenly, there they were.

Four mammoth beings, resembling the smaller incarnations of the elements with which Thrall had worked for so long, moved slowly about. They were tempestuous, wild, and powerful. Even at a distance he could sense their tremendous strength. No, these beings certainly did not have to be concerned if anyone irritated them.

Speaking in a soft, reverent voice, Aggra identified each one. "Gordawg, Fury of Earth. Aborius, Fury of Water. Incineratus, Fury of Fire. And Kalandrios, Fury of Air. If anyone or anything in this land can help you, Go'el," said Aggra, her voice quietly sincere, "it is these beings. Go. Introduce yourself. Ask them your questions."

For a moment Thrall was catapulted back in time to his first encounter with the elements. One by one, the spirits of each element had come to him, spoken in his mind and heart. Now, in a similar fashion, they might do so again. Which to approach first? He chose Kalandrios, Fury of Air, and began moving forward.

Almost immediately he felt that being's power buffet him. He stumbled, the intense wind nearly knocking him off his feet, but pressed onward, lowering his head against the whirling air.

The great Fury looked to him like a living cyclone with strong arms and glowing red eyes. At first Kalandrios ignored him, and then Thrall planted himself against the wind, heavy with sand and leaves that threatened to scour his skin, closed his eyes, and reached out with his mind, as he had been taught.

Kalandrios, Fury of Air . . . I have come a long way to ask your aid. I come from a land that is deeply troubled, but I know not why it suffers. I ask for its aid, and it does not reply to me. On my vision quest, I saw myself unable to save my land. You, who hear the cries of Air here in Outland—can you aid me? Is this vision true and unalterable?

Kalandrios turned his red eyes upon him, and Thrall felt the power of that direct gaze. He spoke, but in Thrall's mind.

What care I for the trials of Air in another land? My own essences suffer here. Air rules the power of thought, Go'el, known as Thrall, son of Durotan and Draka. You are a powerful shaman, for me to even hear your plea. The best I can offer you is to think, and listen. Think on what you saw on your quest. More, I cannot give.

And Kalandrios moved off again, unable to give him any insight. Thrall felt disappointment well up inside him but tamped it down. It would not serve him to grow angry at the Furies. If Kalandrios could have helped, Thrall believed that he would have. Still, he could not shake the notion that there was a flaw in Kalandrios's argument.

He glanced back over at Aggra and shook his head. The Furies were speaking only in his heart; she had not heard Kalandrios. Once, she would have smirked at his failure, he knew. Now he saw her strong face fill with consternation. He moved on to the next Fury.

This was Incineratus, Fury of Fire, and as Thrall approached, the heat roiled off the mighty being with such intensity that Thrall was forced to turn his head and shield his face with his arms. How was he to approach such a being, if doing so would burn the flesh from his bones?

The knowledge came to him gently. Ignoring the painful heat of the Fury's fire, he reached for calmness within himself—from the element of the Spirit of Life he carried inside. He calmed himself, soothed his roiling thoughts, and visualized his skin whole, cool, able to withstand even the mighty Fury's heat. He turned around to face Incineratus, opened his eyes . . . and the heat abated. Now Thrall could move forward and did so, kneeling before the Fury of Fire and repeating his request.

Incineratus turned his full attention upon the orc, and even with his newfound stability, Thrall was forced to close his eyes against the heat the being radiated as he moved to but a few feet in front of him. His throat felt seared as he inhaled, but he did not move away. He was strong enough to speak with this being; he would not be harmed.

I am angry for what you say to me, the Fury of Fire said in his mind. *I am angry that my own kindlings suffer here, and I regret more than you can possibly comprehend that I cannot aid you. Without some essence of Fire from this place, how can I speak with the fires that burn there? How can I know why they suffer and leap in torment, shaman? It is your land, your observations. I feel your passion for your cause, and I grant you my own—the passion to do whatever is necessary so that your world may heal. More, I cannot do.*

A small flicker detached itself and dove down Thrall's throat. He cried out, feeling it burn as it settled into him and seemed to wrap around his heart. It scorched, painfully, but he knew this was no actual, literal flame. He clapped a hand to his chest, over his heart, and fell forward, leaning on his other hand.

Aggra was there, her touch cool and comforting on his shoulder. "Go'el, did he harm you?"

Thrall shook his head. The pain was receding. "No," he said. "Not . . . not physically."

Her eyes searched his, then she regarded Incineratus. The great Elemental Fury was already moving off, having dismissed Thrall. She reached in her bag for a flask of water, but he placed a hand on her arm and shook his head.

"No," he rasped. "Incineratus . . . gifted me with the fire of passion, to do what I need to do."

Slowly Aggra nodded. "As you learned last night, that fire burns within you already. But this is a great gift indeed. Very few have felt the brush of Incineratus's fire."

He knew by what she did not say that she herself had not been so honored. He felt compelled to add, "I do not think the gift was for me. It was for the elements in Azeroth, that I might be better able to help them."

"I have asked for such, to help the kindlings here," she said quietly. "I was not deemed worthy."

He grasped her hand. "You are skilled, Aggra. And it could be that the fire that burns within you already is enough."

Startled, she lifted her eyes to his. He expected her to tug her hand away and make a sharp retort. Instead, Aggra let her hand remain in his, brown fingers entwined with green, for a long moment before squeezing gently and moving away.

"There are two more," she said, once again controlled

and brusque in her demeanor. "While you have a great gift, perhaps Gordawg and Aborius will be able to help you more than Incineratus and Kalandrios could. Give you a little clarity on what you saw, perhaps. I find myself that sometimes their mysteries irritate more than they enlighten."

He was surprised at her irreverence but found himself forced to agree with it. Sometimes Fire and Air were both a little bit flighty.

The metaphysical fire had died down to an ember in his heart now, but he could still feel it. He moved on to Aborius, moving in a circle around the Throne of the Elements, and knelt before the Fury of Water.

She turned around at once. Thrall had not even mentally voiced his plea before he felt the patter of a gentle spray of water across his upturned face. He licked his lips; it was sweet and clean, the freshest water he had ever tasted.

Go'el, your pain and confusion are as my own. Many come here with concerns, but few feel them as strongly as you do. Would that I could aid you, in this world that houses the droplets that are of me and yet not of me. Your heart is already afire with the passion to help, to heal. To put right a world sorely troubled. I cannot give you such a gift as Incineratus did, but I will tell you, do not be ashamed of your feelings. Water shall give you the balance you seek; it shall replenish and restore. Do not be afraid of anything you feel in this journey to save your world. Neither be afraid of the wound within your own soul, which you must heal.

Thrall was confused. *I? I have no wound, great Fury, save the pain at the torment my world is in.*

He felt a brush of compassionate humor. *One faces one's burdens when one is ready, not before. But I say again unto you, Go'el, son of Durotan, son of Garad—when the time comes that you are ready to heal your wound, do not be afraid to dive deep.*

Water was running down his face now. Again Thrall opened his mouth to taste the sweet liquid, but instead found it to be warm and salty. Tears. He was weeping, openly, and for a moment Aborius allowed Thrall to feel the element's own empathy for him.

He sobbed, unashamed, knowing that what he felt was good and true. Tears were part of the gift that loving Taretha Foxton had given him, as had been so poignantly revealed to him last night. Even more than wanting to liberate his people from the camps, even more than wanting them to have a land where they would be safe and happy, Thrall realized that he wanted the world in which he had been born to be whole. Only then would the other things follow. Only when Azeroth had recovered from this strange, angry hurting that was causing it to shake and quiver and weep, only then could the Horde, or, indeed, the Alliance, truly grow and thrive. This was why he had felt called to come to Outland. This was why he had left the Horde behind, the Horde he had loved and helped create. It truly had been the only choice.

He got to his feet, shaking, dragging an arm across his eyes, and turned to the final Fury.

Gordawg was perhaps the most imposing of the Furies, even more so than the fiery Incineratus. The Fury of Earth was like a mountain come to life, and as Thrall approached, the earth beneath him trembled.

Gordawg seemed to take no notice of Thrall, instead striding away from him as the orc hastened to follow. Thrall reached out imploringly with his thoughts. Finally Gordawg came to a halt so abruptly that Thrall almost ran into him.

Massively, slowly, he turned and gazed down at the orc, so small in comparison.

What you wish of Gordawg?

I come from a land called Azeroth. The elemental spirits there are troubled. They voice their pain in wildfires, floods, earthquakes.

Gordawg peered down at him, his glowing eyes narrowing.

Why so pained?

I do not know, Fury. I ask them, but their replies are chaotic. All I know is that they suffer. Your fellow Furies have been unable to help me solve this mystery so that I can aid the elements of Azeroth.

Gordawg nodded, as if he had been expecting this.

Gordawg want to help. But other land far away. Cannot help without knowing land.

Thrall was not surprised. It was the same reason the other Furies had given for being unable to help: it was not their world, and they did not know it.

A thought came to him. *Gordawg, there is a portal between Azeroth and what remains of Draenor. Once, it was closed so that the destruction of Draenor would not pass to my world. Now, the illness of my world could pass to yours, if I do not stop it. Can you do nothing to help me? And in helping me, perhaps protect Outland?*

Gordawg hears what you say. Gordawg understands the

need. And yet Gordawg says again—of this world, Gordawg knows. The great being knelt, scooped up a handful of earth, and popped it into his maw before Thrall's startled gaze. *I taste. I can tell where this earth has been, what its secrets are.*

Thrall's eyes widened as an idea came to him. Could it be so simple?

He always carried with him a small transportable altar—a feather to represent Air, a small chalice for Water, flint and tinder for Fire . . .

. . . and a small rock for Earth. Now he fumbled in his pouch with fingers gone shaky with hope and fear commingled. Finally his hand emerged, holding the small rock in his palm.

It was an actual piece of an element of Azeroth; the other items—flint and tinder, a chalice, a feather—were only symbols. But this *was* the element it represented.

Gordawg . . . here is a stone from my world. If you can glean anything from it, I ask you, please tell me.

Gordawg stared. The rock was small. He bent over, extending his giant hand, and Thrall dropped the stone into it.

Not much for Gordawg to taste, he grumbled. *But Gordawg try. Gordawg wish to help.*

The stone was but a tiny speck on his hand, and Thrall watched it vanish into the massive gullet. He glanced over at Aggra, who spread her hands and shrugged. She was as confused as he.

Suddenly Gordawg growled. *Not the way of the earth. Not right. Angry, frightened stone here. Something has made it so!*

Thrall listened, barely breathing.

Something that was once right, but now is wrong. Was of the world, but now is unnatural and dark. Was wounded, once, but now is healed in a way—but the healing also wrong. Is angry. Wants to make others wounded. Will hurt the earth to do so. Must be stopped!

He stamped his foot, and the earth shook.

This . . . something, Thrall thought. *It is in Azeroth?*

Stone fears its coming. Not there, not yet. But stone is afraid. Poor stone. He lifted a hand and extended a finger, pointing it at Thrall. *You hear cries of frightened stone. Of all the elements. These quakes of the earth, giant waves, fires—that is the elements telling you they are afraid. You must stop them from being wounded . . . maybe destroyed completely!*

How do I do that? Please tell me!

Gordawg shook his enormous head. *Gordawg not know. Perhaps other shaman who also hear the frightened stone might know. But I tell you this. I have tasted something like this fear before. Almost kind of fear I taste in the earth right before this world ripped to pieces. Is fear of being broken. Being shattered.*

Gordawg turned and strode off. Thrall stared after him, shocked.

"He ate the stone you gave him," Aggra said, stepping up beside Thrall. "Was he able to help?"

"Yes," said Thrall, his voice a whisper. He cleared his throat, shook his head. "He told me that the stone was afraid. That all the elements are afraid. They know something dreadful is coming. Something that was once good and in harmony with the world, but now is unnatural. It's been hurt, and it burns with the desire to hurt other things."

He turned to her. "And one final thing. I have to go back to Azeroth. I don't think they would have helped me if I couldn't do something. I have to see if I can figure out what exactly the elements are so terrified of . . . and do all in my power to stop it. Because that stone was emitting a similar kind of terror to what Draenor felt before—"

"—before it was shattered," Aggra finished, her own eyes wide with fear. "Yes, Go'el. Yes! We must not let such a cataclysm happen twice!"

Once the bloodlust and the thrill of victory over Cairne had passed—Cairne Bloodhoof, a legend, one of the great figures of the Horde's history in Azeroth—Garrosh was somewhat surprised to find himself dealing with mixed emotions.

Cairne had been the one to challenge him. Garrosh still wasn't exactly sure why. Cairne had hurled accusations about—something about some attack on druids somewhere. Garrosh had had no idea what he was talking about, but once that humiliating blow had been struck and Cairne had invoked the challenge, there had been no turning back. For either of them. The old bull had fought well. Garrosh would never admit it, but he had been worried that he might not survive the fight. But he had. Garrosh bore the blood of the tauren high chieftain on his hands, yes, but there was no guilt. It had been a fair fight, each combatant had been aware that only one would walk away alive, and honor had been satisfied.

And yet . . . while there was no guilt, Garrosh found there was regret. He had not disliked Cairne, although the two had clashed repeatedly over their beliefs in what was best for the Horde. It had been a shame that Cairne simply could not wrap his old-fashioned mind around what needed to be done.

After the wild celebrating of those who had been supporting Garrosh had died down and the night was moving toward dawn, Garrosh found himself back at the arena. Cairne's body had been removed almost immediately, to where, he did not know. He wasn't sure what the tauren did with their dead. Bury them, burn them?

There was still blood on the floor of the arena. Garrosh supposed someone would have to come clean it up. He would see to it on the morrow. For now, he was embarrassed that he had neglected the vital task of cleaning his blade for too long. Speaking of . . . where was—He looked around, becoming increasingly worried when he did not see the axe.

"Are you looking for Gorehowl?" The voice startled Garrosh. He turned to see one of the Kor'kron standing there, holding out his cherished axe and bowing. "We retrieved it and put it in a safe place until you wished it."

"My thanks," said Garrosh. He was a little uncomfortable with the nearly constant and yet often unnoticed presence of the elite unit of bodyguards. But he had to admit, they were handy at times like this. He was angry that he had allowed himself to be so carried away as to forget Gorehowl. It would not happen again. He waved the bodyguard away, and the Kor'kron bowed again and moved into the shadows, leaving Garrosh alone with the axe that had been his father's.

As he regarded the axe, and the blood on the arena where Cairne had fallen, he heard a voice behind him. An orc's—but not one of his bodyguards.

"This is a loss to the Horde, and I know you know it."

Garrosh turned to see Eitrigg sitting up in the stands. What was the old orc doing here? He couldn't remember seeing Eitrigg during the combat, but surely he had to have been present. Garrosh found he didn't remember much about the actual fight itself; it was no wonder that he hadn't been paying attention to who else was watching. He had been rather occupied at the time.

He debated chastising the other orc, but found he was strangely weary. "I do know it. But I had no choice. He challenged me."

"Many saw the challenge. I don't dispute that. But did you not notice how quickly he fell?"

Unease stirred in Garrosh. "I do not remember much. It was . . . fast, and heated."

Eitrigg nodded. Slowly, for Garrosh knew his joints pained him, Eitrigg rose and descended to the floor of the arena, speaking as he went. "It was. How many blows did you receive? How many did Cairne deal? Many. And yet he fell so quickly from just one."

"It was a good blow," Garrosh said, his voice sounding petulant in his own ears. Had it been? It had been right across the chest. Hadn't it? The bloodlust hazed everything—

"No." Eitrigg spoke bluntly. "It was a long but shallow cut. And yet he did not defend himself when the death strike came." By now Eitrigg stood beside him. "Do you not think that odd? I certainly did. And I am not alone in my observation. Cairne died far too quickly, Garrosh, and if you didn't notice it, others did. Others like me, and Vol'jin, who came to me just a short while ago. Others who wonder how it is that such a fine warrior fell with just a glancing blow."

Garrosh was starting to grow angry. "Out with it!" he growled. "What are you trying to say? Are you saying I did not win this fight fairly? Would I have let him give me these wounds had I been attempting to cheat?"

"No. I do not think you fought dishonorably. But I believe someone did." Eitrigg extended a gnarled finger and pointed at Gorehowl. "You received a shamanic blessing with sacred oil on your blade."

"So did Cairne. So does everyone who chooses to fight in the mak'gora," Garrosh said. "It's *part* of it. That is not dishonorable!" He was starting to raise his voice, and a strange emotion was churning inside him. Was it—fear?

"Look at the color of the oil," Eitrigg said. "It is black and sticky. No—in the ancestors' names, *do not touch it*!"

Most of the blade that had taken Cairne Bloodhoof's life was coated with dried blood. But in one small spot along the edge, Garrosh could now see a tacky-looking, black substance that did not in any way resemble the golden, glistening oil with which blades were usually anointed.

"Who blessed Gorehowl, Garrosh Hellscream? Who blessed the axe that slew Cairne Bloodhoof?" Eitrigg's voice held anger, but it was not directed at Garrosh.

A sick feeling twisted Garrosh's gut. "Magatha Grimtotem," he said, his voice a hoarse whisper.

"It was not your skill in battle that killed your opponent. It was the poison of an evil schemer who sought to destroy an adversary and used you, like a pawn, to do so. Do you know what has happened in Thunder Bluff? While you were out celebrating?"

Garrosh did not want to hear. He stared at the blade, but Eitrigg pressed on.

"Grimtotem assassins have taken over Thunder Bluff, Bloodhoof Village, and other tauren strongholds. The teachers, the powerful shaman, and druids and warriors—all dead. Innocent tauren slaughtered in their sleep. Baine Bloodhoof is missing and is probably dead, too. Blood pours from a peaceful city, because you were too full of pride to notice what was happening literally right in front of your eyes!"

Garrosh had been listening in increasing horror, and now he bellowed, "Enough! *Silence,* old one!" They stood there staring at one another.

And then something broke in Garrosh. "She robbed me of my honor," he said quietly. "She took my kill from me. I will never know now if I would have been strong enough to defeat Cairne Bloodhoof in a fair fight. Eitrigg, you must believe me!"

For the first time that night, the old orc's eyes held a glimmer of sympathy. "I do, Garrosh. No one has ever questioned your honor in battle. If Cairne knew what was happening to him as he died, I believe he knew you were not to blame. But know that doubt has been sown here tonight. Doubt that you fought fairly—and they are speaking of it, in hushed whispers. Not everyone is as understanding as I and Cairne Bloodhoof."

Garrosh stared again at the blood- and poison-coated weapon he bore. Magatha had stolen his honor. Had stolen his respect in the eyes of the Horde he so loved. She had used him, used Gorehowl, too, a weapon his father had once wielded. It had been coated with poison, the coward's weapon. It, too, had been dishonored. And Magatha, in performing such a base, deceitful act, had spat in the face of her shamanic traditions. And Eitrigg was telling him that there were some who believed he would willingly be involved in this?

No! He would show Vol'jin and any others who voiced their lies exactly what he thought of them. He closed his eyes, clenched his hand on the hilt of Gorehowl, and let the rage take him.

TWENTY-SEVEN

Jaina's first instinct upon seeing Anduin materialize so unexpectedly, almost literally in front of her, had been to contact his father. While Moira had been doing an excellent job of keeping a tight hold over communication going in and out of Ironforge, complete isolation was difficult to obtain. Rumors had begun circulating after only a day. Varian had immediately tried to contact his son by sending urgent letters. When they were not answered, he had become both worried and angry.

Jaina was not a parent, but she had an idea of what Varian was going through, both as the father of a son he had only recently reunited with and as a king fearing for the security of his kingdom. But more urgent than putting Varian's fears to rest had been the calming of a potentially explosive situation. Sometimes politics began and ended with two people. While she had never met Baine, his reputation preceded him. She had certainly known, respected, and liked his father. Baine had come to her, risking everything, trusting that she would aid him. Jaina *did* know Anduin, quite well, and knew that if the initial shock and suspicion could be quelled, productive conversation would ensue.

And so she had assuaged their fears, and gotten them to speak, both to her and each other. The news each bore was dreadful in its own way. Baine spoke of the murder of his father at the hands of Garrosh and Magatha and the ensuing slaughter of a peaceful people in one of the bloodiest coups Jaina had ever heard of. And Anduin spoke of a returning daughter whose rightful claim to the throne did nothing to mitigate the fear at the utterly tyrannical way she had swept into a city and taken away the liberties of its citizens.

Both, each in his own way, were fugitives. Jaina had made the promise to keep them safe and support them however she could, though the plans as to how exactly she would do that had not yet been formed.

Now voices were growing hoarse from speaking, and heads, including Jaina's own, were starting to nod. But she felt good about what they had done here. Baine had told her that those who had accompanied him would be expecting his return, and if it did not happen, they would likely assume treachery. Jaina had understood; she would have assumed the same. She opened a portal to the site he requested, and he stepped through, leaving Anduin and Jaina alone.

"That was . . ." Anduin struggled for words. "I feel so bad for him."

"I do, too . . . and for all those poor tauren in Thunder Bluff and Bloodhoof Village and all the other sites that came under attack. And Thrall . . . I don't know what he's going to do when he gets the news." It would crack the orc's noble heart, she knew. And indirectly, it was all because of his decision to appoint Garrosh as leader in his absence. Thrall would be devastated.

She sighed and shook it off, turning to Anduin and giving him the affectionate hug she'd not given him upon his arrival. "I'm so very glad you're safe!"

"Thanks, Aunt Jaina," he said, returning the hug and then pulling back. "My father . . . can I talk to him?"

"Of course," Jaina said. "Come with me."

The walls of Jaina's small, cozy room were, not surprisingly, lined with books. She stepped up to one shelf and touched three of them in a particular order. Anduin gaped as the bookshelf slid aside to reveal what looked like a simple oval mirror hanging on the wall. He closed his mouth as he caught a glimpse of his own reflection; he looked rather idiotic staring with his jaw open.

Jaina didn't appear to notice. She murmured an incantation and waved her hands, and the reflection of Anduin, Jaina, and the room disappeared. In its place was a swirling blue mist.

"I hope he is nearby," Jaina said, frowning a little. "Varian?"

A long, tense moment passed, then the blue mist seemed to take on a shape. A topknot of brown hair, features in a lighter shade of blue, a scar crossing the face—

"Anduin!" cried Varian Wrynn.

Jaina could not help but smile, despite the direness of the situation, at the love and relief in Varian's voice and expression.

Anduin was grinning. "Hello, Father."

"I've heard rumors. . . . How did—of course, the hearthstone," said Varian, answering his own question. "Jaina—I owe you a tremendous debt of thanks. You may have saved Anduin's life."

"It was his own cleverness that made him remember to use it," Jaina demurred. "I just gave him the tool."

"Anduin . . . did that witch of a dwarf hurt you?" Varian's dark brows drew together. "If she did, I will—"

"No, no," Anduin hastened to assure his father. "And I don't think she would. I'm too necessary to her. Let me tell you what happened."

He filled his father in on all that had transpired, quickly, concisely, and accurately. They were almost the exact same words he had used earlier to Baine and Jaina. Not for the first time Jaina found herself admiring the cool head on the young man's shoulders, especially given the fact that he—along with Jaina herself—was operating on very little sleep and under extremely tense circumstances.

"So you see, her claim is legitimate," Anduin finished.

"Not that of empress," Varian retorted.

"Well, no. But princess, yes, and queen, once she's had a formal coronation. She doesn't have to be doing this . . . trapping everyone like this."

"No," the king replied. "No. She doesn't." His eyes flickered to Jaina. "Jaina, I'm not about to tip my hand to Moira and let it be known that Anduin escaped successfully. Let her stew for a bit. That means I have a favor to ask."

"Of course he can stay here with me," Jaina replied before he could even voice the question. "No one's seen him yet, and the few who will are completely trustworthy. Whenever you're ready for him to come home, just let us know."

Anduin nodded. He had been expecting such a decision, but Jaina saw a flicker of disappointment cross his face. She didn't blame him for it. Anyone in his position would have wanted to go home and be done with all this.

"Thank you," said Varian. "And of course I'll continue to publicly appear as baffled as she wants me to be."

"As will I. We'll let Moira think she's succeeded in hiding her coup. And in the meantime—"

"Don't worry." Varian smiled coldly. "I've got a plan."

And with that, his face vanished. Jaina blinked at the abrupt dismissal.

"He looked angry," Anduin said quietly.

"Well, I'm sure he is. I was angry when I heard about all this, too, and the danger you were in. And he's your father."

Anduin sighed. "I wish there were something more I could do to help the people of Ironforge, or the tauren."

Jaina resisted the urge to ruffle his hair. He wasn't a child anymore, and although he was probably too courteous to protest, she suspected he wouldn't like it. She contented herself with giving him a reassuring smile.

"Anduin, believe me when I say that, somehow, I'm certain you'll find a way."

Anduin was surprised but pleased when he learned that Baine Bloodhoof had actually requested his presence at the next night's meeting with Jaina. Although the sitting room where they had spoken last night seemed a strange place for such weighty negotiations, Anduin didn't object when Jaina suggested it again. And neither did Baine, although it was obvious that nothing in the room was ever intended for one of his bulk. Anduin wondered if somehow Baine, too, sensed the comfort of the room, even though it was so far removed from what Anduin understood to be the tauren lifestyle. But here friends had often gathered to ward off the chill of a cold rainy day with lively conversation, hot tea, and cookies. Maybe some of that good cheer lingered and was perceived by Baine.

It was an odd way to conduct negotiations, Anduin thought, remembering the summit at Theramore long ago. No formal declarations, no weapons to lay down, no guards. Just three people.

He decided he liked it.

Baine and Jaina were already there when Anduin came to join them. To Anduin, the tauren seemed a little calmer, but sadder, than he had last night. Anduin greeted Baine politely and sincerely, bowing the correct distance to an equal. Baine made his own gesture of respect, touching his heart and then his forehead. Anduin smiled. It began as an awkward smile, but as he regarded Baine, it softened into an easy, sincere one.

Baine, Jaina, and Anduin again sat on the floor. Anduin's back was to the fire, and the heat beating against him was comfortable. Jaina brought in a tray of tea, placing it in the center between all of them. This time, Anduin noticed, she had an oversized mug for their guest.

Baine noticed it, too, and made a small, gentle, snorting sound. "Thank you, Lady Jaina," he said. "I see the details do not escape you. Thrall does well to put his trust in you, I believe."

"Thank you, Baine," Jaina said. "Thrall's trust means a great deal to me. I would never jeopardize it—or yours."

Baine took a swallow from the mug, which, even though large, still looked small in his great hands. He stared into the cup for a moment. "There are some among the Forsaken who read tea leaves," he said. "Do you know such an art, Lady Jaina?"

Jaina shook her bright head. "No, I do not," she said. "Although I'm told that used tea leaves make a fine compost."

It was a weak joke, but they all smiled. "It is just as well. I do not need to have an oracle tell me what my future holds. I have been thinking, praying for direction from the Earth Mother. Asking her to guide my heart. It is full of pain and anger now, and I do not know if it is altogether wise."

"What does it tell you?" Jaina asked quietly.

He looked up at her with calm brown eyes. "My father was stolen from me by treachery. My heart cries out for vengeance for that despicable action." His voice was steady, almost a monotone, but even so, Anduin found himself instinctively shrinking from it. Baine was not anyone he would ever want charging at him demanding vengeance.

"My heart says: They took from you, take from them. Take the Grimtotem who entered a peaceful city of their own kind in the dark of night, and who slew by smothering or stabbing victims too deep in slumber to fight back. Take their matriarch who placed poison on a blade instead of sacredly anointing it. Take the arrogant *fool* who dared fight my father and who could only win by stooping to—"

Baine was beginning to raise his voice, and the calmness in his eyes was slowly being replaced by anger. His hands tightened into fists the size of Anduin's head, and his tail began to lash. Abruptly he halted in midsentence and took a deep breath.

"As you see, my heart is not wise at this moment. I am in agreement with it on one thing. I must retake my people's territory—Thunder Bluff, Bloodhoof Village, Sun Rock Retreat, Camp Mojache, any other village or outpost where they have made incursions and spilled innocent blood."

Anduin found himself nodding. He agreed completely, for many reasons. The Grimtotem shouldn't be rewarded for such violence and cruelty, Baine would be a better leader than this Magatha, and besides, any hope of peace with the Alliance would only be made with this brave young tauren at the head of his people.

"I think you should as well," Jaina said, but Anduin caught the note of caution in her voice. He knew she was wondering what exactly he intended to do—and what would be asked of her. She must be willing to help in some way, or else she would never have permitted Baine to come speak with her in the first place. He held his tongue and let Baine continue.

"But there is something I cannot, I must not do. Even

though my heart drives me to it. I cannot do this thing because I know my father would not wish me to, and I must honor his wishes—what he fought for, what he did with his life—rather than my own emotions." Baine heaved an enormous sigh. "Much as I long to . . . I cannot attack Garrosh Hellscream."

Jaina relaxed almost imperceptibly.

"Garrosh was appointed by my warchief, Thrall. My father swore loyalty to Thrall, as did I. My father believed in his heart Garrosh was responsible for the attack against the Sentinels in Ashenvale and also an attack on a peaceful gathering of druids. He therefore issued the mak'gora against Garrosh, for the good of the Horde, and even stood by his challenge when Garrosh changed the rules and made it a battle to the death. In that situation, I believe what he did was right. His motives were not anger, or hatred, or vengeance."

Baine's voice broke, ever so slightly. "His motives were love of the Horde, and a desire to see it safe. He was willing to risk his life for it—and it was with his life that he paid."

Anduin found the words tumbling out of his mouth before he could stop them. "But no one would deny you your right to vengeance, especially if you can prove that Garrosh let Magatha poison his blade! And the attack on the druids—"

Jaina wasn't happy with his outburst, and Baine appeared startled. He swung his large head around to face Anduin for a moment.

"Yes. But what you do not understand—and even you might not, Jaina—is that my father issued the challenge of the mak'gora. The outcome determines the matter once and for all. The Earth Mother has spoken."

"But if Garrosh cheated—"

"We have evidence that Magatha poisoned the blade. None that Garrosh consented. There was no doubt in my father's heart. There *is* doubt in mine. If I challenge him without absolute faith that I am right, I then ignore the ancient tradition of my people. I say, I do not like these laws, so I will not obey them. I deny the Earth Mother. What does that make me, young Anduin?"

Anduin nodded his fair head slowly. "You can't say it's a fair way to determine right or wrong one day, and then say it's unfair the next because you don't like the outcome."

Baine snorted gently in approval. "You do understand, then. Good. My father challenged Garrosh to try to heal the Horde. Yet if I do so, I will be ripping it apart. I would be destroying the tauren way of life, everything for which they have striven, in a misguided effort to protect that very thing. That is not what Cairne Bloodhoof gave his life for his son to do. And so . . . I shall not do it."

Anduin felt a chill run down his spine. He knew what many humans and, indeed, other races in the Alliance thought about the tauren, about the Horde. He'd heard it muttered often enough—sometimes shouted. Monsters, the Horde were called. And the tauren, little more than beasts. And yet Anduin knew that in all his admittedly short time in this world, he had never been witness to such integrity under strain.

He also knew that Baine was not entirely at peace with his decision. He knew what was right, but he did not want to do it. Anduin realized, without understanding how that realization came, that Baine . . . didn't think he could.

Baine didn't believe he could be the tauren his father was, and underneath the words that were clearly bought with such anguished thought and pain was a fear that, somehow he would fail.

Anduin knew what it was like to live in the shadow of a powerful father. It was obvious to anyone with eyes and ears that Baine and Cairne had been very close. Anduin felt a shameful wave of envy at the realization; he was not close with Varian now, although he once had been and longed to be again. How would he feel if his father had been so brutally taken away from him? How had Varian felt when his own father had been murdered? Had Varian not had the wisdom of Anduin's namesake, Anduin Lothar, to guide him, what would he have done?

Would either Wrynn have been able to feel the hurt—for assuredly Baine was not pretending it did not exist—and still choose the path that best served his people rather than his personal needs?

"I'll be right back," Anduin said suddenly. He rose and bowed, then, feeling the curious glances behind him, raced to the room Jaina had been letting him use. Under the bed was the pack he had brought with him when he had used the hearthstone to escape Ironforge and the gilded cage Moira had wrought for him. He grabbed the pack and hurried back to Jaina and Baine. Jaina had the little furrow between her brows that told Anduin she was slightly annoyed with him. He sat down again and reached inside the bag, pulling out something carefully wrapped in cloth.

"Baine . . . I don't know. . . . Maybe this is a little forward of me, and I don't really know if you care what I think, but . . . I want you to know I understand why you're choosing this path. And I think it's the right one."

Baine narrowed his eyes speculatively but did not interrupt.

"But . . . it feels to me . . ." Anduin groped for words, heat rising in his face. He was guided by an impulse he did not fully understand, and he hoped he wouldn't end up regretting it. He took a deep breath.

"It feels to me like you yourself don't believe the path you've chosen is the right one. That you're worried that . . . you might not be able to walk it. That you won't be the best leader of your people, like your father was."

"Anduin—" Jaina's voice was sharp, a warning.

Baine held up a hand. "No, Lady Jaina. Let him finish." His brown eyes bore intensely into Anduin's blue ones.

"But . . . *I* believe in you. I believe that Cairne Bloodhoof would be very proud of what you've said here tonight. You're like me—we were born to become rulers of our people. We didn't ask for it, and anyone who thinks our lives are fun or easy . . . they don't know *anything* about what it means to be us. To be the sons of leaders, and to have to think about leading ourselves. Somebody believed in me once, and gave me this."

He unwrapped the item that was lying in his lap. Fearbreaker caught the light of the fire and glimmered brightly. Anduin caressed the ancient weapon as he spoke. His hand ached to close around it, but he resisted the urge.

"King Magni Bronzebeard gave this to me the night before—before the ritual that killed him. It's an ancient weapon. Its name is Fearbreaker. We were talking about duties, and sometimes the things everyone expects of us aren't what we're really meant to be doing." He looked up at Baine. "I think the tauren will be as angry and as hungry for vengeance as you are. Some aren't going to be happy that you're not out for blood. But you know you're on the right path—for you, and for them, too. They just won't see it now. But they will, one day."

He lifted Fearbreaker, holding it carefully in two hands. Magni's words floated back to him: *It's known th' taste o' blood, and in certain hands, has been known tae also stanch blood. Here, take it. Hold it in yer hand. Let's see if it likes ye.*

He didn't want to let it go. *If ever a thing was meant fer someone, that weapon was meant fer ye,* Magni had said with certainty.

But Anduin wasn't so sure. Maybe it was meant for him for only a short time. There was only one way to find out.

He lifted the weapon and handed it to Baine. "Take it. Hold it. Let's—let's see if it likes you."

Baine was puzzled, but obeyed. The mace was too large for Anduin, and yet it looked small in Baine's huge hands. Baine regarded the weapon for a long moment. Then he took a long, deep inhalation and sighed, letting the breath go, letting his body relax a little. Anduin smiled softly at Baine's reaction to the weapon.

And sure enough, a few seconds later, Fearbreaker began to glow, ever so slightly.

"It *does* like you," Anduin said quietly. He felt a sense of loss. He had never even had the chance to wield the weapon before it had wanted to be passed on. But at the same time he had no regrets about what he had done. In some way that Anduin didn't quite understand—and perhaps never would—the weapon had chosen Baine, just as it had chosen him.

"It thinks you are making the right decision, too. It has faith in you—just like I do, just like Jaina does. Please take it. I think I was meant to have it so I could give it to you."

For a moment Baine did not move. Then his large fingers curled tightly around Fearbreaker.

Anduin felt the Light tickling gently at the center of his chest, within his heart. Still unsure, he lifted his hand. It flashed brightly, and Baine was suddenly bathed in a gentle glow that disappeared as quickly as it had come. Baine's eyes widened. He took another deep breath, and before Anduin's eyes, settled into calmness.

Now Anduin recognized the feeling—except this time, it was coming from him, to be bestowed on Baine, not from Rohan to be bestowed on him. Baine was feeling the same peace that Anduin had felt when Rohan had blessed him with a ward against his own fear. Baine lifted his head.

"An honor, from you, Anduin, and from Magni Bronzebeard. Know that I will treasure this."

Anduin smiled. Beside him, Jaina was looking at him with an expression akin to awe. Her eyes, wide and bright, looked from him to Baine and back again, and her face curved into a gentle, tender smile.

The tauren gazed at the glowing weapon. "Light," he said. "My people do not think the darkness is evil, Anduin. It is a naturally occurring thing, and therefore right. But we, too, have our own Light. We honor the eyes of the Earth Mother, the sun, and the moon—An'she and Mu'sha. Neither is better than the other, and together they see with balanced vision. I feel in this weapon a kinship to them, even though it comes from a culture very different from my own."

Anduin smiled gently. "Light is light, whatever its source," he agreed.

"I wish I had something comparable to give you in return," Baine said. "There are certainly honored weapons that have been handed down in my line, but I am in possession of very little at the moment. The only thing I can give you is some advice my father shared with me.

"Our people were once nomads. It is only recently, in the last few years, that we have halted our wandering and made a home for ourselves in Mulgore. It was a challenge. But we created villages and cities of peace, of tranquility and beauty. We imbued the places in which we dwelt with a sense of who and what we are. And that is what I wish to restore now. My father once said, 'Destruction is easy.' Look what havoc the Grimtotem were able to wreak in a single night. But creating something that lasts—that, my father said, was a challenge. I am determined to make sure that what he created—Thunder Bluff and all the other villages, the goodwill between the members of the Horde—I will devote my life to seeing that they last."

Anduin felt his heart both swell and calm at the words. It was indeed a challenge, but he knew Baine, son of Cairne, was up to the task. "What else did your father say?" Cairne, as described by his son, seemed so very wise to Anduin, and he hungered for more.

Baine snorted slightly in laughter that was warm and genuine and yet laced with the pain of remembering too early for nostalgia.

"There was something about . . . eating all your vegetables."

TWENTY-EIGHT

The Grimtotem were powerful and uniquely trained. From early childhood, while others their age were learning to be in harmony with nature and learning the rites of the Great Hunt, the Grimtotem were taught how to fight one another. They learned to kill, quickly, cleanly, with hands, horns, and whatever weapon was at hand. In any given conflict, the odds were with a Grimtotem to win a fight. They did not fight honorably; they fought to win. But their numbers were not inexhaustible. Magatha was able to target only certain places, and she had chosen to focus primarily on seizing the main city from which Cairne had led, the heart of Mulgore, which was the first real "home" the tauren had ever known, and on slaying the son he had fathered. The first victory had been obtained. Dawn had shone light on hundreds of corpses in and around Thunder Bluff. Their goal had been twofold: to eliminate those most highly positioned to oppose them, and to strike utter, crippling terror into the tauren population by slaughtering anyone who lifted a weapon to them.

Their enemies lay stiffening in congealing pools of blood, as did many who were simply in the wrong place at the wrong time. But those deaths, too, were a powerful propaganda tool. Magatha and the Grimtotem held Thunder Bluff. They held all of that city's resources and hostages with which to negotiate. The recent attacks combined with the loss of Cairne and the disappearance of his son had left the tauren people unsettled. She felt certain that, in a desperate attempt to find normalcy again, the tauren would acknowledge her as their leader.

Baine, however, had slipped through their fingers. A spy had informed her that one of her own, Stormsong, had turned traitor. As Magatha sat in the lodge that had once been Cairne Bloodhoof's seat of power, she fumed quietly. She had, of course, marked Stormsong for assassination but did not entertain any notions that he would be easily located. Doubtless he was with the pretender, as she had taken to calling (and encouraging others to call) Baine since the Grimtotem uprising. Stormsong would die with him, once Baine was found, but likely not until that anxiously awaited hour.

And as she had expected, for Magatha was no fool, the tauren in more far-flung places such as Feralas and of course the druidic stronghold Moonglade had already begun their rebellion. Couriers from other tribes brought word of their defiance, facing the expected immediate execution after bearing such bad news with a stoicism that irritated Magatha.

Other rumors were flying as well. That the pretender was in hiding in the Moonglade. That he had struck a deal with the Alliance in exchange for free trade with a recaptured Thunder Bluff. That he had the power of the Earth Mother behind him, and that his shaman and druids were able to harness trees to march and fight alongside them.

Of all these, there was one thing of which Magatha was certain: Baine was gathering reinforcements, and when he was strong enough, he would challenge her.

So lost in thought was she that it took Rahauro two tries to get her attention. She snorted, angry at woolgathering, knowing that among the younger ones it would appear as senility. She started to direct her anger not at her faithful servant but at the young orc courier who stood before her. Then her ears lifted as realization struck her. An orc meant . . .

She waved a hand. "Speak."

"Elder Crone Magatha, I come from the acting warchief of the Horde, Garrosh Hellscream."

Her eyes widened. Two days ago she had sent out a plea to Garrosh for assistance, knowing that at some point—and probably sooner than later—Baine would come, and many would come with him. The letter had been full of sincere-sounding compliments and praise for how he had managed the Horde. She had also dangled the lure of a formal alliance between the Grimtotem and the Horde if Garrosh lent his support in this venture. Surely Garrosh could use the Grimtotem's unique . . . methods. Magatha had hoped that a response would come in the form of troops marching to assist her in defending Thunder Bluff, but apparently Garrosh had some questions, or else he wanted to apprise her of his thoughts.

Either way, she was pleased at the swift response. She smiled kindly at the orc.

"You are welcome here, courier. Please—take a moment to refresh yourself. Then read what your master has to say to me."

She settled back in the chair, folding her arms across her belly, and waited as the orc gratefully took a long pull on the waterskin but declined food. Then, with a bow, he retrieved a leather tube from his pack, withdrew a scroll, and read in a strong, clear voice:

"Unto Elder Crone Magatha of the Grimtotem,
Acting warchief of the Horde, Garrosh Hellscream,
Sends his most sincere wishes for a slow and painful death."

A gasp rippled around the room. Magatha went very still, then with a speed that belied her age she bolted from the chair, backhanded the courier, and held the scroll at arm's length to accommodate her increasingly poor vision to read it for herself.

It has come to my attention that you have deprived me of a rightful kill. Cairne Bloodhoof was a hero to the Horde, and an honorable member of a usually honorable race. It is with disgust and anger that I discover you have caused me to bring about his death through accidental treachery.

Such tactics may work well for your renegade, honorless tribe and Alliance scum, but I despise them. It was my wish to fight Cairne fairly, and win or lose by my own skill or lack of it. Now I shall never know, and the cry of traitor will dog my steps until such time as I can sport your head on a pike and point to you as the real traitor.

So . . . no. I will not be sending any truehearted orcs to fight alongside your treacherous, belly-crawling tribe. Your victory or your defeat is in the hands of your Earth Mother now. Either way, I look forward to hearing of your demise.

You are on your own, Magatha, as friendless and disliked as you have ever been. Perhaps more. Enjoy your loneliness.

Her hand had begun to shake halfway through the reading, crushing part of the letter. When she had finished, she threw her head back in an angry bellow and thrust her hand in front of her. A single bolt of lightning speared down from the sky, blasting through the thatched roof to strike the courier dead.

The acrid smell of burning flesh filled the room. Everyone stared for a moment at the green body with the charred, black chest, then two Bluffwatchers moved, without needing to be told, to pick up the corpse and bear it out.

Magatha was breathing heavily, snorting in fury, her fists clenched.

"Elder Crone?" Rahauro's voice was tentative, cautious. Seldom had he seen his mistress so angry.

With an effort, Magatha composed herself. "It seems that Garrosh Hellscream refuses the Grimtotem any aid whatsoever." She would not shame her tribemates with the blistering insults with which Garrosh had freely peppered his missive.

"We are on our own, then?" Rahauro looked slightly worried.

"We are, as we always have been. And always we have endured. Do not worry, Rahauro. I planned for this eventuality as well."

In actuality, she had not. She had been convinced that the young Hellscream would continue to be easy to play. This stupid "honor" thing that the orcs—and, truth be told, her own race—were so obsessed with had been a serpent lurking in the grass, ready to bite her when she least suspected it. It was unfortunate that the Kor'kron had been swift to recover Gorehowl before she had had a chance to clean the poison off herself.

Still, all that was needed was to destroy Baine Bloodhoof and reestablish order in Mulgore. The tauren would quiet down and accept her as their new leader. And then, from a place of strength, she would see if Garrosh Hellscream might be willing to change his mind.

In the meantime, she would need to prepare for the pretender's inevitable attack.

There was a cool marine breeze circulating through the room at the top of Jazzik's General Goods. The tauren who paced there nervously, his black coat and white markings clearly identifying him as a Grimtotem, was glad of it, although the openness bothered him. Still, this was where he had been told to come.

"Heya, you made it, good," came a voice behind him.

The tauren turned and nodded as Gazlowe, the goblin leader of Ratchet, climbed the stairs and gave him a wave. "Don't worry. This is my town. Long as you're here, you're safe. I understand your boss has a proposition for me."

The Grimtotem nodded. "Indeed."

Gazlowe indicated a table and two chairs. The tauren sat down, carefully at first, then a little bit more confidently as he realized the chair would support his much greater weight.

"We need several items."

Gazlowe fished out a pipe from his jacket pocket and a small pouch of herbs. He filled it as they spoke. "I can get you most anything, but not for free. Nothing personal, just business, you know?"

The tauren nodded. "I am prepared to pay for your services. Here is our list." He shoved a small, rolled-up parchment across the table at the goblin. Gazlowe wasn't about to be rushed, though, and finished tamping down the herbs and lighting the pipe before he reached out a green hand and accepted the list. His eyes widened.

"*How* many bombs?"

"You can read, friend goblin."

"I thought there was an extra zero. Or maybe two." His mouth curled around the stem of the pipe. "My, my. Looks like I might be able to buy myself an additional vessel. Maybe an additional *town*." His eyes flitted to the Grimtotem's. "You're sure you can pay?"

For answer, the tauren untied a sack from his belt. It was larger than his mammoth fist and made a pleasant clinking sound as it landed on the table. "Count it all, if you like. I was told you charged a fair rate."

"Even a fair rate would be a small fortune," Gazlowe said. He opened the pouch. The afternoon sunlight caught the glint of gold. "Holy smoke."

"Can you get me all the items on the list?"

Gazlowe scratched his head, clearly torn between an honest response and the one he wanted to give. "Maybe," he said after a moment. He took a pull on his pipe and let the smoke trickle out of his large, hooked nose. "Maybe."

"Within a few days."

Gazlowe coughed, smoke coming from his mouth in short billows. "What?"

The Grimtotem pulled out a second pouch, not as large as the first, but still quite respectable. "My . . . boss understands that one needs to pay extra for rush jobs."

The goblin whistled softly. "Your boss is smart," he said. He eyed the list again and sighed. "It's going to be tough, but—yeah. Yeah, I can get all this for you." He hesitated. The Grimtotem sat patiently. A private war was clearly going on inside the goblin's head.

With a sigh that was low and pained, Gazlowe pulled out a fistful of coins from the second pouch, then shoved the rest back at the tauren. The Grimtotem looked up at him, confused. A goblin, not taking money freely offered?

"Listen," Gazlowe said. "Don't spread this around, but . . . I, uh . . . support what you are trying to do."

The tauren blinked. "I . . . am glad."

Gazlowe nodded, then rose. "I'll have them for you in four days. No sooner."

"That is acceptable." The tauren rose, too, and turned to leave.

"Hey, Grandpa?"

The Grimtotem turned.

"Tell Baine I always liked his dad."

Stormsong Grimtotem smiled softly. "I will."

The army was on the move.

Although Baine was secure in his decision to not seek revenge against Garrosh Hellscream, he was not about to ask that rash orc for aid. That meant that he was on his own. Fortunately, the story of Magatha's treachery was beginning to spread. Camp Mojache had not fallen to the Grimtotem yet, but everyone there was desperately fighting. They could spare no reinforcements. But Freewind Post had managed to rebuff an assault and stayed loyal to the Bloodhoof line. Everyone there who could fight had volunteered the first night that Baine had asked for sanctuary. He had two dozen healthy, fit warriors, and others who were desperately in need of training but whose enthusiasm and passion could not be denied. Cairne had been well loved and his son respected and honored. There was no question that any tauren who was not a Grimtotem—or living in fear of them—would rally to Baine's side.

He wore Fearbreaker proudly, although he did not explain who had given it to him. He had no wish to jeopardize Anduin in any way. The weapon had not seen the light of day for decades, perhaps centuries. It would not be noted as a distinctively dwarven weapon although it was small. Nearly every weapon was small to a tauren.

When asked, he merely replied, "This was given to me by a friend, as a gesture of faith in me and my cause." That explanation seemed enough to satisfy most.

They were marching up the Gold Road toward Camp Taurajo. Word had come from Sun Rock Retreat. They had repulsed an attack and were sending troops to meet him there. Baine marched openly, sending a strong message to any Grimtotem spies that might be observing that he and his supporters were not afraid. Indeed, their numbers swelled as they left the stagnant marshes of Dustwallow behind and entered the dry lands of the Barrens.

More than tauren had come to join their cause. There were several trolls among the ranks, a few orcs, and even one or two Forsaken or sin'dorei. The Forsaken who had come had expressed owing a debt to the tauren who were, after all, the ones who had pushed to allow them into the Horde at all. Most of the rest were mercenaries; however, thanks to Jaina, who had given him a considerable amount in untraceable gold, he was able to hire them. Their skills would, Baine was certain, prove vital.

The shape of a kodo appeared on the road, a small dot, and as it drew closer, Baine recognized its passenger as Stormsong. He drew his large mount alongside Baine, who went on hoof.

"Good news?" asked Baine.

"As good as possible," Stormsong said. "Gazlowe agreed to provide all we need in four days. And he did not even accept the full amount. He said to tell you he always admired Cairne and supported our cause."

"Really?" Baine glanced up at him, surprised. "A true declaration of loyalty from a goblin. I am pleased."

Hamuul had been talking with his fellow druids. Now he stepped forward. "As you predicted, they know we are coming. We have spies who inform us that Thunder Bluff is preparing for a siege. The good news is, they are gathering all their resources and warriors there and not attacking us on the road."

Baine nodded. "They think Thunder Bluff impossible to claim and that any challenge on the road will be a waste of Grimtotem lives."

Stormsong snorted. "You should have seen Gazlowe's face when he read the list. The matriarch and her followers will be in for a very great surprise."

The reinforcements from Sun Rock Retreat were not numerous, but they were apparently very swift. They were already waiting for Baine when he approached the path that led westward from the Southern Gold Road toward Mulgore. His heart lifted as a cry of welcome went up, and he could make out the chanting: "Baine! Baine! Baine!"

"Listen to them," Hamuul said to him quietly. "You bring them hope. Your plan is audacious and risky," he admitted, "but that is precisely why I believe it will succeed. You have your father's steadiness and your own imagination, Baine Bloodhoof, and you will be victorious in this battle."

"I pray you are right," Baine said. "If we fail, I tremble for the fate of our people."

* * *

Thunder Bluff, once filled with the sounds of raucous celebration, was now silent. The first victory, won by stealth in the night, had been fairly easy, but the Grimtotem now were preparing to fend off an army headed by a very popular leader, not slaughtering slumbering victims. Thunder Bluff was an excellent place for defense, and they could handle a long siege. Still, Magatha was not looking forward to it.

It had been foolish for Baine to be so open about his approach. Perhaps it had won him a few more followers, but it had also given his enemy time to prepare. And Magatha had not wasted the opportunity.

Scaling Thunder Bluff was not impossible, but it was very difficult, especially for tauren and even more so if said climbers were expected. The lifts were key—and if they were rigged to explode at the push of a button, as the engineers of the tribe were working on doing, it would be a challenge for Baine's troops to do anything other than camp at the base and wait it out. And if things were timed correctly, the explosion might also take several of Baine's followers with it. Magical methods of infiltration, such as portals, were already warded against.

And it would be a long wait. The several days' notice that Baine had given them had enabled the Grimtotem to bring in a great quantity of food and other supplies. She had recalled all her people from Bloodhoof Village and the unsuccessful Sun Rock Retreat attack to defend this, the capital. Yes, the more Magatha thought about it, the calmer she grew. Baine would be defeated, as his father had been, and her stranglehold on the tauren would be certain.

She drifted to sleep in the lodge that had belonged to Cairne Bloodhoof. Her pleasant dreams were interrupted by a sudden flash of brilliant light and a roll of answering thunder that shook the very earth. Rain sluiced down on the lodge as Magatha bolted upright, snorting. Another blinding flash of lighting. A shaman and a tauren, Magatha was no stranger to storms. But this one had a powerful fierceness to it. She sniffed and listened, senses alert. Perhaps she was imagining things. Still, she had not lived this long by ignoring her instincts, and so she threw on some robes and a cape to guard against the torrential downpour.

Magatha squinted as rain pelted her face, peering upward. The sky was black and gray, with thunderclouds blotting out the stars. Nothing unusual. This place was called Thunder Bluff, after all. Satisfied that it was nothing more than a particularly violent storm, she reached to slip the hood further down over her face.

And then she saw it. It emerged from its cover, as garishly colored as the concealing thundercloud had been subdued, an airborne ship with a bright purple balloon hovering over it. Then came another . . . and another. She gasped with the crash of recognition.

"Zeppelins!" Magatha cried.

TWENTY-NINE

No sooner had Magatha uttered the word than ropes were lowered from the sides of the zeppelins, and several tauren, orcs, and trolls shimmied down them. Such was the surprise that many of the enemy were able to drop safely to the earth before the Grimtotem could gather guns and bows to defend themselves.

Once on the ground, the enemy rushed to attack. Three of them were heading directly for Magatha. Fully awake now, she frowned and reached into a small pouch she carried by her side. Her fingers closed on one of her totems. The elements responded—the sky was suddenly ripped open by jagged bolts of lightning, several of which shot like spears directly at the enemy. Many of them fell at once. But in the chaos that ensued, another zeppelin moved into position and unloaded its dangerous passengers.

Magatha snarled and lifted her hands to the sky. Lightning speared one of the zeppelins. It caught fire immediately, the blaze racing hungrily along, devouring the enormous rigid balloon frame in seconds. The pilot somehow managed to steer it so that it careened right into the flight tower.

Magatha swore. The wyverns trapped within would be of no use to them as burned corpses. The late goblin pilot had made the destruction of his ship count.

But there was no time to ponder the incident. A huge explosion rocked High Rise of Thunder Bluff. The remaining zeppelin was dropping bombs. Bodies and pieces of bodies flew up into the air, illuminated by the dim, incongruously pink light of dawn. Rahauro grabbed his matriarch and steered her back from the conflict. She struck him angrily and returned to the fray.

"Get what wyverns we have and attack from the air!" she cried. "We've downed one of the zeppelins; let's get the other one!"

"Other . . . two," Rahauro corrected.

A huge storm crow landed beside Baine. It shapeshifted, twisted, and Hamuul told his chieftain, "We lost one of the zeppelins. But all their attention is focused on High Rise. Stormsong's thundercloud worked perfectly."

Baine nodded his approval. The first wave was the most dramatic. They had the element of surprise, of shock and startlement, and Magatha and her best fighters were swarming over that level now. They were fighting the several dozen who had been lowered from the zeppelins to attack and distract them from the slower, but harder to stop, rogues stealthily moving to Hunter, Elder, and Spirit Rises. Baine was giving the Grimtotem a taste of their own medicine—cutting them off from one another. Except whereas the Grimtotem had slain the shaman, druids, and hunters, Baine's troops were merely cutting the ropes of the bridges that connected the smaller rises to the main rise. Some arrows, bullets, and spells would reach across the space between the rises, but the vast majority would not.

Several of the mercenary trolls he had hired were also hard at work. They were swiftly and implacably scaling the sheer bluff. Bombs had been carefully placed for just such an attempt; these were carefully defused.

The lifts, not surprisingly, were set to blow. These were more complicated and were taking much longer. For the moment the distraction on High Rise had worked, and no one had thought to blow the lifts.

Yet.

What wyverns were left were swiftly prepared for flight, and the Grimtotem took the fight to the zeppelins. Grimtotem hunters mounted on the winged, lionlike creatures were able to fire directly on the crew and fighters on the deck—even those druids who had assumed storm crow form and were swooping down for the fight. But the Grimtotem were met with equal force as guns and arrows were fired directly at them. Magatha watched as one Grimtotem hunter was sprung upon by a great horned cat that sank its teeth in the hapless tauren's throat. Druid and hunter both toppled from the wyvern, the druid changing into storm crow shape a scant few feet above the rise. The hunter struck the ground hard and lay still.

Corpses were everywhere. It was time to retreat.

There were Forsaken magi in a cavern containing bodies of water known as the Pools of Vision; they could, if properly persuaded, create a portal to whisk Magatha away to safety. The traditional ramp that led down to each level had been bombed by a zeppelin and was still smoking. Magatha gestured, then turned and leaped down to the second rise. Rahauro and several others followed her, weapons in hand. Bloody hand-to-hand combat was rampant as well. A shadow fell over her, and she glanced up to see one of the two remaining zeppelins.

"To the Pools of Vision!" she cried. "And the lifts—detonate the bombs, then join me!"

"At once, Elder Crone," Cor said. The bombs had been his plan, and now he hurried off to carry out her orders.

Magatha hastened up the lodge that led to the bridge. In the space of a few more heartbeats she would be—

She skidded to a halt, her hooves slipping on the well-worn wood. Gorm reached out a hand just in time to keep his matriarch from falling down into the chasm that yawned below.

"They've cut the ropes!" Gorm yelled, tugging Magatha back to safety.

"I can see that, you stupid—" She was interrupted by an explosion. She turned back to the rise to see smoke coming up from where one of the lifts was, and smiled to herself. Now the next one. She waited for the highly anticipated sound. True, it would mean Thunder Bluff would be officially under siege for some time, but they were prepared for that.

The sound did not come.

The lift reached the top, and Baine Bloodhoof rushed forward so fast that Rahauro could not even move to intercept him. Hard on Baine's hooves were a charging bear, a Grimtotem, and several other warriors. Magatha reached for a totem, but before her fingers could close on it, Baine was upon her. He swung—not a sword, but what looked to be a mace, far too small for him.

Breath rushed out of her in a whoosh as the small mace slammed into her side. She had not had the chance to don armor, and the impact sent her flying. Pain shot through her, and before she could even struggle to breathe, let alone rise, Baine Bloodhoof was crouching over her, holding the peculiar weapon high. "Yield!" he cried. "Yield, murderess and traitor!"

She opened her mouth, and nothing came out. She still could not inhale to speak. Baine's brown eyes narrowed in . . . pleasure? Panic shot through her as she realized, in her silence, she had given him permission to strike.

"I . . . yield!" she gasped, the words barely audible over the cacophony of battle.

Baine lowered the mace. But out of the corner of her eye, she saw him clench his other fist, and then she knew nothing more.

Baine stood and gazed out over the Grimtotem he had taken prisoner. Some Grimtotem had died in the fight to retake Thunder Bluff, and many of those who had survived were injured. He had ordered their wounds treated, and there were white bandages on the black fur. Their numbers had been reduced during the fierce battle, but they had died in fair combat trying to hold a city they had taken by treachery and stealth, and he did not mourn them.

The question before him was, what to do with those who remained? Especially their leader?

Magatha was among the wounded, but it did not appear to have damaged her pride any. She stood as straight and tall as ever, flanked by two Bluffwatchers who appeared to be longing for any excuse to attack and finish her off. Part of Baine shared that longing. To strike off her head and impale it on a pike at the foot of the bluff as a warning, as had been done with the heads of dragons . . . yes, he admitted it would satisfy him greatly.

But it was not what his father would have done, and Baine knew it.

"My father let you stay here, in Thunder Bluff, Magatha," Baine said, not using her title. "He treated you fairly, hospitably, even though he knew that you were more than likely plotting against him."

Her eyes narrowed, and her nostrils flared, but she did not speak in anger. She was too smart, curse her.

"You repaid that consideration by smearing poison on Garrosh Hellscream's weapon, and watching as my father died ignobly and in agony. Honor would demand a life for a life, or the challenge of mak'gora—a challenge issued to you, not to Garrosh, who I think was nothing but a pawn in your game."

Magatha tensed, ever so slightly, waiting for the challenge. Baine smiled bitterly. "I believe in honor. My father died for it. But there is more that a leader must respect. He must also know compassion, and what is best for his people."

He strode down from the lodge until he was eye to eye, hoof to hoof with her, and it was she who drew back slightly and flattened her ears.

"You like comfort, Magatha Grimtotem. You like power. I will let you live, but you will taste neither." He held out his hand. One of the Bluffwatchers gave him a small pouch. Magatha's eyes widened as she recognized it.

"You know what this is. It is your totem pouch." He reached inside and brought forth one of the small, carved totems—the links Magatha had with the elements she controlled. He held it between two powerful fingers and crushed it to pieces. She tried, and failed, to not show her horror and fear at the gesture.

"I do not think for a moment this will completely sever your connection to the elements," Baine said. Nonetheless, he repeated the gesture with another totem, and another, and finally a fourth. "But I know it will anger the elements. And it will take you time—and abasement before them—to regain their favor again. I think such groveling and humility are fine things for you to taste. In fact, I will contribute even more of such things.

"You will be sent from this place to the harsh Stonetalon Mountains. There you may eke out an existence as best you may. Harm no one, and no one will harm you. Attack, and you are the enemy, and I will put no restraints on anything anyone wishes to do to you. And stir up treachery again—then, Magatha, I will come for you myself, and even the spirit of Cairne Bloodhoof urging me to calmness will not stop me from cutting off your head. Are we clear?"

She nodded.

He snorted, then drew back, eyeing the others. "There are some among you who were uneasy with the bloodshed, as Stormsong Grimtotem was. Any of you who wish to come forward and swear loyalty to me, the tauren people, and the Horde, and publicly disassociate yourselves from the stain that spreads whenever the name Grimtotem is mentioned, as Stormsong has done, you will receive a full pardon. The rest of you, go with your so-called matriarch into the wilderness. Share her fate. And pray you never see my face again."

He waited. For a long moment no one moved. Then a female, clutching the hands of two little ones, stepped forward. She knelt before Baine and bowed her head, her children imitating her.

"Baine Bloodhoof, I had no part in the slaughter of that night but confess that my mate did. I would have my children grow up here, in the safety of this peaceful city, if you will have us."

A black bull moved toward the female, placing a hand on her shoulder, then kneeling beside her. "For the sake of my mate and children, I present myself to your judgment. I am Tarakor, and it was I who led the attack against you when Stormsong deserted. I have never seen mercy in my life, but I ask it for my innocent children, if not for myself."

More and more came forward, until fully a quarter of the Grimtotem were kneeling before Baine. He was not so trusting as to think they would not need to be watched. When sharing Magatha's banishment, shame, and powerlessness was the only other option—for he intended to strip all of them of their ability to fight back, at least temporarily—he imagined many would have a sudden change of heart about their past deeds. But some of them, he also knew, were genuine in their desire. And perhaps others would become so. It was a risk he would have to take, if true healing were to happen.

He took a small, petty pleasure in the look on Magatha's face as more and more of her so-called loyal Grimtotem abandoned her. He suspected his father would be all right with that.

"Any more?" he asked. When the rest of the Grimtotem stayed where they were, he nodded. "Two dozen Bluffwatchers will escort you to your new home. I cannot honestly say I wish you luck. But your deaths at least will not be on my head."

They moved toward the lifts. He watched them for a moment. Magatha did not look back.

My words were not idle, Magatha Grimtotem. If I see you again, even though An'she guides me, I will not stay my hand.

Garrosh had once been ashamed of his heritage. It had taken time for him to understand, embrace, and finally celebrate who he was and where he had come from. Filled with that confidence, he had legitimately won much honor for himself and the Horde. Since then he had grown accustomed to adulation. But now, as he and his retinue climbed up the winding ramp to the appointed meeting site in Thousand Needles, he felt the gazes of the tauren on him and stiffened slightly.

It was not a good sensation, to feel that he had not been in the right. And truly, he knew that he had wished to fight Cairne in an honorable way that showed respect both to himself and to one he regarded as a noble warrior. Magatha had robbed him of that, cast an ugly shadow on his reputation in the eyes of many—too many. Why, *he* was as much a victim as Cairne.

So he forced his head higher, and quickened his pace. Baine was waiting for him. He was bigger than Cairne, or perhaps he simply stood straighter than the aging bull had. He stood quietly, holding his father's enormous totem at his side. Hamuul Runetotem, Stormsong Grimtotem, and several others waited a slight distance behind Baine.

Garrosh eyed Baine up and down, taking his measure. Large, powerful, with the calmness that Garrosh recognized from Cairne, he waited almost placidly.

"Garrosh Hellscream," Baine said in his deep, rumbling voice, and inclined his head.

"Baine Bloodhoof," Garrosh replied. "I think we have much to discuss."

Baine nodded to Hamuul. The elderly archdruid caught the eye of the others standing behind Baine and gestured to them. They inclined their heads and walked several paces away, giving the two what privacy they could atop this barren needle.

"You robbed me of more time with my father, whom I loved," Baine said bluntly.

So this was how it was to be played. No false courtesies, which Garrosh despised. Good.

"Your father challenged me. I had no choice but to accept that challenge, or my honor—and his—would forever be sullied."

Baine's expression did not change. "You used trickery and poison to win. That sullies your honor even more."

Garrosh was tempted to retort hotly but instead took a deep breath. "Much as it shames me to admit it, I was deceived by Magatha Grimtotem. It was she who poisoned Gorehowl. I will never know if I could have defeated your father in fair combat, and so I am as cheated as you are."

He wondered if Baine would understand what that admission cost him.

"You stand there with your honor tarnished because she tricked you. I stand here, bereft of my father, gathering up corpses of innocents. I think one of us has lost more than the other."

Garrosh said nothing, his cheeks growing hot, with what emotion, he did not know. But he knew what Baine had said was true. "I will expect the same challenge from the son as the father, then," he said.

"You will not have it."

Garrosh frowned, not understanding. Baine continued. "Do not think that I would not enjoy fighting you, Garrosh Hellscream. Whatever was on the blade, yours was the hand that cut down my father. But tauren are not so petty. The true killer was Magatha, not you. My father issued the mak'gora, and the argument between you and he is settled, even if, due to Magatha's treachery, the fight was no fair one. Cairne Bloodhoof always put the tauren people first. They need what protection and support the Horde can provide, and I will do all in my power to see that they get it. I cannot claim to honor his memory and yet disregard what is best for them."

"I, too, loved and respected my father, and have striven to honor his memory. I did not *ever* seek to dishonor Cairne Bloodhoof, Baine. Your understanding of that despite the treachery that slew him speaks well of you as a leader of your people."

Baine's ear twitched. He was still angry, and Garrosh did not blame him in the slightest.

"Yet—your mercy to the Grimtotem confuses me. I have heard that although you have driven them out, you did not exact revenge on them either. Here, the mak'gora or even stronger revenge seems appropriate. Why did you not execute the Grimtotem? Or at least their deceitful matriarch?"

"Whatever the Grimtotem are, they are tauren. My father suspected that Magatha might prove treacherous, and he kept her here so he could watch her. He chose that path so as not to cause division and strife. I honor his wish. There are other ways to punish than killing. Ways that are perhaps even more just."

Garrosh struggled with that for a moment, but he knew in the end, he would want to honor his own father's wishes just as Baine had. He contented himself with saying, "It is good, to honor the wishes and memory of one's father."

Baine smiled coldly. "As I have ample proof now that Magatha is a traitor, she has been banished and her power crippled. The same punishment is shared by all Grimtotem who chose to go with her. Many have repented of their actions and stayed. There is a separate Grimtotem faction now, led by Stormsong, who saved my life and has proven himself loyal to me. Magatha and any Grimtotem who follow her will be killed on sight if they trespass into tauren territory. That is sufficient vengeance. I am not going to waste time on revenge when my energy is better spent toward rebuilding."

Garrosh nodded. He had learned all he needed to about the young Bloodhoof and was impressed.

"Then I offer you the full protection and support of the Horde, Baine Bloodhoof."

"And in return for that protection and support, I offer the loyalty of the tauren people." Baine said the words stiffly, but sincerely. Garrosh knew he could trust this tauren's word.

He extended a hand. Baine took it in his three-fingered one, enveloping Garrosh's completely.

"For the Horde," Baine said quietly, although his voice trembled with emotion.

"For the Horde," Garrosh replied.

THIRTY

It began as a thunderstorm.

Anduin had grown used to frequent, and sometimes violent, rainstorms in Theramore. But this one had thunder that rattled his teeth and shook him awake and lightning that completely illuminated his room. He bolted up in time to hear another crash of thunder and the sound of rain pounding so fiercely against his window that he thought the drops alone would shatter it.

He got out of bed and looked out—or tried to. Rain was sluicing down so heavily it was impossible to see. He turned his head, listening as the sound of voices in the hallways reached him. He frowned slightly and threw on some clothes, poking his head out to find out what the commotion was.

Jaina rushed past. Clearly she, too, had just awakened and tossed on clothing. Her eyes were clear, but her hair had not seen a comb yet.

"Aunt Jaina? What's wrong?"

"Flooding," Jaina replied succinctly.

For an instant Anduin was hurled back in time to the

avalanche in Dun Morogh, to another instance of angry, distressed elements venting their rage upon the innocents. Aerin's cheerful face swam into his mind, but he forced it aside.

"I'm coming."

She drew breath, probably to protest, then gave him a strained smile and nodded. "All right."

He took another minute to tug on his tallest boots and throw on a hooded cape, then he was racing outside along with Jaina and several servants and guards.

The rain and the whipping wind almost halted him in his tracks. It seemed to be coming sideways rather than straight down and took his breath away for a moment. Jaina, too, was having difficulty walking. She and the others stumbled almost as if drunk as they descended from the elevated tower to ground level.

Anduin knew there was a full moon, but the heavy clouds obscured any light it might have provided. The guards bore lanterns, but the illumination was feeble. Fire would have been no use whatsoever in the deluge. Anduin gasped when his feet sank ankle-deep in water so cold he could feel it even through his heavy but now sodden boots. His eyes were adjusting to the dimness, and he realized that the entire area was covered with water. It was not too deep—not yet.

Lights were on at the inn and the mill, and there was more shouting, barely heard over the tremendous pounding of the rain and thunder. The inn was on a slight hill, but the mill was now several inches deep in water.

"Lieutenant Aden!" Jaina cried, and a mounted soldier wheeled his steed and splashed toward her. "We're opening the doors of the citadel to anyone who needs refuge. Bring them in!"

"Aye, my lady!" Aden shouted back. He yanked on the head of his horse and headed for the mill.

Jaina paused for a moment and lifted her hands to the sky, then moved her hands and fingers. Anduin couldn't hear what she said, but her mouth was moving. A heartbeat later, he gasped as the image of a giant dragon head appeared beside her. It opened its jaws and breathed a sheet of flame across the water, evaporating a large patch. Of course, the water rushed in again to fill the void, but the dragon head seemed tireless. It continued to breathe fire, and Jaina nodded in satisfaction.

"To the docks!" she cried to Anduin, and he followed her, gamely running as fast as he could through the water. It grew deeper as the ground sloped downward. Up ahead, Anduin saw a sight that might have been humorous at any other time but now only contributed to the chaos: All the gryphons had flown to perch atop various buildings. Their wings and fur were drenched, and they cawed defiantly at the flight masters who were alternately railing at them and pleading with them to "Please, come down!"

The water was up to Anduin's knees now, and he, Jaina, and the guards were grimly slogging their way forward. People, like the gryphons, had gotten to the highest ground possible. Their instincts were sound, but the lightning was furious and frequent, and what had seemed like wisdom at first was now revealed as potentially even more dangerous. Anduin and the guards were now helping frightened merchants and their families climb down to safety.

Anduin was starting to shiver. His cloak and boots were sturdy, but they were never meant to keep him warm or dry while actually *in* water. The water was utterly frigid, and he couldn't feel his legs below his knees. Still, he pressed onward. People were in trouble, and he had to help them.

He had just opened his arms to receive a sobbing little girl when a lightning bolt turned night into day. He had been looking over the girl's shoulder as she clung to him in the direction of the docks and saw a bright white zigzag strike the wooden pier. A deafening clap of thunder came immediately afterward, along with the horrible sound of people screaming and the groaning of shattered wood. Two ships that had been docked there rocked violently, tossed about as if by an angry giant child.

The girl shrieked in his ear and clutched his neck as if trying to strangle him. There was another flash of lightning, and it looked to Anduin as if a giant wave had come out of the sea, almost like a hand about to slam down on the docks. Anduin blinked, trying to clear his vision from the rain pouring like a river down his face. He couldn't be seeing what he thought he was, he simply couldn't.

Another nearly blinding flash, and the strange wave had disappeared.

So had the Theramore docks and the two ships. He had seen what he thought he had after all. The lightning had sheared off most of the Theramore docks, the ocean had completed the task, and now he could even glimpse fire despite the pummeling of the rain.

Jaina grabbed his shoulder and placed her mouth next to Anduin's ear. "Take her back to the citadel!"

He nodded and spat out rainwater in order to speak. "I'll come right back!"

"No! This is too dangerous!" Jaina again yelled in order to be heard over the storm. "Go and take care of the refugees!"

Anger and impotent frustration suddenly welled up in Anduin. He wasn't a child. He had strong arms and a calm head; he could help, dammit! But he also knew Jaina was right. He was heir to the throne of Stormwind, and he had a responsibility not to put himself foolishly in harm's way. With a muttered curse he turned back toward the citadel, wading through the icy water.

He was past shaking by the time he slogged into the citadel, where some of the servants were busily wrapping blankets around the flood victims and offering hot tea and food. Anduin carefully turned over the child to an older woman who rushed up to take her. He knew that he was drenched, that he needed to change out of the wet clothes, but he just couldn't seem to move to do so. One of Jaina's assistants looked up at him, did a double take, and frowned at his expression. Anduin stared back, chilled to the bone, blinking almost stupidly. In a distant part of his brain, he realized he was probably going into shock.

"Wish I had Fearbreaker," he murmured. He was dimly aware of the servant pulling him into a side room, helping him out of the sodden clothes and thrusting a too-large shirt and pair of pants at him. Before Anduin quite realized what had happened, he was wrapped in a rough but warm blanket in front of the fire with a mug of hot tea in his hand. The servant vanished—there were many others who needed immediate care. After a few moments Anduin began shivering violently, and after a few moments more, he began thinking about the idea of perhaps being in the vicinity of being warm.

After a while he felt well enough to be of help, rather than simply taking up a spot on the floor. He went to his room, threw on his own clothing, and returned to help others as he had been helped, providing hot liquids and blankets and taking their soggy clothes to hang up on lines quickly strung about the rooms.

The rain did not let up. The waters rose, despite Jaina's dragon head trying to keep them at bay. Jaina was pushing herself well past the point of exhaustion, renewing the spell every few minutes, issuing orders, and aiding the refugees. As the waters climbed, more and more people sought refuge in the citadel, sitting on the wooden floors of its many stories. Eventually Anduin was fairly certain that the citadel, the guard quarters, and the inn housed everyone who lived in Theramore.

Finally, toward dusk of the second day, Jaina resigned herself to sitting down and eating and drinking something. She had changed clothes several times, and this current change of clothing was now sopping wet. Anduin drew a seat for her by the fire in her small, cozy room and brought her some tea. Jaina was shaking so badly that the cup rattled in the saucer as she lifted bloodshot, exhausted eyes to him.

"I think you need to return home. There's no knowing when the flooding is going to stop, and I can't risk your safety."

Anduin looked unhappy. "I can help," he said. "I won't do anything foolish, Jaina, you know I won't."

She reached out as if to tousle his blond hair but seemed too weak to complete the gesture. Her hand fell limply into her lap, and she sighed.

"Well, it's not as if you'd see your father," she murmured, taking a sip of tea.

"What do you mean?"

Jaina froze, the cup halfway to the saucer. She lifted wide eyes to Anduin, and he saw the look of someone desperately searching for a comforting falsehood but too exhausted mentally to find it.

"What about my father? Where is he?" And then he knew. He stared at her, horrified. "He's going to attack Ironforge, isn't he?"

"Anduin," Jaina began, "Moira is a tyrant. She—"

"Moira? Come on, Aunt Jaina, you have to tell me what he's doing!"

In a voice that was heavy with resignation and trembling with weariness, Jaina spoke, confirming his worst fears.

"Varian is taking an elite strike team to Ironforge. Their mission is to execute Moira and liberate the city."

Anduin couldn't believe his ears. "How are they getting in?"

"Through the Deeprun Tram passageway."

"They'll be spotted."

Jaina rubbed her eyes. "Anduin, we're talking SI:7 people. They won't be spotted."

Anduin shook his head slowly. "No, they won't. Jaina, you're right. I do need to leave Theramore."

She frowned, the little crease on her forehead more prominent with her weariness. "No. You are *not* going to Ironforge!"

He almost growled in exasperation. "Jaina, listen to me, please! You've always been reasonable; you've got to be reasonable now. Moira's done some bad things—locked down the city, put innocent people in jail. But she *didn't* kill King Magni and she *is* his daughter. She's the rightful heir, and her son after her. Some of the things she wants to do, I approve of—she's just trying to do the right things the wrong way."

"Anduin, she is holding a whole city—Ironforge, the dwarven *capital*—hostage."

"Because she doesn't know them yet. Doesn't trust them. Jaina, in some ways, she's just a frightened little girl who wanted her father to love her."

"Scared little girls who rule cities do dangerous things, and they need to be stopped."

"By being killed? Or do they need to be guided? She wants the dwarves to take another look at their heritage. To reach out to the Dark Irons as the brethren they are. Is that worth being murdered for? And maybe her child along with her? Listen to me, Jaina, please. If Father carries out this attack, a lot of people are going to die, and the succession will be thrown into confusion. Instead of coming together as a people, the dwarves are going to find themselves in the midst of another civil war! I've got to try to stop him, don't you see? Make him understand that there's another way."

"No, absolutely not! You are thirteen years old, with insufficient training, and the heir to the throne besides. Do you think it would help Stormwind if you got yourself killed?" She took a deep breath and paused, thinking hard. He stayed silent. "All right. If you are set on doing this—and you might be right—I'm coming with you. Give me a few hours to contain the situation here and—"

"He's on his way now. We don't have the luxury of a few hours, you know that! I know Father, and so do you. You know that whatever is going to happen, it's going to be bad, and it's going to happen quickly. I can help. I can save lives. Let me do this."

Jaina's eyes filled with tears, and she turned away. He didn't press her. He had faith in her and knew she would do the right thing.

"I . . ."

"One day I'll be king, and not just for a short time. One day Father will be gone, and no one knows when that day will be. It could be as early as tonight—Light knows I hope not, but you know that, and I know it. And so does Father. Ruling Stormwind is my destiny, what I was born to do. And I can't face that destiny if I'm being treated like a child."

She bit her lower lip, then dashed her hand across her eyes. "You're right," she said quietly. "You're not a little boy anymore. We both still want you to be, your father and I, but you've already seen so much, done so much. . . ."

Her voice broke and she paused. "You take the utmost care not to get caught, Anduin Wrynn," she said in a voice that was hard and angry. For a second he was startled, then he realized she wasn't angry at him—she was angry that there was no other way. "And you stop your father. You make it worth the risk, do you understand?"

He nodded mutely. She caught him up in her arms and hugged him tightly, as if she were holding him for the last time. And maybe, in a way, she was, trying to give a final farewell to the boy he had been. He hugged her back, feeling a cold brush of fear. But even stronger than the fear was a calm, quiet feeling in the center of his being that told him he was doing the right thing.

She drew back and patted his cheek, the tears streaming down her face as she forced a smile.

"May the Light be with you," she said. Stepping back, she began to cast the spell to create a portal.

"It is," Anduin said. "I know it."

And he stepped through.

They were shadows, nothing more, as they slipped along the dark streets that were deserted this hour of the night. They were heading north, into the smoky Dwarven District.

Heading for the Deeprun Tram.

The station was utterly deserted, and of course the tram itself was nowhere to be seen. When it had been running, bright spotlights had been placed every few yards along the track for the safety and pleasure of the commuters. Now that the tram was "closed for repairs" at its Ironforge departure site, Varian had ordered all the lights in the Stormwind jurisdiction extinguished. The eighteen other men and women who now dropped down onto the tracks and ran lightly along the metal path, their feet making barely a sound, were accustomed to maneuvering in the darkness, and the path was a straight shot. Varian's feet, however, did make some slight sounds, and he frowned to himself. He was in this instance the weakest link in the chain. His training had been much different from those of his compatriots. While he was unquestionably as deadly as they, his manner of attack was quite different, and he was more than willing to let himself to be guided and corrected. All nineteen of them wore masks to protect their identities.

The leader of this part of the mission was Owynn Graddock, a dwarf with darkly tanned skin and black hair and beard. He had been handpicked for the job by Mathias Shaw, head of SI:7. Though most were human, there were several other dwarves and a few gnomes among the company. Varian had insisted they be included. Every trained assassin could do the job, but dwarves and gnomes would stand to benefit the most from regaining control of Ironforge.

Prior to the mission, Graddock had scouted out almost the entire length of the tram's tunnel himself, so the group knew what to face.

"There's nae break in th' glass keeping the water from th' lake out," Graddock had reported. "I half-expected that—it would flood the tunnel but good, an' thus prevent the sort o' thing we're attempting here. But I figure

Moira eventually wants to be able to use th' tram—maybe tae mount an attack on Stormwind. At any rate, we're lucky with that.

"Now, about here . . . I saw some Dark Irons lurkin' about. So . . ." He had looked up, his solemn brown eyes regarding Mathias and Varian. "Here's where th' battle begins."

Now they ran, swiftly and for the most part silently, until they reached the subterranean lake. Varian did not spare the wonders of the lake, visible through strong glass, a second glance. His mind was utterly on the mission.

On they ran, no one growing even slightly out of breath. A scent reached Varian's nostrils—thick and sweet and cloying. Pipe tobacco. He smiled beneath his mask at how his enemies had so obviously given themselves away. At once he slowed, as did his companions. In the dim light he saw Graddock gesture for them to prepare for battle.

The assassins drew various weapons—daggers, awls painted with poison, gloves with special devices built inside them. Varian tightened his mask more firmly so that it would not slip and reached for his own weapons, two shortswords. He was loath to forego the more familiar Shalamayne, but it was instantly recognizable, and he wished no one to suspect his identity until he chose to reveal it.

Another gesture from Graddock, and they moved forward, slowly, and this time even Varian's feet did not make noise on the creaky metal. He was learning. Now he could glimpse the dwarves up ahead. There were five of them. They were sitting on folded blankets. Tankards of ale and trays heaped with the remnants of a meal surrounded them, and—Varian couldn't believe it—they were playing cards.

Graddock held up his hand and brought it down once, twice, three times.

The assassins sprang.

Varian wasn't sure how they communicated, but it was almost as if the attack was choreographed. Each dwarf had a black-leather-clad killer atop him before he could do more than gasp in surprise. Varian had charged forward, swords at the ready, biting back a yell, but by the time he was there, the five had been quickly and quietly killed. One had a knife in his eye. Another's neck had been snapped. A third's face was swollen in reaction to a swift-acting poison, froth still dripping from his mouth. A gnome male named Brink, balding and oddly dangerous looking for one of his race, and a human female now rose, cleaning their blades emotionlessly and efficiently, from the final two kills.

They moved on to the next group. They were closing in on Ironforge.

THIRTY-ONE

"Anduin!" Rohan's voice was filled with warmth and surprise as he peered at the boy, who had suddenly appeared in the Hall of Mysteries. "We'd heard ye escaped. Why in th' world have ye come back here?"

Anduin stepped out from the portal and quickly ducked into a corner of the hall. Rohan followed, speaking quietly and urgently.

"Moira's on th' warpath for ye. She's searched here twice already an' has got her lackeys scouring every inch of Ironforge. She's nae said anything, o' course, but we can tell who she's looking for."

"I had to come back," Anduin said, keeping his voice low. "My father is mounting an attack to sneak into Ironforge, and I've got to stop him. He plans to kill Moira. He thinks she's a usurper."

Rohan's white brows drew together in a frown. "But she's not. She's a lousy queen, that's fer sure, an' she's thrown some good people in jail. But she is the rightful heir, and so is the wee bairn after her."

"Exactly," Anduin said, grateful that Rohan understood what he was getting at. "What she's doing is wrong. I of all people can see that. She was trying to keep me prisoner. She was never intending to let me go. But that doesn't mean my father can just murder her. It's not his place, and he will accomplish nothing other than dwarven outrage and another civil war. Besides, some of what she wants to do is the right thing."

"How did ye learn of this? Are ye certain yer information is accurate?"

Anduin didn't want to implicate Jaina, so he just nodded. "As the Light guides me, Father Rohan, I trust that what I have been told is true."

"Well, ye are a prince, not a humble priest like meself, so if you think it is the truth, then I do, too. And ye're right. Murderin' our leaders is nae the right thing t' do . . . and there are folks that like some o' what she's been saying. I'll help ye, lad. What do ye need of me?"

Anduin realized he hadn't thought that far ahead. "Um," he began, "I know my father's coming via the Deeprun Tram tunnel. I don't know when he's supposed to get here. We should try to intercept him."

"Hm," said Rohan, "like many things, easier said than done. Ye're a lad yet, but ye're no dwarf-sized. And th' Dark Irons are on the lookout for ye."

"We'll just have to be careful," Anduin said. "And I'll have to stoop. Come on!"

The eighteen assassins and the king of Stormwind scrambled out of the Deeprun Tram track and onto the platform. They were met by several Dark Iron dwarves. It was a one-sided fight, and the SI:7 team quickly and ruthlessly dispatched Moira's guards. The fight had attracted some attention, and a little crowd of mostly gnomes now stared at the men and women in masks and black leather, unsure if they were rescuers or new foes.

"Dinna worry," Graddock reassured them. "We've come fer Moira and her people, not the good folk of Ironforge."

The gnomes, who had been clustered together, gave a cheer.

They hurried on, heading toward the Hall of Explorers, which would be quiet at this time of night. From there, it was a straight shot across the Great Forge to the High Seat. The gnome named Brink scouted ahead and reported back.

"Twenty-three," he said in a gravelly voice. "Ten are Dark Iron guards."

"Only ten? I expected more," Graddock said. "Let's go."

In the end Anduin did not have to stoop. One of the priestesses was an alchemist and had readily agreed to mix up an invisibility potion. "It will nae last very long," she cautioned. "An' it tastes nasty tae boot."

"I can run pretty fast," Anduin assured her, taking the small vial. He uncorked it and coughed at the fumes. The priestess was right—it certainly smelled nasty.

"Bottoms up," he said and lifted it to his lips.

"Hold a moment, lad," Rohan said. "There's summat going on out there. . . ."

There was a commotion out in the main area.

Various guards were running about, looking grimmer than usual.

"Och, I hope ye've not been spotted," Rohan said quietly. One of the guards started jogging toward the Hall of Mysteries, and Anduin crouched back in the shadows, prepared to chug the potion, if need be.

"Healers! Come quickly, ye're needed!"

"What is it?" Rohan said, giving a fairly good impression of someone who had just been roused from sleep.

"There's been fighting at the Deeprun Tram," the Dark Iron guard said.

"Really?" Rohan kept his voice pitched loud for Anduin's benefit. "How many? And is th' site contained?"

"About ten, and nay, there seems to be fighting in th' Great Forge area, too. Bring all yer priests! Now!"

Rohan cast a quick, apologetic glance over his shoulder, then gathered his supplies and hurried off along with the other priests. Anduin was on his own.

"Too late," he murmured to himself. If Varian and the team of assassins were already at the forge—

His mouth set in a grim line, then he lifted the potion to his lips and gulped it down, grimacing at the taste.

Then Anduin Wrynn ran as fast as his legs could carry him toward the High Seat, Moira . . . and his father.

The first few guards were dispatched quietly. The group skidded to a halt and caught their breaths, melding with the shadows. Right across the forge was the High Seat . . . and there were several Dark Irons in the way.

"We'll split into two groups. You," and Graddock

pointed to nine of his followers, "stay wi' me. We'll tackle th' guards at th' forge. The rest of ye, go wi' Varian. Get him tae Moira, no matter the cost. Is that clear?"

They all nodded. Despite the odds that stared them in the face, none of them looked particularly distressed. As Varian watched, Brink even yawned and stretched. He supposed this was all in a day's work for them, just as slaughtering foes twice his size had been his "job" as a gladiator.

"All right, then. Let's be about it."

And with no further warning, the first group moved forward. Varian, whose eyes had gotten used to seeing them after the hours they had spent together this night, blinked as they became indistinguishable from the shadows. And then the cries started as the assassins attacked—cutting throats, picking up the startled dwarves and hurling them into the molten liquid pools of the forge.

"Go, go!" It was Brink, elbowing Varian in the thigh. He needed no further urging. His group began to run at full speed along the length of the Great Forge. The Dark Iron guards stationed there met them halfway, roaring challenges. Pleased to finally be in an open, one-on-one swordfight after sneaking around all night, Varian shouted a battle cry and fell eagerly on the first one. Swords clashed against axe blade and shield, striking sparks in the dim light. The Dark Iron was good, Varian had to give him that. He managed to block Varian's blows fully four times before the king dodged a counterattack and stabbed the dwarf through the gap in his armor between arm and breastplate.

He whirled, sweeping one sword parallel to the ground, biting through the armor of another guard. This one cried out in pain, falling to his knees. Varian kicked him in the face, then severed his head from his shoulders with the second sword. He didn't even see the head strike the ground, his eyes searching for where the next attack would be.

His team was already inside the High Seat, quickly and ruthlessly dispatching any opposition they found there. Of course, at this hour Moira would not be sitting on her stolen throne. She would be in one of the private back rooms, asleep, with her brat of a child.

Varian rushed forward, his focus narrowing so that the door to the false queen's private rooms was the only thing he thought of. He ran full tilt toward it, turning at the last minute to slam it with a plated shoulder. It did not yield. Again he slammed into it, and again, and then two more assassins were there, putting their shoulders to the task.

The door splintered, and they half-ran, half-fell inside. They were attacked almost at once. Varian heard a woman screaming and the shriek of a frightened infant. He paid it no mind, slashing out with his swords at the two dwarves who charged him. They fell quickly, their blood spattering him. One of his swords was lodged firmly in the midsection of one, and after a quick attempt to tug it free Varian abandoned the weapon. He whirled, gripping the remaining sword with both hands, and sought his prey.

Moira Bronzebeard, wearing a nightgown, her hair in disarray and her eyes wide with terror, stood on the bed. Varian ripped off the mask that had covered the lower part of his face, and Moira gasped with recognition. In two strides Varian had her. He seized her arm, hauling her off the bed. She struggled, but his hand had clamped down around her upper arm like a manacle.

She stumbled as he pulled her out of the room, but he didn't care. Varian marched out into the open area near the forge, where crowds were starting to gather, dragging the struggling dwarf behind him. He hauled her to him roughly with one arm.

His other hand was at her throat, pressing the sword against the pale flesh.

"Behold the usurper!" Varian cried, his identity no longer secret, his voice echoing in the vast space. "This is the child Magni Bronzebeard wept countless tears over. His beloved little girl. How sickened he would be to see what she's done to his city, his people!"

The gathered crowd stared. Even the Dark Irons did not dare make a move, not with their empress in such immediate jeopardy.

"This throne is not yours. You bought it with deceit, and lies, and trickery. You have threatened your own subjects when they have done nothing wrong, and bullied your way to a title you have not yet earned. I will not see you sit upon this stolen throne one moment longer!"

"Father!"

The voice cut through the haze of Varian's rage, and for just an instant the blade he held to Moira's throat wavered. Then he recovered. He did not take his eyes from the dwarf as he replied.

"You shouldn't be here, Anduin. Get out. This is no place for you."

"But it *is* my place!" The voice was coming closer, moving through the crowd toward him. Moira's gaze darted from Varian to, presumably, his son, but she made no attempt to beg for aid. Probably because she knew any movement other than her eyes would result in the sword's being plunged deep into her pale throat.

"You sent me here! You wanted me to get to know the dwarven people, and I have. I knew Magni well, and I was here when Moira came. I saw what turmoil her arrival brought. And I saw that things got far too close to civil war when people reached for weapons to solve their problems with her. Whatever you may think of her, she *is* the rightful heir!"

"Maybe her blood's right," snarled Varian, "but her mind's not. She's under a spell, Son; Magni always thought so. She tried to keep you prisoner. She's holding a bunch of people for no reason." Making sure his grip was solid, he turned his head slightly. "She's not fit to be leader! She's going to destroy all that Magni tried to do! All that he . . . he died for!"

Anduin stepped forward, a hand outstretched imploringly. "There's no spell, Father. Magni wanted to believe there was rather than the truth—that he drove Moira away because she wasn't a male heir."

Varian's black brows drew together. "You spit on the memory of an honorable man, Anduin."

Anduin didn't flinch. "You can be an honorable man and still make mistakes," he continued implacably. His father's cheeks darkened, and he knew he didn't need to say anything else. "Moira was accepted among the Dark Irons. She fell in love, she married within the laws of her people, she bore her husband a child. She's the rightful *dwarven* heir of the *dwarven* people. They need to decide whether to accept her or not. It's not our place."

"She held you hostage, Anduin!" Varian's voice echoed, and Anduin flinched slightly. "You, my son! She can't be allowed to get away with that! I won't let her hold you and a whole city prisoner. I won't, do you understand?"

His boy, his beautiful son . . . it was hard not to simply bellow in anger and plunge the blade into the usurper's neck. To not rejoice in the feel of hot, wet blood spurting over his hand. To know that the threat to his son was forever ended. He could do it. He could do all that. And how he wanted to.

"Then let her answer to the law, to her people, for what she has done to them. Father—you're a king, a good one, one who wants to do the right thing. You believe in the law. In justice. You're not some—some vigilante. Destruction . . ." Anduin paused in midsentence, a strange but calm look coming over his young face, as if remembering something. "Destruction is easy. Creating something good, something right, something that lasts—that's what's hard. It'd be easy to kill her. But you have to think of what's best for the people of Ironforge. For the dwarves—all of them. What is wrong with the dwarves' deciding how much or how little they want to participate in the world's politics? What's wrong with reaching out to the Dark Irons if they are amenable?"

There were some slight murmurings. Varian looked around, nostrils flaring. Rohan cleared his throat.

"The lad speaks true, Yer Majesty. Summat o' what Moira says is wisdom. Now, how she's gone about it—

right foolish. But she's *our* princess, in the end. And once she's proper crowned, our queen."

"If Moira dies and there is no clear heir, civil war will erupt!" Anduin continued. "Do you think that's what's best for the dwarven people? Do you think that's what Magni would want? This might bring Stormwind into the war, too—or the night elves, or the gnomes. Can you make the decisions for them, too?"

Varian's hand was trembling slightly now, and Moira let out a little squeak as the blade nicked her throat. A single drop of red blood dewed the sword.

You're not some—some vigilante.

Destruction is easy.

I do want to do what's right—what's just, Varian thought wildly. *But how do I create something that lasts? She is the rightful heir, and, yes, the dwarves might turn on one another. It's not my place to do this. This is their city, their queen or their pretender. If we could only find Brann or Muradin, we—*

He blinked.

"Much as I wish it weren't true," he said harshly to Moira, who stared up at him with wide, terrified eyes, "yours *is* the rightful claim to the throne. But just like me, Moira Bronzebeard, you need to be better than you are. You need more than just a bloodline to rule your people well. You're going to have to earn it."

He shoved her away. She staggered back but made no attempt to flee. How could she? She was encircled by the populace of the city she had tried to rule with a cruel, arrogant hand.

"You obviously can't be trusted to have free rein over Ironforge. Not by yourself, not yet. You've made that amply clear. These people aren't just the Dark Iron dwarves you're used to lording over. The dwarves have three clans. Dark Iron, Bronzebeard, and Wildhammer. You want to bring the dwarven people together? Fine. Then each of those clans needs a representative. A voice, which, by the Light, *you will listen to*!" He was working it through as he spoke. The Wildhammers, it was true, had demonstrated little interest in Ironforge and had their own holdings elsewhere. They were their own nation; Moira would not be their queen.

But this was about more than her title. It was about the dwarves as a people. It was about preventing, as Anduin had said, civil war. It felt right—right enough to be given a chance to see if it worked. In the end, the dwarves themselves would decide that.

Moira said nothing, only looked around with wide, fearful eyes. She looked like nothing more than a scared little girl, standing there in her nightgown. . . .

"Three clans, three leaders. Three . . . hammers," Varian said. "You for the Dark Irons, whom you married into, Falstad for the Wildhammers, and Muradin or Brann or whoever we can find for the Bronzebeards. You will listen to their needs. You will work with them for the betterment of the dwarven people, not your own selfish ends. Do you understand me?"

Moira nodded . . . carefully.

"We'll be watching you. Very. Closely. Instead of bleeding your life out here on the floor of the High Seat, you've got a second chance to prove that you're ready to lead the dwarves." He leaned over her. "Don't disappoint them."

He gave a curt nod. The blades of the SI:7 team were sheathed as quickly as they had been drawn. Moira's hand went to her throat and tentatively touched the nick there. She was visibly shaking, all her chilling elegance and false sweetness gone.

He was done with her. He turned to Anduin, saw his son smiling and nodding with pride. With two strides Varian closed the distance between them and hugged his son. As he held Anduin tight, he heard the first smatterings of applause. It built, grew, was joined by shouts and whistles of approval. Names were called— "Wildhammer!" "Bronzebeard!" And, as Anduin and Rohan had said, even "Dark Iron!"

Varian looked up to see dozens, perhaps hundreds, of dwarves smiling and cheering at him and his decision. Moira stood alone, her hand still to her throat, her head bowed.

"See, Father?" Anduin said, pulling back to look up at him. "You knew exactly the right thing to do. I knew you did."

Varian smiled. "I needed someone to believe that for me, before I could," he replied. "Come on, Son. Let's go home."

Thrall and Aggra hurried back to Garadar, only to find a grim-faced welcome. Greatmother Geyah in particular looked extremely sad, rising to embrace Thrall. A tauren stood by, tall and straight. Thrall recognized him as Perith Stormhoof, and he felt the color drain from his face. "Something terrible has happened," Thrall said, the phrase not a question but a statement. "What is it?"

Geyah laid a hand on his heart. "First, you know here that you were right to come to Nagrand. Whatever has happened in your absence."

Thrall glanced at Aggra, who looked as upset as he felt. He forced himself to be calm. "Perith. Speak."

And Perith did, his voice calm, breaking only at certain points. He spoke of the treacherous murder of innocent druids gathering peacefully, and of an outraged Cairne challenging Garrosh. Of the great high chieftain's death that was subsequently determined to be from poison administered by Magatha Grimtotem. Of the slaughter at Thunder Bluff, and Bloodhoof Village, and Sun Rock Retreat. When he had finished, he held out a rolled-up scroll. "Palkar, Drek'Thar's attendant, sends this as well."

Thrall unrolled it with hands he forced to not tremble. As he read Palkar's words—words that revealed that, contrary to what all had thought, Drek'Thar, while his mind sometimes wandered, still had true visions—his heart sank. The ink had spotted as Palkar wrote of Drek'Thar's latest utterance: *The land will weep, and the world will break. . . .*

The world will break. As another world had done once before . . .

Thrall swayed, but refused offers to sit. He stood, his knees locked into position as if welded there. For a long moment he stood, wondering, *Was I right to come? Was this bit of knowledge I have gleaned worth the loss of Cairne? Of so many innocent, peaceful tauren? And even if I was right—am I in time?*

"Baine," he said at last. "What of Baine?"

"No word, Warchief," Perith said. "But it is believed he is still alive."

"And Garrosh? What has he done?"

"Nothing, so far. He appears to be waiting to see which side is victorious."

Thrall's hands clenched into fists. He felt a brush, featherlight, and looked down to see Aggra's hand touching his. Not knowing exactly why he did so, he opened his fist and permitted his fingers to twine with hers. He took a deep breath.

"This—" His voice broke, and he tried again. "This is grievous news. My heart breaks for the slain." He looked at Geyah. "Today, I learned things from the Furies that I believe will help me aid Azeroth. I had hoped to leave in a few days, but now surely you understand that I must depart immediately."

"Of course," Geyah said at once. "We have already packed your things."

He was both glad of this and not, as he had hoped to have a few moments to compose himself. Geyah, shrewd female that she was, realized this at once. "I am sure you will wish to take a few moments in meditation before you go," she said, and Thrall seized upon the opportunity.

He strode outside Garadar a short way to a clump of trees. A small herd of wild talbuk eyed him, then with a flip of their tails galloped a short distance away to resume grazing in peace.

Thrall sat down hard, feeling a thousand years old. He was having difficulty absorbing the scope of the catastrophic news. Could it all really be true? The killing of the druids, of Cairne, of untold numbers of tauren at the very heart of their land? He felt almost dizzy and placed his head in his hands for a moment.

His mind went back to his last conversation with Cairne, and pain shot through his heart. To have exchanged such words with an old friend—and to have those words be the last thing Cairne had from him . . . this single death seemed to strike him harder than all the innocent lives lost as a result of Cairne's murder. For murder it was. Not a fair death in the arena, but *poisoned*—

He jumped as he felt a hand on his shoulder and whirled to see Aggra sitting beside him. Anger stirred inside him and he snapped, "Have you come to gloat, Aggra? To tell me what a poor warchief I am? That my divided loyalties have cost the life of one of my dearest friends and those of countless innocents?"

Her brown eyes were unspeakably kind as she shook her head, remaining silent.

Thrall exhaled loudly and looked off to the horizon. "If you did, you would be saying nothing I have not already thought."

"So I assumed. One doesn't often need help in beating oneself up." She spoke quietly, and Thrall suspected he was hearing the voice of experience. She hesitated, then said, "I was wrong to so sit in judgment of you. I apologize."

He waved a hand. In light of what he had just heard, Aggra's tart comments were the least of his worries. But she pressed on.

"When we first heard of you, I was excited. I was raised on stories of Durotan and Draka. I admired your mother in particular. I . . . I wanted to be like her. And when we heard of you, we all thought you would come home to Nagrand. But you stayed in Azeroth, even when we, the Mag'har, joined the Horde. Made alliances with strange beings. And . . . I felt betrayed that Draka's son would forsake his people. You did come back. Once. But you did not stay. And I could not understand why."

He listened, not interrupting.

"Then you came again. Wanting our knowledge, knowledge that was bought with such pain and effort—not to help the world that birthed our people, but to help this strange, alien place. I was angry. And so I was harsh to you. It was selfish and shallow of me."

"What changed your mind?" he asked, curious.

She had been looking away, to the horizon, as he had been. Now she turned her face to his. The slanting afternoon light caught the strong planes of her brown, so very orcish face. And Thrall, used to finding harmony and pleasing beauty in the faces of human woman, as he had grown up among that race, was suddenly struck by hers.

"It was starting to happen before the vision quest," she said quietly. "You had already begun to change my mind. You did not rise to the bait to be hooked like a fish. Neither did you use your influence with the Greatmother to replace me as your teacher. And the more I watched and listened to you, the more I realized . . . this truly does matter to you.

"I walked with you, and saw how you lived the elements, like a true shaman does. I saw, and I shared, your pain, and joy. I watched you with Taretha, with Drek'Thar, with Cairne and Jaina. You live what you believe, even if you didn't understand it until you underwent the vision quest. You are not a power-hungry child seeking a new, better challenge. You are striving to do what is best for your people—all of them. Not just orc, or Horde, but you even want what is best for your rivals. You want," she said, and placed a brown hand flat on the earth in a loving gesture, "what is best for your world."

"I am not sure that what I have done is best for it," Thrall admitted quietly. "If I had stayed—"

"Then you would not have learned what you have."

"Cairne would be alive. And so would the tauren who lived in Thunder Bluff and—"

Her hand shot out and gripped his arm, the nails digging angrily into the flesh. "What you have learned could save everything. Everything!"

"Or nothing," Thrall said. He did not pull his arm back, instead watched as blood began to seep from beneath her nails.

"You chose possibility over certainty. The possibility of success over certain defeat. If you had done nothing, then you would not have been a warchief. You would have been a coward, unworthy of such an honor." Her face hardened slightly. "But if you want to wallow? Cry, 'Poor Go'el, woe is me'? Then by all means do so. But you will have to do it without me."

She began to rise. Thrall caught her wrist, and she glared at him.

"What did you mean?"

"I meant, if you choose the path of self-pity over action, that you would prove my change of heart to be wrong. And I would not go back to Azeroth with you."

He tightened his grip on her wrist. "You . . . were planning on returning with me? Why?"

Emotions flitted across her face, and finally Aggra blurted, "Because, Go'el, I found that I did not wish to be apart from you. But it seems I was wrong, because you are not what I thought you were. I will not go with one who—"

He pulled her down into his arms and crushed her to him. "I would have you come with me. Walk with me wherever this path may take us. I have grown used to your voice letting me know when I am wrong, and . . . I like to hear it when you speak gently. It would pain me, to not have you near. Will you come? Be at my side?"

"To—advise you?"

He nodded, his cheek resting against the top of her head. "To be my wisdom, as Air, my steadiness, as Earth . . ." He took a deep breath. "And my passion and my heart, as Fire and Water. And if you would have it so, I would be these things to you."

He felt her trembling in his embrace: she, Aggra, strong and courageous. She pulled back a little and laid her hand on his chest, her eyes searching his. "Go'el, as long as you have this great heart to lead—and to love—then know that I will go with you to the ends of any world and beyond."

He placed a hand on her cheek, green skin against brown, then leaned forward slowly to rest his forehead gently against hers.

THIRTY-TWO

The funereal cloth in which High Chieftain Cairne Bloodhoof had been lovingly wrapped was exquisite. It had been woven in the hues of the Earth Mother—tans and browns and greens.

As was traditional among the tauren, the dead were cremated with ceremony and ritual. The bodies were placed atop a pyre, and a raging fire was lit beneath them. The ashes would fall to the earth; the smoke would rise to the sky. Earth Mother and Sky Father would thus both welcome the honored dead, and An'she and Mu'sha would witness their passing.

Thrall wore, as he almost always did, the armor that the late Orgrim Doomhammer had bequeathed to him. Its weight hindered him somewhat, and Thrall was forced to climb slowly atop a ridge so he could be on the same level as the body and look at what remained of Cairne with vision made blurry because of tears.

Thrall had rushed back to Azeroth. He and Aggra had met briefly with Baine, and Thrall had requested some time alone with Cairne. The request had been granted.

Later there would be long conversations, and planning, and preparations. But for now Thrall sat near his old friend for a long time, while the sun made its languid path across the blue sky of Mulgore. Finally Thrall took a deep breath and said quietly, "Cairne, my old friend . . . are you still here?"

Both tauren and orcs believed that the spirits of the beloved dead sometimes spoke with those they had loved in life. They imparted warnings, or advice, or simply blessings.

Thrall would have been grateful for any of these.

But his words were taken by the soft, fragrant breeze and borne away, and nothing, no one, stirred to answer him. Thrall lowered his head for a moment.

"And so I truly am alone, and you truly have departed, my old friend," he said. "And so I cannot ask your advice, or your forgiveness, as I should have been able to."

Only the soft sigh of the wind answered him.

"We parted in anger, you and I. Two who should never be angry at one another, two who should have been old enough to know that this is a bad way to part. I was frustrated in my inability to solve my own challenges, and I turned from you when you spoke wisdom. Never had I done so before, and now see what has happened. You lie here, slain by treachery, and I cannot look you in the eye and tell you how my heart is breaking at this sight."

His voice, too, was breaking, and he took a moment to regain his composure, although there was no one here to see him save the birds and beasts of the land. The armor felt heavy and hot on him.

"Your son . . . Cairne, I would say to you, you would be so proud of Baine, except that I already knew how proud you were of him. He is truly your son, and will carry the legacy of all you fought for to another generation. He did not let his pain rule his head. He has kept your people safe, at the cost of his own burning desire. The tauren are at peace once again, which I know was all you ever wanted for them. Even in the depths of horror, such as that dreadful, dark night—even then, your people, and the spirit of the Horde survived.

"The Grimtotem are now open enemies, instead of deceivers you held to your heart, who took your trust and still coldly planned to strike. The tauren will not be taken unawares by them again—ever. As for Garrosh . . . I truly believe that he did not know of Magatha's treachery. He's many things, but a deceitful, scheming murderer is not one of them. He'd want to know he'd won fairly, so he could legitimately revel in the honor. He . . ."

His voice trailed off. Thrall was terribly distraught at the murder of his friend and the slaughter that had followed Cairne's death. He was glad the tauren were again at peace, under such a fine leader as Baine. But other than that . . .

"Cairne," he said slowly, "I built this Horde. I inspired them, gave them purpose, direction. And yet . . . it seems as though this duty, this purpose . . . it is no longer the one that calls to me. How can I lead them well when my focus is elsewhere?"

His instincts, once so certain, were no longer as
as they once were. He buried his face in his
black armor creaking with the gestur

Torn. He again saw himself standing in the mist of the vision quest, his armor cracking and falling off him as he stood in the grip of fear and helplessness. He realized with a jolt that if he continued to lead them thusly, with his mind and heart and attention elsewhere, that he would eventually take the Horde down the path of civil war. Whatever his disagreement with Garrosh about what had happened in his absence, it had been he who had appointed young Hellscream acting warchief. It was his responsibility as much as Garrosh's, and, in the end, all that could be proven was that the youth had done nothing worse than accept a challenge and up the consequences. He would not force the Horde to watch him and Garrosh struggle over that.

"I never told you this before. I wish I had. Do you know," he continued quietly, "that to my mind, you always held the heart of the Horde, Cairne? You, and the tauren. When many others in the Horde hungered for war and darker paths, you listened to the wisdom of your Earth Mother, and counseled us to try other ways, other ideas. You reminded us of forgiveness and compassion. You were our heart, our true spiritual center."

Thrall knew, as he clumsily formed the words, that it was time he trusted his own heart. It was leading him away from Orgrimmar, from the Horde, to a fierce and passionate young shaman named Aggra and the proud orcish ways she represented.

s leading him to the very heart of the world.
his eyes in pain. He did not *want* this deci-
ht one. It was too hard; it would cause
rt too many people. There were

many reasons he should stay, all sound and logical, all important and vital. And there was only one reason he should go, and that reason was mystical and mysterious and far from clear to him.

But it was the right choice. It was the *only* choice. A wind came, tugging at his hair gently, tugging at his soul more firmly. His skin prickled. And he realized that his choice had already been made.

He had been shown, very clearly, what to do. If he continued to walk the path of warchief, he would fail. There was only one way he could save the Horde—and his world.

He knew what to do.

Slowly Thrall rose. The setting sun—An'she, to the tauren people—in its riot of color bathed the black plate. Then, slowly, Thrall began divesting himself of it. First he unfastened and then slipped off the shoulders. They fell to the soft, green grass with a musical, clanking sound. Next, he began unfastening the breastplate. It had once been dented by the blow that had cost Doomhammer his life. That blow had been a cowardly one—it had come from behind, a spear strike that had shattered the back plate and dented the breastplate from the inside. Thrall had ordered it repaired, so that it could be worn again.

Piece by piece, the armor of Orgrim Doomhammer, the armor of the warchief of the Horde, was removed and placed with reverence on a growing pile. Thrall reached into his pack and pulled out a simple brown robe, pulling it over his head, and then draped the string of prayer beads about his neck. Aggra's words came back to him: *We do not wear armor in our initiations. An initiation is a rebirth, not a battle. Like the snake, we shed the skins of who we were before. We need to approach it without those burdens, without the narrow thoughts and notions that we have held. We need to be simple, clean, ready to understand and connect with the elements, and let them write their wisdom on our souls.*

He removed the boots and rose, his bare, green feet on the good, solid earth, his arms outspread, his head tilted back, his blue eyes closed. He greeted the arrival of twilight not as the warchief in ceremonial garb. It was not who he was, not anymore. They had shown him, the elements. But he had perhaps acted in time—he was choosing to shed the armor and the title of warchief rather than having it torn from him. The choice was in his hands—and he made it freely, calmly.

Thrall was a shaman. His responsibility no longer lay only with the Horde, it lay with Azeroth itself, and the elements that cried out to him for aid, to save them from the dreadful catastrophe that loomed ahead, or to heal them if it turned out he was not in time. The wind, still warm and gentle, picked up, as if caressing him in approval.

He lowered his head and opened his eyes. His gaze fell upon the body of his friend one last time. As An'she set in the west, making a striking silhouette of Thunder Bluff, a final ray seemed to fall upon the body. Arranged atop Cairne's broad chest were all the ritual adornments he had worn in life—feathers, beads, bones. And something else. Pieces of wood, broken, with blood and carvings to adorn them.

Thrall realized that he was looking at pieces of the legendary Bloodhoof runespear that Gorehowl had shattered when Garrosh dealt the killing blow.

And with the realization came a wave of loss, fresh and raw, and Thrall understood that the pain he had felt up until this moment was a pale shadow. And he had a lifetime left to endure without his old friend's kindness, wisdom, and humor.

Impulsively Thrall leaped gracefully onto the pyre. The poles used to create it swayed a bit but held beneath his weight. Thrall reached out a hand and placed it on Cairne's brow, then, gently, reverently, picked up the smallest piece of the broken runespear. He turned it in his hand, and a shiver went through him.

The piece he had selected bore the single rune: *Healing.* He would keep this, to remember Cairne by. To always be in touch with his heart.

Thrall jumped lightly to the earth and began to walk slowly toward the setting sun. He did not look back.

The wind was slightly chill after the sun had gone, Thrall reflected. There was much that yet needed to be discussed with Baine, much planning that still needed to be done. Yet before that Thrall desired a little time to sit with Aggra in this peaceful land. She had never been here, but like him had responded to the gentleness and tranquility of the place. She—

A continent away, Drek'Thar, who had been dozing, bolted upright. A scream was torn from his throat.

"The oceans will boil!"

The ocean bed cracked open, and miles away, the

tide drew back from Stormwind Harbor like a curtain. Ships were suddenly grounded, and citizens of that city out for a pleasant afternoon stroll along the beautiful stone harbor paused, shielded their eyes against the light of the setting sun, and murmured to one another, idly curious.

The ocean drew in upon itself for but a moment. Then what had pulled back began to return, with a lethal intensity. A towering wave bore down upon the harbor. The great vessels that had sailed to such exotic, faraway places as Auberdine and Valiance Keep were smashed to so much kindling, like toy ships beneath an angry child's foot. Debris and bodies now crashed into the docks, destroying them just as easily and quickly, sweeping away the now-screaming pedestrians as the water rushed implacably forward. The water rose, drowning engines of war and crates of medical supplies with equal ruthlessness.

It did not stop there. It continued to climb, until even the mighty stone lions that stood watch over the harbor were completely submerged. Only then did it seem to halt.

Miles to the south, a crack in the earth off the coastline of Westfall had created a huge sinkhole. The ocean was angry, and frightened, and it vented its terror upon the land, and the land responded in despair.

Drek'Thar clung to Palkar, shaking him, shouting, "The land will weep, and the world will break!"

The earth split beneath Thrall.

He leaped aside, landing and rolling and getting

swiftly to his feet only to be knocked off them again. The ground beneath him surged upward as if he were riding the back of a great creature, lifting him up and up. He clung to it, unable to rise and flee, and even if he did flee, to where?

Earth, soil, and stone, I ask of you calmness. Share with me what it is you fear, name it, and I will—

The earth did have a voice, and now it screamed, a rumbling, agonizing cry.

Thrall felt the rip in the world. It was not here, not in Thunder Bluff, nor even in Kalimdor—it was to the east, in the midst of the ocean, in the center of the Maelstrom. . . . This, then, was what the elements had been so afraid of. A shattering, a cataclysm, breaking the earth as Draenor had been broken. Through his connection with them, their terror surged through him, and he, too, threw back his head and shrieked for a long moment before unconsciousness claimed him.

He awoke to the tender touch of beloved fingers on his face, opening his eyes to see Aggra looking down at him with a worried expression. She relaxed as he gave her a weak smile.

"You are tougher than you look, Slave," she teased him, though her voice conveyed her relief. "I thought you had decided to join the ancestors there for a few moments."

He looked around and realized he was in one of the tents atop Thunder Bluff, maybe in Spirit Rise. Baine was standing beside him.

"We found you lying on the earth, a short distance

from the funeral grounds, and brought you here, my friend," said Baine. He smiled slightly. "My father loved you in life, Thrall, son of Durotan," he said. "But I do not think he would have you join him in death quite so soon."

Thrall struggled to sit up. "The warning Gordawg gave us," he said. "We were too late."

Her eyes were compassionate. "I know. But I also know exactly where the wound was made."

"In the Maelstrom," Thrall said. "I got that much before I . . ." He grimaced.

She touched his shoulder, feeling the texture of the soft robe. "You do not wear your armor," she said quietly.

"No," said Thrall. "I do not." He smiled gently at her. "I have shed my skin." He turned to Baine. "If you would—I would ask that you send someone for it. Though I no longer wear the armor of a warchief, I would have it brought to Orgrimmar. It is an important part of our culture."

"Of course, Thrall. It shall be done."

Aggra sat back, glancing at him and Baine. "So what do we do now?"

Thrall reached up and grasped the young Bloodhoof's hand. "Baine . . . you know I came back with the hope of both helping the Horde and the elements. And I believe I can still do both these things. Just . . . I can no longer achieve both goals as warchief."

Baine smiled sadly. "I have no love for Garrosh Hellscream, although I do believe him innocent in the poisoning of my father. I confess I would prefer to see you again leading the Horde. But after what has happened,

I understand that you must go. Reports have been coming in—every place with a shoreline facing the South Seas is reporting tidal waves and storms. Theramore, Stormwind, Westfall, Ratchet, Steamwheedle Port. The Undercity has had massive quakes. Fires burn in Ashenvale from lightning strikes."

Thrall closed his eyes. "Your understanding makes this easier, Baine. I love the Horde. Along with your father, I built it into what it is today. But there is a greater need, and it is that need I must attend to. Immediately. I will send word to Orgrimmar and then prepare to set sail to investigate this . . . wound to the world. The Horde must get along the best it can without me."

Drek'Thar wept, tears falling from blind eyes. Palkar knew better than to doubt him. He felt nothing, at least not here, not physically, but he could sense the world's distress. And so when Drek'Thar inhaled a sobbing breath and turned his face up to his young caretaker, Palkar waited for what the seer would impart. The younger orc's blood seemed to run cold in his veins at the words.

"Someone is breaking down the door! Bar it! *Do not let him in!*"

Drek'Thar had been right before. He had been right about everything. There was no doubt in Palkar's mind that he was right about this.

The only question was—who was the mysterious intruder?

EPILOGUE

Thrall breathed the sea air, letting it stir his hair and beard. Above, in a sky still pink with dawn, seagulls wheeled and called. The little town of Ratchet was quiet at this early hour, although a few people had roused themselves and had come to see him off on his journey. Thrall closed his eyes and exhaled, smiling a little.

"I like to see you smile," said Aggra, standing beside him.

He opened his blue eyes and gazed down at her, the smile widening. "You should get used to it, for with you, I seem to smile much more often."

The words were true, but even though Thrall's heart was full and his mind at peace with his decision, there were many uncertainties and, he was sure, trials yet to come. He took her hand in his and squeezed it.

They had come to Ratchet from Thunder Bluff, sending word ahead to Orgrimmar and the port town while he and Aggra finalized their plans. One of the greatest sailing vessels of the Horde fleet had been prepared at lightning speed for the journey to the Maelstrom. As Thrall and Aggra rode their wolves down to the dock, they were greeted by Gazlowe. He looked a bit bleary-eyed, and Thrall suspected he had not yet seen his bed, but he gave them a wide, sharp-toothed smile nonetheless.

"Your courier told us to get this ship ready, and we did!" Gazlowe said. "Fresh water, a few barrels of beer and grog, plenty of supplies—you're all set for your voyage, Warchief!" He did a double take at Aggra and then bowed low. "Hel-*lo*, you must be the lovely young shaman I've heard so much about."

"I am a shaman, and my *name* is Aggra," she said, eyes narrowing. "And you might be?"

"Gazlowe. Me and that big lug of yours go way back," the goblin said, beaming. Clearly either he hadn't noticed Aggra was irritated, or else he simply was unperturbed by it. "Like what you've done with his style. Simple brown robes—understated, sharp. It's a good look for the big guy. Always happy to have the warchief and, now, his lady come to visit."

"I am not the warchief," Thrall said, "not for some time anyway. Garrosh will continue as acting warchief in my absence."

Gazlowe grumbled a bit. "Bad business that, with Cairne."

Thrall sobered. "True," he said. "A tragedy that has lessened us all. But Garrosh did not act dishonorably. And that is all I will say on the matter. You say the ship is ready?"

"Ready and waiting," Gazlowe said. As they approached, Aggra saw the name of the ship.

"Draka's Fury," she said, grinning. "A good choice for our journey."

"It seemed to fit," Thrall said. "I wanted to honor the strong orc females who have blessed my life."

Aggra actually blushed and looked a little flustered. "It will be a long journey."

"But the right one," Thrall said. He did not have a second thought. He had been called, and he would go. Not as warchief, but as himself.

As Thrall.

Son of Durotan and Draka.

Shaman.

Notes

The story you've just read is based in part on characters, situations, and settings from Blizzard Entertainment's computer game *World of Warcraft,* an online role-playing experience set in the award-winning Warcraft universe. In *World of Warcraft,* players create their own heroes and explore, adventure in, and quest across a vast world shared with thousands of other players. This rich and expansive game also allows players to interact with and fight against or alongside many of the powerful and intriguing characters featured in this novel.

Since launching in November 2004, *World of Warcraft* has become the world's most popular subscription-based massively multiplayer online role-playing game. The *Wrath of the Lich King* expansion sold more than 2.8 million copies within its first twenty-four hours of availability and more than 4 million copies in its first month, breaking records to become the fastest-selling PC game of all time. More information about the upcoming expansion, *Cataclysm,* which continues the story of Azeroth where this novel ends, can be found on worldofwarcraft.com.

Further Reading

If you'd like to read more about the characters, situations, and settings featured in this novel, the sources listed below offer additional pieces of the story of Azeroth.

- Thrall's intriguing background—depicted in *Warcraft: Lord of the Clans* by Christie Golden—has allowed him to form strong bonds with humans such as Jaina Proudmoore. You can find more information about Thrall and Jaina's friendship in *World of Warcraft: Cycle of Hatred* by Keith R. A. DeCandido as well as in issues #15–20 of the monthly *World of Warcraft* comic book by Walter and Louise Simonson, Jon Buran, Mike Bowden, Phil Moy, Walden Wong, and Pop Mhan. Additional insight into the lives of Thrall's ancestors is revealed in *World of Warcraft: Rise of the Horde* by Christie Golden.

- In this novel, Prince Anduin Wrynn struggles to cope with the violent and short-tempered "Lo'Gosh" side of his father, Varian. Further details about Anduin's relationship with Varian, as well as his life as the prince of Stormwind, are depicted in the monthly *World of Warcraft* comic book by Walter and Louise Simonson, Ludo Lullabi, Jon Buran, Mike Bowden, Sandra Hope, and Tony Washington.

- The headstrong Garrosh Hellscream appears alongside Thrall in issues #15–20 of the monthly *World of Warcraft* comic book by Walter and Louise Simonson, Jon Buran, Mike Bowden, Phil Moy, Walden Wong, and Pop Mhan. In addition, a glimpse into Garrosh's life before he became a praised hero of the Horde can be seen in *World of Warcraft: Beyond the Dark Portal* by Aaron Rosenberg and Christie Golden.

- The treacherous events of the Wrath Gate, including the tragic death of the Horde hero Saurfang the Younger, are portrayed in the short story "Glory" by Evelyn Fredericksen (on worldofwarcraft.com).

- Orgrimmar's arena has seen many brutal battles, one of which was between Garrosh Hellscream and Thrall. The reasons behind their duel and its outcome are shown in issue #19 of the monthly *World of Warcraft* comic book by Walter and Louise Simonson, Mike Bowden, Phil Moy, Richard Friend, and Sandra Hope.

- Drek'Thar is an aging and absentminded orc shaman in this book, but he once acted as Thrall's tutor in *Warcraft: Lord of the Clans* by Christie Golden. Drek'Thar's past is also described in *World of Warcraft: Rise of the Horde* by Christie Golden.

- Jaina Proudmoore strives to mediate conflicts between the Alliance and the Horde in the monthly *World of Warcraft* comic book by Walter and Louise Simonson, Ludo Lullabi, Jon Buran, Mike Bowden, Sandra Hope, and Tony Washington, as well as in *World of Warcraft: Cycle of Hatred* by Keith R. A. DeCandido. You can read about Jaina's earlier years before she became the ruler of Theramore in *World of Warcraft: Arthas: Rise of the Lich King* by Christie Golden.

- Even before the world-altering events of this novel, King Varian Wrynn's life was plagued with difficulties. *World of Warcraft: Tides of Darkness* by Aaron Rosenberg, *World of Warcraft: Arthas: Rise of the Lich King* by Christie Golden, and the monthly *World of Warcraft* comic book by Walter and Louise Simonson, Ludo Lullabi, Jon Buran, Mike Bowden, Sandra Hope, and Tony Washington all offer insight into Varian's background, including his mysterious past as Lo'Gosh and his relationship with his son, Anduin.

- King Magni Bronzebeard plays a minor role in issues #9–11 of the monthly *World of Warcraft* comic book by Walter Simonson, Jon Buran, Jerome

Moore, and Sandra Hope. Additionally, *Warcraft: Legends volume 5—Nightmares* by Richard A. Knaak and Rob Ten Pas reveals Magni's fears about his daughter, Moira, and the Dark Iron dwarves when his dreams are plagued by foul magic from the Emerald Nightmare.

- Before becoming one of Thrall's most trusted advisors, the orc Eitrigg led a life of solitude. Eitrigg's intriguing history and the events that led him to join Thrall's side are depicted in *Warcraft: Of Blood and Honor* by Chris Metzen.

- High Priest Rohan, Anduin Wrynn's wise dwarven ally in this novel, plays a role as a member of the new Council of Tirisfal in issues #23–25 of the monthly *World of Warcraft* comic book by Walter and Louise Simonson, Mike Bowden, and Tony Washington.

- Further details of Magatha Grimtotem's tenuous relationship with Cairne Bloodhoof are disclosed in issue #3 of the monthly *World of Warcraft* comic book by Walter Simonson, Ludo Lullabi, and Sandra Hope.

- Archdruid Hamuul Runetotem is featured in issue #3 and issues #23–25 of the monthly *World of Warcraft* comic book by Walter and Louise Simonson, Ludo Lullabi, Sandra Hope, Mike Bowden, and Tony Washington. The venerable archdruid also plays a minor role in battling the foul magic of the Emerald Nightmare in *World of Warcraft: Stormrage* by Richard Knaak.

- The inspirational story of Thrall's mother, Draka, and her struggle to overcome her own frailty is portrayed in *Warcraft: Legends volume 4—A Warrior Made: Part 1* and *Warcraft: Legends volume 5—A Warrior Made: Part 2* by Christie Golden and In-Bae Kim.

The Battle Rages On

Azeroth's elementals are in disarray; tenuous political ties among the Alliance and the Horde are on the verge of shattering to pieces, and the very surface of the world has been ripped and torn asunder. The Cataclysm has begun. . . .

Now that you've glimpsed the dire fate that awaits Azeroth, you can play a role in sparing the world from impending doom in *World of Warcraft*'s upcoming third expansion, *Cataclysm*. The previous two *World of Warcraft* expansions, *The Burning Crusade* and *Wrath of the Lich King,* take players to the alien world of Outland and the icy wastes of Northrend. In *Cataclysm,* players will witness the return of the corrupted Dragon Aspect Deathwing as he awakens from his subterranean slumber and erupts onto the surface of Azeroth, leaving ruin and destruction in his wake. The future hangs in the balance, and as the Horde and Alliance race to the epicenter of the Cataclysm, they will require the help of any and all adventurers willing to risk their lives.

To discover the ever-expanding world that has entertained millions around the globe, go to worldofwarcraft.com and download the free trial version. Live the story.

ABOUT THE AUTHOR

New York Times bestselling and award-winning author Christie Golden has written thirty-five novels and several short stories in the fields of science fiction, fantasy, and horror. Among her many projects are more than a dozen Star Trek novels and several original fantasy novels. An avid player of World of Warcraft, she has written two manga short stories and several novels in that world (*Lord of the Clans, Rise of the Horde, Arthas: Rise of the Lich King,* and *The Shattering: Prelude to Cataclysm*) with more in the works. She has also written the StarCraft Dark Templar Trilogy, *Firstborn, Shadow Hunters,* and *Twilight*. Forthcoming is *Devil's Due*, a StarCraft II novel focusing on the unlikely friendship between Jim Raynor and Tychus Findlay. Golden is also currently writing three books in the major nine-book Star Wars series, Fate of the Jedi, in collaboration with Aaron Allston and Troy Denning. Her first two books in that series, *Omen* and *Allies*, are on shelves now. Golden currently lives in Colorado. She welcomes visitors to her website, www.christiegolden.com.